# The Stones of (

Chris Crockford

For Heather

And With Thanks to

Ginnie
Dave
Erin
Richard
Alex

Without your help, I never would have got here.

Cover Design by Mike Smith

Find out more on Facebook.

Search for "Stones of Gunjai"

# Chapter One

## Unexpected Help

Molly ran through the maze of filthy streets, the sounds of pursuit loud behind her. The overnight rain had made the dirty cobbles slippery and she almost fell as she dipped round a corner and pressed herself flat against a rough brick wall, trying to catch her breath. The three men chasing her thundered past and she tried to merge into the brickwork, making herself as small and inconspicuous as possible. Luckily they didn't see her. She watched them go, their shouts dying as they headed away to be replaced with the bustle of the city and the nearby docks. Wiping a lock of her shoulder length tangled blonde hair out of her eyes, she let out a small sigh of relief. That had been close.

Her pinafore dress may have once been blue but it was so stained and grubby it was difficult to tell. It was also too short, reaching only to just below her knees while the top had been badly patched and altered to make it fit across the shoulders and chest.

Reaching a dirty hand into a pocket, Molly took out the apple she'd stolen. Holding it in front of her like it was a trophy she hesitantly took a bite. It had been close but it was worth it. She hadn't eaten properly for two days and the taste was pure heaven.

She closed her eyes and savoured the moment, leaning back against the wall with an ecstatic sigh. She took another bite, the juice dripping down her chin. It was a thing of beauty.

'Got you, you little thieving...'

She cried out and dropped the apple into the mud as a heavy hand dropped on her shoulder. Instinctively she lashed out and caught him on the ankle with a booted foot.

He swore and let her go, just as his friends came up the road.

'Get the bitch.' shouted the man as she ducked under his grasp and ran off into the dockside crowds.

She jinked right into a dirty alley, trying to lose them again but she knew she was in trouble.

Unseen by the people on the streets a hooded figure dressed in black watched the girl and her pursuers from high on the roof of one of the warehouses that backed onto the dock.

Reaching a decision, a smile played across its lips before it stood and followed across the rooftops, effortlessly keeping pace with the group as they headed through the dirty streets.

They were close. She could hear their pounding feet and she dared not look behind her as she weaved through the people and alleys that made up the maze that was the docks. Seeing an opening to her left, she changed direction at the last minute and cut across the road in front of a horse and cart. The animal reared up but the men weren't stopped for long.

They followed right behind her, their shouts loud in her ears. A sharp right and she found herself in a yard behind some run down shops. A dead end. Now she was in trouble.

'Got you now.'

She whirred round and began backing away from the mouth of the yard until she bumped into a pile of crates. The men fanned out, cutting off any escape. There were three of them, all dressed in scruffy shirts and trousers. They were rough and she didn't like the way they were looking at her.

'Steal from me would you?'

The man in the centre stepped forward, grinned evilly, showing a mouthful of rotten teeth.

'I'm starving.'

'So? What do you want me to do about it?'

'I'm sorry.' she said.

'Sorry?' he laughed. 'I'm going to give you something to be sorry about and then maybe my brothers will want an apology too.'

He glanced back at them and they grinned, looking forward to the sport that was to come.

Suddenly the girl feinted left and then made a dash to the right but the lead man lunged quickly and wrapped a hand in her dirty blonde hair. She screamed and kicked out as he dragged her towards him.

'Now. How about you pay for that apple and show me how sorry you are?'

Again, she lashed out with her legs but he slapped her hard with the back of his free hand and she fell, the fight leaving her in an instant. He hauled her up by the hair again before hitting her once more.

'Touch her again and you'll regret it. Leave her alone and walk away while you still can.'

All three men turned as a lithe figure wearing a heavy black cloak with a deep hood, dropped softly from the roof of one of the sheds that backed on to the yard.

'This is none of your business.' said the man angrily as he dragged the girl in front of him, his hand still tightly wrapped in her hair. She cried out in pain.

'You're making it my business.'

The voice was accented and foreign but the English was perfect. The figure threw back the hood and unbuckled the clasp at its throat, allowing the cloak to fall to the muddy ground.

Underneath was a young woman with a beautiful face. Deep green eyes set in dark skin with long, jet black, hair tied in a ponytail. She was dressed in a black leather jumpsuit and at her back stood the hilt of a sword with another short blade strapped to her thigh. The man laughed.

'And you're going to stop me are you girl? Maybe when I've finished with her I'll have a bit of fun with you. Get her.'

He turned his attention back to Molly and the air rang with another resounding slap as he hit her. His companions however were moving towards the woman in black. Casually she stepped forward and rolled her shoulders, loosening up.

'We're gonna have some fun with you.' leered one of the men as they closed on her.

She smiled tightly at him.

'I don't think so.'

She took a step forward and spun gracefully on her heel to deliver a roundhouse kick hard enough to put the closest man through a wooden crate where he slumped without moving.

The other man hesitated for a second, looking on in shock as if he couldn't quite believe what had just happened. He turned back to the leader.

'Jimmy... She just...' he began

His words remained unfinished as the woman moved quickly, raining in a furious series of punches that dropped him where he stood. She straightened and addressed the last man.

'Let her go. Last chance.'

Jimmy dragged the girl up in front of him and drew a knife.

'I'll kill her.'

The woman in black sighed.

'How tiresome.'

She glanced down at Molly and they locked eyes for a second before the woman nodded
slightly.

'Now.'

As she spoke, Molly twisted in his grip and bit him hard, sending his knife skittering into the dirt. He cried out and slapped her away. She fell heavily, cracking her head on the ground. While he cursed the girl, the woman had closed the ground between them.

He looked back a fraction of a second before she kicked him in the groin. His knees buckled and he bent over but met her knee coming the other way. His nose broke in a spray of blood and he fell backwards. In an instant she was over him, dragging him up by his collar and thrusting him towards the yard entrance.

'If I ever see you again, I will kill you. Do you understand?'

She shoved him again.

'Who are you?' he stammered.

'Your worst nightmare. Leave now while you still can.'

He nodded and she turned to the girl.

'Come on. I think we should be getting out of here don't you?'

Molly looked at her blearily. The woman bent down.

'Up.'

'Behind you!' shouted Molly as the woman help her to her feet..

As soon as her back was to him, the man had pulled another knife and lunged at her. Without looking, she straightened and neatly sidestepped, catching his outstretched arm.

'So predictable.' she said with a shake of her head.

A swift twist was rewarded with a sickening crunch as she snapped his arm. He cried out and stepped back. She turned and with a kick, sent him sprawling. Molly pulled herself to her feet.

'Time to go.'

The man was trying to sit up as they passed and Molly kicked him hard between the legs.

'Bastard.' she spat.

'That's enough. Time to go.'

The woman picked up her cloak and draped it across Molly's shoulders as they walked through the streets and back towards the dock. She was still a bit dazed so the woman put her arm around her and helped her along.

They were only a street away from the waterfront when a shout behind them caused them to turn. The man whose arm she had broken was there, a battered looking pistol held shakily in his good hand.

The woman looked at the girl.

'Go to the wharf. There's a man there called Shakir. Fetch him.'

'How will I know who he is.'

She smiled.

'You'll know. Now go.'

Molly nodded and shed the cloak before she headed off an unsteady run. The woman turned and started to walk towards the man.

'You broke my arm.' he shouted.

'Be thankful I left you with your life.'

'Where's the girl? She owes me.'

'I don't think she does.'

'Stay where you are. I'll kill you.'

His hand was shaking and there was a tremor in his voice. The woman kept walking towards him, reaching behind her shoulder as she moved to draw a long, curved sword from its scabbard on her back.

'Stay where you are! I'll kill you. I swear!'

She smiled at him.

'Go on then. If you can.'

She stopped a couple of feet in front of him, the sword held at her side.

'Are we ready?'

He straightened his arm and tried to steady the gun.

The girl ran onto the dock, piles of crates littered the quay and horses and carts went to and fro amongst the bustle and noise and a mass of men were unloading a large ship with three masts.

She looked around in a panic until she saw him. It must be him. He was huge! He was dressed in a white army uniform with gold braid and a huge bushy beard that hid most of his face. On his head, there was a tall hat that looked like it was made of wrapped cloth and at his side hung a heavy sword.

She ran over to him but pulled up short when he looked at her intensely. His face was stern.

'Are you, um, Shakir?'

'Yes.'

'The woman in black needs you. She's in trouble.'

He looked at her for a second longer before answering, his accent thick and foreign.

'I seriously doubt that but show me.'

He followed at a jog as she dashed off in front.

'Go on then.' she told him, lifting her sword in front of her.

She watched his eyes and his trembling hand and, as he went to pull the trigger, she batted the muzzle of the pistol away with the flat of the blade. The gun went off with a crack, the shot burying itself in the woodwork of a door across the street.

She moved quickly, spinning on the balls of her feet with her sword out before her at head height. The man barely had time to register the movement before she took his head, the blade passing through his neck and out of the other side without a pause. Shock in his eyes, his body crumpled to the floor in a spray of blood while his head rolled a few feet in the muddy road.

'Nareema!'

She turned to see Shakir striding towards her, Molly close behind. She sighed and for the first time, felt the wetness on her face. She reached up and seemed surprised when it came away bloody.

'Damn.'

He stopped just in front of her.

'We've been off the boat for barely an hour.'

'It's a ship.'

Shakir looked at her and then pointed at the body. Around them a crowd had gathered.

'I suppose you want me to do something about that.'

Nareema smiled at him.

'Yes please.'

He sighed.

'Go. We have unloaded most of the luggage. The coach will take you home.'

She stood on tiptoe and gave him a kiss on the cheek.

'Thank you.' she turned to Molly. 'Are you coming too?'

'Will you kill me if I don't?'

Nareema smiled.

'No. You just look like you could do with something to eat and I can help with that.'

Molly looked at her before a rumble in her stomach made the decision for her. The woman laughed.

'Come on.'

She headed off towards the dock with the Molly in tow. Shakir looked down and sighed again at the bright red patches of blood on his previously spotless white uniform.

Molly followed Nareema to the dock where a black coach and horses waited. There was a large iron bound trunk on the roof and several other cases and trunks nearby.

'Here. Hold this.'

Nareema handed Molly the sword and began rooting through one of the trunks. She held the blood-soaked weapon at arms' length as if it were likely to explode.

After a few moments Nareema pulled out a couple of neatly folded cloth bundles before taking it back.

'Come on.'

They got into the carriage and the driver headed off. Nareema wiped most of the blood from her face with the one of the cloths and then began to clean the blade with the others. They rode in silence for a while before curiosity got the better of Molly.

'Who are you?'

Nareema laid the sword across her lap.

'I am Princess Nareema Kareen Vashti. First daughter of his Highness Hanka Nessa Vashti, Maharaja of the Sunjian province.'

'Oh.'

'Although my friends just call me Nareema.'

The girl looked at her, sword on her lap and drying blood on her face and in her hair.

'You've got friends?'

Nareema laughed.

'I do. So, who are you and why were those men chasing you?'

Molly had never met a Princess before so she didn't really know what to say.

'I'm Molly, Your Highness.' she said eventually.

'Your name is Molly Your Highness?'

'No. Molly Carter.'

'Why were they chasing you?'

'I stole an apple.'

Nareema just looked at her but said nothing.

'And a wallet.'

Still Nareema said nothing. Molly felt compelled to fill the silence.

'I'm starving. I haven't eaten in two days. I had to do something.' she said defensively.

Nareema raised her eyebrows and she looked down.

'Your Highness...'

'Was it worth it?'

Molly reached into a pocket in her dress and pulled out a battered leather wallet. It was empty.

'No. And I dropped the apple.'

'Not a very good thief, are you?'

'I get by.'

'Most of the time.'

'Why did you help me?'

'You looked like you needed it. And I needed to stretch my legs. We've been at sea for weeks.'

'Where did you learn to fight like that?'

Nareema smiled at her.

'Do you have a place to go? Family?'

'No.'

'How old are you?'

'Seventeen.'

They rode in silence for a little while.

'Where are you from?' asked Molly.

'India.'

'Why are you in England?'

'To see a very dear friend. I have something very precious that I need him to take a look at.'

'Is it in the trunk on the roof.'

'No. That's just clothes. I keep it safe.'

'What is it?'

'Nothing that you need to worry about.'

They were silent for a moment.

'I wouldn't try to steal it, whatever it is. Not with that man guarding it. He's scary. And massive.' said Molly

Nareema unbuckled the scabbard from her back as she spoke.

'Shakir? He's a pushover. And besides, he's not guarding it.'

She smiled and slid the sword into the scabbard with a click.

'I am.'

Molly opened her mouth to say something but then remembered what she'd already seen. The woman had bested three men without breaking a sweat. She closed her mouth and Nareema gave her a sly grin.

Where are we going?' asked Molly.

'Home.'

## Chapter Two

Homecoming

The coach eventually came to a stop outside a large double fronted house on an expensive looking road and Nareema was out even before it finished moving. She gracefully swung herself up onto the roof and began to undo the straps holding down the luggage.

Molly stayed in the carriage until Nareema stuck her head in the door, ponytail dangling behind her upside-down face.

'Will you go and knock on the door please. Get Simcox to come out here and give me a hand.'

The head disappeared again and Molly hesitantly got out and went to the door. It was black and highly polished with a solid brass door knocker in the shape of a huge bird. Tentatively she reached up and swung the knocker hard against the wood.

After a moment, the door swung open to reveal a smartly dressed butler with receding hair and a hard face. He looked down his nose at her as he took in her scruffy dress and dirty face.

'Yes?'

Molly opened her mouth but a shout from the coach caught his attention.

'Simcox. She's with me. Can you give me a hand?'

'Nareema?'

He broke into a grin before dashing out into the road to grab the end of the trunk as it swung off the roof.

'Why didn't you tell us you were coming? Is Shakir with you?'

He wrestled the trunk to the ground and then offered a hand to Nareema to help her down. She just grinned at him before dismounting with a somersault.

She reached into the carriage and took out her sword then gave him a hug.

'Just a flying visit. We're going to see Uncle Tobias.'

He broke from the hug and put his hands on her shoulders.

'You've grown.'

'It's been three years.'

Simcox took in the blood on her face and on her clothes.

'Look at the state of you. Is that blood?'

'It's not mine.'

She reached down and grabbed one of the handles of the trunk.

'Leave that.' he told her.

'It's fine.'

Simcox looked like he was going to protest but in the end, he took the other handle and between them they carried it inside.

Dropping it in the hall, Nareema motioned for Molly to come in. Simcox called down the hallway.

'Alice... I mean, Mrs Kettering. Come quickly.'

He turned back to Nareema.

'You should have written to us. Let us know you were coming. We'd have...'

She cut him off.

'We didn't want to put you out. Besides, as I said, we're on the way to see Uncle Tobias. This is really only a stopover.'

Down the hallway came an aging woman with a friendly face. Her greying hair was hidden under a mop cap, she was muttering under her breath.

'What do you want? Shouting the place up...'

She stopped in her tracks when she saw Nareema.

'Nareema?'

'Hello Mrs Kettering.'

They both grinned and Mrs Kettering gave her a huge hug. 'You should have...'

'Simcox has already been through that.'

'I'll make up your room. What's that all over you? Is that blood? Is Shakir with you? '

'When is he not? He's finishing the unloading then he's coming here.'

'And who's this?'

Mrs Kettering looked at Molly who felt uncomfortable. A bit like an intruder at a family gathering. Absentmindedly she tried to smooth out her dirty dress in an effort to look more presentable. Nareema grinned at her.

'This is Molly Carter. I would appreciate it if you would find her something to eat, then probably a bath and some clean clothes. Then please send her to see me.'

'Of course. Do you want me to run a bath for you as well?'

'Thank you but not right now. I've a few kinks to work out.'

Nareema turned to Simcox.

'Is the summer house...'

'Yes. I won't say "just as you left it" as it is now tidy and in one piece.'

There was no denying the admonishment in his voice but his smile said everything.

'Perfect. Molly, go with Mrs Kettering. She'll sort you out.'

Nareema headed down the corridor leaving Molly standing in the hallway.

'Is she really a Princess?' Molly asked between mouthfuls. She was sat at the kitchen table with a mound of chicken, cheese and bread in front of her. Mrs Kettering turned from where she was busy at the stove.

'Yes. She is.'

'She doesn't act like one.'

'And I bet you've met lots of Princesses in your time?' laughed the older woman.

Molly smiled.

'You know what I mean. She's... different. Not all posh dresses and waving and stuff.'

Mrs Kettering put a large pot of tea on the table before sitting down and pouring for both of them.

'No. She's not like anyone else I've ever met.'

'Do you work for her?'

'Yes. But she's away a lot so most of the time Mr Simcox and I just keep the place tidy and running.'

'What about Shakir?'

'Him? He doesn't work for anyone but her father. He's there to protect her.'

Molly choked on a bit of bread and grabbed her tea to help wash it down.

'She doesn't seem to need much protection.' she spluttered.

'Is that how she found you?'

Molly put down the bread and tea before looking dejectedly at the table.

'Yeah. She saved my life. She beat three men and then... Then she killed one of them. She made it look like the easiest thing in the world.'

They were silent for a moment. Molly felt uncomfortable.

'Thank you for the food. I'd better be going.'

Mrs Kettering stood up.

'Oh no. I've my instructions. The Princess asked me to feed you, sort you out a bath and some clean clothes. Then she wanted to see you. So that's what I'm going to do. Come on.'

Molly went to protest.

'Do you want to tell her you're leaving? If you leave without speaking to her she'll find you and then you'll find out whatever it is she wants whether you like it or not. She's very determined like that.'

An hour later Molly had bathed and Mrs Kettering had

found her a dress. It was a pale green and the finest thing she had ever worn.

'That'll do for now. It's a bit big but I'm sure the Princess will find you something that's a better fit.'

Molly looked down at herself.

'It's perfect as it is.'

Mrs Kettering laughed.

'You're easily pleased.'

'It's better than my other one.'

'That it is. Sit down and I'll sort out your hair.'

Molly sat while Mrs Kettering ran a brush through her recently washed hair, pulling out the tangles.

'How old are you girl?'

'Seventeen.'

'Family?'

She tried to shake her head.

'Keep still.'

'Sorry.'

There was a knock at the front door and they heard a deep baritone voice, heavily accented and thick.

'That'll be Shakir.' said Mrs Kettering as she stood back and looked at her handiwork.

Molly was scrubbed, washed and presentable.

'Go on and find the Princess. She's in the summer house which is at the bottom of the garden. I'll say hello to Shakir and then be waiting for you in the kitchen. Hurry up. You don't want to keep the Princess waiting.'

'Thank you.'

Molly stood and headed out into the garden. It was tidy and well cared for with a stone path leading up to a large single story building at the end. The entire garden was surrounded by a high wall and a few trees were dotted around. Their blossom was fragrant in the early summer sun and it was peaceful and quiet.

Nervously she walked up and knocked on the door. After receiving no reply, she pushed it open and went in.

The building was open plan with plain panelled wood walls and a solid wood floor covered in a woven reed mat. Along the back wall were several racks holding weapons of all kinds and a large padded sack hung from the ceiling to the left. To the right stood a heavy wooden post with smaller poles sticking out from it at various heights and angles. It was in front of this that Nareema stood.

She had changed into a pair of deep green silk trousers with a matching loose fitting top that was held closed with a heavy black belt tied around her waist. The black leather suit she had worn earlier lay casually discarded in the corner. Molly watched, fascinated. The Princesses' arms were a blur as she struck the smaller wooden poles hard enough to rattle them using her fists, palms and forearms as she worked her way round the large pole.

She was drenched in sweat, the blood from earlier mingled with it to run down her face leaving red smears on her skin and she seemed completely oblivious to Molly's presence. Her full concentration was on the pole in front of her as she repeatedly hit it from every conceivable angle.

Molly watched for a minute before she coughed politely.

'You wanted to see me?'

Nareema ignored her for a moment longer before she leapt back and kicked the wooden pole hard enough to split it. Breathing heavily, she turned to Molly. Her face was as hard as stone. Expressionless.

'Can you read?' her voice matched her face.

'No... But I can write my name.'

'That's a start. Do you want a job? I'll give you somewhere to live, feed you, clothe you, teach you to read and write and maybe a few other things as well.'

Nareema kicked the pole again, splitting it further.

'What will I do? Do you need a maid?'

'No. I need someone to... Be my eyes and ears in certain circumstances. Help me with day to day things.'

'Why me?'

'Why not you?'

She jumped and spun in the air to deliver a huge kick which sheared the top from the post. It crashed to the ground and Molly took a step back.

'Hand me that towel.'

Molly looked round and saw a folded white towel on the floor. She grabbed it and passed it to Nareema who took it and wiped the sweat and blood from her face.

'So. What do you think?'

Molly didn't know what to say. The violence of the last five minutes was astonishing and she felt a little scared. Nareema dropped the towel on the floor.

'You don't have to. I thought you might be interested.'

'No. Thank you. I am interested. I would like a job.' she said hurriedly.

Nareema grinned, the hardness falling from her face and bringing back the woman Molly had met earlier.

'Good. Please go and ask Mrs Kettering if she would run me a bath, then tell Simcox I've broken the dummy.'

Molly wasn't sure how to respond now she was employed by a Princess so she attempted a curtsey.

'Yes Your Highness.'

'Stop that now.' said Nareema sternly. 'My name isn't Your Highness, or Your Majesty or anything like that. It is Nareema. And don't curtsey. It really doesn't suit you and you're not very good at it.'

Molly smiled nervously.

'Thank you.'

'Go.'

She turned and headed out into the garden and back down to the kitchen. Mrs Kettering was waiting.

'Well?'

'She offered me a job.'

'Did you take it?'

'Yes.'

'But?'

'She was different. Harder. Scary. I don't know.'
Mrs Kettering stood up.
'She is different to us. You'll get use to her.'
Molly smiled tightly.
'Um, she asked me to see if you would run her a bath.'
'Of course.'
'I also need to tell Mr Simcox she's broken the dummy. I think it's that wooden post thing. She kicked the top off it.'
'Already? She's only been back an hour.'
Mrs Kettering shook her head.
'I'll tell Mr Simcox. Come on, let's find you a room. I assume you're staying with us?'
Molly shrugged. She hadn't given it any thought.
'I expect so. This house has eight bedrooms. Mr Simcox and I only use one of them. It'll be good to have some people around the place.'
She saw Molly's face.
'Don't look like that. We're not married but he and I don't mind. Nareema doesn't either and to be honest it's nobody else's business.'

Ten minutes later Molly looked around her room. Her room! She'd never had a room of her own. It was light and airy with a huge four poster bed. Her bed! She couldn't believe it.

There was a wash stand near the window that looked out over the garden and a huge wardrobe and dresser. Both were empty but Mrs Kettering had promised to take her shopping. Nareema didn't shop and somehow Molly wasn't surprised.

She sat on the bed. It was soft and had thick blankets covering it. This wasn't the way she would have imagined her day to go in her wildest dreams. Molly jumped up and sat in the deep leather armchair that was near the fireplace. The leather was a dark cherry red and smooth under her touch.

Unable to sit still with the excitement of the whole thing she stood and looked out of the window. Nareema was striding down the path, still dressed in the green silk top and trousers with her sword held in her hand.

She looked deep in thought until the huge shape of Shakir came out of the house. He met her half way and there were words exchanged.

Even though she couldn't hear what they were saying she could tell that he was angry. It was in his body language. Nareema said something and stepped back, drawing her sword, flinging the scabbard to the ground. Shakir also stepped back and drew his own weapon. It was a huge curved blade that made Nareema's look like a butter knife.

The big man swung the sword directly at Nareema's head but she jinked deftly out of the way and countered, her blade being deflected by an overhand swipe from Shakir.

They were going to kill each other!

Molly dashed out of the room and down stairs. She reached the kitchen where both Mrs Kettering and Simcox were standing by the window watching the fighting pair in the garden.

'Nareema is fighting Shakir.' she said breathlessly.

'We know.' said Simcox.

'They're going to kill each other! Why are they fighting?'

'I don't know. They'll keep going until one of them submits. Last time she was here it was almost always Nareema that won.'

Molly stepped up to the window as Nareema flicked her blade underneath Shakirs strike and rested the point against his throat. He spread his arms wide, yielding to her.

'That was quick.' commented Simcox.

Nareema turned and headed back into the summerhouse.

Mrs Kettering turned to Molly and handed her a glass of water and a towel.

'Take this out to her.'

She nodded and went out into the garden. Shakir still

looked angry. He slammed his sword into its scabbard and stalked inside as Molly came out.

She skirted around him and quickly headed up the garden. Nareema had put on her leather suit and had her back to the door as she went in.

'Don't.' her voice was hard.

She turned and picked up her sword, slinging it across her back.

'I'm going out.'

'But what...'

'I said don't.'

Nareema strode past her. Her face was thunderous.

'Mrs Kettering said... Here.'

Molly held out the glass of water. Nareema looked at her for a second before slapping the glass out of her hand, smashing it against the floor.

'Get out of my way.'

She left the building and Molly heard her climb onto the roof and then head out over the high garden wall. She swallowed. She'd been in a few scrapes in her time but Nareema had scared her. The look on her face... The anger... She stood there for a moment before Mrs Kettering came in.

'Are you alright?'

'I.... I broke the glass.'

Mrs Kettering looked at her before she put her arms around her and pulled her into a hug as she broke into tears.

Molly tossed and turned in bed. She couldn't sleep. It was one thing to have a bed, another to get used to the soft mattress and covers. She'd slept where ever she could for such a long time that this seemed un-natural. She was also going over earlier in her mind.

After Nareema had left, Mrs Kettering had taken her down to the kitchen and waited with her until she had stopped crying. Molly couldn't remember the last time she had cried like that. The ferocious look in Nareema's' eyes. The anger in her face. It was something else. She was something else. Was she always that angry?

With a sigh, she rolled over to face the wall. It was no good. She couldn't sleep. Would she be allowed to go and get a drink of water?

Her usual haunt for the night had been a stable near the river. It had been warm and she'd felt safe there. The horses hadn't minded if she shared their water either. Molly decided that she would go down to the kitchen and see.

She rolled over again and almost cried out when she saw Nareema sitting in the leather chair by her bed with her sword was laid across her lap. Molly was sure she hadn't been there a moment ago. She sat up.

'I didn't mean to wake you.' Nareema said softly.

'You didn't. I can't sleep.'

'Why not?'

'I'm not use to a real bed. It's soft.'

Nareema smiled but it didn't reach her eyes.

'I'm sorry about earlier. I wasn't angry with you. I...'

'It doesn't matter.'

'It does.'

They were silent for moment.

'Why were you fighting?' asked Molly tentatively.

'He disagreed with my decisions.'

'But you're a Princess. Doesn't he have to do as you tell him?'

Nareema laughed quietly.

'No. He speaks with the voice of my father. It is I that should do as he says. But we're both stubborn and neither will back down. However, it is rare that we come to blows like we did this afternoon.'

'You could have hurt each other.'

Nareema didn't reply.

'What were you fighting about?'

'You.'
Molly felt her stomach sink.
'Me? Why me? I'm nobody.'
'He said that what we are doing is important. More important than giving you a chance to live.'
'He wants to kill me?'
'No. I meant live your life. Live it free of hunger and fear with a chance to grow. He forgets that what I want to give you is what my father gave him.' she sighed. 'He is right though. What we are doing is important.'
'Do you want me to leave?' Molly asked, dreading the answer.
'No.'
Silence descended once more.
'What are you protecting?'
'Something beautiful but powerful. It would be dangerous if it fell into the wrong hands.'
The Princess stood.
'Get some sleep and we will talk more in the morning.'
'Your Highness...'
'Nareema.' she corrected.
Molly smiled.
'Nareema. Would it be allowed for me to go and get a drink?'
Nareema looked at her quizzically.
'Of course. Why wouldn't it be? In fact, are you hungry?'
Molly shrugged.
'Come on. We'll go and see what Mrs Kettering has in the pantry.'
'Won't she mind?'
'Probably. But what's life without a little danger every now and again.'
'I don't want to get in any trouble.'
'You won't. I promise. Come on.'

Molly grinned and got out of bed to follow the Princess downstairs.

The creak of floorboards woke Molly. She snapped awake just as the curtains were pulled back and light flooded the room. Confusion reigned. Where was she?

'Come on young lady. Time to be up and about.'
Mrs Kettering turned from the window and was surprised to see Molly's bed empty. Her brow furrowed for a second until she saw a blanket poking out from beneath the bed. She lifted the sheets and peered under.
'Why are you under the bed?'
Molly looked at her blankly for a second until she realised who she was.
'I couldn't sleep. It's too soft.'
Mrs Kettering shook her head.
'Come on. Up. Wash and get dressed. Nareema is taking breakfast in the dining room. Although how you two can eat breakfast after the amount you ate last night I don't know.'
Molly unwrapped herself from the blankets she had dragged under the bed and slid out.
'Sorry. She said it would be alright if we...'
Mrs Kettering shook her head.
'Ten minutes and I'll be back.'

Fifteen minutes later, Simcox escorted Molly into the dining room. Nareema was there, sat at the head of a huge table that could have easily seated twenty people. To her right was Shakir. He was carefully peeling a hardboiled egg and glanced up at her as she came in. She hesitated for a second before Nareema waved her over to the seat on her left. The Princess looked refreshed and relaxed, dressed in a silk gown with gold edging.
'Good morning.'

'Good morning Your Highness.'
She glanced nervously at Shakir.
'Sir.'
'My name is Nareema. Please don't call me Your Highness.'
'Sorry.'
The big man looked up at her.
'And I am Shakir.' his voice was gruff and thickly accented.
Molly nodded and spoke softly, the man was intimidating even when he was sat at the breakfast table.
'Sorry.'
Nareema smiled.
'Stop apologising. Would you like some breakfast?'
'Yes. Yes please.'
'What would you like?'
'I... I don't know.'
'How about an egg?'
Molly nodded and Simcox headed off to the kitchen. When he was out of the room Shakir took a bite from his egg and studied her. There was something intense about his gaze. As if he were reading her soul. Eventually he spoke.
'Nareema and I have been talking. Do you know what we are doing?'
Molly shook her head.
'We are going to see a man in the country. We have something very precious to show him and hopefully he can help us.
'What is it?'
He hesitated and looked at Nareema, who nodded slightly, before he continued.
'Something that would be very dangerous in the wrong hands. People have died to protect it and I fear that more may lose their lives before our journey is complete.'
'Oh.'

Molly glanced at Nareema who smiled sadly. Shakir looked at them both then sighed.

'I cannot argue with Nareema's sentiment but her timing leaves a lot to be desired. If you stay, you must know these things. It will be dangerous but I promise you little one, that I will protect you with my life. Just as I have sworn to protect Nareema.'

'Thank you.' stuttered Molly.

Nareema placed a hand on her arm.

'*We* will protect you. If you still want to stay.'

Molly nodded.

'Good.' said Nareema as Simcox returned with a boiled egg and some toast. He also had in his hand a heavy cream envelope which he handed to Nareema.

'This arrived for you.'

She picked up her knife from the table and slit the paper open. Inside was a gilt-edged card.

'How tiresome. I've only been in the country for a day and already the invitations have started to come in. How do these people know? Haven't they got anything better to do with their time that to have parties?'

Shakir took the card from her.

'It looks good to their friends if a Princess attends their event. It's all about looking better than everyone else.'

He handed the card to Molly. It was heavy and covered in a neat handwritten script but the words didn't mean anything. She handed it back to Nareema.

'Have you ever been to a ball?'

'No.'

'Would you like to?'

'I don't know.'

'Well we're heading to see Uncle Tobias in a couple of days. But tomorrow night. Why not? It will be an education. Teach you how not to do things.'

Shakir rumbled a laugh.

'You two have fun. But don't be back late.'

'We'll have you to tell us when it's time to leave.'
'Oh no you don't. I know how these things go.'
Nareema smiled at Molly and gave her a wink.
'We'll see.' she turned to Simcox who was still standing by the table.
'Will you please take Molly to see Mrs Hopkins this morning. Ask her to make an outfit in the same specifications as last time, but for Molly. Then can you find her something appropriate to wear to a ball?'
'Of course.' he turned to leave but Nareema stopped him.
'Simcox?'
'Yes?'
'Relax. You don't have to fuss around me so. I would have been quite happy to eat in the kitchen.'
He grinned.
'I know. It's for the look of the thing. You know how these things go and besides, the dining room doesn't get that much use these days.'

After breakfast Simcox and Molly left in the carriage to see Mrs Hopkins and as it pulled to a stop, Molly realised she knew where she was.
They had stopped at a small dressmakers' shop near the river. It was on the corner of two narrow streets with flaking green paint on the door and a small, badly worn sign, over it.
Molly hesitated as Simcox took a couple of bolts of fine silk from the carriage and went to the door.
'Come on.'
'I don't...'
'Now. Please.'
His tone was insistent and brooked no argument. She followed reluctantly. Simcox went in and the door opened with a jingle from the bell.
'Hang on a minute. I'll be there.'

The voice floated from the back room and after a moment Mrs Hopkins appeared. She was a small thin woman with grey hair but knowing brown eyes. She smiled as she saw who it was. Molly stayed near the door and looked at the floor trying her best to be inconspicuous. Mrs Hopkins glanced her way once before giving him a gap-toothed grin.

'Mr Simcox. How's business?'

Simcox smiled back and placed the two bolts of silk on the counter. One was deep green, the other red.

'With compliments of Princess Vashti.'

Mrs Hopkins ran the material through her fingers.

'Very nice. So what can I do for you?'

'The Princess would like another suit made.'

'Like the last one? No problem. I've still got her measurements.'

'This one isn't for her.'

Mrs Hopkins eyes flicked to Molly and Simcox nodded. Suddenly she became serious.

'We'll be a while Mr Simcox.'

'Of course. I'll be back later. I have some things to attend to.'

'Come 'round the back when you do. I'm closing up.'

Simcox nodded again and left.

Mrs Hopkins followed him to the door and locked it behind him.

'Right. You'd better come with me.'

Molly followed Mrs Hopkins into the back room, still looking at the floor.

'Look at me.'

She lifted her eyes to look at the older woman and was shocked by a slap to the face. Her hand went to her stinging cheek.

'You steal from me again Molly Carter and you'll get more'n that.'

'I don't know...'

Mrs Hopkins raised her hand again and Molly flinched.
'Don't think that posh dress fools me madam.'
'I'm sorry.' stuttered Molly, tears forming in her eyes.
The older woman sighed.
'Why'd you do it? I ain't got much. I'd been looking forward to that pie all week. Don't come across cuts of meat like that very often round here. Then all of a sudden it's gone. From my very kitchen table. Buggers didn't take anything else. Just my bloody pie.'
'I was starving. I...'
'Then why'd you not ask for help? Too bloody stubborn I bet. I'm not likely to bite your head off. If you need help, ask for it. Won't hurt nothin' but your pride. And pride'll kill you, believe me.'
'I'll pay for it.'
'Will you now? What with?'
Molly swallowed. She didn't have any money.
'Thought so.'
Mrs Hopkins walked around her, looking her up and down as if inspecting a soldier on parade.
'Where'd you get that dress? It don't fit properly.'
'I got it yesterday. It was the closest thing they had that would fit me.'
'Who's they?'
'The Princess and...'
'Ah. Now we're getting somewhere. You fallen in with the Princess?'
Molly nodded.
'Could have done worse. She the one that killed Jimmy Gatling?'
'Yes. And she gave his brothers a beating too.'
'I heard that. They're after her blood.'
'I don't think that it's her blood they should be worried about.'
Mrs Hopkins smiled and picked up a tape measure.
'You're probably right. Take your dress off.'

'What? Why?'

'I can't make a suit if I don't have your measurements. And I can't do nothin' about the fit of that dress if you've got it on.'

'Why do I need a suit?'

Mrs Hopkins shrugged.

'I don't ask. Which is why I gets me business. And it'll probably do you good not to ask either.'

'Oh.'

Molly spent the next half an hour being measured in every way possible and it was with some relief when she was told to put her dress back on.

'That'll do. You'll have to come back for a fitting but I expect to have it ready for next week.'

'Thank you.'

Mrs Hopkins looked at her as she began to pin the dress, taking it in around the waist and bust.

'You don't strike me as the sort that goes with Princesses. You're too... rough.'

'I thought you didn't ask questions?'

Mrs Hopkins gave her a grin and cackled a laugh.

'Molly Carter, I like you. Do you want a cup of tea?'

'Yes please.'

An hour later, the dress had been altered to bring it in a bit.

'Not the best fit but it's better'n it was.'

'Thank you.'

There was a polite knock at the back door and Simcox came in.

'Are we ready?'

'She'll do. Bring her back next week for a fitting and we'll see.'

'Thank you, Mrs Hopkins.' replied Simcox.

He handed her a bag of money and they left.

'Next week.' called Mrs Hopkins from the doorway as they walked to the waiting coach.

Nareema was in the drawing room when they got back to the house, drinking a spicy tea that filled the room with exotic smells. Simcox led her in, carrying a large box under his arm.

'Did everything go as expected?' asked Nareema putting her cup down.

'Yes.' he told her. 'She has a fitting next week.'

'Good.'

'I also took the liberty of buying this. I hope it is suitable.'

He placed the box on a table by the wall

'If there's nothing else...'

'Thank you Simcox.'

He left and closed the door behind him. Nareema stood up and went to the box.

'So, let's see what he's bought then shall we?'

She removed the lid and took out the most beautiful dress Molly had ever seen. It was a deep royal blue and inlaid with sparkling gems. There was also a pair of matching long silk gloves and satin shoes. Nareema held it up.

'Perfect. Here. Go and try it on.'

She handed it to her.

'I can't wear this.' she said as she held it against herself.

Nareema cocked her head and looked at her quizzically.

'Why not?'

'It's too much. I don't think...'

Nareema cut her off.

'Look. Am I taking you to your first ball tomorrow? Something, that I understand, is a very important part of an English girl's education and something she should remember for the rest of her life.'

'Not this girl. But yes, you are.'

The Princess smiled at that.

'And am I employing you?'

'Yes.'

'Then you need to look the part. I can't have my eyes and ears looking like something that the cat dragged in.'
'But...'
'Enough. Go and try it on.'

Molly opened her mouth to say something else but Nareema raised her eyebrows so all she managed was a 'thank you' before she headed upstairs to change.

## Chapter Three

## The Ball

  Molly came down the stairs where Nareema and Shakir were waiting in the hallway. He was dressed in a white army uniform with gold braid and his sword hung at his side. His hat, which Molly had learnt was called a turban, was white with a sparkling cluster of gems at its centre and his chest positively bristled with medals.
  Nareema was wearing a white silk sari edged with silver. Her long black hair was tied in an intricate braid that was held in place by gold rings spaced down it. Around her head sat a thin circlet made of twisted gold and in the centre, was a sapphire the size of a man's thumb which rested against her forehead.
  'You look fabulous.' said Nareema
  Molly blushed and looked down. Mrs Kettering had done her hair, curling it and tying in blue ribbons that matched the dress. And the dress... it was something else. She had never imagined that she would get to wear something like this. If she had thought the green dress was impressive, this was in another league all together. Nareema came up to her.
  'I have one more thing for you.'
  Shakir stepped forward holding a solid wooden box. He opened it to reveal a diamond necklace nestled on a bed of red velvet. There were four small gems set around a larger stone, all encased in finely worked silver.
  Gently Nareema took it and placed it around Molly's neck, it was heavy and felt cold against her skin.
  'This was my mothers. I would like you to wear it.'
  Molly touched the gems.
  'I can't wear this.'
  'Please.'

Nareema looked a little sad as if the necklace had triggered an old memory.

'What?'

The Princess shook her head.

'Nothing. I would like you to wear it. It finishes off your outfit. You can't arrive at your first ball looking half-dressed now can you? Shall we go?'

She turned to leave only to be confronted by Shakir. He was stood in front of the door, hand held out in front of him.

'What?'

'You know.'

'I don't know what you mean.' she replied innocently.

'Nareema.' his voice was strict.

The princess sighed and heaved her gown up in a very unladylike manner to undo the buckles of the knife she had strapped to her thigh. Molly suppressed a laugh as she slapped it into his palm.

'And the other one.'

She rolled her eyes and then fished out the smaller knife that was hidden in the folds of the silk.

'Thank you.' he said before turning to Molly, 'How about you little one? Are you armed?'

Molly shook her head quickly. Why should she be?

'No.'

'Maybe you should.'

He handed her the small knife that he'd just taken from Nareema. She took it tentatively.

'Why do I need this?'

'Just in case.' he replied as he stepped aside, pulling the door wide open for the women. They moved past him towards the waiting carriage before he spoke again. His voice was heavy with mirth.

'Oh, and Nareema, you may keep the ones you have in your hair.'

Instinctively her hand shot up to touch what looked like long, but thick, ivory hairpins.

'Come.' he said with a smile. 'Time to go.'

They had been in the coach for almost an hour before they pulled up outside a grand manor house set in a huge expanse of land. Nareema had spoken to Molly as they came to a stop.

'These people are arrogant, tedious and very fond of the sound of their own voices. The women especially. Keep your wits about you.'

She nodded. She was nervous but excited. This wasn't like anything she had done before.

The gravelled area in front of the house was crowded with coaches and horses. Molly looked out of the window at the scene of composed chaos that it seemed to be. People were headed in a steady stream towards the huge grand doors of the manor.

'Ready?' asked Nareema with a smile.

Molly nodded again as the coach stopped and a valet opened the door. Shakir got out first, turning to help Nareema, and then Molly, out.

The early summer air was pleasant but promised a chill later on. Molly tried to take it all in as Shakir lead them inside. A butler met them in the hallway and escorted them to a huge room full of people.

At the far end a small string quartet was playing and a table positively groaned under the weight of more food that Molly had ever seen in one place. Smartly dressed servants carried drinks around the assembled guests and several couples were dancing in the middle of the room. They were all dressed in their finest.

The men were polished and smart and the women wore dresses of every colour imaginable, adorned with jewels and baubles that sparkled in the light of the huge chandeliers that lit the vast room.

The butler cleared his throat and announced them loudly.

'Her Royal Highness Princess Vashti of Sunjian. General Shakir Peynan Commander of the Royal Guard and...' he hesitated and glanced at Molly before continuing. '...um, Miss Molly Carter.'

As he spoke, all conversation in the hall stopped and in the sudden silence, three hundred pairs of eyes flicked their way. Nareema beamed and stood tall. Molly just blushed at the attention. It only lasted a moment before the hostess bustled up and introduced herself and the hubbub of conversation restarted.

'Lady Samantha Banton Your Highness.' said the woman with a deep curtsey. She was short and dumpy with a badly fitted wig and a pale blue dress.

Nareema smiled graciously.

'Lady Samantha.'

Lady Samantha straightened.

'May I offer you a drink Your Highness?'

Nareema nodded.

'Thank you.'

'And for your...' the hostess floundered as she looked to Molly. She could feel her eyeing up the necklace around her neck. It was probably worth more than the house.

'My ward.'

'Your ward. Of course.'

She turned and headed off to find a servant with some drinks. As she headed away, Nareema turned to Molly.

'They're all talking about us you know.' she whispered.

'Why?'

'I doubt they've ever seen anyone from India before. To be honest I doubt if they've ever seen anyone like you either.'

Shakir cleared his throat and bowed to them both.

'Nareema. Little one. If you will excuse me I think I'm going to go and see what they've got to eat.'

'Why does he call me that?' asked Molly as he left them.

Nareema smiled sadly.

'It's what he use to call my sister.'

'Use to?'

Her answer was interrupted by Lady Samantha who was practically dragging a servant along bearing a tray of drinks.

For the next hour, Molly stuck close to Nareema as she was gently guided between groups of expensively dressed men and women who just seemed to talk about nothing in particular.

The men fawned over the Princess and the women just seemed to give her odd looks. Molly had said little, allowing Nareema to answer any questions that were directed at her, for which she was eternally grateful. These people lived in a different world from the poverty and struggle she was used to.

She shook her head and let her attention wander, turning to watch the dancing. The men and women twirled gracefully around the floor, spinning in time to the music. That bit at least was just as Molly had imagined a ball would be.

After a few minutes a handsome man in a red army uniform marched up to Nareema and saluted smartly before bowing low. He had tousled brown hair with a strong chin, pale blue eyes and a thin moustache which he probably thought was dashing.

'Captain Marcus Kane at your service Your Highness.'

Nareema smiled.

'Captain.'

He took a breath.

'If Your Highness will permit me. Would it be acceptable if I were to ask your, um... May I ask your...' he was flustered and Nareema just smiled more which seemed to make him even more uncomfortable.

'Would Your Highness allow me to dance with the young lady?'

'Why don't you ask her? She can speak for herself you know.'

'Of course. My apologies.'

He bowed again before turning to Molly.

'Would do me the honour of this dance?'

Molly blushed as he held out his hand and couldn't miss the hard looks she was getting from a group of girls that were stood nearby which made the whole thing worse.

'I... I don't know how.' she replied hesitantly before blushing further.

He cocked his head quizzically.

'Really?'

'Yes. Really. I've never danced before. Not like this.'

'Then please permit me to show you.'

Molly could feel Nareema grinning beside her as she tentatively took his outstretched hand.

'Thank you.'

As he led her onto the dance floor she whispered to him.

'I really don't know how.'

He turned and looked at her before whispering back.

'Just follow my lead.'

The music started and he took her into hold before whirling her across the floor. As they spun to the music, Molly couldn't help but laugh with joy. This was fun!

'So how can a beautiful girl like you not know how to dance?' he asked her as they moved.

'It just hasn't come up before. It's not something I've needed to do.'

'Why?'

'It just hasn't.'

He twirled her around.

'We've not been formally introduced. Captain Marcus Kane at your service my lady.'

'Molly.'

'I'm sure I've never seen you at one of these tedious gatherings before. I would recognise you anywhere.'

Molly blushed.
'I've never been to one before.'
'Really?'
'Yes. Really.' said Molly with a touch of anger in her voice.
The Captain rallied.
'I do apologise if I offended you. I'm just surprised, that is all.'
'Why?'
'I can't imagine where such a beautiful young lady has been hiding herself.'
Molly could feel herself turning red with embarrassment.
'Captain...'
As they moved, Molly glanced over his shoulder and saw Nareema staring off down one of the corridors with a stern expression. Marcus spun her again and she just caught sight of her walking away from the hall. Something wasn't right. She stumbled and Marcus caught her.
'Could we please sit down for a moment. I feel dizzy.'
'Of course.'
He led her to a nearby chair.
'Let me fetch you a glass of water.'
She nodded and he turned and headed across the hall. As soon as he was out of sight, Molly stood and followed Nareema.

Nareema watched Molly dance with the Captain for a moment. She looked happy and distractedly Nareema wondered how long it had been since she had smiled and laughed like that.
She sighed inwardly as Lady Samantha came up and watched the dancing with her, prattling on about how her own daughter was waiting for the imminent proposal of marriage from the Captain. Nareema glanced back at the dance floor.
'I wouldn't be so sure.' she muttered to herself.

The woman bristled.

'I beg your pardon Your Highness?'

Nareema ignored her as she saw someone she recognised through the crowd. A thin oriental man with slicked hair and thin wireframe glasses. He smiled and nodded cordially to her before he left the room.

'What's he doing here?'

'Who?' asked Lady Samantha.

Nareema looked at her angrily and the woman took a step back. She took a deep breath and tried to calm herself, forcing her anger down, before smiling tightly.

'I'm sorry. Would you excuse me for a moment.'

With that she turned on her heel and left the hostess standing speechless behind her.

Cutting through the assembled crowd like a knife, she headed to the corridor where the man had gone.

The crowd thinned as she saw him, waiting for her, a glass of champagne in each hand. As soon as he was sure she had seen him he nodded once more then turned and headed to the right through a pair of large double doors.

Taking a breath, Nareema followed him. She pushed the doors open to find herself in a library. He was stood in the middle of the room.

'Princess Vashti. What a pleasant surprise.' his accent was clipped but his English was well pronounced.

She strode into the space and cursed herself as she felt movement behind her and heard the doors close. Turning slowly she took in the four other men behind her. All were armed with swords. Her slow circle finished with her face to face with the man.

'Tong Li.'

He smiled.

'Champagne?' he asked, holding up a glass.

Nareema made no move to take it. She could feel the men behind her move closer. He took a sip from his drink.

'I do so hate these affairs. They're so boring. Don't you

agree?'

She didn't answer so he sighed.

'Let's cut to the chase. Give me the Air Stone and I'll let you live.'

'Is that what you told my sister?'

He sipped his drink and made a hurt face.

'Harsh. She wouldn't give me the Fire Stone. I had to take it. Her death was quick.'

Placing the glass on a table of books he walked over to her.

'Give me the Stone.'

'No.'

She felt the point of a blade at her back.

'Then I shall take it.'

The pressure in her back from the blade increased slightly as Tong Li reached up to take the circlet and sapphire from Nareema's brow.

Molly headed out of the hall and down a side corridor just as a pair of large double doors closed. As quietly as she could she went up to them, pressing her ear against the wood. There were voices but they were muffled and she couldn't make out any words.

She bent down to look through the keyhole. She could see Nareema stood talking to a thin man with glasses. Behind her stood another man who was holding a sword to her back.

'Peeking through keyholes isn't very ladylike.'

Molly started at the sudden voice and whirled round to come face to face with the Captain.

'Captain Kane. You made me jump.'

'Sorry. What are you doing? I was looking for you. I went to get you a drink and then you were gone.'

'I had to find the Princess.'

'Is she in there?'

'Yes. No.' Molly bit her lip. She had to do something.

'Captain...' she said coyly.
'Yes?'
She grabbed his lapels and spun him so his back was to the door. His protests were barely out of his mouth before she kissed him deeply. He floundered for a moment and she pushed him backwards into the doors which sprang open. The men in the room turned at the noise. Molly giggled like a school girl.

'Oops. I'm sorry. We seem to have gotten the wrong room.'

Marcus was still reeling from the kiss.

'Dreadfully sorry...'

It was then that Nareema moved. Like lightning, her hands went to her hair, coming back with the two small daggers. The first slashed at Tong Li, opening up a cut across his palm while the second she buried deep in the throat of the man behind her. He gurgled as he fell back, dropping his sword as he tried to stem the blood sprouting from the wound in his neck. Nareema scooped up the weapon and shouted to Molly.

'Go and find Shakir. Captain. Go with her.'

Molly grabbed his jacket and hauled him away.

'We can't leave her there.'

'Come on.'

Stumbling, they both crashed into the hall, knocking over a waiter with a tray of drinks. Everyone looked up at the noise.

'Shakir!'

He heard Molly shout and began to run towards them, drawing his sword as he went. Around them the party erupted into a mass of shouting and screaming. Some of the more bold men followed him.

'What?'

'Nareema. There were five of them. In the library. She killed one.' Molly told him breathlessly as the Captain helped her up.

He nodded and pounded down the corridor to the library. The doors were open and Nareema stood with her sword buried deep in the last of the assailants. Her pristine white dress looked like it belonged in a butchers shop.

'What seems to be....' began the Lady Samantha as Nareema pushed the dead man from the blade with her foot.

'Oh my.' she said before she fainted dead away.

Shakir went to her, Molly and the Captain pushing through the crowd to follow.

'Dear god...' said Marcus.

'What happened?'

'Tong Li.'

'He is here?' the disbelief obvious in Shakirs voice.

'He was here.'

She pointed to an open window with the sword before bending down to pick up the circlet from the floor, the metal and sapphire slick with blood. Shakir rushed over to the window but there was no one to be seen.

'Damn him. How did he know?'

'I don't know.'

'You're hurt.'

Molly pointed to a long cut across Nareema's left arm. It was bleeding heavily.

'Go and fetch my bag from the carriage. It's under the seat.'

She nodded and hurried away, pushing back through the gathered crowds at the doorway.

'Wait. I'll come with you.'

It was the Captain. He had picked up a sword from one of the dead men and was close behind. They headed back to the hall quickly but Molly pulled up short.

'Hang on.'

She put a hand on his shoulder to steady herself before she reached beneath the dress and pulled off the satin shoes.

'That's better.'

All eyes were on them as they moved through the room. She glanced across the hall to the gossiping group of girls from earlier. They stared at her in disbelief as she dashed towards the door, shoes in hand.

Marcus entered the entrance hall first with his sword raised, causing gasps from the people milling around.

'How did the Princess do that? There were five of them.'

'She'd probably say something like "Practice", but I don't know where she learned to fight.'

'She's a very capable woman.'

He glanced at Molly.

'So are you if you don't mind me saying.'

'Captain...'

'You surprised me you know. Not many women can do that.'

'How did I surprise you.'

'You really can't dance.'

They pushed their way out to the gravel outside the house and headed for the coaches. Staff and servants bustled about, they knew something was up but not what it was.

'I thought I did quite well.'

'My toes beg to differ my lady.' he said with a smile.

She shoved him playfully.

'I'm not a lady.'

'You certainly don't act like one. Or speak like one. I haven't heard you mention your dress once this evening and I'm sure I've never been kissed like that at one of these things before.'

Molly blushed.

'It was the first thing I could think of that would be a distraction.'

They slowed as they reached Nareema's coach. It was the last one in the line. The driver was nowhere to be seen.

'Not that I'm complaining you understand.' he said hurriedly as he turned to her.

'Good.' she said as she pulled open the coach door and clambered inside.

'Although if you would like my advice Captain. I would lose the moustache. It tickles and looks a bit silly. Like you've drawn on your top lip.'

His hand went to his face.

'I say...'

Nareema watched them go before turning away from the gathered crowd. They were all stunned by the bloodshed that was in front of them. Shakir turned to them.

'There has been an attempt on the Princess's life. Please leave.'

He shut the double doors in their faces before returning to Nareema. She had put the sword on the table and sat herself next to it, absentmindedly she wiped her hands on her dress smearing more blood into the silk.

'Let me have a look at you. Are you hurt?'

She shook her head.

'No.'

Shakir bent down and tore a strip from the bottom of her dress which he quickly wrapped around the cut on her arm.

'He was here.' she said after a moment. 'And I walked right into his trap.'

'You couldn't have known.'

'I should have. He has the Fire Stone. He almost got the Air.'

'Tobias should have found where the other two Stones are by now. We will have to make sure we get to them before he does.'

Shakir stood up.

'That'll do for now.'

Nareema stood and smashed her fist against the table angrily, sending the glass of champagne flying.

'He was here.'

'Calm yourself. There is nothing more you can do now.'

She whirred round, her face as hard as stone.

'Calm down? I had him in front of me. I could have...'

Her words were cut short by a scream from somewhere outside. Nareema grabbed her sword.

'Molly.'

She ran headlong for the door and flung it open. The people milling outside quickly saw the look on her face and got out of the way. She was from a nightmare. An avenging angel swathed in blood.

At a run she headed for the front door, bursting out of it into the night. Quickly she headed along the line of coaches and as she neared the end of the line, she saw the Captain laid flat on the floor with a bloody gash on his temple. Next to him was a long leather holdall and her mothers' diamond necklace, but of Molly or the coach there was no sign.

Nareema rolled him over and checked his pulse. He was alive. She grabbed him and hauled him to his feet.

'Where is she?' she shouted.

He blinked blearily at her.

'Who?'

She cried out in anger as she slammed him bodily against a nearby tree.

'Molly. Where is Molly?'

He touched the cut on his temple and seemed surprised when his fingers came away bloody. Nareema slammed him into the tree again.

'Where is she?'

'Nareema! Let him go.'

She glared angrily at Shakir before turning back to the Captain.

'If I find you had anything to do with this, I *will* kill you.'

With a final push she turned and left him, picking up the bag and necklace on the way back into the house.

'There were four of them I think. A thin one with glasses and some others. They hit me from behind and as Molly passed me the bag out of the coach, they hit me again. After that I don't know what happened.'

They were sat in the kitchen of the big house. Shakir had chased the staff out. There were too many people upstairs for them to get some peace.

'I've killed her.' said Nareema quietly.

'You don't know that.' snapped Shakir as he looked at the wound on the Captains head. He took out a small jar from the bag and scooped out a wad of foul smelling brown ointment.

'This is going to sting a little.' he said as he applied it to the cut.

Marcus jumped and cried out.

'Damn. That hurts. What is that stuff.'

'It will keep the wound clean and closed until it has had a chance to heal.'

Shakir turned to Nareema who was sat at the other end of the table.

'Now you.'

She looked at him for a moment before nodding and undoing the makeshift bandage from around her arm. Shakir applied more of the ointment to the cut and although she set her jaw, she made no sound. Once he was done, Nareema stood up.

'I'm going to find her.'

'Nareema...'

'No. If it wasn't for me she would still be here.'

'She would be dead. Those men would have killed her. Or worse...' said Shakir softly.

'What men? What are you talking about?' asked the Captain.

'I'm going.'

She delved in the bag, pulling out her leather suit and then beginning to strip off the ruined dress.

'I say... Your Highness...' began Marcus.
She stopped and glared at him.
'I'll wait outside.'

The kitchen door opened a few minutes later and Nareema strode out. Her face was a grim mask. Marcus looked at her in disbelief as if he couldn't comprehend what she was wearing and doing. She ignored him walked up to Shakir.

'Go home and get Mrs Kettering and Simcox. Take them to Uncle Tobias. If Tong Li has come here he might go after them too.'

'Nareema...'

'No. I'm going to find her. We will come to you.'

He nodded sadly.

'Be careful.'

'Am I not always?'

The words were light but her voice betrayed her. Shakir bent and kissed her cheek.

'Find her.'

She nodded and headed back upstairs. Footsteps followed her and she turned to see the Captain, sword in hand, coming up behind her.

'Where are you going?'

'With you.'

'No.'

'I feel responsible for this. I should have protected her. I should have been more aware of the danger...'

Nareema looked at him, seeing the determination in his face.

'Do you know how to use that?' she asked, indicating the weapon in his hand. He looked down at the sword for a second before nodding.

'Much to my shame, yes. I was at Waterloo.'

She sighed.

'Try to keep up.'

She turned and headed to the hall which was still crowded

with gossiping people. Nareema headed for Lady Samantha who took one look at how she was dressed and went white.

'I need a horse.'

She opened and closed her mouth a few times as if searching for the right words.

'Take mine.' said a man standing nearby when it was obvious no answer would be forthcoming from her ladyship.

Nareema nodded her thanks and turned to leave, the man trailing behind her to take her to the animal. As she left she couldn't help but smile as she heard Marcus address the hostess.

'Lovely party. Thank you for the invitation. Haven't had this much fun in ages. Got to dash now however, damsel in distress and all that. '

'She thinks you're going to ask her daughter to marry you.' said Nareema as he caught her up.

He shrugged as behind them the Lady Samantha fainted once more. Once outside, the Captain mounted his own steed and Nareema jumped up onto her mount.

'Are you sure you want to do this?' she asked him.

'Yes.'

The princess gave him a hard look.

'Come on. But don't get in my way.'

Before he could ask her what she meant, she shouted, kicked her horse into a gallop and headed off into the night.

## Chapter Four

### Fire

Molly woke suddenly. It was dark and she was lying on her side on a dirt floor. There was a rough cloth tied over her eyes and another was pulled between her lips as a gag. Wherever she was smelled of animals.

Fighting a rising panic, she tried to sit up but someone had tied her arms behind her and ankles together. She tested the ropes at her wrists, but they were securely bound. Slumping back down Molly tried to remember what had happened.

She had been getting the bag for Nareema from the coach. The Captain had taken it when someone hit him from behind. She had screamed as hands came through the door behind her and grabbed her head. She'd bitten one of them and then that was it. Judging from the way her head hurt, they must have hit her as well.

She wriggled some more before she heard footsteps coming towards her.

'I'm going to take off your blindfold and gag. Scream or make any sound at all and I will kill you. Do you understand?'

Molly lay still for a moment before nodding. The movement caused her head to spin.

There was a brief conversation in a language she didn't understand before rough hands took away the blindfold and gag. She looked up at her captor. It was the man with the glasses she had seen in the library with Nareema. His hand was bandaged and behind him stood half a dozen armed men.

'What... What do you want. I haven't got money...'

He knelt down close to her and produced the dagger which Shakir had given her. He rested it against her cheek.

'Little girls shouldn't play with knives. They can be dangerous. As for what I want?' he smiled darkly. 'Nothing you have. Although... I'm sure my men can find something they might be interested in.'

He carefully ran the blade down her skin to her breast and she shuddered at the look in his eyes.

'Your friend the Princess has something I want. I will offer to trade your life for it. She's probably on her way here now. We've left her enough clues.'

'What is it?'

'A stone. A precious gem. One of the four Stones of Gunjai. With that Stone, I can find the others. And then the Crown. And then... well... the world is my oyster...'

He stood up and smiled humourlessly before saying something else in the foreign language. A moment later one of the men grabbed her and forced the gag back in to her mouth and slipped the blindfold back. She struggled but the thin man spoke softly to her.

'Be still and quiet and I promise I won't let my men have you before I kill you.'

Nareema stood on a rooftop overlooking the cattle market. Marcus clambered up beside her breathing hard.

'How the hell did you get up here so fast?'

'Practice.'

She squatted down.

'This is too easy. Tong Li wants me to find her. He left pieces of her dress all the way here.'

'It's a trap.'

She glared at him.

'Of course it is.'

'Does he think you'll fall for it?'

'I doubt it. Which is why there is probably a back way in. Which will certainly be an ambush.'

'So what do we do.'

'I knock on the front door.'

Nareema stood.

'Captain. Go around the back. Find Molly and get her out. I'll give them something to think about.'

Before he could reply she stepped off the edge of the roof. He scrambled to the edge in time to see her begin to stride purposefully towards the cattle market.

Nareema had gone no more than a dozen paces before she saw the first guard. He looked up in surprise as she fell upon him with a short knife in each hand. It was over in an instant and she left the body where it had fallen. Stealth was something she wasn't trying for. The next two men were also dealt with quickly and she stepped into the wide doorway.

'Tong Li!'

Her shout echoed back and forth across the market. Wooden stalls where the animals were penned stretched away on her left and right, with a wide walkway down the centre. The entire place smelled of dung.

She stepped further into the building and called again. There was movement at the far end. Four men were walking towards her, one was hauling Molly along with him. Her dress was torn, her wrists bound behind her and she was blindfolded and gagged. Nareema stopped.

'Let her go.'

Molly looked up at the sound of her voice and struggled in her captors grip. He struck her hard and she fell to her knees.

'Molly. Are you alright?'

There was dried blood in her matted and dirty blonde hair but she managed a nod. Tong Li stepped forward slightly, an amused look on his face.

'Princess. You accepted my gracious invitation.'

'Let her go.'

'Give me the Stone.'

'Do you really think me that stupid?'

'You're here aren't you?'

He shouted in Chinese and, sensing movement, Nareema turned to meet the three men running in from behind her. As the first man reached her she dropped and spun, sweeping his feet out from under him. He hit the ground hard but Nareema was already rising to meet the second, a knife in her hand. The blade caught him under the chin, her momentum pushing it up through the roof of his mouth and into his brain. He was dead before he hit the floor.

She let the knife go and drew her sword. The first man had managed to struggle to his knees before she kicked him hard in the face. He slumped backwards and she followed, driving her sword into his chest. The third slowed as he saw what she had done to his friends.

Nareema faced him with her sword in her hand. Tong Li shouted at him and his eyes flicked from the Princess to him and back again. He hesitated for a second before he dropped his own weapon and ran for it. Nareema let him go. She turned to face Tong Li.

'Give me the Stone. Or she dies.'

He waved his hand and the man with Molly hauled her back to her feet before pressing a knife to her neck. Nareema hesitated but she reached inside her suit and took out the sapphire.

'Let her go.'

'The Stone.'

Casually, she threw gem towards him. It landed halfway between them in the dirt.

In the shadows behind the men she could see the Captain. He was almost behind Molly.

Tong Li stepped forward and picked the gem up, holding it to the light and examining it.

'Kill them.' he said.

As he spoke, Marcus plunged his sword into the man holding Molly and as soon as he had struck, Nareema launched herself at Tong Li. She covered the ground between them in a second. He turned as she swung her sword at him. The blade missed his head but caught the gem, sending it spinning across the market.

He swore and kicked out, catching Nareema full in the chest and sending her sprawling. She rolled and jumped back up, putting herself between him and the Stone. To her left, Marcus had dealt with one of the remaining men but was locked in a brutal fight with the last.

The man screamed as he fell, taking Molly with him. Marcus grabbed her and dragged her back up.

'It's me. Marcus. Get behind me.'

With an uncermonious shove he pushed her out of the way to meet the incoming blade of one of the other men.

As Marcus had pushed Molly she had fallen hard, banging her already sore head. She cried out but the fall dislodged the blindfold over one eye. She peered past the cloth to see Nareema and Tong Li circling each other, swords raised and Marcus fighting his own battle.

Scrabbling to her feet she launched herself at the closest man. He turned at the last second to see her coming but couldn't do anything about it and they both crashed to the ground in a heap. A moment later, she was bodily hauled out of the way before Marcus drove his blade into the prone man's chest.

Marcus ripped the gag and blindfold from Molly's head before using his sword to cut the ropes at her wrists.

'Are you alright? Did they hurt you?'

She shook her head, still feeling a little dizzy.

'No. I'm fine.'

Molly looked up as Nareema and Tong Li met in a flurry of sword strokes. Each thrust was parried and deflected with a practiced ease from both of them. A heavy swing from Tong Li locked their blades for a moment and they were stood face to face, both trying to push their opponent off balance and gain an opening. Nareema's face was a mask of tension as slowly but surely the man forced her back.

Suddenly she sagged and jumped to the side, his forward momentum continued and he sprawled on the floor.

'Molly, grab the Stone. Get out of here.'

Nareema kicked the gem towards her and leapt back as Tong Li recovered and tried to hack at her legs as he stood back up. Molly dived forward and grabbed the sapphire.

Tong Li had risen to one knee when he saw Molly take the gem. He let out a curse and reached inside his shirt to pull out a ruby on a silver chain. It was about the same size as the sapphire.

'You have no idea just what power the Stones have.' he spat at Nareema as she edged away from him.

He ripped the chain from his neck and gripped it tightly in his left hand before he flicked his head back and let out a huge roar to the sky. The sound was more than a man should have been able to make. It reverberated around the market and above him the wooden beams charred and then burst into flame.

Nareema watched in horror and his body burst into fire which enveloped him, continuing up his sword until it was swathed in dancing flame. As he stood, she caught his eyes which were deep pits of raging fire. He roared again and the wooden stalls behind her began to catch light as a blast of ferocious heat swept in all directions. Nareema covered her face as the blast ripped past her.

'Now I'm going to kill you.' he roared.

With that, Tong Li launched himself forward, bringing his flaming sword down towards her head. She managed to block the swipe but the power behind it drove her to her knees. His strength was incredible! Around them the fire was spreading fast, the straw and wooden fences quickly turning to an inferno. Nareema rolled to the left to avoid another strike and flipped to her feet.

'Marcus!  Get her out.'

Her shout was almost lost in the growing sounds of the fire.  He nodded and grabbed Molly's arm

'Come on.'

'We can't leave her!'

Even as she spoke, Tong Li feinted with his sword before delivering a powerful backhand that caught Nareema in the chest and sent her flying.  She hit one of the uprights supporting the roof hard with her shoulder and dropped to the floor.

Tong Li roared in victory and around him the fire burnt harder.  Nareema struggled to her hands and knees but couldn't get her breath as Tong Li advanced, grinning madly.  He kicked her in the stomach and she dropped to the floor again before he raised his sword high.  Molly watched in horror.

'No!'

As she shouted, the gem in her hand grew warm and her words turned into a vicious wind.  It swarmed out of nowhere and picked the fiery monster up, flinging him a full thirty feet to crash heavily into the wall.

Marcus rushed over to help Nareema to her feet.  She cried out in pain and her right arm hung uselessly at her side.  Across the market, Tong Li was getting up.  He shook his head to clear it, roared again and around him the building burned.

'We've got to get out of here.'  Marcus shouted to Molly as part of the roof collapsed.

'This way.'

She hurried towards the back of the building and began stamping on the dirty floor.

'What are you looking for?'

After a few seconds, Molly's stamping was rewarded by a hollow wooden sound.

'This.  Help me.'

Marcus carefully sat Nareema down and helped Molly clear the dirt and straw from a worn looking trap door. There was a bestial roar from behind them. Tong Li was trying to get to them but around him the building was coming down. He seemed untroubled by the flames, smashing burning beams and stalls from his path as he advanced.

'Quickly.'

They heaved the trapdoor open. Marcus covered his nose.

'God. What is that smell?'

'Do you know how much shit a market full of cattle makes? We're near the river. There's a barge that comes up underneath the market and they just shovel it in.'

'Right. What do they do with it?'

'How the hell do I know?' snapped Molly.

'I was only asking.'

She looked at him and shook her head.

'Come on.'

'Are you sure.'

'No. But it's better than burning to death.'

'Right.' Marcus didn't sound convinced but a crash from their left that spat burning embers across them changed his mind.

Molly took a deep breath before she jumped into the hole and a second later there was a splash. Marcus helped Nareema to her feet again and hugged her tightly.

'Sorry Your Highness but…'

'Just jump you idiot.' she muttered through gritted teeth.

He took a deep breath and plunged into the darkness a second before a pile of burning timbers crashed down to cover the trapdoor.

They fell for a moment before hitting freezing water. He spluttered to the surface and dragged Nareema with him.

'Marcus. Over here.'

There was a small jetty to one side and Molly had hauled

herself into it. He splashed his way over and between them the dragged Nareema onto the damp and slimy wood.

Above them they could feel the heat of the fire and above the crack of timbers and burning wood, they heard a roar of anger.

'We've got to get out of here.'

There was a narrow stone path that ran towards the river. Molly stood and helped Nareema up.

'Come on. I think I know a place we can go.'

Marcus looked at her for a second before nodding and leading the way into the dark.

Twenty minutes later the trio were stood in a small walled yard. A woodpile was to the left and a tired looking green wooden door led to a house. In the distance, they could see the flames from the market as it burned. They were wet and tired. Molly went up to the door and knocked loudly. There was no answer so she knocked again and again until there was a voice from the other side.

'I'm coming. Hold your horses.'

The door opened a crack and the face of Mrs Hopkins peered out.

'What?'

'Mrs Hopkins. It's me. Molly Carter. I need your help.'

The woman hesitated before she opened the door wide, gasping in surprise as she saw Nareema slumped against the Captain.

'Come in.'

She quickly ushered them inside and shut the door.

'She's hurt. I didn't know where else to go.'

Mrs Hopkins cleared the small table in her work room.

'Lay her down.'

Marcus helped Nareema up onto the table and Mrs Hopkins checked her over. As she touched the shoulder the princess shouted in pain.

'She's bruised a couple of ribs and dislocated her arm. I'm going to have to put it back. Hold her down.'

As Marcus and Molly put their weight on Nareema, Mrs Hopkins spoke softly to her.

'I'm going to put your shoulder back in. It's going to hurt.'

Nareema nodded through gritted teeth and Mrs Hopkins stepped back.

'Hold her. On the count of three. One... Two...'

She pulled and twisted Nareema's arm and she cried out, bucking against the two people holding her against the table.

'Almost got it.'

She yanked hard again and with an audible pop her shoulder snapped back in. Nareema cried out once more before she fainted.

'Three.' finished Mrs Hopkins.

She stepped forward and put her hand on Nareema's forehead.

'She'll be alright. You.' she pointed at Marcus. 'Take her upstairs and lay her on the bed. First room on the left.'

He nodded and picked up the unconscious Princess and carried her out of the room. Mrs Hopkins looked at Molly.

'Thank you.'

'Don't make a habit of it. Now I think you need to get out of what's left of that dress and into something that's dry and doesn't stink of shit.'

Molly smiled despite herself.

'Come on. I've got some things in the shop that'll do for now. I can probably find something for your man too when he comes back.'

'He's not my...'

'Of course not.' she said with a wry smile. 'Stoke up the fire and put the kettle on.'

Mrs Hopkins left Molly adding wood to the fire and went into her shop. A moment later Marcus came down the stairs.

'She's asleep.'

Molly looked up at him.

'Thank you.'

'For what?'

'For coming to find me.'

'I'm sorry I didn't protect you in the first place.'

'I don't need protecting.'

They stood and looked at each other for a moment, neither knowing what to say. The silence between them was broken by Mrs Hopkins who came back in.

'Here.' she said, throwing a pair of trousers and a shirt to Marcus and a dress to Molly.

'Get out of those wet clothes. You can change in there.' she said, indicating to the shop with her head.

'Of course. If you will excuse me.'

Mrs Hopkins waited until he was out of earshot.

'So where'd you meet him? Looks pretty good.'

Molly took her ruined dress off.

'At a ball. We've only known each other for a few hours.'

'A ball? All high and mighty all of a sudden.'

'It's not like that.'

'I know. I'm only playing with you.' grinned Mrs Hopkins

Molly smiled sadly.

'Looks like a good man. Keep hold of him.'

'He's not...'

'No. You said. Sorry. Got to humour an old woman. Right, I don't know about you but I could do with some tea.'

# Chapter Five

## The Stones

Molly dozed in a chair by the fire not really asleep but feeling dog tired. Across from her, Marcus slept in his own chair. Mrs Hopkins had taken herself off upstairs a while ago. It had been quite a day. Soft footsteps on the stairs woke her and she looked up as Nareema came down. She rotated her shoulder a few times, wincing as she did so. Molly sat up and spoke quietly.

'Are you alright?'

Nareema smiled tightly as she came over and sat in front of the fire.

'I'll live. How are you?'

'I'll live too.'

They both went quiet. The only sounds were the crackling of the fire and the light snoring from Marcus.

'I'm sorry about this evening. If I had known Tong Li was going to be there I would...'

'It doesn't matter.'

The Princess smiled tightly again and they lapsed in to silence.

'How did you control the Stone?' asked Nareema eventually.

Molly shrugged.

'I don't know. It just happened.'

'It's yours now. It has never spoken to me like that. I found it and have protected it ever since but now I will protect you, and it, with my life.'

'Nareema, you don't need...'

'No. I do.'

They were silent for a moment.

'What are the Stones?'

Nareema looked at Molly through tired eyes, the firelight catching her face to make her look older. She sighed heavily.

'A thousand years ago there was a small settlement in the foothills of the Gunjai mountains. There had been a terrible drought. The cattle were dying and those that were left would not give milk. The crops failed and the people were starving. In desperation, the chief of the village prayed to the Gods for help. They heard his plea and sent him four gemstones. One for each of the elements.'

'An emerald for the Earth and with it he made the land fertile. A diamond for the Water so he could bring the rain and make the crops grow. Sapphire was for the Air so he could control wind and clouds and a ruby for Fire to protect his people.'

'With the help of the Stones, his village prospered and quickly became a town and then a city. The people forgot their hunger and suffering and lived. But as with all things, men sought the power for their own ends.'

Nareema paused and looked into the fire.

'The chief had a son who, as he grew, craved the power of the Stones for himself. He murdered his father for them and declared himself King. He had a crown fashioned using dark and evil magic and set the Stones within it.'

'His rule signalled a change for his people. Nothing could stand before him as he raised and army and conquered everything that he saw. Farmers turned into bloodthirsty warriors and they rampaged across the land, taking what they pleased. Against this stood only one group. The only light in the darkness. These were the Daughters of Kali.'

'They were not powerful enough to take the King on as an army but they were schooled in more subtle arts. One of the Daughters made her way through the court until she was the concubine of the King and as they made love one night she, killed him. Stabbed him through his black heart with a dagger blessed by the gods. As he lay dying she took the crown and made her escape.'

Molly had shifted to the edge of her seat.

'Then what happened?'

Nareema looked at her.

'The Daughter rode hard to the monastery of Kali but eventually had to stop to rest. It was then that she was ambushed by bandits. Though she killed many of their number she was slain. The robbers didn't know what they had. They took the Crown, separating the Stones and spreading them to the four winds. The Daughters of Kali have been looking for them ever since.'

'Are you a Daughter of Kali?'

'Yes.'

'Who are they?'

'It doesn't matter.'

Nareema looked at the fire, unable to meet Molly's gaze.

'My mother was the first to find one of them. She found the Fire Stone, a ruby, in a temple in the east. She took it back and became it's protector. From clues in the temple and help from Uncle Tobias, I was able to find the Stone of Air. The sapphire. It had become part of a necklace owned by a French noblewoman. I took it back. She did not deserve what she had.'

'Did you kill her?'

Nareema didn't answer.

'How did Tong Li get the Fire Stone?'

'He killed my mother for it. He got into the palace one night and tried to take it. She was a skilled warrior and not easily cowed. As they fought, she gave the Stone to my sister and brother. She told them to run.'

She looked into the fire sadly.

'Mother gave her life to allow them to escape but it wasn't enough. Tong Li tracked my sister and brother down. They had fled the palace and were in the city but he still found them. My brother, Ramesh, tried to protect his sister but he was no match for Tong Li.'

'Did he die?'

Nareema shook her head.

'No. He was badly injured and almost bled to death. Pakau ran but Tong Li cornered her in an alley. He murdered her. She was seven years old.'

Molly put her hand to her mouth, unsure what to say next.

'I will kill him for that.'

Nareema's voice was like steel.

'Where are the other Stones? And the Crown?'

'I don't know. No one does. But we must find them before he does. He will usher in a reign like no other the world has ever seen.'

'Tong Li said that with this one he could find the others.'

'Did he? I didn't know that. Maybe Uncle Tobias will have an answer.'

Molly took the sapphire from her pocket.

'Maybe I can find them?'

Nareema shifted to her knees before Molly.

'Maybe you can.'

Taking a breath, Molly held the gem in the palm of her hand.

'What do I do?'

'I don't know. Try thinking of one of the Stones.'

Molly closed her eyes and thought of the gem that Tong Li had. In her palm the sapphire began spinning slowly, changing colour to become a vivid blood red. It came to rest pointing towards the east.

'The Fire Stone is towards the docks. Think of the Earth. It was an emerald. A green gem.'

Taking another deep breath, she concentrated hard. The stone in her hand began to spin until it pointed south west. Its colour had changed to be a weak green.

'What does that mean?'

'The Stone is that way but I think it may be a long way off. We need to go to see Uncle Tobias.'
'Who is he?'
'A dear friend and the one person that knows the most about the Stones.'
'Oh.'
Nareema studied her for a moment.
'You look tired. Get some sleep. It's been an eventful day.'
Molly nodded and smiled. Nareema stood and turned to go.
'You were right.' said Molly.
'About what?'
'My first ball was something I'll never forget.'
Nareema laughed and glanced at Marcus.
'In more ways than one. Get some sleep.'

Molly woke suddenly. The fire had burnt itself out and across the room Marcus still slept. There was no sign of Nareema.

She stretched and tried work out which bits of her didn't ache. Eventually she decided that there were so few of them that it didn't make much difference. Quietly she headed outside to the yard. The smoke from the cattle market hung heavily in the early morning air. On the horizon, the sun was just beginning to rise but dark clouds to the south promised rain later.

She shivered and turned to go back inside picking up some more wood for the fire from the pile. She had lit it and was on her knees in front of it when Marcus woke up.
'Morning.' she said quietly.
He smiled and let out a groan as he stretched.
'How are you this morning?' he asked.
'Stiff. You?'
'The same. I must say that when I accepted Lady Samantha's invitation I didn't expect such an eventful

evening.'

'Or waking up in a chair in a dressmakers' shop.'

'I've woken up in worse places than this. Where's the Princess?'

Molly shrugged.

'I don't know.'

Marcus stood and stretched.

'What happened last night? How did that man make all that fire? I've seen some magic tricks in my time but nothing like that. And how did you make the wind come?'

Molly shrugged again.

'I don't know. It sort of happened. It's all to do with this.'

She held out the sapphire for him to see.

'Very nice. What is it?'

'Nareema said is it one of the Stones of Gunjai.'

Marcus sat back down again.

'What?'

Molly repeated what Nareema had said about the Stones and he sat quietly, listening to the whole story. She didn't mention that the Princess was a Daughter of Kali.

'He killed her mother and sister?'

Molly nodded.

'And nearly killed her brother.'

'Poor girl. No wonder she was angry.'

They lapsed into silence for a moment

'So who is this Tobias character then?'

'I don't know that either. Nareema called him Uncle so he must be a relative of hers. Maybe he can tell me how to control the Stone and then I can use it to find the others and stop Tong Li. So, I guess I need to see Tobias. Whoever he is.'

'We.'

'Pardon?'

'You said *you* were going to stop him. You should have said *we*. I'm coming along too.'

'You can't do that.'

'Why not?'

Molly looked at him, trying to find a way to dissuade him but couldn't think of anything. Marcus stood up and came over to the fire where he knelt next to her.

'I won't have it said that I didn't give my wholehearted assistance to a damsel in distress.'

Molly blushed as he looked at her. He smiled and took her unresisting hand. They looked at each other for a moment, both lost in their own thoughts.

'We'll have none of that, thank you very much.'

They turned as Mrs Hopkins came down the stairs and both looked embarrassed as they saw the amused look on her face.

'Go out and get us some bread. Molly and I have things to do. Here.'

She flicked a coin to Marcus who caught it deftly and threw it back.

'Thank you for your hospitality. I will buy the bread. It is the least I can do.'

Mrs Hopkins shrugged.

'Fair enough. And if you could see your way to some tea and me' be a little drop of gin that would be nice too.'

Marcus grinned and then snapped off a salute before bowing low.

'As you wish my lady.'

They watched him go before Mrs Hopkins ushered Molly into the shop. Carefully she checked the front door was locked and pulled across the curtain.

'Here.'

She reached under the counter and took out a leather suit like the one Nareema wore.

'I made a spare for the Princess.' she explained. 'You're a bit taller than she is and there's a little more to you but I've adjusted it so it should fit. Try it on.'

Molly took it and ran it through her fingers. The leather was soft and supple. She bit her lip and began to take off her dress.

'It feels like I'm not wearing anything.'
'You'll get use to it.'
Molly spun to see Nareema standing in the doorway.
'It looks good on you. You just need a good pair of boots and you'll be set. Where's Marcus?'
'He went shopping. Where have you been?'
'To the market. It's completely destroyed. There is no sign of Tong Li.'
They were silent for a moment.
'I'm sorry I got you into this.'
Molly's reply was lost as Marcus opened the door. He was laden down with bread, cheese and all sorts of other things. Nareema couldn't help but notice the way Molly's face lit up when she saw him or the look of astonishment that crossed his. He hesitated for a second before rallying and dropping the shopping on the table.
'I'm back ladies. Breakfast is secured.'
He grinned at them both.
'So, what's the plan?'
'We're going to see Uncle Tobias.' replied Nareema.
'Where does he live?'
'Somerset.'
'It'll take us a good few days of riding to get there.'
Molly held up her hand.
'I can't ride a horse.'
Marcus looked at her with a quizzical look on his face.
'Really?'
Molly sighed angrily.
'Yes really. My name is Molly Carter. A few days ago I was homeless and starving. I can't read or write, I can't dance and I don't know how to ride a bloody horse. It hasn't been high on my list of things to learn to do. Just

making sure I had somewhere safe to sleep seemed more important. I'm not one of your pampered ladies. I've got nothing and until Nareema showed up nobody could have cared if I lived or not.'

'Molly...' began Marcus.

'Don't. I don't want sympathy.'

She stormed past them both and out into the yard.

'I didn't know.' said Marcus defensively but obviously stunned. 'She didn't...'

Nareema shook her head.

'You were doing so well.'

'Why didn't she say anything?'

'We really haven't had time but what did you expect? Not everyone is born to privilege. I helped her and I'm trying to give her a chance. But I'm not doing too well at the moment. I've gotten her kidnapped and almost killed.'

'I'm going to talk to her.'

He turned to go.

'Wait. Be kind. She's been through a lot this last couple of days.'

Marcus nodded and followed Molly outside.

She heard the door open and wiped the tears from her eyes with the back of her hand before she turned around. Marcus was stood by the door.

'Go away.'

'I'm sorry. I just assumed that as you were with the Princess you were... I don't know... I'm sorry. I never imagined that someone...'

'Someone what? Common? Penniless?' snapped Molly.

'Different. Special.'

Marcus sighed and stepped towards her.

'Please forgive me.'

Molly looked at him angrily for a second and then burst into tears. He put his arm around her and held her close.

'If you'll permit me I would be delighted to teach you to dance.' he whispered.

Molly laughed and sniffed, wiping her eyes again.

'You can teach me to ride a bloody horse too.'

'I can do that.'

They left Mrs Hopkins after they'd eaten, Marcus headed to his own home to pack a few things and Nareema took Molly with her. They had arranged to meet him at nightfall on the western road near the Queens Arch. Mrs Hopkins had found Molly a pair of shoes as she had lost the satin ones somewhere and had given Nareema a dress to wear. She slipped it over her leather suit but kept her sword in hand. Molly did likewise and they quickly made their way across the town to Nareema's house. They cautiously approached.

'It looks quiet.' said Molly.

Nareema nodded.

'What now?'

'Come.'

Nareema led them towards the house but instead of going through the front door they went round the back to the high wall that surrounded the garden.

'Come on.'

Nareema stripped out of her dress and began to effortlessly climb the wall. She reached the top in moments and straddled it.

'It's easy.' she whispered before dropping out of sight down the other side.

Molly looked left and right, feeling mightily embarrassed and nervous before she too stripped off her dress and scrambled up the wall. The climb was more difficult than the Princess had made it look but shallow hand holds had been cut into the bricks and once you knew what you were looking for it became easier. Still, she was still breathing hard by the time she got to the top. Uncurremoniously, she kicked her leg over the wall and dropped heavily onto the roof of the summerhouse.

'Nareema?' hissed Molly.

'What?'

Molly almost cried out as she answered from right behind her.

'How do you do that?'

'Practice.' replied Nareema with a smile.

They dropped off the roof and went inside. The summerhouse was empty. Quickly Nareema hurried over to the racks of weapons and began picking them up. Two short knives went at the small of her back and another on her upper arm. A short sword was strapped to her thigh and finally a set of throwing knives fixed to the straps holding the scabbard for her sword to her back. Molly looked at her in astonishment.

'Are you expecting trouble?'

Nareema smiled.

'I always expect trouble but this time I know it'll be coming. Here.'

She handed Molly a sword that was the twin of the one on her back and a short sword for her thigh. Molly drew the sword and held tentatively in front of her. It was about three feet long but thin and slightly curved with a lethally sharp edge.

'I don't know how to use a sword.'

Nareema began helping her fix the scabbard to her back.

'The pointy end goes into the person who's trying to kill you.'

'I don't want to kill anyone.'

Nareema stepped back and sighed sadly.

'Sometimes it's not about wanting to. Sometimes it is necessary.'

'How many people have you killed?'

'Enough.'

'Were they all necessary?'

Nareema turned away from her.

'This isn't the time for this conversation.'

'It...'

'No.' her tone was hard.

She turned back and put her hand's on Molly's shoulders, her voice softer.

'I will talk to you about this. But not now. We don't have time. If Tong Li gets the other Stones then it won't matter. Please understand.'

Molly sighed and nodded.

'Good. I promise we will talk.'

Nareema turned and headed to the wooden dummy in the corner.

'Help me with this.'

Molly put the sword away and helped Nareema pull the heavy wooden frame to the side. Underneath was a trap door which Nareema flung open to reveal a deep pit with rungs set into the side. She swung herself over the edge.

'Come on.'

'Where does this go?'

'Into the house. A secret entrance.' said Nareema with a grin.

She disappeared into the dark and with some trepidation, Molly followed. She had descended about twenty feet before she hit a stone floor.

'Hold on.'

There was a scratching sound and then a second later Nareema lit a small lamp. Its light casting shadows around the edge of the room they were in. It was made of stone and about ten feet square and seven high. There was a small wooden table in the centre on which sat the lamp. An iron door sat in front of them, while to the left there was a low tunnel.

'I like to be able to get in and out if I need to.' explained Nareema. 'The door leads to the cellar of the house and the tunnel goes to the sewer.'

Molly stepped further into the room and could feel a chilly draught coming from the tunnel.

'Who built this?'

'Don't know. Simcox arranged it.'

The door was solid with a handle but no lock. Nareema stood in front of it and began counting the bricks that ran around its edge.

'I can never remember where the lock is.'

She stopped at a brick that was just above her shoulder height and gave it a press. There was a clunk and the door swung open slightly to reveal a dark passage on the other side. Heaving the door open, Nareema picked up the lantern and drew her sword. Molly followed her into a long corridor that ran straight ahead, drawing her own sword and holding it tightly.

'Relax your grip.' said Nareema from in front of her.

'What?' whispered Molly.

'Don't hold the sword so tightly. Relax your grip a bit.'

'How did you...'

'I can hear the bindings on the hilt creaking from here.'

Even though Molly couldn't see her face she knew Nareema was grinning. The passage was about eighty feet long and ended in another iron door. Nareema passed the lantern to Molly and pressed her ear to the cold metal. She was silent for a moment before she again started counting the bricks around the door. Finding the brick she wanted she gave it a shove and was rewarded with a soft clunk.

'Douse the lantern.'

Molly quickly put it out and they stood in the dark. She could barely hear Nareema move as she swung the door open and stepped into the cellar. A weak light filtered in through a small window near the ceiling and from it she could see that the room was empty.

'Come on.'

Putting the lantern down, Molly followed Nareema towards the stairway that led up to the hall by the kitchen.

Carefully they ascended, Nareema pausing by the door at the top to listen for a second before opening it. It swung noiselessly on well-oiled hinges. The women moved out into the corridor.

'Go and check the dining room.' whispered Nareema.
'What for?'
'Mrs Kettering or Simcox or...'
'Tong Li?'
Nareema hesitated.
'He wouldn't be here.'
'Are you sure?'
'No. That's why I'm sneaking into my own house.'
'That makes me feel better.'
Nareema laughed softly.
'Just be careful. If you see anything, shout.'
Molly nodded and turned to go. Suddenly she turned back.
'Hang on. We can see if he's here without searching the house.'
The princess looked at her quizzically. Molly quickly reached into a pocket on her suit and took out the sapphire. She placed it in the palm of her hand and concentrated on the Fire Stone. The sapphire span in her palm for a moment before pointing south west and glowing a dim red.
'I don't think he's here.'
Nareema looked at the gem and then at Molly.
'We should be alright but it's better to be safe than sorry.'
Molly nodded and turned towards the dining room.

Ten minutes later they had checked every room in the house. It was deserted.
'Where is everybody?'
Nareema bit her lip before heading off upstairs with Molly right behind her. She opened the door to her room and climbed onto her four-poster bed. It was made of heavy dark wood and ornately carved. Reaching up she

unscrewed one of the finials that decorated the end of each post. Inside there was a piece of paper.

'Good old Shakir.' she said with a smile

'What is it?'

'Another secret. Somewhere to leave messages where they won't be found.'

She sat down heavily on the bed and began to read the message.

'What does it say?'

Nareema glanced up.

'He's gone to Uncle Tobias. He's taken Mrs Kettering and Simcox with him.'

'That's good.'

'It is. At least they're safe.'

Nareema jumped up and then began to root around under the bed. With a bit of effort she hauled a large wooden trunk out from underneath and opened it.

'Here.'

She threw a black leather backpack to Molly. Rolled up and strapped to the bottom was a thin blanket and bedroll.

'And these.'

Molly caught the pair of solid knee length boots that came her way.

'Go and see what food they've left us please.' Nareema asked as she fished another backpack from the trunk.

Molly pulled the boots on before she headed downstairs to the kitchen. She had just begun looking through the pantry when she heard voices outside. Carefully she crept up to the window and looked into the garden. There were men climbing over the back wall. Armed men. She ducked down and hurried upstairs.

'Nareema. We've got trouble.'

The Princess ran to Molly's room and glanced out of the window.

'Quickly.'

They grabbed their backpacks and headed down stairs. The men were cautiously trying the back door.

'Into the cellar.'

They closed the cellar door behind them as the glass in the back door was broken. Nareema bolted the door from the inside and they went down stairs and into the secret tunnel. The door swung shut and Nareema lit the lamp. Ahead there were voices.

'We left the hatch open in the summer house. We'll have to move fast.'

They ran up the tunnel and arrived in the stone room. Molly could see the feet of a man coming down the ladder and another was already there.

Nareema didn't hesitate, with a single move she jumped and skidded across the table. Her boots caught the man in the chest and sent him flying. He cried out but she was up and on him before he had finished moving, her sword driving deep into his chest. The man on the ladder tried to come down faster but he didn't have chance to turn around before Nareema cut his legs off at the knee. He fell the last four or five feet screaming in agony.

'Into the tunnel. Go.'

Molly didn't need any more urging. She headed quickly into the dark and draughty tunnel, Nareema close behind with the lantern. There were more shouts from behind them.

'Keep going.'

Molly ran, the shaky light from the lantern showing her the way. She slowed as out of the darkness loomed a heavy iron gate. There was no lock or handle. Nareema put the lantern down and drew her short sword.

'Open the gate.'

'How?' asked Molly.

'Third brick from the left on the right-hand side.'

'What?'

There was a shout as two men rushed down the corridor towards them. The Princess turned and met the first with a kick which knocked him to the ground.

'Get it open.'

Molly rushed forwards and began randomly pressing the bricks around the edge.

'I can't find it.'

'Press them all.' grunted Nareema as she deflected a blow from the second man, pirouetting to kick the first man in the face as he rose to his knees.

Frantically Molly pressed every brick she could see.

'It's not working.'

'Try the other side.'

She shifted to the other side of the gate and began shoving the bricks. After a moment she was rewarded with a resounding thunk and the gate swung towards her. She heaved it open and dashed through.

'Nareema it's open. Come on.'

The Princess risked a glance over her shoulder before dropping and sweeping the legs out from under the second man. He hit the stone floor hard but she didn't hesitate. She jumped back and darted through the gate, slamming it behind her.

'Move!'

She and Molly pounded down the tunnel away from the shouting men. Glancing over shoulder at the princess, Molly called out.

'How far does this...'

Her words turned into a scream as the floor beneath her dropped away sharply and she found herself sliding uncontrollably down. Sliding for a second, the ground beneath her disappeared and she plunged into a pool of freezing water. She stood up in the waist deep water as Nareema followed. Her landing was far more graceful and she didn't even get her hair wet.

'Sorry. Should have mentioned that.'

She smiled widely and headed off to a narrow stone walkway at the far side of the pool. Wiping water from her face Molly followed, muttering to herself.

They followed the tunnel and eventually came to a ladder which emerged in a narrow alley. As Molly pulled herself out of the manhole, Nareema effortlessly climbed up onto the roof of one of the low buildings that framed it. Grunting with the effort, Molly followed.
'I don't think they're following us.' she said as Molly crouched next to her.
'What now?'
'We get ourselves some horses and meet the Captain.'
Molly sighed.
'Yes I know you can't ride yet but you're going to have to learn fast. Can you do that?'
'How hard can it be?' asked Molly with a shrug.
She was rewarded with a smile.
'Good. Go and wait by the Queens Arch for the Captain. When he gets there head away from the city. There is a small wood a few miles down the road. I will meet you both there later with some horses and supplies.'
'I can't walk across the city like this! I'm practically naked.'
Nareema grinned.
'Then keep to the high ground.'
With that she stood and headed east across the roof. Molly watched her jump gracefully from roof to roof before she dropped out of sight. She sat back on the tiles.
'Keep to the high ground. That's easy for you to say.'
She sighed then stood up.
'Right. You can do this.'
She crawled to the edge of the roof and looked over. The ground was about ten feet down.
'You *can* do this.'

She took a deep breath and glanced up to the roof of the next building. The gap was about four feet. Slowly Molly stood and took a couple of steps back.

'Right.'

Taking a run up she closed her eyes and launched herself across the gap with a shout. The instant she left the roof she knew that closing her eyes had been a bad idea. She hit the neighbouring roof hard, her momentum throwing her forward onto her stomach.

'Shit.'

Trying not to panic, she slid forward towards the edge of the building. She rolled onto her back and flung her arms out, her fingertips catching a broken tile as her feet slipped over the edge of the roof. Hanging on for all she was worth, Molly rolled once more and scrambled up from the edge. She was breathing hard she lay on the roof for a moment before hauling herself back up to the top.

'That was close.'

She looked at the next roof. It was flat and looked like a single storey extension on a larger house whose roof stood another storey up. Molly shook her head.

'Don't think so.'

As she looked for a way down she saw some washing in the yard. A maid was hanging out several dresses to dry in the sun.

'That'll do.'

She jumped onto the flat roof, taking her time and judging the distance better this time and waited for the maid to go back in. As soon as the door closed she dropped into the yard and took one of the dresses from the line, scrabbling quickly over the wall. On the other side she slipped it over her head. It was wet and a little big but it would do. She took another deep breath, checked the coast was clear and then headed off to meet Marcus.

# Chapter Six

## Uncle Tobias

Marcus rode up the road and waited by the Queens Arch which sounded grander than it was. Built hundreds of years ago it was now not much more than half a crumbling arch in the road. Small houses and sheds had been built either side to create a maze of alleyways but it was still almost out of the city. He looked round for a moment before dismounting. There was no sign of either Molly or the Princess. He shook his head.
'I hope nothing's happened to them.'
'Nothing's happened to who?'
He jumped and spun round to see a grinning Molly. She was dressed in a figure hugging black leather jumpsuit and had a sword at her back, just like the Princess.
'Don't sneak up on people like that! It's not lady like.'
Molly smiled even more.
'I'm not a lady.'
'So you told me. You certainly don't dress like one.'
She smiled at him and did a little twirl.
'Don't you like it? I hear it's all the rage with royalty at the moment.'
'It's very...' he struggled to find the right words and felt himself beginning to blush.
'Revealing? To be honest, I'm not sure about it myself yet but it does allow a certain freedom of movement you just don't get in a dress.'
'I'll have to take your word for that I'm afraid.'
Molly grinned.
'There's a wood a mile or so down the road. Nareema said to wait there for her.'
'Where is she?'

'Getting some horses. That's another thing that I'm not sure about yet either.'

Marcus got on his own horse.

'Well we'd better start you off then. Have you ever been on a horse?'

'No.'

He shifted back in the saddle to make room for her.

'Here.'

He held out his hand and helped her clamber up in front of him.

'This is cosy.'

Marcus blushed further as he felt her warmth against him, but uncomfortable at the sword that was strapped to her back. He cleared his throat.

'Excuse me.'

He reached round her and took the reins in his hands. She gently placed her hands on his.

'How do we make it go?'

'Him. How do we make him go. His name is Lucius. And we make him go like this. Hold on.'

He dug his heels into the animals flanks and it took off down the road. They rode for a mile or two before peeling off the road and into the woodland. Finding a small clearing shielded from the highway by a thick stand of trees they made camp. Molly made a fire and they shared some of the food Marcus had brought with him.

'So how do you know the Princess?' he asked her as they ate.

'She saved my life. There were three men and she stopped them from hurting me.'

'Why would they want to hurt you?'

Molly smiled sadly.

'Sometimes you have to steal or starve. I should have been more careful who I stole from.'

'Don't you have any family?'

She shook her head.

'No. I was orphaned when I was three. Ran away from the workhouse when I was ten. I've been on my own since. I get by.'

Marcus looked at her but didn't say anything. She sighed sadly then tried to change the subject.

'How about you? What do you do?'

'I am a Captain in His Majesties South Essex. Currently on leave.'

'Have you seen any fighting?'

'Yes. I was with Colonel Sharpe at Waterloo. It was... Unpleasant.'

Now it was Molly's turn to remain silent. He wiped his hands on a cloth and stood, holding his hand out to her.

'Enough of the past. If you would do me the honour of this dance m'lady.'

She giggled.

'I'm not a lady.'

Marcus smiled as he took her into hold.

'Left foot first.'

He began humming softly as he guided her around the fire. She laughed.

'Is there no Mrs Kane you should be with now?'

'No.'

'There must be lots of girls who would like the job.'

'I didn't realise that it would be such an onerous position that I would have to hold interviews.'

'What does onerous mean?'

Marcus laughed.

'You still surprise me Miss Carter.'

'Are you making fun of me?'

'I wouldn't dream of it.'

He began humming again and they danced slowly around the fire, getting closer together with each movement.

Nareema watched them from a nearby tree and smiled sadly to herself. Molly looked happy. She closed her eyes for a moment before silently dropping out of the branches to the ground and heading back to where she had tethered the horses.

Making as much noise as she could she stomped towards the small camp they had made. Molly quickly broke away from Marcus and they both looked embarrassed as she approached. Nareema pretended not to notice.

'Found you at last. I've been looking for ages.'

'Have you eaten?'

Molly began to cut some of the meat they had been eating.

'No. I'm fine. Thank you. I found you a horse.'

She handed the reins of a dappled grey mare to Molly who eyed it suspiciously.

'What's it called?'

'She. What is she called.' corrected Nareema.

Molly shrugged.

'I don't know what she is called. I didn't stop to ask the man I stole her from so I guess you can call her what you like.'

Marcus looked at the Princess in shock.

'Stole?'

'Yes. I didn't have much time and it was the easiest option. Killing him would have been too messy.'

'Your Highness...'

Nareema grinned.

'I wouldn't have killed him but I did steal them. They're not the first things that I've taken without asking and I doubt they'll be the last. And please don't call me Your Highness. My name is Nareema.'

Marcus looked uncomfortable.

'But...'

'Na-Reem-A. Try it. It's easy when you know how.'

'But...'

Molly looked at him.

'Let it go.'

He sagged and sat down by the fire looking lost. Nareema guided Molly and her new horse to where Marcus had tethered his.

'So what are you going to call her?'

'Don't know. I'll think of something.'

Nareema nodded.

'Dance lesson go well?' she asked innocently.

Molly blushed and glanced back at the Captain.

'We were...'

' Don't worry about it. He's handsome in a very British kind of way. He should do something about that moustache though. It looks like someone has drawn on his face.'

'I said the same thing last night.' giggled Molly.

They camped in the woods and the next day they began their journey towards Somerset. Marcus and Nareema had given Molly some pointers about riding but by the time they stopped for the night she thought she'd never walk again. Her back and bottom were sore and her legs stiff. She hobbled to the fire Nareema had made.

'It'll get easier. Keep upright more and move with the horse.' said Marcus as she slowly lowered herself to the ground.

'I'm trying.' she groaned

Nareema rooted around in her backpack and threw her a small pot.

'Rub some of this into your back where it hurts. It will help ease the stiffness and pain.'

Molly nodded and took the lid off.

'This stinks!'

'Yes but it works.'

Hauling herself to her feet Molly moved away from the fire so she could apply some of the ointment to her aching body.

'She likes you.' Nareema said quietly when Molly was out of earshot.

'I'm sorry?'

'Molly. She likes you.'

'She is a very capable young woman and...'

'And you like her to don't you Captain?' Nareema looked at him directly and raised her eyebrows. Marcus blushed.

'It isn't proper to discuss such matters Your Highness.'

Nareema grinned but left it at that.

They rode hard and the journey took them six days but eventually they reached a large manor house set in its own sprawling grounds. A set of wide stone steps led to a veranda and Shakir came striding out of the house as they approached. Nareema jumped from her horse and gave him a hug.

'We didn't know what had happened to you. We feared the worst. What happened?'

'Where is Tobias? I'll tell you both all about it.'

Uncle Tobias turned out to be an aging Englishman with a shock of wiry grey hair and a permanently confused look about him. Shakir had led them all to his study which was strewn with papers, maps and books of all description.

'Uncle Tobias.'

He greeted Nareema with a hug which he carried over to Molly and then a slightly disconcerted Marcus. He sat down in a large leather chair while Nareema shoved some books out of the way and sat down opposite him on a matching leather sofa. Molly and Marcus stood, as did Shakir.

'You've grown. What are you now? Fourteen? Fifteen?'

'I'm twenty two Uncle.'

'Twenty two? No. Where does the time go?'

He sighed.

'Did you find the Fire Stone?'

Nareema nodded.

'My mother did.'

Tobias looked down.

'Shakir told me about your mother and sister. I'm very sorry. Please pass my condolences on to your father.'

'I will.'

'Well we know that there's at least one Stone around. We just have to find the others.'

Nareema smiled at him.

'We have the Air.'

He sat up straight.

'Really? Here?'

'Yes.'

'May I see it?'

Nareema looked at Molly who reached inside her suit to produce the sapphire. Tobias took it and held it up to the light, squinting.

'Fantastic. It's just like the descriptions in the books. Where was it?'

With a glance at Molly, Nareema spoke.

'It was in a necklace. I took it from its owner.'

Marcus didn't miss the disapproving glance that Molly gave her.

'Fantastic.'

'We have more than that Uncle. Molly can talk to it.'

He looked up at Molly, surprise written across his face.

'Really? May I see.'

Molly smiled tightly under the obvious excitement and scrutiny of Tobias. She took the sapphire from him and placed it in her palm. Closing her eyes she thought of the Fire Stone that Tong Li had. In her hand, the gem span for a few seconds before pointing east and glowing a dim red.

Tobias grinned manically.

'That, I must say, is fantastic.'

His enthusiasm even made Shakir laugh.

'Can you make it do anything else?'

Molly shrugged.

'I made the wind come but I don't know how I did it and I don't know if I could do it again.'

'Give it a try.'

Closing her fist around it she concentrated on the wind. The gem grew warm in her hand and suddenly a blast of wind flashed from her fist and hit Tobias in the chest. The force of the gale knocked him and his chair over backwards, scattering papers all over the study. Molly instantly let the gem go and rushed to his side.

'Oh. I'm so sorry.'

He stood up, grinning like a madman.

'Amazing. Fantastic. How did you do that?'

'I don't know. The first time, Nareema was in trouble and it just happened. Then I just thought about the wind and it came. I don't know how to control it.'

'I think I'll need to study this further.'

Tobias righted his chair and sat down heavily, dragging some of the papers towards him before he began scribbling furiously.

'We don't have time for that Uncle. Tong Li has the Fire Stone and we need to get to the others before he does.'

Tobias looked up.

'Of course. Do you know where they are?'

'No. We were hoping you could tell us.'

He looked confused for a moment.

'Ah, yes. Hang on.'

He stood and went to a large pile of books near the window, picking them up in turn and then casually throwing them over his shoulder when they weren't the one he was looking for. Eventually he settled on a large book covered with dark red leather.

'Here we are.'

Grasping the thick tome in his hands he went and sat at his desk, putting on a battered pair of spectacles before he began to flick through it.

'As you know, the Stones have a spotty history. They turn up every now and again and sometimes with someone who can talk to them. I've found a reference to an emerald that seemed to be able to cause wilting flowers to bloom.'

'That's it.' said Nareema.

'This reference is three hundred years old. It was in a church in Portugal. Somewhere near the coast. I can probably work out where if you give me a few minutes. Did I say that it was in Portugal?'

'Yes. You did.'

'Ah. Right. They thought it was a miracle.'

'Is it still there?' asked Marcus.

Tobias shrugged.

'I don't know. As I said, this reference is three hundred years old.'

Molly concentrated on the Earth Stone. In her palm the sapphire spun once more to point south.

'It's south of here. Where is Portugal?'

'South.' said Marcus with a smile.

'Then that's where we need to go.'

'What about the Water Stone or the Crown?' asked Shakir.

'What sort of gem was the Water Stone?'

'It was a diamond.' answered Tobias and Nareema together.

'What do they look like?'

'Like the ones in my mothers' necklace.'

Molly closed her eyes and concentrated. In her hand the gem spun before coming to rest pointing north and glowing with a weak white light.

'That way I guess.'

'What about the Crown?' asked Tobias.

'What does that look like?'

Tobias pulled a piece of paper towards him and began sketching out a rough picture.

'As far as we know, it was a circle of gold with a raised front, into which the stones sat. They are all pretty much the same shape, so the end of the teardrop pointed inwards when they were in place.'

She imagined the Crown in her mind but in her palm the sapphire remained still.

'Nothing.'

'Try again.' urged Tobias.

Taking a deep breath, Molly closed her eyes and gripped the gem in her fist. Suddenly she was no longer in the dusty study, she was deep underground in a circular rock cavern. She looked around. A large tunnel bracketed by some heavy stone doors led off in one direction but in the centre stood a raised pedestal with the Crown on it. The cavern was damp and cold and Molly could hear the dripping of water somewhere nearby.

She stepped towards the pedestal, her footsteps loud in the empty space. It looked as Tobias had described, a gold circle with space for four gems in a raised part at the front. However there was a small impression in the middle of the gems. A space for something else.

She span as there was a loud noise from the tunnel. As if something heavy was being dragged along the stone floor. She turned back to the Crown, feeling suddenly afraid.

Slowly she reached out to touch it but her vision clouded and she swam back to the study to be greeted by Marcus's concerned face.

'Are you alright? You seemed to...'

'What did you see?' Nareema pushed her way in front of him.

'I saw the Crown. It was in a round cave. It had spaces for the four stones but there was another space in the middle. It looked like something else went in there.'

'Fantastic!' Tobias's excitement was undeniable.

'Did you get a good look at where it was?'

'No. Somewhere underground. What happened?'

Somehow she had moved from standing by the desk to lying flat on the sofa.

'You fainted. Gave me... us... quite a scare.' said Marcus.

'Did you see anything else?'

Molly shook her head.

'No. But I had the feeling of... I don't know... It was as if something wasn't quite right about it. It was a bad place.'

'Are you alright. You've gone very pale?' said Marcus.

Molly sat up and her head swam.

'I feel a bit tired. I think I might need a lie down.'

Tobias stood up.

'Of course my dear. I'll find you and your husband a room and then you can get some rest. You'll dine with me tonight of course. It's not often that I get visitors and I want to talk with Nareema and catch up. It's been a few years since I last made it out to India to visit.'

Both Molly and Marcus looked at each other and then at Tobias before speaking at the same time.

'We're not married.'

'Really? Well I have plenty of rooms. You can have one each. Unless you wanted to share. I don't mind really. Very broadminded. Travel broadens it you understand. I think...'

Nareema interrupted him.

'Uncle. I'll take Molly and find her somewhere to lie down. Why don't you take the Captain and show him around?'

'What? Of course. You'll have to forgive me my dear. I tend to ramble a bit.' he said as he pushed his spectacles up onto his head.

Molly smiled tightly and stood but swayed slightly. Marcus was at her side in an instant with an arm to steady her.

'Are you sure you're alright?'

'Yes. I'm fine.'

Nareema took her hand.

'Come on.'

She led her out of the room. Tobias watched them go before standing.

'Fantastic. Very pretty wife you have Major.'

'Please call me Marcus, I'm only a Captain and we're not married.'

'Oh, of course. You did say.' Tobias patted his pockets. 'Now where did I put my glasses?'

Molly came down for dinner later that evening. She was still feeling a little tired but nothing that wouldn't be sorted by something to eat and an early night. Mrs Kettering had packed some clothes for her and Nareema before she had left so it was with some relief that she didn't have to go to dinner wearing her leather suit.

Marcus was waiting in the hall as she came down stairs. He had changed into a simple blue velvet jacket with cream trousers.

'How are you feeling?' he asked as he met her at the foot of the stairs and offered her his arm.

'I'm fine. Thank you.'

'Are you sure?'

'Yes. Don't fuss. I can look after myself you know. Until a week ago I had to do it every day. There was none of this dinner at seven malarkey. I was lucky if I got dinner at all.'

Marcus smiled.

'Sorry. Of course. I forgot.'

She raised her eyebrows at him and smiled.

'Shall we Captain?'

Dinner was a lavish affair. Mrs Kettering had practically taken over the kitchen and laid on a feast that would have put the finest houses in England to shame. Marcus escorted Molly to her seat then went to sit opposite her with Shakir next to him. Tobias was at the head of the table and

Nareema placed herself on Molly's left. Molly had been slightly overwhelmed when she sat at the table. There were more knives, forks, spoons and glasses than she'd seen in one place before.

'Just start with the cutlery at the outside and work your way in, or do what I do, pick one set and just use that all night.' whispered Nareema.

As they ate, talk turned to the Stones and to Tobias. He had travelled extensively in India where he had bumped into Nareema's father. Quite literally it would have seemed.

'So there I was, running away from them when I rounded a corner and came smashing into the Maharajah. We both went sprawling and his guards were on me in an instant. He waved them away and that was that. Very understanding chap.'

Molly glanced at Nareema who looked down, a sad expression on her face.

'What's the matter?' she whispered.

The Princess shook her head.

'Nothing.'

Tobias continued.

'Anyway, there we are. I've been back a few times since, but not since my dear Jenny passed on. That was a few years ago now.'

He looked down at the table and went quiet.

'How is Elizabeth?' asked Nareema, trying to lighten the mood.

'Oh, she's well. Married of course. Had a little boy called Nathanial. They come up from Exeter every now and again. Her husband is something to do with publishing. Can't see a future in that but they're happy so that's good enough for me.'

'How did you come across the Stones?' asked Marcus.

'Funny story that.' replied Tobias. 'After I'd fallen in with the Maharajah, I was poking around his library and stumbled across some old scrolls. Now ancient languages are a bit of a hobby of mine so I took to translating them and got a bit carried away. Nareema's mother found me after a day and a half, I hadn't realised the time, and she asked me for help in locating the Stones. I've been looking ever since. Become a bit of an expert if you don't mind me blowing my own trumpet. Not that I can play the trumpet. More of a violin person really. Not that I can play that either although I do have a tinkle on the old piano every now and again...'

'Can you teach me to control the Stone?' asked Molly, interrupting him.

Tobias shrugged.

'Don't know. I haven't seen anything that would give me any idea on how to do that. No instructions. I think it may be a bit of a trial and error process I'm afraid.'

He looked at Nareema.

'Maybe your father has some more scrolls?'

She shook her head.

'No. You've seen all that he has and all that the Daughters have too.'

'That's a pity. Ah well, I've got an appointment next month with the curator of the British museum. He's an old friend and hopefully I'll get a look at the latest shipment of curios from India he's had in. He wrote to me a few weeks ago. Seemed very excited about a set of stone friezes that he had found.'

'Maybe they can help.' said Marcus.

'Maybe.' replied Tobias 'but I don't think they'll be in the country for a few weeks.'

He turned to Molly.

'How does that sound dear? You and your husband are welcome to stay here with me until then.'

Molly smiled.

'Thank you but I need to find something that will help me stop Tong Li before it is too late.' Nareema looked at her for a second.

'Molly, you can't stop him.'

'I'm the only one that can control the Air Stone, sort of, I have to try.'

'I can't ask you to do this. This is something that will be dangerous and I would fear for your safety.'

Molly looked Nareema in the eye.

'Your Highness. You promised to teach me to read and write, neither of which you have done yet, I am coming with you.'

'You can't read?' asked Tobias.

Molly sighed.

'Why is that such a surprise to everyone?'

Nareema smiled.

'Thank you.'

'I will too.' said Marcus. 'How can I let my damsel in distress get into more distress?'

'I'm staying here. I might be able to find out where the other Stones are. Now I know the Water Stone and it's north somewhere I can narrow it down a bit.' said Tobias after a moment.

Nareema smiled and turned to Shakir.

'Go back to London. Take Tobias, Simcox and Mrs Kettering. Protect them.'

Shakir bristled and took a deep breath to reply.

'Don't argue. Please. I know you're supposed to protect me but I need to know they are safe.'

After a moment, he nodded.

'I will.'

'Thank you.'

Nareema turned back to Molly and the Captain.

'Have you ever been on a ship Molly?'

## Chapter Seven

## Away to Sea

'I'm still not comfortable with this Your Highness.'
A few days later Marcus was sat with Nareema and Molly in a coach at the dockside in Plymouth. They had booked passage on a ship to Portugal, and after a little shopping for the voyage, they were here.
'I can see the sense in wanting to keep a low profile but really...'
'Enough Captain. Shakirs' plan is sound. We want to get to Portugal in one piece and try not to attract any more attention to ourselves than absolutely necessary. Travelling as a Princess will not do that.'
'But a servant...'
'It is more likely that an English army Captain and his young wife would have an Indian servant than any other combination. That is the end of the conversation.'
Marcus took a breath but a stern look from Nareema silenced any further protests. He sighed in defeat.
'Yes Your Highness.'
'Stop calling me that. My name is Nareema.'
Molly smiled. She was nervous, never having been on a ship before, but more so at the duplicity they were employing. She glanced at her left hand to the wedding ring that she wore. It was the twin of the simple gold band that Marcus wore for appearances sake. They were supposed to be newly married. Nareema placed a hand on her knee and leant forward.
'It will be fine. Ready?'
Molly nodded.
'Yes. I think so.'
'Captain?'
He nodded too.

'Yes.'
'Good.'

Marcus got out of the coach and turned to help Molly and then Nareema. He offered Molly his arm and they walked towards the ship. It was a large merchant vessel called the Endurance. It's crew were busy loading the last of their provisions for the trip. The master was a large Yorkshire man with a bald head and a scar across one cheek which gave him an almost piratical appearance. Seeing them walking towards the ship he quickly headed to the foot of the gangplank to meet them.

'Captain Kane.' he boomed.

Marcus snapped to attention and gave him sharp salute.

'At your service sir.'

The Captain waved his formality away and shook his hand.

'We'll have none of that.'

He turned his attention to Molly and Marcus quickly introduced her.

'This is Molly, my wife.'

The Captain bowed low before he took Molly's hand and gave it a kiss, causing her to flush red.

'A pleasure my lady. Captain Owain Brody at your service.'

'Thank you sir.'

He straightened.

'And this is, um, my wife's maid. Nareema.'

The Princess bowed lightly. Brody gave her a quizzical look for a second before he led them on board.

'I'll have some of my men help your maid with the luggage. You and your wife have a cabin near mine. The servant will be below decks.'

'I would appreciate it if she could have a cabin near mine Captain.' said Molly hurriedly.

He thought for a moment.

'We have no other passengers on this trip. There's a small

cabin next to yours. She can have that.'

Marcus took his hand and gave it a shake, Molly couldn't help but notice the coins change hands as they did so.

'Thank you. My wife and I appreciate your understanding.'

Brody nodded before bellowing orders to the crew.

'Davis, take the Captain and his good lady to their cabin. Johnson, Skippy you go and help with their luggage. Move!'

The men scurried to obey.

'If you will excuse me, I have final preparations to make.'

'Of course.'

He gave Nareema another odd look before he bowed theatrically and headed off, leaving an old, thin sailor called Davis to show them the way. They were led them to a spacious cabin with a plain wooden bed and furniture.

'Here y'are sir.'

'Thank you.'

Marcus pressed a coin into his hand.

'Please make sure my wife's maid finds her cabin with the minimum of fuss.'

'Right y'are sir.'

He tugged at his forelock and quickly headed off. Marcus looked the cabin over.

'I'm afraid the sleeping arrangements may be difficult. I will sleep on the floor.' he announced.

Molly looked at him.

'Why? There's a perfectly good bed.'

'But then where would you sleep?'

'In the perfectly good bed.'

He looked aghast at the prospect which made Molly smile. She stepped close to him and took his hands.

'We are supposed to be husband and wife. It will look suspicious if we take separate beds.'

He opened his mouth to say something but was interrupted by a knock on the door.

'Come.'

Davis hurried in carrying some of their luggage, followed by another couple of sailors with the rest. Nareema calmly walked behind them.

'Put it over there.' Marcus pointed to a spot near the wall. The sailors deposited their burdens and left.

'I'm not interrupting anything am I?' asked Nareema with a grin.

Molly blushed.

'We're setting sail soon. Captain, why don't you go up on deck and see if you can be of any assistance. I will help my mistress unpack.'

Marcus hesitated, clearly uneasy.

'Right. Yes of course.'

Nareema and Molly couldn't help but laugh at the look on his face as he left.

'Please don't call me mistress.'

'Why not? What would you have me call you?'

'My name is Molly.'

'It wouldn't be appropriate in these circumstances. And besides, I do like the way it rankles the Captain.'

Molly laughed again before helping her unpack.

Marcus returned an hour later. They had set sail with the tide and were making progress towards Portugal. He opened the cabin door he knew something wasn't right. Molly was sat on the bed with her head in her hands and Nareema was knelt on the floor next to her.

'What's wrong?' his voice was full of concern.

'Sea sickness.' said Nareema as Molly heaved into a bucket.

'Oh.'

'Lie back. It'll get better.'

Molly did as she was told and flopped back onto the bed.

'I'll find her some water.'

Marcus nodded as Nareema left. He went and sat on the bed.

'Is this a storm?' asked Molly pathetically, she had never felt so ill.

He laughed despite himself.

'No. This is just a calm day. Storms are something else.'

'Can you make the room stop moving?'

'Afraid not.'

'Then can you stop my stomach flipping around.'

'I can't do that either.'

Her reply was lost as she sat up suddenly and dived for the bucket.

'I'll tell Captain Brody that we will have to decline his kind offer of dinner this evening.'

He gently patted her on the back.

'It will get better. I was a sick as a dog the first time I went to sea.'

Molly lay back down again.

'That really doesn't make me feel any better.'

It was four days before Molly felt well enough to leave the cabin. Marcus and Nareema escorted her up to the deck for some air. Brody saw them and waved them up to the wheel.

'Feeling better?' he asked.

'A little.' replied Molly with a weak smile.

'Glad to hear it. Now that you're up and about would you two like to dine with me tonight?'

'Of course sir. It would be our pleasure.' answered Marcus.

All Molly could manage was another tired smile. Food wasn't something high on her list at the moment but she had hardly eaten since they left England.

'Seven o'clock.'

Marcus bowed slightly and escorted Molly back to the cabin.

Seven o'clock came round quickly. She had spent most of the day with Nareema who had begun to teach her to read. Only small words but she was a quick learner and was picking it up fast.

'Is this too much?' asked Molly as Nareema helped her get dressed.

'No. You are dining with the Captain of this ship. He will expect you to dress accordingly, as will your husband.'

'He's not...'

Molly stopped herself.

'Of course. I hope it's nothing too heavy. I don't think I can manage much.'

'You'll be fine.'

Nareema stepped back to look at her. She was wearing a red silk dress that sparkled in the light. There was a knock at the door and both Molly and Nareema spoke at the same time.

'Come.'

Marcus opened the door. He had already changed into his full military regalia. Red jacket and white trousers with his hat under his arm. Buttons and boots polished to perfection and shining.

'You've shaved.'

He looked embarrassed and touched his top lip.

'My wife told me she didn't like it, so it had to go.'

Both Nareema and Molly grinned.

'Shall we?'

He offered his arm to Molly who took it.

'Are you sure that you don't want to come with us?' asked Molly for the hundredth time.

Nareema shook her head and gave her the same answer.

'It wouldn't be correct for a servant to dine with the captain. I will be fine.'

Molly nodded and let Marcus led her out of the room.

'You look fabulous by the way.' said Marcus quietly as they walked.

'You don't scrub up too badly yourself.'

They were both smiling as they reached the Captains' cabin and Marcus knocked smartly on the door. Brody opened it with a flourish.

'Captain Kane.'

He turned to Molly and took her hand, kissing it theatrically.

'Mrs Kane. Please come in. It will be only simple fair I'm afraid. We don't stand too much on ceremony.'

He escorted Molly to a seat at a round table set for three. He pulled out her chair for her to sit.

'Would you like a glass of wine?'

'A small one please. I'm still feeling a little, um, delicate.'

Brody grinned and poured them all a drink.

Nareema watched them go. They really did make a lovely couple. Maybe when this was all over she would have a word with Marcus. She smiled to herself and straightened the bed before she headed up to the deck to take in some air as she had done on most nights.

The sea was calm and the moon was hanging heavy and bright in the sky. Around her some of the sailors were attending to their duties while across the deck an old seaman began to play a soulful shanty on a battered looking fiddle. Nareema sighed. Molly would be fine. Marcus would look after her tonight.

She stayed, staring out across the waves for a while until a chill in the air caused her to shiver. It was getting cold. Time for bed she decided and headed below to her cabin.

As she opened the door, a pair of rough hands grabbed her from behind. One went across her mouth and the other grabbed her breast. With a shove she fell headlong into the room, her attacker coming with her. He landed heavily on her and cracked her head on the wooden planks of the floor.

'Keep still and this'll be over quick.' he whispered viciously.

Keeping still was far from Nareema's mind. She rolled and tried to get to her feet but the man banged her head against the floor again. Dazed she heard another voice.

'Come on. We ain't got much time.'

Molly smiled at the men.

'I think I may have had a little too much wine.' her speech was slightly slurred.

'If you gently men will excuse me I think I might retire for the evening.'

She swayed slightly as she stood, Marcus was straight to her side. She waved him away.

'I'll be fine. You two carry on.'

'Are you sure?'

'Yes.'

She pecked a quick kiss on his cheek before heading out of the door. As she closed it behind her she wondered why the floor was moving so much.

'Maybe I *have* had too much wine.' she said to herself.

Swaying slightly she headed to her own cabin but saw that Nareema's door was open. Molly called out softly.

'Nareema?'

Getting no answer she went up to the door and screamed at what she saw. There were two men in her cabin. One had her on the floor and was trying to get her dress off while the other watched.

At Molly's scream, the other man turned and launched himself at her. She turned and ran but his outstretched fingers caught the hem of her dress.

'Get off me.' she shouted as she turned and aimed a kick at him.

He tried to pull her back but the thin silk tore and she was free. She hammered down the corridor to run straight into Marcus and Captain Brody. They had heard her scream and had come running.

'What is it?'

'Nareema. Help Nareema.'

Marcus and Brody pushed past Molly and ran towards Nareema's cabin. The man still standing outside saw them coming and turned to run but was tackled heavily by Marcus, sending them both crashing to the ground. Brody skidded to a halt and bodily hauled the other man off Nareema.

As soon as he was lifted from her, she leapt up and kicked him hard in the groin. He crumpled and was met with a kick to the face before Brody dragged him out of the room. The Captain bellowed for help while Molly forced her way past and to Nareema. It was obvious from her face that she was furiously angry.

'Are you alright? Did they hurt you?'

Nareema shook her head.

'I'm fine.'

'You're bleeding.'

She touched her forehead, fingers coming away bloody from a small cut.

'I'm fine.'

Several other sailors came running to answer Brody's shouting.

'Get them out of here.' he yelled at them.

As the two sailors were dragged away, Marcus and Brody stood in the doorway. It was plain that the ships' Captain was angry.

'I can only apologise. I will have them flogged. This is not the way I expect my crew to behave. '

'Molly, are you alright?' asked Marcus.

Molly nodded and looked down at her torn clothing.

'I've ruined another dress.'

She glanced at Nareema.

'Come next door. Please. Let me look at that cut.'

Nareema gave her a hard stare then closed her eyes for a second, trying to get her anger under control. Eventually she nodded.

'Marcus, Captain Brody. Please excuse us.'

Both men stepped out of the way and Molly led Nareema to her cabin. As they went she heard the captain apologising again.

'I'm truly sorry Captain. I assure you and your wife that they will be punished.'

Molly sat Nareema on the bed and crouched down in front of her.

'Are you alright?' she asked softly.

Nareema closed her eyes for a second before replying.

'No.'

Molly took her into her arms as the tears began in a flood. She held the Princess for a minute until they were interrupted by a soft knock on the door. Nareema gently pushed herself away from Molly and wiped her face as Marcus came in.

'Are you both alright?'

He looked like he was going to say something else but the look Molly gave him changed his mind.

'I thought I'd... Right... I'll sleep next door tonight. You two stay here.'

He closed the door behind him and Nareema smiled sadly.

'You've already mastered the stare I see.'

'The what?'

'I've seen married women give their husbands that look before. The look that says "go away and find someone else to bother".'

'I didn't...'

'You did. And he reacted like every other husband.'

'That's rubbish. We're not married.'

'No but you play the part well. Both of you do.'
Molly changed the subject.
'Let me have a look at that cut.'
Nareema let out a long breath.
'It's fine. Honestly. I am fine too. It was a bit of a shock. That is all. I wasn't paying attention and they took me from behind. There was no room for me to move and...'
'You don't need to explain.'
Nareema sighed.
'Thank you.'
'What for?'
'Saving my life again.'
'I didn't.'
'You did. They would have killed me.'
'You've saved mine twice so I think it only fair that I try to help.'
The Princess took a deep breath which she let out slowly.
'Thank you anyway.'
'Are you sure you're going to be alright?'
'Yes.'
Molly nodded.
'Why don't you get some sleep?'
Nareema nodded and lay back on the bed.
'I'll just go and check on Marcus.'
'Ever the doting wife.' said Nareema with a smile.

Captain Brody's promise that the men would be punished was realised the next day. The entire ships company was mustered on the deck and the men were brought up from below in chains. Molly was stood next to Marcus. There was no sign of Nareema.

'I gave you both a chance to serve on this ship. We carry cargo and passengers. I don't expect those passengers to be attacked in their own cabins. Twenty lashes each and I will be putting you ashore at the first opportunity.'

'She was only a servant!' protested the man Nareema had kicked.

Brody stepped forward and shouted at him.

'Only a servant? Her master had paid her way fair and square. I don't expect my passengers, servant or not to be treated in that way. It'll ruin the reputation of this ship and put us all out of work. Mr Davis. Please begin.'

Molly stood next to Marcus as the ships bosun secured the man's wrists to a heavy grating leant against the forecastle and then ripped his shirt off. After checking the bindings once more, he unfurled a long multi tailed whip.

The crew looked on silently as the first stroke was delivered. The man screamed out in agony as it wrote half a dozen bloody lines down his back. After the second, Molly buried her head in Marcus shoulder, unable to watch. He put his arm around her and held her close. Eventually they reached twenty and the man was cut down and dragged away, his back a bloody mess.

'Next.'

The other man put up more of a struggle, having just witnessed his colleagues fate but within moments he was tied to the frame. Davis stepped back and raised the whip.

'Wait!'

The crew turned as one to see Nareema stride onto the deck. She was dressed in her leather suit with sword at her back. The look on her face told Molly all she needed to know.

'Oh no.'

Completely ignoring the crew she walked up to the man, drawing a knife from her belt to cut his bindings.

'Hey...' began the Brody but he was silenced by a glare from Nareema.

She turned back to the freed man who turned, rubbing his wrists.

'You wanted me. Here I am.'

He stood dumbly looking at her without moving.

'Come on.' Nareema slapped his face hard.
He bristled but didn't move.
'Come on. You wanted me last night.'
She slapped him again, this time he glanced at Brody who was watching open-mouthed.
'Fight me. If you win you can have me with no repercussions. If I win...' she left that hanging in the air.
He glanced at the Captain again and the around at the crew. They were all looking confused.
'He'll kill her.' whispered Brody.
'Please Nareema. Don't.' begged Molly.
She turned away from the sailor.
'He tried to take something sacred from me and he will pay for that.'
She turned back.
'No repercussions. No flogging. Come on. Do you want me or not?'
The sailor looked once more at the Captain and crew before he made up his mind and suddenly rushed at her. She nimbly somersaulted backwards out of his way.
'Is that the best you've got?'
Slowly they began circling each other. He stepped forward and swung a ham sized fist at her but she dropped underneath his swing and swept his legs out from under him. He hit the deck hard.
'Come on. You can do better than that.'
He stood and rolled his shoulders before lunging again but this time she spun gracefully and kicked him hard in the face. He fell onto the deck, blood spurting from his broken nose.
'Enough!' bellowed Brody.
Neither of them took any notice. The sailor shook his head and stepped forward again, his anger rising, but all he found was Nareema's boot coming the other way hard enough to send him crashing into the assembled crowd.

Ten minutes later he fell for the last time, unable to get up, a bleeding and beaten mess. As soon as he went down Nareema straddled his back and grabbed hold of his hair. Fishing a knife from her belt she hauled his head back and pressed the blade to his throat.

'Nareema. No!'

She looked up through her anger to see Molly clutching Marcus tightly.

'Please. Don't kill him. Please.'

Nareema hesitated for a moment before she cried out with rage and let go of the unconscious sailor, smacking his head on the deck. Straightening she stepped before the stunned crew. Not one of them had moved since she had started and only the Captain could look her in the eye. Nareema turned slowly so they could all see her face before she spoke with a voice like stone.

'If anyone touches me again I *will* kill them. Unlike her...' she pointed to Molly with the knife she still had in her hand. '...Unlike her, I am not merciful.'

To emphasise the point she kicked the downed man again before stalking back below decks. The assembled crew watched her go in stunned silence.

'I must see if she's alright.' said Molly, letting go of Marcus and following her.

Captain Brody stared after them.

'How did... Where...?

Marcus shook his head. Brody recovered from his shock quickly and began bellowing orders. The crew snapped out of their daze and it to their ordered tasks. Marcus watched as the unconscious man was dragged away.

'Captain Kane. May I have a word with you.'

There was no mistaking the building anger in Brody's voice.

Molly ran to Nareema's cabin. She knocked but there was no answer. Tentatively, she opened the door and went in.

The Princess had her back to her and was in the process of taking off her suit.

'I do not wish to be disturbed.' her voice was full of anger and had an edge like steel.

Molly's hand went to her mouth at what she saw.

'Oh my god.'

Nareema had a huge black raven tattooed between her shoulder blades, its wings spread and an evil look in its eyes. But that was not what caused her pause. Nareema's back was covered in criss-crossing scars and after what she had just witnessed she knew exactly what they were. As soon as Molly had spoken, Nareema began to pull the suit back up again.

'You've been flogged.'

The Princess let out a long sad sigh and finished pulling it on.

'Yes.'

Molly sat on the small bed and after a moment, Nareema did the same.

'Why? Who would...'

'Shakir did it.' she said, as if it was the most normal thing in the world.

'Shakir?' she couldn't keep the surprise from her voice. 'He loves you like a daughter...'

'It was under orders from my father. He and my brother protested but he was given no choice. I was taken to the market square, stripped and publicly lashed.'

'Why?'

'I failed my father. He sent me to kill a man but I couldn't. He was surrounded by his children. I couldn't kill him in front of them.'

'But why did he have you flogged? Surely...'

'A week later, that man murdered my mother and sister.'

Molly didn't know what to say.

'I failed and it cost me my family. I haven't spoken to my father since. I think it should have been more but Shakir cut me down after thirty and helped me back to the Daughters of Kali.'

'How could he? Your father?'

'He was angry. They had lost his wife, his daughter and nearly his only son.'

'But...'

Nareema shook her head.

'No. I failed. I deserved to be punished for that failure. Justice needed to be done.'

'What about Tong Li. Doesn't he deserve punishment? How could your father hurt you like that?'

Nareema sighed.

'I don't question my father's decisions. It hurt though. It was more pain than I have ever experienced but if I thought I could bring them back I would have a thousand more in a heartbeat. As for Tong Li? I will just have to settle for his head.'

'Is that why you fought the sailor? To prevent him from the pain?'

Nareema looked at her.

'No. He deserved to die but my honour demanded I gave him a chance.'

'Oh.' Molly paused, unsure what to say next. 'Thank you for not killing him.'

'He won't appreciate your kindness.'

They lapsed into silence.

'I didn't kill her you know.'

'Who?' asked Molly.

'The French woman. The one that had the sapphire. I didn't kill her. I stole it while she slept. I think she thought the third story of a house was a safe place for her jewellery box.'

Molly smiled and went to speak but was interrupted by a knock on the door.

'Come.'

Davis opened the door a fraction, eyeing Nareema warily.

'Cap'n would like you to join him in his cabin. If'n it's not too much trouble.'

Nareema stood and he backed away quickly as she picked up her sword.

A few minutes later they were stood in front of Captain Brody. He had calmed down slightly, having vented most of his anger at the crew and then some at Marcus, but he was still not a happy man. He stood and rested his fists on his table.

'I'm responsible for discipline on this ship. I don't take kindly to people taking matters into their own hands.'

'It wasn't you he tried to rape.'

Brody looked down for a second before glancing back up.

'No. But he is still part of my crew and I will deal with any insurrection in my way. I don't need people causing trouble like that. What sort of Captain let's his crew get beaten to a pulp? And by a woman at that!'

Molly felt Nareema tense next to her and touched her arm to stop her doing anything rash.

'I've a good mind to have you all thrown overboard now.'

'You could try...'

There was no disguising the venom in her words. Brody and Marcus both spoke at the same time.

'I don't take kindly to threats...'

'Your Highness...'

Brody looked at him sharply as Marcus realised what he had said.

'Highness?' he said as he sat down heavily in his chair. 'I think you'd better start telling me what the hell is going on.'

Nareema stood straight and gripped her sword.

'My name is Princess Nareema Kareen Vashti. First daughter of his Highness Hanka Nessa Vashti, Maharaja of the Sunjian province.'

Brody didn't look impressed.

'I am also a Daughter of Kali.'

He sat back and nodded.
'That explains a few things.'
'You've heard of us?'
'You can't travel as much as I do without picking up a few rumours. Never believed them until now.'
Marcus looked at them.
'Like in the story about the Stones?'
'Yes. I'll tell you later.' whispered Molly.
Nareema stepped to the table.
'My friends and I are travelling to Portugal on our own business. The sooner you get us there, the sooner we will be off your ship.'
With that, she reached into a pouch at her belt and pulled out a small velvet bag which she threw to Brody.
'For the inconvenience.'
Without giving him a chance to reply she turned on her heel and left, slamming the door behind her. Molly and Marcus looked on as Brody opened the bag and emptied its contents into his hand. Around three dozen small diamonds landed in his palm. He let out a sigh before addressing Marcus.
'Why didn't you say something?'
'We are trying to keep a low profile sir.'
Brody waved at the door angrily.
'How in the hell is that keeping a low profile?'
The ship's master sighed again and looked at the diamonds.
'Join me for dinner this evening.'
'Of course sir.' said Marcus.
The pair turned to go but Molly turned back as they reached the door.
'Would you please keep this a secret. We don't want...'
Brody looked at her for a moment.
'Aye. I'll keep your secret for now.'
'Thank you.'

Nareema was sat in her cabin alone. Molly had tried to talk to her but she wasn't in the mood for company so had chased her away. She had cleaned her weapons three or four times and now sat in silence with an open book on her lap. She hadn't read a single word but had just stared at the wall, running over the last day in her mind. She felt as if she was getting sloppy. There was no way those men should have been able to sneak up on her like that. Her thoughts were interrupted by a heavy knock at the door.

'I do not wish to be disturbed.'

It opened anyway to reveal Brody. He stepped in and closed the door behind him. She looked at him venomously.

'If you are looking for an apology then you are going to be disappointed.'

'To be honest, I wasn't expecting one.'

Nareema stared at him for a second before turning to look at the wall.

'May I? he asked.

She closed her eyes and gave him a curt nod. Brody sat next to her on the bed.

'Drink?'

He held up the bottle of wine and two silver cups he had brought with him. Nareema sighed before she turned to look at him.

'Yes. Please. That would be nice.'

Brody poured them both a drink and handed one to Nareema. She sipped it and made an approving face. Brody smiled, his scar twisting it to something humourless.

'Just because I run a ship doesn't mean I don't know a thing or two about wine. Picked this up last time I was in the south of France. Been saving a bottle or two for a special occasion.'

'And why is this special?' enquired Nareema politely.

'It's not every day I get a Princess on board. Or a Daughter of Kali for that matter.'

'I am flattered but I do not consider who or what I am to be special.'

They sipped their drinks in silence for a moment.

'I knew you weren't a servant from the moment I laid eyes on you.' said Brody eventually.

'How so?'

'It's the way you move. You're too graceful. Too light on your feet. Like a fighter.'

'I shall have to try harder.'

Brody waved his cup in the air.

'And what a fighter! I've never seen anything like that and I've been in a brawl or two in my time.'

'I'm glad you found me entertaining Captain.' her tone was icy.

'I didn't mean it like that and you know it.'

Nareema sighed again.

'Yes Captain. I apologise. Sometimes I let my anger get the better of me.'

'Like this morning?'

'Yes.'

'Would you have killed him?'

She was silent for a moment before answering as if she were deciding what to say.

'Yes. And I will if he comes anywhere near me again.'

'What stopped you?'

'Molly.' she replied simply.

Brody took a swig from his cup and poured another, offering the bottle to Nareema who shook her head.

'No. Thank you.'

'There's something about her too. Can't put my finger on what it is though.' he shook his head. 'I suppose they're not married either are they? All part of the disguise.'

'No. They're not.'

'They play the part well though. Well enough to fool me at any rate. There's love there I think.'

The Princess smiled but it didn't reach her eyes.

'I think so. They need to work it out for themselves. In all honesty they only met each other a few weeks ago. They saved my life and have hardly been apart since.'

'What's so special about Portugal?'

'I can't say Captain. I have enemies. Powerful enemies and I don't want to inconvenience you any further.'

Brody sighed and reached into his coat to pull out the velvet bag. He handed it to Nareema.

'Here. I've a feeling you may need these more than I will.'

The Princess took the bag without comment.

'Now I just need to work out what I'm going to tell the crew. Gossip is already rife. I've heard that you were going to drink his blood after you'd slit his throat.'

Nareema smiled.

'Not before breakfast.'

Brody laughed before going silent and staring into his wine.

'I suppose that Captain Kane picked you up on the way back from his last trip to India did he? And that, knowing he was getting wed before being posted abroad again, he hired you to look after his young wife while he was off with the army. It can be mighty dangerous for a pretty young lady on her own in a foreign country. You never can tell what's going to happen. You're there to sort of see that she doesn't get into any trouble.'

Nareema looked at him.

'Something like that.'

He nodded and stood up.

'Join the Captain and his wife for dinner with me this evening.'

'No. Thank you. It would not do for a servant to be seen in such high circles as the Captain's table.' she replied with a smile.

He grinned back.

'You could consider it an apology for the way you were treated by members of my crew.'

'No.'

'Please. I would be honoured to entertain a Princess at my table.'

'You're not going to take no for an answer are you?'

'Nope. Stubborn is my middle name.'

Nareema laughed softly.

'In such case I would gladly like to join you for dinner.'

'Right you are.'

He turned to go.

'Captain? As the crew will soon no doubt be aware of my...' Nareema hesitated as she chose her words. 'My "protective" roll with Molly would it be alright if I were to give her a few lessons in defending herself? I think that she is going to need them.'

Brody scratched his chin.

'I don't think for a second you'd listen anyway if I said no but as long as you don't kill any of my men you can do what you please. '

He closed the door behind him leaving Nareema feeling content for the first time in a couple of days.

Nareema quietly entered Marcus and Molly's cabin early the next morning. She stood and looked at the sleeping pair. He was sprawled on the bed, covers up to his waist and his left arm flung across the bed. Molly was curled up with her head on his shoulder. The Princess smiled to herself and gently woke the girl.

'Molly. Come. We have work to do.'

'What?'

'Shhh. Find your suit and sword and meet me on deck in five minutes.'

She left Molly rubbing her eyes and trying to wake up. It was ten minutes later before Molly surfaced on deck. She kept looking around and trying not to catch the eye of any of the sailors in her leather outfit. Nareema had no such qualms and was stood in the middle of the deck, her feet planted solidly while she ran through a series of co-ordinated moves with her hands, legs and body that flowed like water.

'Come here.' she said without turning around.

'But they'll see me.'

'Don't be absurd. If they want to touch you they'll have to come through me and I am willing to bet there will be none who dare try.'

Blushing furiously Molly walked over to the Princess.

'What are we doing up so early?'

'I think you need to learn to defend yourself.'

'You're going to teach me to fight? Like you?'

'Yes.'

For the next four days, Nareema woke Molly early and put her through her paces. She began to teach her to move and fight, both with and without a weapon. Several times Brody had to bellow at groups of sailors who had gathered to watch the pair. They would practice for hours and by the time the evening came, Molly would flop, exhausted and bruised, into bed. Marcus spoke to Nareema on the third day after she had knocked Molly on her back for the umpteenth time.

'Don't you think you're pushing her a bit too hard?'

The Princess had smiled.

'Yes. But she keeps getting back up. She will tell me when she's had enough.'

He had made a disapproving noise but said nothing more. It was on the fifth day that the shout went up.

'Land ho!'

All rushed to the port side of the ship to see the coast of Portugal begin to rise from the horizon. Brody came and stood next to Nareema at the railing.

'We'll be putting into port tomorrow or the next day. You

can go about whatever it is you need to do from there.'

'Thank you Captain.'

'If you told me where it was you were going I could probably get you closer than this.'

'This is close enough.'

He nodded and began shouting to his crew who began to get back to their work. Nareema turned away from the railings to see Molly standing, sword in hand, waiting. She was beaded in sweat but ready.

'Are we still practising?'

Nareema smiled and raised her own sword.

## Chapter Eight

## Portugal

At dusk the next day the ship drew into a small harbour. Brody insisted that they spend a last night on board before continuing with their journey. Nareema acquiesced eventually and even took dinner with him alongside Molly and Marcus. As the dawn broke they took their leave of the Endurance and went ashore.

'Thank you Captain.' said Molly as they stood at the top of the gangplank.

She stretched up and gave him a kiss on the cheek. He smiled.

'Take care of yourself lass. And take care of him too.'

'I will.'

He shook hands with Marcus and then offered his hand to Nareema. She looked at it for a moment before she grinned slyly and followed Molly's example, giving him a gentle kiss on the cheek. His hand quickly went to the spot she had touched.

'Thank you for hospitality Captain. Take care.'

Brody nodded and watched as she followed Marcus to the harbour side, hand still on his cheek.

'Glad they're gone cap'n.' said Davis who was stood nearby. 'She gives me the willies that one.'

'What?' muttered Brody, snapping out of his daze.

'Have you got somewhere to be Davis? Come on you lot, make lively. We sail on the tide. Move it.'

He turned back to the quay side to see them climbing into a carriage. Molly waved one last time as it pulled away. Smiling to himself, Brody turned and went to make preparations to put back out to sea.

The carriage took them down the coast for a few days before turning inland to a small town where they bought themselves a wagon to transport them and their luggage the rest of the way. After another week of travel, they were nearly there.

The weather had been fine, barely a cloud in the sky but chilly at night. Molly had enjoyed the open lands, dotted with pretty villages and farms. It was so different from the dirty city she had grown up in. As they neared their destination, Marcus suggested they stop for the night at a local inn set in the middle of a quiet village.

The houses were simple with terracotta roofs and whitewashed walls. Nareema consented eventually, her eagerness to get to the Stone obvious, but seeing the sense in a good nights' sleep. The inn was run by a kindly couple but only had one free room and, much to Marcus's consternation, Nareema refused to take it, repeating that she was the servant and would be more than comfortable in the hay loft. After a good meal, they retired for the night.

'She knows it rankles you. That's why she does it.' said Molly as they lay down in bed.

'I know but I think that the gentlemanly thing to do is...'

'She thinks you're funny. I do too sometimes.'

'And what is that supposed to mean?'

'You have to be a gentleman in everything.'

'I'm an officer in His Majesties army...'

'Who's currently in bed with an unmarried woman.'

He opened and closed his mouth a few times trying to work out what to say.

Molly silenced him with a kiss.

'Go to sleep my gentle man.'

She rolled over and pulled the blankets up and was asleep within moments. Marcus on the other hand, lay and stared at the ceiling.

After about an hour, he quietly got out of bed and dressed. Checking she was still asleep he left and headed out to the stable. Opening the door he was greeted by the smell of hay and animals.

'Your Highness?'

There was no answer. Looking around he saw a ladder leading up to the hay loft.

'Your Highness?' he whispered as he climbed.

Still there was no answer. The hay in the loft had been pressed down and her bag was there but there was no sign of the Princess. He climbed back down again and went outside. There was a chill to the night and it was silent as the grave.

A shrill caw, loud against the night, sounded from above him and made him jump. He shook his head and headed back towards the inn. He jumped again as a hand shot out of the darkness behind him and clamped itself across his mouth. The grip was like steel as it dragged him into the shadows.

'Calm down. It's me.' Nareema whispered in his ear.

Marcus nodded and she let him go.

'What are you doing out here?' she asked him.

'Um, I need to ask you a question.'

The Princess shook her head.

'We haven't got time. There are about forty men heading this way. They're all carrying muskets and don't look friendly. Go and wake Molly. Tell her to dress and arm herself. Grab what you can carry and no more. Hurry.'

'How far away are they?'

'About six miles.'

'Right.'

He turned and headed back to the inn. Quietly he crept into the room and shook Molly awake.

'You've got to get up. There's trouble coming this way. Nareema said you should arm yourself.'

She went from being half asleep to being awake in an instant. Marcus began stuffing clothes and belongings into a couple of small bags. Molly stripped off her nightgown and began to pull the leather suit out of her bag. Marcus sighed, covered his eyes and turned away.

'I wish you'd warn me before you do something like that.'

'Don't be prudish. We've shared a bed for the last I don't know how long.'

'That was different.'

'Why?'

'You've been clothed. I'm going to have a word with the Princess about the habits she seems to be teaching you. They are unseemly. Especially for my wife and a lady.'

Molly grinned as she pulled the leather on.

'I'm neither of those things.'

'So you keep telling me.'

'I'm finished. You can look now.'

He turned back as Molly slipped the sword across her back and began strapping the knife to her thigh.

'Did she say what was wrong?'

Marcus continued putting things in his bag.

'There are armed men coming this way.'

Nodding, Molly grabbed the small leather backpack that Nareema had given her and crammed a few things into it. Quietly they both snuck out of the room, leaving the bulk of their possessions behind. Nareema was waiting outside. She was on a horse with another two next to her. She saw Marcus' look.

'Yes. We're stealing them. Don't start that again.'

'The thought never crossed my mind.'

'Molly. Have you got the sapphire?' Nareema asked as they mounted.

'Yes. Of course. Why?'

'See if you can find the Fire Stone.'

There was something in Nareema's voice that made Molly hesitate.

'You don't think...'

'Just do it. Please. We don't have much time.'

Marcus glanced up the road but couldn't see anything in the darkness.

'How do you know they're coming?'

'I just do. We don't have time. Molly, please.'

Molly reached inside her suit and took out the gem. She held it in her palm and thought about the ruby that Tong Li possessed. The sapphire was still for a second before it span towards the oncoming men and glowed a fierce red.

'It's there.'

'Damn.' spat Nareema.

'How did he...'

'It doesn't matter. Let's get out of here before they arrive.'

She spurred her horse on into a gallop with Molly and Marcus close behind. They rode until the sun came up, trying to put some distance between the village and themselves. Eventually they had to stop to give the horses a rest. They had ridden into a low ridge of hills to the west and found a small stream trickling down a rocky bed.

'We should be safe here for now.'

Molly dismounted and sat down heavily.

'Can we sleep for a bit?'

Nareema looked back in the direction of the village. It was hidden by the hills.

'For a few hours. Then we must be going. We need to get to the church before Tong Li.'

'Molly. Wake up. We've got to move.'

She opened her eyes blearily and shivered.

'What?'

'It's time to go.'

Stiffly she sat up. She had gotten so used to a bed that a few hours asleep on the ground felt like she'd been sleeping on a bag of rocks. The day had moved on and the sun was high.

'Here.'

Marcus handed her a cup of water and some bread.
'Thank you.'
'Where's Nareema?'
'Scouting ahead somewhere.'
Molly rubbed her eyes.
'I can't believe Tong Li is here.'
'No. This has turned into a race. We have the advantage I think. We're on horseback and know where we're going. He is limited by as fast as his men can march.'
'And we have to hope that he doesn't know where the Stone is.'
Marcus nodded.
'Although we only have a vague idea.'
'But it's better than nothing.'
'It is.'
Molly ate in silence for a moment before getting up and stretching tiredly.
'Marcus?'
He looked up from where he was sat by the stream.
'Yes?'
She opened her mouth to say something but was interrupted from a shout from behind them.
'You're awake.'
They both span round to see Nareema coming up the valley.
'Where have you been?'
Nareema sat down and took some water and bread.
'Seeing where we are. We're not far from the church. If we leave now we should get there before nightfall.'
Molly took the sapphire out and held it in her palm. Concentrating, she thought about the Fire Stone. It span to point towards the village and glowed red.
'At least he hasn't moved.'
'No.'
Thinking of the Earth Stone, the sapphire span to point west and glowed a solid green.

'At least we know we're close to the other one.'
Nareema stood.
'Then let us go and get it.'

# Chapter Nine

## Earth

They arrived at the church just before sunset. It was a small single storey building with white walls and blue coving, stood on a cliff overlooking a small fishing village. The sun was going down and the view from the cliff top was idyllic and peaceful. The three of them dismounted and stood for a moment, enjoying the serenity of the place.
'Such a beautiful spot.' said Marcus softly.
He turned to look at them and saw the look on their faces.
'What? Being a soldier doesn't mean I can't appreciate a nice view you know.'
'We never said a thing.' replied Molly with a wry smile.
They led their horses around the back of the building so they would be hidden from the road. Nareema drew her sword.
'Is that really necessary? We're about to enter a house of God.'
'Captain, do you know how many people have died in the name of religion?'
'No.'
'Neither do I but I know it's a lot. And I for one don't want to be another.'
He sighed theatrically but drew his own weapon as well.
'Molly, see if you can find the Stone.'
Molly withdrew the sapphire and placed it in her open palm. The gem glowed a bright green and span in a circle.
'I think we must be close.'
The only entrance to the church was a small wooden door. It was not locked but creaked loudly on rusty hinges and they cautiously entered.
The trio took in the building. An altar with a small wooden cross on it took up one end with rough wooden

pews flanking the sides. The floor was made of large flagstones and the far wall was taken up by a large stained glass window depicting Christ on the cross, which overlooked the altar.

'What now?' whispered Molly.

'I don't know. Have a look around. See what you can find.'

Their search didn't take long. There pews were little more than wooden benches and the altar turned out to be a table with a white cloth on it.

'It's not here.' said Marcus.

'It must be. Molly, try the sapphire again.'

Once more it glowed green and span on the spot.

'It's close. Look again.'

Marcus and Nareema began searching again, checking the walls for concealed niches or buttons. Molly turned and looked at the stained-glass window. The setting sun cast its rays through the coloured glass and it glowed brilliantly as the light flashed through it. It was then that she saw something out of place.

'Nareema! Look!'

She pointed to the window.

'What?'

The Princess came over and looked at the glass.

'Around his neck.'

She stared at it for a second before she saw it. Around the neck of Christ was a simple black thong holding a green tear shaped gem.

'That's it.'

Nareema quickly dragged the altar table close to the window and clambered up onto it. She ran her hands across the figure.

'It's just glass.'

She turned back to the body of the church.

'There!'

From her higher vantage point she saw a stone in the floor that had been underneath the altar. Dropping down she bent over it. There was a deep impression of a tear shaped gem cut into it.

'Give me the sapphire.'

Molly handed it over. Nareema took it and dropped it into the indentation in the brick. It was a perfect fit and as the gem fell into place there was a click but nothing else happened. The Princess frowned.

'This must be it.'

Molly bit her lip before she tentatively reached out and placed her hand over the sapphire. It glowed dimly and grew warm before there was a solid thunk and a deep grinding noise. They all turned to see the flagstones in the middle of the church slip down to form a ramp into a dark hole. Molly picked up the sapphire.

'It looks like it might be this way.'

Nareema grinned.

'Well done. I knew I'd hired you for a reason.'

'You're employing her?' asked Marcus with surprise.

Molly gave him a small shrug.

'Sort of.'

'I don't understand you two at all.'

She gave him a quick kiss on the cheek.

'It's not a husbands place to understand his wife.'

'But you're not my wife.'

'So you keep saying.'

Nareema had headed down the ramp into the darkness. She called back up.

'It looks like some sort of cave. Captain, see if you can find something to make us some torches.'

Marcus looked around, crossed himself and looked up at the stained glass window.

'Please forgive me.'

He tipped the altar table over and broke the legs off before tearing the covering cloth into strips and wrapping it around the legs. He and Molly headed after Nareema.

'These should do.' he said as he handed one of the makeshift torches to the Princess. She took a flint and steel from her belt and lit one of the them.

'Come on.'

The ramp led to a rough cave. Their torches casting a weak light across a maze of stalagmites that littered the floor.

'It looks natural.' said Nareema.

Around the edge of the cave were niches carved into the rock. Each was about six feet long, three deep and a foot or so high.

'I wonder what they're for.' said Marcus.

'I don't like this.' said Molly.

Marcus took her hand and she held it tightly.

'Where now?'

'There.'

Molly pointed to another tunnel on the far side, just visible in the glow of the flames.

The tunnel had been hacked from the stone and led steeply downwards. As it wound its way down Molly noticed that there were more of the niches carved every ten feet or so. Some of them held dusty skeletons.

'I really don't like this place.'

Marcus squeezed her hand.

'They're dead. And have been for some time.'

'Doesn't mean I have to like it.'

'It looks like a burial site. I wonder if these were the priests that served the church above?' commented Nareema who was further ahead.

The passage widened slightly and then abruptly ended in a sharp drop. Marcus walked to the edge and peered over.

'I can't see the bottom.'

He dropped his torch and it fell about twenty feet to land on the rock floor below which sloped away sharply. Nareema looked around. There was a heavy iron ring set just past the edge with a tattered and worn looking rope attached to it. She hauled it up and tugged it.

'We should be alright if we go one at a time. I'll go first. Here. Hold this.'

She handed Marcus her torch before she took the rope and stepped backwards off the edge, bouncing gracefully down the rock face. She reached the bottom in short order.

'Molly next.' she called up to them.

Marcus hauled the rope up and tied it around her waist.

'I'll lower you down.'

She nodded and sat on the edge. Gingerly she eased herself forward as Marcus took her weight and lowered her to the ground.

'I'm here.'

He looked over the edge again.

'Mind out of the way.'

The two women moved back and he dropped his torch over the edge. Molly picked it up and held it above her head.

'Be careful.' she called up to him.

Marcus smiled to himself before he began to climb down the rock. He had made it down about half way before he felt the rope give. The fibres were old and rotten and they couldn't take any more.

'Oh...' was all he managed to say before the rope snapped and he fell.

Molly was staring up at him as he came down the rock. As he got halfway she heard him shout before the rope snapped at the top. He plummeted down, bouncing off the face of the stone.

'Marcus!'

He shouted out as he fell.

'Move!'

Molly heard him but didn't get out of the way in time. He crashed into her and they both fell backwards, tumbling together across the steep floor to crash hard into the wall. Nareema ran after them. Molly brushed a lock of hair out of her face. She was lying on top of Marcus, their faces inches apart. They looked into each-others' eyes for a second before the princess reached them.

'Are you alright?'

Molly could feel herself blushing and was glad of the weak light from the torches. She slowly got up.

'Yes. I think so. Marcus?'

He stood and brushed himself down.

'Yes. Although I'm going to have some bruises in the morning. Are you alright?'

Molly smiled at him.

'Other than having my husband fall on me, I'm fine.'

'I'm not your husband.'

They stared at each other for a second before Nareema sighed and shook her head.

'Come on. We need to keep moving.'

They travelled downwards, deep into the rock of the cliff, for what seemed like an age before Nareema pulled up and stopped.

'Can you hear that?'

Molly listened hard.

'It sounds like running water.'

They moved on and suddenly the tunnel began to widen into a large cave which was split in two by a fast-flowing river. It must have been twenty feet wide and poured savagely from a high ledge and then ran off towards the western side of the cavern. There were more stalagmites and stalactites dotted around the cavern. Some were so big that Molly couldn't have reached around them.

Near the edge of the river stood three heavy stone bowls. Nareema walked over to one and looked at it. It was quite deep and filled with wood and coals. She put her torch to it and it caught almost immediately, filling the area with a bright glow. Marcus lit the other two, illuminating the area further.

'There.'

Marcus pointed across the river. A thin stone bridge, barely two feet wide, straddled the water. There were three more of the stone braziers on the other side and through a maze of stalactites they could just make out another dark tunnel leading off from the cavern.

'I think we'd better go one at a time.' said Nareema as she looked at the bridge.

Marcus nodded.

'It doesn't look too safe.'

The bridge was made of dressed stone blocks but was wet and slippery with a green moss growing on the damp rock.

'I'll go first.'

Nareema stepped onto the bridge and hurried across.

'It's fine. Come on.'

Marcus followed, slightly slower than the Princess but he made it across without a problem.

'Molly, just take it slowly.'

She nodded and began to cross. As Molly reached the middle, one of the stones beneath her feet moved and she fell flat on her face, skidding on the slimy rocks. She shouted out as her feet and then legs slipped off the bridge and she just managed to grab onto the edge before she went over.

'Molly!'

Marcus dashed forward, throwing himself flat and grabbing her wrist.

'Help me.' she shouted.

'I'm trying.'

Slowly he hauled her back up onto the wet rock where they both lay, breathing hard.

'That was close.'

He nodded.

'Too close.'

Marcus rose to his knees and scurried across the bridge to safety, followed closely by Molly. As she moved, one of the stones of the bridge moved with a clunk as her knee pressed on it and then from above a shrieking sound of metal on metal. They all looked up as a heavy stone dropped a few feet towards them. It was as wide as the river and must have weighed a tonne. Above it they could just make out a thick chain holding it up.

'Quickly. Move.' urged Nareema.

Molly dashed the last few feet on her hands and knees and jumped into Marcus's arms.

They looked back up at the stone which swung perilously.

'Looks like some sort of trap. The workings must have rusted.' observed Nareema.

'And thank god they did.' said Marcus as he held Molly who smiled at him.

The Princess shook her head.

'Not now. Come on.'

The princess lit the other braziers and looked around. Ahead of them the cavern narrowed into another tunnel that sloped downwards. Nareema led the way, sword in one hand and flaming torch in the other. After a few minutes the passage levelled out into a corridor made from finely cut and dressed stone.

'This is manmade.'

It ran for about forty feet before opening out into a square room about ten feet to a side. In the middle of the far room was a doorway that was covered by a heavy looking portcullis. Two more of the stone braziers stood in opposite corners. Marcus lit one of them.

'What now?'

'I think we...' began the princess before a grinding noise sounded behind them. They turned in time to see another heavy gate fall down across the door they had just come through. Marcus rushed over to it but it wouldn't budge.

'It's jammed.'

'Hmm.' said Nareema as she took in the rest of the room. There were three apertures in the wall on each side of the room, each about three feet high and two from the floor. She peered into the first one.

'It looks like there's something in here.'

She stood and looked around again before lighting the second brazier. As the flames caught there was another grinding noise and out of each hole, a wooden pole appeared. They were about six inches round and looked very solid.

'Interesting.'

Molly watched as the Princess walked around the room, inspecting the poles.

'Which one do you think we should pull?'

'Is that wise?' asked Marcus.

'Unless you have a better idea?'

He looked like he was going to say something else but in the end just shook his head.

'Here.'

Nareema passed her torch to Molly and put her sword away. She selected a pole and wrapped her hands around it, bracing herself to pull it down.

'Wait!' cried Molly.

In her pocket, she could feel the sapphire pressing warmly against her. She reached in and took it out, holding the brightly glowing gem in her hand.

'Don't. It's a trap.'

'How do you know?' asked the Princess, hands still on the pole

Molly closed her eyes. She could see the poles around the room but there was something else. She opened her eyes and stepped close to the pole that Nareema had hold of.

'Move.'

The Princess stepped away and Molly brought the flaming torch down to touch the wood. In front of their eyes it began to melt in the fire.

'It's made of wax.' said Marcus as he came over too.

'There's more than that.' said Nareema as the wax melted to reveal a sharp steel blade running through the middle.

Marcus picked off some of the wax from the blade. It was soft inside, surrounded by a thin painted veneer that looked like wood.

'You'd have lost a hand if you'd have tried to pull that.'

Nareema looked at Molly.

'How did you know?'

She shrugged.

'I don't know. I just did.'

The Princess regarded her for a moment before smiling.

'Thank you.'

She took the torch from Marcus and tested the other poles. All but two of them were made of wax with a lethal blade in each. Nareema braced herself against one of the others and pulled. There was a clunk but nothing else happened.

'Marcus, pull the other one.'

He moved to the other wooden pole.

'On three. One. Two. Three...'

They both heaved and with another clunk the portcullis at both ends slowly began to rise.

'Shall we?'

Nareema ducked under the portcullis and headed into another corridor made from fine stone. It was about twenty feet long with a carved fresco running down each side. They cautiously walked down.

'This looks like the story of the Stones.' said Nareema, holding her torch high.

The first of the carvings showed a mountain covered in light with a kneeling figure before it. There were four teardrop shaped objects floating in the air above him.

'Tobias would love this.' said Nareema

They continued down the corridor following the story. In front of the mountain a fabulous city had sprung up and at its centre was the figure with the Stones floating above him. Then suddenly the city was in flames. The figure was laid down on the ground with another stood above him, a sword in his hand.

'That must be the son.'

The new figure was then at the head of an army that conquered and enslaved. The Stones no longer floated above him but were in a crown on his head along with a fifth, square stone in the middle.

'Why are there five Stones now?' asked Marcus

Nareema shook her head.

'I don't know. I've only ever heard of four.'

The next pictures showed a bird with talons outstretched stealing the crown, while on the ground lay a body with a knife in its chest. Molly looked at Nareema and could see the recognition in her eyes. The bird resembled the tattoo she had on her back.

'Is that the...'

'Daughter of Kali.' finished Nareema. 'I think it is.'

In the final set of carvings, the bird lay dead with an arrow through its heart while small figures took the stones and headed in different directions. North, south, east and west. A fifth figure had the crown.

'Where is the fifth stone?' asked Molly. 'There are only four in this picture. The one from the crown is missing.'

Marcus stepped back to look at the previous fresco.

'There are only four when the bird steals it too.'

Nareema shook her head.

'We'll have to talk to Tobias about this. For now, we need to get the Earth Stone.'

The corridor ended with a stone block. Marcus ran his hand across the smooth surface.

'A dead end.'

In her hand the gem grew warm again.

'No. There's something else.' said Molly.

Closing her eyes, she placed her open palm on the rock and concentrated. The gem in her hand grew warm and she could feel a tingling in the back of her mind, like a voice in a different room.

'It's here.'

Suddenly there was a flash of light from the sapphire and the rock in front of them began to slowly sink into the ground with a deep rumble. Nareema smiled.

'Well done.'

Molly smiled tightly. Her head was spinning and she could see the flash of light from behind her eyes as if it had been in her mind rather than in her hand.

'Are you alright?' asked Marcus.

She nodded.

'Yes. Come on.'

The door opened to reveal a large square room made from more of the finely dressed stone blocks. In the centre was a low pedestal with a bowl like depression in the centre. In it were hundreds of tear shaped green gems. Marcus picked one up.

'Careful.' admonished Molly.

He held it up to the weak light from their torches.

'I think it's glass. How are we going to work out which is the real one?'

'I could try holding them and see if they talk to me like the sapphire does.'

'There are too many. We don't have time.'

'How about we just take the lot?' suggested Marcus.

'Wait.' said Molly suddenly.

She took a deep breath and then held out the sapphire, concentrating hard on the emerald. In her hand the gem glowed a brilliant green and rotated to point at the pile if green stones. As its colour began to change there was movement in the bowl. One of the gems began to rotate towards the sapphire, its colour changing from green to pale blue.

'That's the one.'

Nareema grabbed it and held it in her hand.

It rotated to point at the sapphire, its colour remaining a pale blue until Molly stopped thinking about it.

'As Tobias would say, that is fantastic.' said Nareema.

Molly looked at her, suddenly nervous.

'You don't think that the Fire Stone does that too do you?'

'Does what?' Asked Marcus.

'The whole spinning and glowing thing.'

Nareema looked back at her with a dawning realisation on her face.

'If it does then we've led Tong Li right to us.'

'We've got to get out of here.'

They quickly headed out of the room and back up to the cavern with the river with Nareema in the lead. As she emerged from the tunnel there was a shout from across the cavern and the crack of muskets erupted.

Molly screamed and Marcus dragged her to the ground as the bullets smashed into the stone around them. Nareema dived to the left and hid behind a stalagmite near the end of the bridge.

'Give me the Stones.'

The shout drifted across the cavern and Molly looked up to see Tong Li stood in the entrance on the far side. Around him stood a dozen men, all frantically reloading their guns.

'Come and get it.' shouted Nareema.

Musket fire flared again, all directed at the bridge.

'Princess. Are you alright?' shouted Marcus.

She turned to him and raised her sword.

'Make sure she gets out of here. Find Shakir. He'll help

you.'

Nareema began to stand.

'No!' shouted Molly.

She began to rise but Marcus dragged her back to the ground.

'Keep down.'

'We can't let her get herself killed.'

More bullets flashed again, chipping the stone and sending a piece searing across her cheek.

'We can't help her.'

'Watch me.'

Molly kicked her way out from underneath Marcus and reached into her suit taking the Air Stone in one hand and the Earth in the other. She began to run towards Nareema who was already halfway across the bridge, seemingly oblivious to the bullets that sang towards her.

'Nareema, duck!'

The Princess looked round before throwing herself flat on the bridge, skidding dangerously close to the edge on the wet moss. Concentrating as hard as she could on the Stones, Molly thrust her hands towards the men on the far side.

The blast of wind from her left hand was so powerful, it knocked her off her feet but sent the men on the other side flying, smashing them hard against the walls. As she fell, the blast surged up to the roof of the cavern. The ferocious vortex caught the big stone above the bridge, and as Molly watched, it began to shift with a hideous grinding noise.

'Move!'

The Princess was up and heading across the bridge towards the men. Her feet had barely cleared the bricks before with a shriek of tearing metal, the huge stone crashed to the ground, smashing the narrow bridge to pieces.

More gunfire erupted but Nareema was running hard, the shots chasing her across the cavern. Molly struggled to her knees and directed the wind against them, sending them crashing down, muskets and bones broken. Tong Li ducked back into the mouth of the tunnel as it swept across towards him.

Relinquishing her concentration on the Air Stone, Molly thought about the emerald. In her palm, it grew warm and she envisaged a block of stone rising up from the ground to block the cavern and seal them away from Tong Li.

Again, the effect was more powerful than she imagined. The ground in the cavern began to shake throwing everyone from their feet. Nareema jumped up, closing the distance between her and their attackers in a second. She launched herself at the closest of them, her sword cutting a deep line across his chest.

Molly concentrated harder and with a roar, the tunnel entrance collapsed in on itself, filling the hole with tonnes of rock and dirt. The earth shook more violently and threw everyone from their feet again. Molly cried out loud as she curled into a ball, covering her ears and forgetting about the Earth Stone, as around her rocks began to fall from the roof. As her concentration was broken the shaking stopped to be replaced with the patter of settling stones and the moaning of the few wounded men on the other side.

Marcus crawled over to her. He was covered in dust and dirt. Miraculously their makeshift torches still burned in the mouth of the cavern, as did the braziers.

'Are you alright?'

Molly nodded and shakily tried to stand up. She didn't think she'd ever felt so tired. Her head was pounding and every muscle in her body ached. She flopped heavily back down to her knees. Marcus looked concerned.

'I'm fine. Find Nareema.'

He hesitated.

'Go on. I'm fine. Honestly.'

She managed a weak smile and then began struggling to her feet and using the wall for support.

Marcus ran across to the river. The falling stone had completely destroyed the bridge and the earthquake had done the rest. Where there once was a fast flowing body of water, there was now a deep hole into which the waterfall plunged down into the darkness. Now that the water was pouring into a hole, the channel it ran down was empty.

'Your Highness... Nareema.'

There was no reply. He scrambled down into the deep river bed which was worn smooth from centuries of fast flowing water and pulled himself up the other side. With a quick glance back at Molly, who was stood leaning against the wall, he called out again.

'Nareema?'

There was movement near the far wall and he drew his sword as he drew close.

'Your Highness?'

Nareema stood slowly, small stones and rocks cascading from her. Marcus couldn't tell her how relieved he was as he rushed over to help her.

'I'm fine Captain.'

She was covered in dust and there were numerous cuts on her skin that were tacky with blood.

'What happened?'

Marcus turned to look across the cavern.

'Molly happened.'

Nareema gave him a hard look before shaking her head.

'The Stones happened.'

She coughed and stretched.

'How are we going to get out of here?'

Marcus pointed to the river channel.

'There. That much water had to go somewhere.'

The Princess nodded in agreement.

'See if you can find something to make some rope and gather some more torches please.'

Marcus turned and began to search the bodies of the Tong Li's men while Nareema headed over to Molly. She looked tired in the flickering light from the flames. Her skin was pale and drawn.

'Are you alright.'

Molly pushed herself off the wall and smiled weakly.

'Yes.'

'How did you do that?'

'I don't know. I think I need some more practice though.'

Nareema smiled tightly as Marcus joined them. One of Tong Li's men had a backpack with torches and rope in it. He slung it over his shoulder and threw a concerned look at Molly.

Nareema followed his gaze, her concern mirrored in his own.

'Let's get out of here.'

It took them the best part of four hours to follow the channel out. It was slick and smooth and sometimes very steep but eventually they crawled out onto the beach at the foot of the cliffs. Molly flopped onto the ground. She was tired. It was a deep down tiredness that filled her completely. Her head pounded and her limbs were like lead. Marcus sat next to her.

'Are you alright?'

Her voice was quiet, as if speaking was an effort.

'Tired.'

He glanced up at Nareema who was looking at the top of the cliff. A thin plume of flame was rising into the darkness of the night.

'Tong Li must have burnt the church.' she sighed. 'We need to move.'

Marcus stood.

'She needs to rest.'

The Princess looked down at Molly who was almost asleep.

'We all do. But not here. There's a wood a couple of miles up the beach. We can rest there.'

Marcus looked at her, his protest on his lips but said nothing. She was right. They were too exposed here. He knelt next to Molly.

'Come on. We've got to go. We can't stay here. It's not safe.'

Molly pushed herself up. Her strength was leaving her fast.

'I don't think I can.'

He hooked an arm around her and hauled her to her feet.

'Yes you can.'

Almost as soon as she was upright her legs buckled and she fell against him. Marcus put her arm over his shoulder and supported her.

'I not leaving my wife behind on a beach so you'd better help.'

Molly barely heard him.

'I'm not your wife.' she mumbled.

Dawn was approaching by the time they reached the wood. It was just up from the beach and both Marcus and Nareema had to help Molly get up to it. She was grimly putting one foot in front of the other but there was no conscious thought about it. It was like she was a zombie, leaning more and more heavily on Marcus.

They headed into the trees and had gone no more than two paces when her foot snagged on a root and she went down hard, taking Marcus with her. He tried to get her back to her feet.

'Can't...'

He looked at Nareema.

'Just a little further. Until we are hidden from the beach.'

Nodding he bent and picked the prone girl up. They moved maybe another half a mile before they stopped. Nareema quickly gathered some wood to make a fire while Marcus laid Molly down on the grass. He stretched and let out a weary sigh.

'She's asleep.'

'I think that's for the best. Is there anything to eat in that pack?'

The captain shrugged the backpack from his shoulders and rooted around in it.

'No.'

Nareema handed him a pile of sticks and her flint and steel.

'Light a fire. A small one. I'll find us some food.'

Marcus nodded and began making a fire and the Princess disappeared silently into the trees.

'That's not really a small fire.'

Marcus looked up sharply from where he was sat next to Molly. He had his sword across his lap but he had been dozing. The day had moved on and the sun was high and warm through the trees.

'I didn't hear you come back.'

'I move quietly when I want to.'

She sat down opposite him and began to clean the rabbits she had caught. He looked at her for a moment.

'How do you do it? You haven't slept or eaten yet you still look fresh enough to take on an army.'

'Practice.'

He shook his head.

'That's not what I meant.'

Nareema smiled sadly.

'It's a front captain. Underneath I am very tired and hungry but I need to keep going. It was one of the first things I learnt. Show no weakness. Show no doubt. Only strength. After a while you believe it.'

'Who teaches things like that?'

Nareema didn't answer him. Marcus watched her clean and gut the rabbits with a practiced ease before spitting them and placing them over the fire.

'Has she woken up yet?'

'No. But she was cold. I mean, really cold. Her breath was like ice. That's why I made the fire bigger.'

'There is a farm on the other side of the woods. I will go later and see if they can spare some blankets.'

Marcus looked down and then across at Molly.

'Does she have any family?'

Nareema shook her head.

'I don't think so.'

The Captain looked up at the Princess.

'We'll eat and then you can get some sleep. I'll keep a watch for a few hours. And before you say anything, consider this an order from your employer and master.'

Nareema grinned at him.

'Then how could I disobey?'

Marcus had woken Nareema as the night had begun to draw in. He had stoked the fire and then lain down to get some sleep. Molly had hardly moved since that morning but some colour had returned to her and her breathing was regular.

After walking around the edge of the wood for a while, the Princess had gone to the farmhouse, returning an hour later with blankets, a ham, bread and cheese. She also had a few bottles of wine that the farmer's wife had given her. Silently she thanked Captain Brody for giving her back the pouch of diamonds. One had been a thousand times more than the value of the farm, let alone what she had got for it but it was worth it. Gently she covered Molly with a blanket and sat down in front of the fire. Marcus stirred as she began to roast some of the meat.

'Smells good.'

He sat up and rubbed his eyes.

'The farmer was more than accommodating. Here.'

She handed him a chunk of bread and a bottle. He nodded his thanks and attacked the food hungrily, washing it down with a good mouthful of the wine.

'Not the best vintage I've ever had but it hits the spot.'

Marcus passed the bottle back to Nareema who took a swig. They sat in silence for a moment.

'Your Highness...'

'Nareema.' she corrected.

'Nareema...' Marcus searched for the right words. 'As Molly doesn't...'

'As Molly doesn't what?'

Both turned quickly to see Molly sit up. She blinked slowly, still obviously tired but awake. They jumped up and went to her.

'How are you feeling?' asked Nareema.

'Tired.'

'We were really worried.' added Marcus.

'Where are we?'

'Safe. Are you sure you're alright.'

'I'm fine. Really. Is there anything to eat? I'm starving.'

She sat, wrapping the blanket around her and moved closer to the fire as Marcus hurried to get her some of the food. Molly ate like she hadn't eaten for weeks before she curled up and went back to sleep. Marcus stood and adjusted the blanket over her.

'I think we should move tomorrow.'

Nareema nodded.

'I agree. We need to get back to England and see Uncle Tobias.'

'I'll go to the village tomorrow and see if I can find some horses.'

'Good idea. The largest port near here is a few days from here. We'll be faster on horseback. Get some sleep. I'll watch for a while and wake you later.'

'Thank you.'

Marcus sat and pulled a blanket over him.

'Captain?'

'What were you going to say before Molly woke up?'

He glanced at her sleeping form and smiled to himself.

'It doesn't matter. This isn't the right time.'
'For what?'
'It really doesn't matter. Good night Your Highness.'
He lay down and was soon asleep. Nareema stood and after adding some more wood to the fire, heard off into the dark woods.

## Chapter Ten

### The Dark Raven

Marcus snapped awake. The fire had burnt itself out and dawn was on the horizon. Molly was still sleeping soundly across to his left but there was no sign of the Princess. He stood and shivered in the morning air. Around him the wood was silent. Nothing was stirring. It was almost as if the trees were holding their breath. He found his sword and looked around. There was nothing there. He slowly moved further out into the wood, stepping cautiously.

'Your Highness?' he whispered.

Glancing back the way he had come he could just make out the sleeping form of Molly. The lack of sound was unnerving.

'Nareema? Damn it, where are you?'

He neared a stand of high bushes when the eerie quiet was suddenly shattered by a loud cawing. He dropped down behind them as the biggest, blackest raven he had ever seen drop down from the trees in front of him. It spread its wings and cawed again, while hopping around in a circle.

Marcus raised his sword, a deep fear flooding him. He'd been scared before but never like this. It was almost primordial.

The raven hopped a step forward and the seemed to fold in on itself. A swirling black mist spread from its feathers and began to whir around its body, drawing up towards the sky until Marcus could no longer see it. A second later the mist began to clear and in the place of the raven stood Nareema. She looked stiff and in pain. She closed her eyes and took a deep breath, a small amount of the black mist escaping from her mouth.

Marcus tried to back away, the fear leaving him but he stumbled and fell. Nareema heard him and in an instant, she crashed through the bush, pinning him to the ground where he had fallen with a knife in her hand.

'What did you see?' she demanded.

'A bird. Then you.' Marcus stuttered, almost afraid to speak with her blade pressed against his throat.

Nareema relaxed slightly and moved the knife but her voice was hard.

'Outside of the Daughters of Kali you are only the second person to see me do that and live. I will kill you if you breathe a word of it to anyone.'

She climbed off him and he hurriedly pushed himself away from her and stood.

'What was it? Are you a witch?'

'Don't be dense Captain. Use your eyes and not an antiquated belief in the supernatural. What did you see?'

Marcus stammered, his heart was pounding.

'Is that really you? The bird... Was that you too?'

'Yes.'

'How?'

'Practice.'

'Why?'

'Sometimes it is necessary. Close your mouth captain, you look like a fish. We should move. Please wake Molly and get ready to go.'

She turned and headed off into the trees. Marcus stood stock still for a second as he tried to get his brain around what he had just witnessed. Hearing soft footsteps behind him, he whirred round, sword at the ready. Molly jumped back in surprise.

'Hey. It's only me. Calm down.'

She took a look at his expression.

'What's wrong? Where's Nareema?'

He took a breath and composed himself quickly.

'Nothing is wrong. I thought I heard a noise.'

'Where's Nareema?'

'Over there.' he pointed with his sword in the direction she had gone.

'How are you feeling?'

'I'm still a bit tired.'

'Come and help me with the things, we're heading to the village and then on to England.'

Molly watched him walk back towards the camp and shook her head. He seemed uneasy.

They caught up with Nareema at the edge of the wood. She was stood staring out across the countryside.

'How are you?' she asked Molly.

'I'm alright. I'm still feeling a bit tired though.'

'The Stones seem to have taken it out of you. We need to talk to Uncle Tobias about this.'

Molly nodded.

'So what's the plan?'

'There is no sign of Tong Li or his men in the village. We go there and find some horses. Then we ride the nearest port and find a ship to take us to England.'

'How do you know he's not there?' Molly asked.

'I checked the village last night.'

Molly heard Marcus make a dismissive snort and gave him a questioning look. He deliberately didn't look her in the eye.

'Come on. We've a few miles to cover yet. Are you up to this?'

Molly nodded.

'Yes. I think so.'

An hour later, Molly wasn't so sure. They were keeping off the main road, walking across fields and through woods. She still felt tired and with every step made it worse. What's more there seemed to be a certain tension between Nareema and Marcus. Neither was talking to the other and every time she asked them what was the matter they both snapped at her.

Eventually she'd had enough. She stopped in the middle of a field and sat down.

'That's it. I don't know what is the matter between you two but I'm not taking another step until you tell me what it is.'

The others pulled up and turned to her.

'Don't act like a child.' said Nareema harshly.

Molly raised her eyebrows.

'Tell me what's the matter.'

Marcus threw a hard look at Nareema.

'Go on. Tell her. Or I will.'

Nareema shifted her stance and turned to him.

'Captain...' there was no disguising the icy warning in her voice.

'She's nearly died for you more than once. She deserves to know.'

'Know what? For Gods' sake. What's going on?'

'She can...' began Marcus

Before he had finished speaking Nareema was upon him. She kicked him in the chest and had her sword at his throat before he realised what was happening.

'Nareema. Don't.'

The Princess turned her head slightly. Molly had risen and had her own sword pressed against her neck.

'Let him go.'

Slowly Nareema removed her sword from Marcus throat and stepped back. Marcus scrambled to his feet and drew his own sword. Molly stepped in between them as Nareema rolled her shoulders and set her feet in a fighting stance.

'Stop it. Now. Both of you. What do you think you're doing? What good will it do if you kill each other? I can't do this on my own.'

'If he wants a fight then I'm going to give him one.'

Angrily Molly reached into her suit and took out the sapphire. She gripped it tightly before flinging her arms out and pointing at each of them. The gust of wind that rushed out caught both of them in the chest and sent them flying.

'Pack it in. Now.'

Nareema jumped to her feet, looked at Molly angrily for a second before she sighed softly and put her sword away. Marcus stood too, watching Nareema warily for a second before sheathing his own weapon. Both rubbed their chests where they'd been struck.

'Better. Now what the hell is going on?'

'I have asked the Captain to keep a secret for me. I also told him I would kill him if he told anyone about it.'

'A secret? Is that is all this is about? I don't care about your secret. But I can't let you hurt each other.'

'Show her.'

Molly threw an angry glance at Marcus and then turned back to Nareema who closed her eyes and sighed heavily.

'I am not a performing monkey, Captain. It is not my place to entertain you.'

'That wasn't entertainment. That was witchcraft.'

'Witchcraft? Grow up. You don't label Molly with the word witch and you've just seen her control the wind.'

'That is different.'

'Really? Why?'

Marcus floundered for a second.

'At least she doesn't sneak around to do it.'

'Sneak? I do not sneak.'

'What do you call it then?'

'Practice.'

Their hands went to the hilts of their weapons. Molly looked at them both and then exploded.

'Right. Kill each other. I don't care.'

She slammed her sword away, picked up the backpack with their belongings in it and stalked away across the field.

'Molly.'

'I don't care. Leave me alone.'

Both Nareema and Marcus watched her go. She'd taken about a dozen steps before she fell hard and lay still. In a second, the argument was forgotten and they were running across the field towards her.

'You're going to have to stop doing that to us.'

Molly opened her eyes. She was lying on a wooden floor with a canvas roof. The floor swayed gently. Nareema was knelt next to her.

'Where are we?'

'In a wagon. We're heading to the port.'

Molly sat up slowly. She was tired and her head ached.

'Are you alright?'

'I think so.'

Molly tried to sit up but her head swam.

'Lie down. Get some rest.'

'Please don't fight with Marcus.'

'We'll talk later. I think we need to be careful with how you use the Stones.'

'You'd have killed him.'

Nareema looked away.

'No. I don't know if I would have.'

'I saw the look in your eyes. You would have done.'

The Princess got to her feet and headed to the front of the wagon.

'Get some sleep. I'll tell Marcus you've woken up.'

'I won't let you kill him.'

There was a determination in Molly's voice that made Nareema pause but she didn't say anything else. Molly slowly sat up. She couldn't believe how much she ached.

'Hey. Are you alright?'

She looked up as Marcus clambered into the back of the wagon.

'I'm fine.'

'I was worried. Those Stones are dangerous.'

'I need to be more careful.'
Marcus didn't say anything.
'Is her secret worth dying for?'
He shook his head as he replied softly.
'No. I've only found one thing that's worth dying for.'
Molly looked at him quizzically for a moment but he didn't say anything else.
'Then keep it. If she wants to tell me she will. I don't think she will hesitate next time. And I don't know if I can stop her.'
Marcus looked at her and took her hand and smiled sadly.
'Get some sleep.'
'Is there anything to eat? I'm starving.'

They travelled south for five days. As the sun began to set on the horizon they crested a hill and the port appeared before them. Molly and Marcus were sat at the front and Nareema was asleep in the back. They had purchased some clothes a couple of days ago but Molly still wore her leather suit under her dress. She turned to the back of the wagon.
'We're here. Almost.'
Marcus reigned in the horse and pulled to the side of the road. He jumped down and then helped Molly dismount. The Princess got down from the rear and joined them.
They stood for a moment looking at the lights in the town. There were numerous large ships in the harbour.
'We should be able to find a ship to take us to England down there.'
Molly turned to Nareema.
'Do you think he is there?'
'Tong Li? I don't know. And no. We're not going to use the Stone to find out.'
'But...'

'But nothing. As soon as we look for him, he will know where we are. I would like to think he's excavating the ruins of the church looking for our bodies.'

'I'll go into town and have a look around.' suggested Marcus

Nareema turned and looked at him hard for a second. She closed her eyes and sighed heavily.

'No. I'll go. Molly come with me please.'

She stalked off the road into a grove of olive trees. Molly looked at Marcus who shrugged but she could sense the unease in him.

'What?'

'It's nothing.'

'Molly!' called Nareema impatiently from the trees.

'I'd better go and see what she wants.'

She headed off after the Princess who was stood in a small clearing in the middle of the trees.

'Do you want to come into the town with me?'

Molly glanced back towards the road.

'I'll take that as a no. Wait here with the Captain. I will be back shortly.'

'No... I'll...'

Her words were cut short as Nareema flung her arms to the sides and began muttering in a language Molly didn't understand but felt deep down. They filled her with an unease that radiated through the trees. The insects in the grass went silent and the rising moon was covered in thick cloud.

'Nareema?' whispered Molly as around the Princess a dark swirling mist began to gather.

It seemed to fall from the sky and in an instant she was lost from sight. Molly wanted to call out to Marcus but her voice wouldn't come. She stood rooted to the spot, the tendrils of fear icily touching her.

Suddenly there was a noiseless explosion, as if the air itself rushed in to fill a void and the mist dissipated as fast as it came. Where Nareema had stood, there was now a huge black bird. It cawed loudly and then with a flap it took to the sky.

Molly took a step back as it leapt into the air and fell down hard on her bottom. As she hit the ground, the spell was broken. Her voice returned.

'Marcus!'

He came running, sword in hand to see her sitting on the floor.

'Where's the Princess.'

'She's... She's gone.'

Marcus took a look at her face.

'Did you see her? Did she change into the bird?'

'Yes. I think so. She was there one minute and then she was gone. I was so scared. I've never felt like that before.'

He helped her stand up.

'You're shaking.'

Marcus took her into his arms.

'I'm sorry.'

'What for?'

Molly shook her head. She didn't know why. There was a feeling of dread that was slowly lifting as he held her. Slowly she leant and kissed him softly. He pulled away fractionally.

'Molly...'

'Don't.' she whispered.

Marcus hesitated for a second before he kissed her back. It started softly but each felt their passion building quickly. After a moment Molly broke away, her heart was pounding. She rested her head on his chest and he pulled her close, feeling his heart beating as fast as hers.

'Miss Molly Carter. Would it be inappropriate for me to say I love you?'

She shook her head as it rested against him.

'Captain Kane, I think it may be.'

'I don't care.'

'That's good. I'm sure it would be just as inappropriate for me to say the same.'
'It would.'
'But who can stop a wife loving her husband?'
'But we're not really married.'
'So you keep saying...'
A chill wind whistled through the trees and Molly shivered.
'Let's head back to the wagon and wait for the Princess.'
Molly nodded and pushed away from him. He offered her his arm and she took it with a smile.

Nareema stalked back into the camp Molly and Marcus had made early the next morning. She didn't look at either of them as they sat close to each other in front of a small fire cooking the last of their provisions. Instead she sat down heavily across the fire from them. There was a tense silence for a moment.
'Would you like some breakfast?' asked Molly tentatively.
'No.'
Marcus bristled.
'I say. That's not on, Your Highness. Molly was only being civil. I would have thought someone of your standing would be more considerate and mindful of her manners.'
Nareema gave him a withering stare before closing her eyes and letting out a long, slow breath as she brought herself under control.
'You're right.' she said eventually. 'I'm sorry. I would like something to eat please.'
Molly smiled and began sorting her out some food.
'I owe you both an apology. What you both saw is something that I don't do often and only Shakir has seen me do before. It is...' she chose her words carefully. '...bad for me to do it but sometimes it is necessary.'
'Why a raven?' asked Molly as she handed a plate of bread

and cheese to her.

'It is traditional. All Daughters of Kali are able to do it. We are taught how when we are marked. It is the link between us and the Darkness.'

'Marked?' asked the captain.

'Your tattoo.' said Molly.

Nareema nodded.

'How does it work?'

The Princess sighed.

'It is dark magic. Old magic. We can call the bird from the night. It comes to us and we become it. The transformation is painful and it takes me to a dark place. My mind is in the bird but my body is in limbo. Suspended in perpetual night and tormented ceaselessly...'

She shuddered, as if just talking about it hurt her. Marcus looked at Molly questioningly. Concern obvious in his face.

'By what?'

'By the souls of the people I have killed. Every life I take binds their soul to me. It is the price that I have to pay. The price all Daughters of Kali pay for what we do. For what we are given.'

Nareema looked down and hugged her knees to her chest.

'Would you go and see to the horse please?' Molly asked Marcus quietly.

He glanced at her and the back at the Princess before nodding.

'Of course. If you will excuse me.'

He left them by the fire and Molly moved to sit next to Nareema. Gently she put her arm around her and pulled her close. Nareema didn't resist, she leant in and rested her head on Molly's shoulder.

'It doesn't matter you know.'

'He doesn't like it. I don't like it.' whispered Nareema.

'Then why do it?'

'Sometimes it is necessary.'

Molly didn't say anything.

'I forget.' said the Princess after a while.

'Forget what?'

'How many people I've killed. It's so easy to do now. I don't think about it. Not until I call the Darkness. Then... Then I...'

Molly hugged her tighter as a slow tear ran down her face.

'Don't. I don't care. I can do things too. I think I need to learn a bit more control though.'

Nareema sniffed and motioned towards the horse.

'You should care. He cares.'

Molly glanced towards Marcus who was putting the reins on the horse.

'Leave him to me.'

'You're making a good wife.'

'You'll never guess what.' said Molly, trying to lighten the mood.

'What?'

'Last night. After you'd gone, he told me that he loved me.'

Nareema sat up and wiped her face.

'Really? And how do you feel about that?'

Molly shrugged but smiled coyly.

'Maybe you really will be Mrs Kane?'

'No.' replied Molly with a sad sigh.

'Why not? He loves you, you love him. What else is there?'

'It wouldn't work. He's a gentleman. An officer in the army. He has money, and has been brought up to know it. I'm a nobody with nothing. I'm never going to be the high born lady that he deserves. I'd only end up embarrassing him. What use is there for a wife that can't read or write? I don't know how to behave at a dinner or a ball. The last one I went to was a bit of disaster.'

Nareema smiled.

'That was my fault and as for the other things, those can be learned. If he truly loves you then he won't care what you've got or where you're from. Love will be enough. And besides, I didn't see him rush to ask anyone else to dance at the ball. Don't put yourself down so.'

'That's easy for you to say. You're a Princess. You understand these things.'

Nareema laughed softly.

'I don't understand at all. But if that's what is bothering you then after this is all over come to India with me. You can be a Princess in all but name.'

Molly glanced at Marcus who was coming back towards them.

'I'm sure there will be place for him too.'

'But what...'

'I'll talk to him about it.'

Molly nodded and gave Nareema a hug. The both looked up as Marcus coughed politely.

'We're ready to go when you are.'

'Thank you Captain.'

They broke camp and headed down towards the town as the sun rose higher. Before they set off, Nareema had told them what she had seen the night before.

'There are four ships that look like they would take us to England, but one more so than the others.'

'Why?' enquired Marcus.

'It's the Endurance.'

'Captain Brody?'

Nareema had nodded.

'Yes. I will talk to him when we reach the port.'

'What else did you see. Is Tong Li there?'

'I don't think so. At least, I saw no sign of him.'

Molly saw something in her face. A doubt.

'But?'

'But I am sure I saw Uncle Tobias going into an inn on the quay. There were lots of men and I only saw him for a

fraction of a second but I think he was there.'
  'Why would Tobias be here?'
  'I don't know and that worries me.'

## Chapter Eleven

The Endurance

The wagon rumbled onto the quay and Marcus brought it to a halt. Molly was sat next to him and Nareema was in the back. She spoke quietly to them.
'Captain, find someone to sell the wagon to. I don't care how much you get for it. We don't need it anymore. I'm going to find Captain Brody.'
'What about me?' asked Molly.
The Princess handed her some coins.
'See that tavern over there? That's where I thought Tobias was going. Go and see if you can find anything out.'
Molly looked at the gold in her hand.
'But what if...'
'Meet me on the Endurance in an hour. We'll decide then.'
Nareema slipped out of the wagon and disappeared into the shadows of the alleys that connected to the quay. Marcus looked at Molly who shrugged before jumping down.
'Be careful.' he told her.
She blew him a kiss with a grin before heading off towards the inn.

Nareema worked her way to the far side of the harbour before she slipped into the water. Keeping to the shadows of the boats she swam across to the Endurance. There were lots of sailors and noise on the quay and on the deck and nobody noticed as she pulled herself out of the water and climbed one of the mooring lines.
After a final look around she dropped lightly onto the deck above the captains' cabin. There were footsteps and two sailors, one she recognised as Davis, began to climb the steps to the wheel. They were engaged in a loud

conversation.

'So I sez to him, you better get that out of the way before cap'n sees it or there'll be hell to pay.'

Neither man noticed the shadow move over the back of the boat and climb down. One of the windows was open and she cautiously checked the room was empty before she swung herself gracefully in.

She looked around for a moment before heavy footsteps sounded from down the corridor and she quickly dived behind the door as it swung open. Brody turned and addressed a man in the corridor.

'Get Davis and then go and find Skippy. He's probably drunk somewhere but I need him as he can speak Portuguese better'n me. I want those provisions bought and loaded by tonight so we can sail on the tide in the morning.'

'Aye sir.'

Brody stepped into his cabin and shut the door. He let out a deep breath and headed over to his table where he poured himself a large drink. The cup was to his lips when Nareema spoke.

'Hello Captain.'

He spun round, hand reaching for a knife on his belt until he saw who it was.

'Princess. I don't know why but I had a feeling I'd see you again.'

She walked over to stand in front of him.

'Then I'm glad I haven't disappointed you.'

'And what do I owe the pleasure of you sneaking into my cabin?'

'I do not sneak. Your men just aren't very attentive.'

'Looks like sneaking to me. Drink?'

She shook her head.

'No. Thank you.'

He sat on the edge of the table.

'So?'

'Where are you headed next captain?'
'Italy.'
'Could you be persuaded to head to England instead?'
'Won't get much for my cargo there.'
'I will pay you double what it's worth if you take us to England.'
'Us?'
'Mr and Mrs Kane and myself of course.'
'They get married yet?'
'No. The last church they were in burnt down.'
Brody saw the smile in her eyes.
'I don't suppose I want to know why do I?'
Nareema shook her head.
'Probably not.'
He sighed.
'You're not going to go away are you?'
'Maybe. There are other ships in the harbour.' replied the Princess with a shrug.
'But none that you know.'
Again, she shrugged.
'I'm sure I could make them come round to my way of thinking.'
The Captain laughed and shook his head.
'You're as much of a rogue as me.'
He thought for a second and looked at her hard, studying her. She just stood there and stared back. Eventually he spoke.
'Alright, I'll take you where you need to go but I need a couple of things from you.'
'What are they?'
'The truth. Tell me what's really going on.'
'And the second thing?'
'Tell the lads who you are.'
Nareema raised her eyebrows in surprise.
'Don't look like that. Most of 'em have been with me for years. I trust 'em and the servant story isn't going to wash

this time. They've all heard the stories of the Daughters of Kali. We've been around and you pick these things up. They deserve to know who they're sailing with.'

She sighed and considered his offer for a moment before holding out her hand.

'You have a deal Captain. However Molly and Marcus will still be Mr and Mrs Kane.'

'Agreed.'

He shook her hand.

'Now would you like a drink? While you tell me what this is all about?'

Nareema sighed again.

'Yes. Please.'

Across the harbour, Molly sauntered towards the inn. It was a low whitewashed building with terracotta slates on the roof. Outside hung a sign with a black boar roughly painted on it.

There were sailors lounging around outside in various states of drunkenness. Some of them whistled and jeered as she came close. She just smiled sweetly back and gave them a wave.

The door was open, a dark rectangle in wall, through which wafted thick, pungent smells of smoke, liquor and men. She glanced around one last time, took a deep breath then stepped in.

The place was dark and it stank. Rough tables and chairs dotted the room, each full of women and drunken men. A fiddle player was sat across the room and several women were on tables dancing a jig to his tune, cheered on by a group of sailors.

One of the women glared hard at her as she entered and jumped up to meet her half way across the floor. The conversation stopped and all eyes turned to the two women. Molly smiled but just got an angry tirade in a language she didn't understand. Even though the speech was different, the indication was obvious. Molly wasn't welcome here.

The woman prodded Molly and pointed at the door, giving her another blast of angry words. When Molly made no move to leave the woman gave her a shove, sending her crashing into a table of drunken men. They cheered loudly and groped at her before pushing her back towards the centre of the room. She stumbled and fell to her knees, and some of the coins that Nareema had given her hit the floor with a chink.

The woman shouted again and pointed at the money. Molly took a deep breath and stood, her heart was pounding and mouth dry. Gingerly she handed the gold to the woman and as soon as the exchange was made, her attitude changed. Molly was ushered to the bar and a bottle slammed down in front of her.

The woman took a swig and handed the bottle to Molly who did the same, coughing as the strong liquid burnt its way down her throat. A cheer went up and then the raucous drinking and singing began again. The woman took the bottle back and introduced herself.

'Madame Teresa.'

'Molly'

'Engleesh?'

Molly nodded and Teresa slapped her on the shoulder.

'Engleesh!' she shouted and raised the bottle high in the air as another cheer went up. Teresa handed the bottle back to Molly, slapped her on the shoulder again and went back to the group of men she had been with.

Glancing around she saw several groups of men eyeing her up hungrily. There was only one thing they had on their mind. She raised the bottle to them and took a swig.

'I wouldn't drink too much of that, little one, not if you want to get out of here alive.'

Molly spun quickly and peered into the shadows.

'Shakir?'

He sat forward and motioned towards Teresa with his head.

'She thinks you are a whore. Girls don't come in here if they know what's good for them. You've paid your dues to the mistress of the house and now you can do as you please. For the sake of appearances, smile and come over here.'

Molly glanced around before picking up her bottle and going over to Shakir. He pushed his chair out and patted his knee. She looked at him for a moment before sitting on his lap. Shakir took the bottle from her, had a drink and then wrapped his arms around her.

'Where's Nareema?' he whispered.

'Finding us a ship. What are you doing here.'

He kissed her neck, his beard scratching her skin.

'Slap me and then storm out. There is a stable adjoining the inn. Wait for me there.'

'What?'

'Do it.'

Molly pushed him away roughly. He went to grapple with her but she shot up and slapped him hard. Teresa looked across with obvious amusement. She slapped him again and then stomped away and out of the door.

Shakir rubbed his face, waited for a minute and then followed her outside. To the right of the inn was a large wooden door. He pushed it open and went in. Molly was waiting for him.

'Little one...' he began but was cut short as Molly punched him.

'How could you?' she demanded angrily.

'How could I what? We needed to make it look like...'

'Not that. How could you do that to Nareema?'

He caught her hand as she tried to hit him again. Holding her arm tightly he spun her around and shoved her down into the hay. He checked his jaw where she'd hit him.

'I see that Nareema has been teaching you well.'

He sat down next to her and for the first time, she got a good look at him. He looked old and tired. His turban was gone, showing a lank mane of greying hair and his clothes were dirty and stained.

'You want to know why I hurt her?'

Molly looked down at her hands, suddenly uncomfortable, but nodded.

'I did it to save her life.'

'Flogging her doesn't seem like a good way of doing that.'

'You don't understand.'

'Then tell me. What happened?' she asked quietly.

Shakir let out a long sigh.

'After his wife and daughter were killed and he'd nearly lost his only son, her father blamed her. His rage was incredible. Nareema was taken from the palace at dawn to the market square. She didn't resist. She blamed herself and she still does. She was stripped, gagged and tied between two poles. The sun in India is hot and it was not kind to her. During the day one man had tried to offer her some water but he was beaten severely by the guards and after that, none helped. Only the bonds and her stubbornness made sure she was still standing when her father arrived seven hours later to witness the punishment.'

He sighed again and looked at his hands.

'I begged and argued with him not to go through with it but his mind was set. I had to stand and watch as one of the guards unfurled the whip and laid the first across her back. She tried not to scream but it cut her deep. I couldn't stand to see her suffer like that so I took the whip from him and did it myself. I pulled as many of the blows as I could but after ten she couldn't stand and after twenty, the hours in the sun and the pain had become too much and she passed out.'

Molly swallowed. How much had that hurt her?

'Her father went down, woke her and gave her some water. He spoke but I do not know what was said. She has never mentioned it and I have never asked. After that, he watched me lay one more on her before he left, leaving me to finish the punishment. I had to give her some more before I was sure we were not being watched. Then I cut her down and got her away.'

'But why did you have to do it?'

'Little one, she barely survived thirty. If I had let one of the other guards to do it she would have received the full amount her father had decreed and she would be dead.'

'How many...'

Shakir looked at her.

'Five hundred.'

Molly's hand went to her mouth.

'Five hundred?'

He nodded.

'Why so many?'

'I don't know. Rage and loss is one thing but...'

He shook his head, as if trying to dislodge and uncomfortable thought.

'I did my best but I hurt her beyond measure. She doesn't blame me for it but I blame myself. So I try to protect her the best I can to make it up to her. Although that is not as easy as it sounds sometimes.'

They were both quiet for a couple of minutes.

'I don't think you had any choice.' said Molly eventually.

'No. Sometimes we have to do what we can and hope for the best.'

Molly laid a hand on one of his.

'I'm sorry I hit you. I didn't know. Nareema didn't tell me.'

He stood up.

'She doesn't know herself how much her father wanted her to suffer and I would like to keep it that way.'

'I won't tell her.'

'Thank you. Come. We must find Nareema. I have news that she's not going to like.'

He headed out of the stable with Molly close behind.

'Alright. I'll take it.'

Coins were exchanged and Marcus handed over the reins to the horse, picked up their meagre belongings from the back and headed back towards the harbour. He wandered down the busy streets of the town and thought about how his life had changed.

A few weeks ago he was preparing himself for Lady Samantha's ball. Even considering asking her daughter for her hand in marriage. Jane was a sweet girl but too much like her mother who was almost bordering on obsession with finding a the girl a "proper" husband. Still, she was quite pretty and would have looked good on his arm. Then Molly had walked into the room and it had all changed.

Marcus smiled to himself as he remembered. She had looked beautiful. Scared, lost and way out of her depth. But now that he had got to know her he knew why. She was so much more than any other girl that had been at the ball. She couldn't have cared less about finding a husband or about anything more than making it through the evening. And that's why he'd fallen for her. There and then. Just like that.

Molly was so different and so much stronger than any other woman he'd ever met. Maybe apart from the Princess. She was something else entirely. Hard and sometimes she scared the living daylights out of him. But Molly? She was perfect.

Pretending to be man and wife was one thing, but he wanted it to be real. He would ask her to be his wife. He was snapped out if his revere by a familiar voice.

'Well I say that is fantastic!'

Marcus ducked into a narrow alley as he saw Tobias walking up the road with a pretty girl on each arm. Behind him came a dozen armed men and bringing up the rear was Tong Li. The girls steered Tobias down a side street and then into a house, the armed men following closely behind.

Tong Li spoke to two of them and they remained outside, alert and hands resting on sword hilts. What was Tobias doing here? Why was he with Tong Li. Marcus headed away from the house quietly and back towards the harbour. He needed to talk to the Princess about this.

Brody was sat in his cabin with Nareema. She had told him everything. Why they were in Portugal, about the Stones, everything. He hadn't said a word as she spoke but when she finished he sat back.

'And you really expect me to believe that?'

'I don't care what you believe Captain. It is the truth.'

'Magic stones? What type of idiot do you take me for?'

Nareema's reply was cut short by a knock on the door.

'What?' snapped Brody.

A nervous looking sailor opened it and stuck his head in, the surprise obvious on his face when he saw the Princess who shot him a venomous look.

'Uh, cap'n...'

'What is it?'

'It's that Mrs Kane. She wanted to see you but we tried to stop her coming on board. She's already knocked Hudson off the quay and when Billy tried to grab her she kicked him in the privates and then broke his nose. She's very angry that we won't let her on the ship.'

Brody looked at Nareema who shrugged but there was definitely a smirk on her face.

'Is Captain Kane with her?'

'No. Just some bloody big Indian bugger.' he glanced at Nareema and saw the look she gave him. 'Beggin' your pardon.'

'Let them on and show them up here.'

'Aye sir.'

He threw another nervous glance at the Princess before ducking out.

'Big Indian bugger?'

Nareema shrugged but there was a doubt in her mind. A few minutes later the sailor knocked again and Molly stormed in followed by a giant of a man who had to stoop slightly.

'Mrs Kane.' said Brody.

'Shakir!'

Nareema dashed over to him and gave him a hug.

'What're you doing here?'

'It's Tobias.'

Her face fell.

'What's happened...'

There was another knock at the door.

'What now? shouted Brody.

The sailor opened the door again, looking very put upon.

'It's Captain Kane sir...'

'Bloody show him up too. We're having a proper little family reunion here.'

He turned to Nareema.

'Anyone else coming? Your parents? Uncles? Second cousins?'

'I would appreciate it if you didn't make light of this Captain.' her voice was so icy Brody hesitated before speaking again.

'Everyone take a seat. I don't know about anyone else but I could do with another drink.'

They sat at his table as Marcus was shown in. He looked on in surprise as he saw Shakir and no one missed Molly's face light up when he came in. Brody held up a bottle.

'Drink?'

'I wouldn't mind Captain.' said Marcus. 'And I'm very sorry for the intrusion.'

Brody shook his head and poured a couple of large glasses of wine.

'Anyone else?'

No one answered so he just put a few silver cups on the table along with the bottle before sitting down.

'What the hell is going on? I've had some...' he hesitated and glanced at Nareema before continuing. 'Some... story about magic stones that I'm not sure I believe and now you lot turn up in my cabin. Again.'

He turned to Molly.'

'Please don't attack my crew. They're good lads and I don't appreciate you breaking them.'

She looked down, suddenly embarrassed.

'He shouldn't have grabbed me like that.'

Brody sighed and shook his head.

'What did you do?' whispered Marcus.

Molly grinned at him and raised her eyebrows.

'I'll tell you later.'

'Right. Enough. Mrs Kane, the Princess says you have some magic stones. Show me and then I'll believe any of the other rubbish she's been spouting. If I didn't know who she was I would have thrown her off the ship.'

Marcus laid a hand on Molly's arm.

'Don't.'

She looked at him.

'I'll be careful.'

He held her arm for a second before letting it go. Molly reached inside her dress and took out the sapphire and emerald which she passed to Brody.

'Here.'

He held them up to the light.

'Nice. Very pretty. Don't look very magical to me.'

Molly glanced at Marcus and held out her hand.

'I'll show you Captain.'

'Please don't ask Molly to do this. The Stones...' Marcus tried to think about what to say next.

'What?'

'They take a lot out of her. More each time I think.' finished Nareema.

'It's fine.' said Molly.

Captain Brody hesitated before handing them back.

'Now I don't want you to do anything to hurt yourself.' he said, sounding unsure.

She took the sapphire and closed her fist around it.

'Honestly, it's fine. Although I might stand back if I were you.'

The people at the table shifted their chairs back slightly and Molly concentrated on the silver cups on the table. Thinking of the wind, she tried to muster enough of it to knock them over. Slowly she held out her hand towards them and in her palm the stone grew warm. She could feel the power rushing towards her and instantly she knew it was too much.

'Duck!' she shouted as a ferocious wind tore from her outstretched hand and across the table. Everyone flung themselves to the ground as the cups were picked up and, with the speed of a bullet, were sent smashing through the windows at the back of the captains' cabin. Molly sagged in her seat and slowly let the gem go.

'Are you alright?' asked Marcus as he got up.

She nodded and smiled tightly.

'Bloody hell.'

Brody stood and went to the back window. The panes were smashed where the cups had exited.

'They were bloody silver! How...?'

He looked at Molly who had gone very pale.

'Are you sure you're alright?'

'I think I may need a lie down.'

Molly stood and then almost immediately fell into Marcus's arms as he legs gave way from underneath her.

'Tenby!' bellowed Brody.'

The door opened a second later and the thin sailor stuck his head around the door.

'Yes cap'n?'

'Take Mr and Mrs Kane to their cabin. Then bring us some more wine and some of that salted beef.'

Tenby glanced at the people around the table before nodding hurriedly. Marcus picked up Molly and followed the sailor as he led them away.

'Is it always like that?' Brody asked.

'She can't control it. Every time she uses it, the Stone seems to take more from her.'

'Bloody hell. Alright. I believe you. I'm sorry that she did that and I don't wish any harm to her but...' he shook his head. 'Bloody hell.'

They fell into silence, each lost in their own thoughts until Marcus returned a few minutes later.

'She's sleeping.'

'I'm sorry Captain. If I'd have known...'

Marcus smiled tightly.

'Perfectly understandable. If I hadn't seen it with my own two eyes, I wouldn't have believed it either. I've seen a lot of things recently which defy explanation. So more so than others.'

He glanced at Nareema as he spoke. Shakir sat forward and look at them sternly for a second before speaking.

'Tong Li has taken Tobias.'

Nareema looked shocked.

'He came to the house and took him. Mrs Kettering had quite a scare.'

'Is she alright?'

'She's fine. Tong Li knew what he was looking for. Swept in and took Tobias and his books. Simcox and I were in town. It was all over by the time we got back. I've followed as best I could. They've moved quickly.'

'That explains how he knew where the Earth Stone was. I knew I'd seen him last night.'

'He *is* here. I've seen him. This very morning.' said Marcus.

'Where?

'In a house in town. He didn't look like a prisoner. Pretty girl on each arm, he looked like he was having a whale of a time.'

'I don't like it.' said Shakir.

'Neither do I.' added Nareema.

'Who's Tobias? Will someone tell me what's going on?' Nareema turned to Brody.

'Tobias is a dear friend of mine. A bit scatty but he knows more about the Stones than anyone. He's the one that led us to the emerald underneath the church.'

'With a bit of help from Molly.' added Marcus defensively.

'Yes. With a lot of help from Molly.' replied Nareema with a smile.

'So what are we going to do?' asked Shakir. 'If Tong Li has Tobias then he will find out where the Water Stone is.'

'We must rescue him.'

'If he needs rescuing.' said Brody. 'From what Captain Kane has said it doesn't sound much like he does.'

'There were armed men. A dozen or more. They followed Tobias into the house.'

'It's a trap.' said Nareema after a moment.

'Of course it is. Tong Li is going to use Tobias as bait for you. He knows you'll come after him.'

'Then I'd hate to disappoint him.'

Nareema stood up and drew her sword.

'Captain Kane. Will you tell me where the house is please? I'm going to get my Uncle back.'

'I can't let you do that on your own.'

'Why not. They won't see me coming.'

'At least let me...'

'No.' Nareema's voice was stern. 'Captain. You need to be here for your wife.'

Marcus sagged before standing straight and addressing Nareema and Shakir.

'Your Highness, Sir, with respect, she's not my wife. But...' he hesitated. '...but I have feelings for her and would like to address that. As far as I understand it, you are the closest thing that Molly has to a family. Therefore I humbly request your permission to ask for her hand in marriage.'

Shakir rumbled a laugh.

'You English. You really know how to pick your moments. Honestly.'

Brody looked at him.

'There's a time for this lad and from the sounds of it, this isn't it.'

'If I don't do it now then I may not get another chance. I'm coming with you Your Highness whether you like it or not and I'd like to know before I do. Just in case.'

Shakir sighed.

'I don't think for one second that you need my permission, but if it means that much to you then you have it.'

'Thank you Sir.' he looked at the Princess who stared back.

'When we have rescued Tobias, you can ask me again.'

Marcus looked like he was going to say something else but decided against it and just nodded.

'As you wish. But I'm still coming with you.'

Brody spoke.

'I'll look after your wife Captain. She'll be safe here.'

'Thank you.'

Nareema looked at them all.

'We need to get Tobias. As soon as Tong Li has what he wants he will kill him. Marcus, tell me what you saw.'

## Chapter Twelve

### Escape

Shakir, Marcus and Davis hid in the shadows across the road from the house Tobias had been taken to. Brody had offered some of his men to help but Nareema had refused.

'We need stealth, not force. I don't want the whole town involved.' she had said.

He had eventually agreed but insisted that Davis go with them. If there was trouble he could run to the ship and get some help. She had agreed once both Shakir and Marcus pointed out the tactical sense in the plan.

Now they waited. Darkness was falling and the guards had lit torches which sat in sconces either side on the door. Their smoky light illuminating the narrow street.

'They look ready for trouble.' said Shakir.

'That they do Sir.'

'Don't call me that.'

'You're a General, I'm a Captain. It's right and proper.'

Shakir shook his head with a smile.

'You Englishmen. I will never understand your fascination with right and proper.'

'Where is the Princess?'

'I don't know, she said to wait for her signal.'

'What is the signal?' asked Davis who was beginning to realise there was more to this than he had been told.

'I don't know that either. But knowing Nareema, it will be more than obvious.'.

The door opened and they ducked further back into the shadows. Tong Li stepped out, followed by half a dozen men. Marcus began to draw his sword but Shakir put a hand on his arm.

'Let him go.'

'But I could kill him now and end it once and for all.'

'You can't. There are seven of them and three of us. You wouldn't get close and if you did you won't beat him. His skill is almost unsurpassed. There is only one person among us that stands a chance of killing him.'

'The Princess.'

Shakir nodded.

'Yes and she has already sworn to take his head. Tong Li is hers and hers alone.'

Marcus slid his sword back into the scabbard as above them there was a loud caw. Tong Li paused and looked up for a second before continuing down the road and away from the house. The caw came again and Marcus shuddered despite himself.

'You know about that then?' whispered Shakir.

Marcus nodded.

'Yes. I found out by accident and I can't say it sits well with me.'

Shakir said nothing

'Found out about what?' asked Davis, eager to know what was going on.

Both men turned to him but Marcus spoke.

'We can't say. If we were to tell you then the Princess would kill you. I'm sure you wouldn't like that now would you?'

He hastily shook his head.

'No sir. But beggin' your pardon, I thought she was your servant, not a Princess.'

'She is a Princess. That is all for now.'

Davis shook his head. What sort of man had a Princess for a servant?

The raven circled the house a few times before perching on the roof. It spread its wings wide and cawed again before it was enveloped in a dark mist which dispersed as quickly as it had come and left in its place was Nareema.

She squatted down on the tiles to get her bearings and let out a long slow breath, the dark mist escaping from her lips in a thin stream. Tong Li had left and headed towards the quay with some of his men. If Marcus' information had been correct then there should be fewer than ten people in the house.

Quietly she moved across the roof to one of the small dormer attic windows that was set in the eaves and leaning around, she looked inside. The small room was empty. A door stood ajar on the right-hand side but all was silent. Nareema reached to her belt and took out a knife which she inserted into the gap between the window panes. With a quick flick upwards the catch on the window popped open and she slipped inside.

Sheathing the knife, she drew the short sword from her thigh. It was much easier to use in the tight confines of a building than the sword she had at her back. Treading carefully she made her way across the rough wooden floor to the door where she paused to listen. There was no sound so she pushed it open slowly.

The door opened into a narrow corridor which ran down to some stairs on the left. Opposite was another door which presumably was for the twin of the room on the other side of the house. She stepped close and listened at the door. There was no sound coming from the room but she still slowly opened the door to check. It was empty.

Closing the door again she began to move down the stairs. The staircase was narrow and ended in a locked wooden door. Nareema crouched in front of it, weighing up the need for silence and surprise over speed. In the end, she put her shoulder against it and forced it open. The lock was old and gave way with a loud shriek.

Immediately there were voices from down the corridor. Quickly she moved to stand behind the first door and as it opened, she plunged her blade into the throat of the first man to appear. He staggered back, blood gurgling from his neck while the other occupant scrabbled to draw his sword from where it lay on one of the rough beds. She closed the gap to him in a second and kicked him hard in the chest. He flew back and went through the bedroom window with a crash.

The trio, who were still waiting in the alley across the road, heard a smash and looked up to see a body come tumbling down from the second story window. It landed heavily with a sickening crunch right in from of the guards at the door.
'I think that was our signal. Wait here.' Shakir told Davis as he drew his sword. 'If I call I want you to run like hell itself is chasing you and get some help.'
Davis nodded.
'Aye sir.'
Shakir glanced at Marcus.
'Ready.'
'Yes.'
With a shout, they both charged. The guards, who were still looking in shock at the body, didn't see them coming until it was too late. Shakirs sword sang through the air and decapitated the first man while Marcus dealt with the second. They glanced up at the window to briefly see Nareema look down. She gave them a quick thumbs up before disappearing again.
'I think we should knock.' said Marcus with a smile.
Shakir grinned as they put their shoulders to the door and heaved. It gave way with a crash and they dashed inside, catching the man guarding the hallway completely by surprise.
'Captain, check upstairs and find Nareema. I'll find Tobias.'

Up in the room, Nareema heard a commotion coming from down stairs and turned to go. As she did so, the whole street seemed to shake as a terrific explosion and huge plume of fire erupted from the harbour.

She dashed back to the window as another swath of fire blossomed into the sky. This one however moved as if it was being blown by a ferocious wind and in an instant she knew she had fallen for another trap. But this time it wasn't for her.

Molly had woken suddenly and sat up. Her head was spinning and it took her a moment to work out where she was.

'Slow down lass. You're safe.'

She glanced across to see Captain Brody sat in a chair by the door.

'Where's Marcus?'

'Not here. He's gone with the Princess and the big bugger to get Tobias.'

'Tobias?'

'Apparently. Someone called Tong Li has him.'

At the mention of his name Molly drew a sharp breath and began to swing herself off the bed.

'I need to go and help.'

Brody stood and went to the door.

'I promised your husband that I'd look after you and letting you run around town isn't going to do that. I'll have Tenby bring you something to eat in a minute.'

He left and Molly heard the door lock. She jumped up and went to the door.

'Hey. Let me out.'

She banged on the wood but there was no answer.

'Bastard.'

Fuming, she turned and looked around the room. Someone had dropped her belongings off in the corner so Molly pulled out her leather suit and sword. Ten minutes later she heard the lock turn and Tenby came in, carrying a tray with some food and wine on it.

'Cap'n said...'

He didn't get a chance to finish the sentence before Molly hit him from behind with the chair. He fell to the ground with a crash as it smashed across his shoulders.

'Sorry.'

Opening the door fully she was confronted by Brody.

'Thought you might try something like that.'

'Let me out. I need to help them. Tong Li can control the Fire Stone. If they've gone against him they're going to get killed.'

'I'd lay a fair bet with the Princess on that score.'

Molly stalked back to the bed and then turned around.

'Please move Captain. I don't want to have to hurt you but you can't keep me here.'

'Watch me.'

She reached inside her suit and took out the sapphire.

'You've seen what I can do with this and you know I can't control it very well. So which side of the ship don't you want?'

Brody held her gaze for a moment before sighing resignedly.

'You're just as bloody stubborn as she is. Alright, I won't stop you but I'm coming with you. And so are some of my men.'

Molly went to protest.

'Don't argue or I'll have you tied and gagged before you can blink.'

She took a deep breath.

'Deal.'

He shook his head.

'Why do I think I'm going to regret this?'

Ten minutes later, Molly strode down the gangplank where Brody and six of his men were waiting.

'Captain Kane said the house was towards the north side of the town. If we head that way I'm sure we'll be able to find it. It'll be the one that the people are running away from. Are you sure you're ready for this?'

'Yes.'

He looked at her doubtfully.

'Come on. If we run into any trouble, stay out of the way. We'll deal with it.'

She nodded and glanced round at the sailors, each held a sword and a grim expression but none would look her in the eye. They had only reached the black boar inn when she saw him. Tong Li was walking calmly towards them.

He was smiling as he walked underneath the large stone arch that covered the main entrance to the port as if it were a spring day and he was walking through the park. Molly pulled up short, Brody and his men taking a couple of steps forward before they realised she had stopped.

'What?' asked the Captain.

'It's him.'

Suddenly fear gripped her. He was here. Where were Nareema and Marcus? Were they dead? Tong Li saw her and smiled evilly. Stopping a score of yards away he shouted to her.

'And so we meet again Miss Carter. Or should that be Mrs Kane? I'll make this easy for you. Give me the Stones and I'll kill you quickly.'

'Where's Marcus and Nareema?'

Tong Li shrugged.

'Probably trying rescue that tiresome Tobias man. I do hope they find the little gift I left for them in the basement. However it wasn't him that I wanted. I made sure that he was seen so she would rush off to his aid, leaving the poor Molly defenceless. She's nothing if not predictable.'

Molly slowly drew the sword from her back.

'I'm not so defenceless.'

'Fighting spirit. I do like that in a woman.'

He shouted in a foreign language and the half dozen men drew their weapons and charged.

Brody watched them for a second before snapping into action and bellowing at his men.

'What are you bloody waiting for? Get them!'

The sailors hefted their weapons and rush towards the oncoming attackers. Brody drew his own sword and put himself between Molly and the fight. Tong Li smiled, drew his own blade and started towards them.

'Get behind me.' shouted Brody as the men met with a crash of metal on metal. One of his men dispatched his opponent and swung his sword at Tong Li who parried easily before he pirouetted and cut the man's head from his shoulders without breaking his stride. His eyes were fixed on Molly and his face had a dark smile. Brody moved forward and raised his own weapon.

'You want her, then you'll have to go through me.'

'As you wish.'

The Captain barely managed to deflect the first blow. He countered but the shorter man moved quickly out of the way before spinning, their blades met with a clang. Tong Li was grinning as he moved away. They circled each other.

'I don't believe we've been properly introduced.'

'No. But I know a murdering bastard when I see one.'

'Charming. How much would it take for you to leave this fight? You can't win. How about you step aside and give her to me? I'll let you walk away and you and your crew can leave the harbour in one piece?'

'I don't think so.'

'Are you sure? It would be a terrible waste for me to have to kill every single member of your crew before sinking the pile of crap you call a boat.'

'It's a ship.'

Brody swung his blade at Tong Li but he danced out of the way before savagely thrusting with his sword. Brody brought his own weapon up again just in time, but only managing to veer the point away from his throat and across his bicep, the blade cutting him deeply. He cried out in pain and swung wildly but was met by a heavy kick to his knee and he dropped to the floor.

Another kick flashed in, catching Brody under the chin and sending him crashing onto this back. Tong Li raised his sword once more to finish him off.

'Get off him!'

He turned just in time to meet the blast of wind that picked him up and threw him fifty feet across the quay. He crashed heavily through the doors of one of the warehouses that lined the harbour, disappearing into the darkness beyond them. Molly rushed over to Brody who was trying to sit up. His nose was broken and blood was flowing freely from it.

'Come on. We've got to get out of here.'

She manhandled him to a sitting position and looked around. The sailors and Tong Li's men were still locked in a vicious fight but the sailors were winning. Two of them lay dead but four of Tong Li's were down. Brody touched his nose and blinked, trying to clear his head.

'Damn. That bloody hurt.'

'We've got to find...'

Molly's words were cut short as a huge ball of fire ripped across the quay. The warehouse that Tong Li had crashed into exploded, sending fire and burning debris in all directions.

Molly threw herself flat before glancing up in horror as Tong Li strode out of the flames. His eyes were deep burning pits of rage and fire enveloped his body. He looked directly at her and roared.

'I'm going to enjoy ripping your pretty head off.'

Around him the fire burned intensely, the other buildings around the harbour quickly catching alight. It spread quickly and people began to rush out on to the quay. With another roar, Tong Li began to walk towards Molly, smashing and cutting down anyone who got in his way.

As he closed he raised his arm and a stream of fire spat from his hands. Molly screamed and flung her own arms out towards him, the blast of wind catching the fire and directing it upwards but the heat was incredible. She sagged as the attack ended, her head spinning and body like lead.

'You need to learn to control that power girl.'

Again another flash of fire spat towards Molly and again she deflected it with the wind. The fire slashed off into the harbour, setting the anchored ships alight. Tong Li grinned as Molly dropped to her knees.

'Come on.'

Brody stood and helped her up. She leant heavily against him as her legs didn't seem to want to work. They hurried towards the arched gateway that led into the town but it was a burning inferno. They were almost there when there was a roar from behind them and a line of fire struck the arch, shattering it and sending burning stone crashing into the road.

'You can't run from me.'

Molly pulled herself up straight and turned to face him.

Nareema crashed out into the hallway and began to fly down the stairs two at a time. Marcus met her halfway.

'Your Highness...'

She cut him off.

'It's Molly. He's gone after Molly and I've let him.'

His face went white.

'Captain, get Tobias and get back to the ship.'

She saw the look on his face.

'Don't argue. Just do it.'

She didn't give him time to answer before she pounded down the stairs and out into the road. As she ran, she began to mutter under her breath, the black mist spreading out behind her. With a cry, she leapt into the air, transforming into the raven and heading straight towards the harbour.

Marcus hurried back down stairs to find Shakir. Evidence of his passing was everywhere, a body here, a smashed door there. He eventually caught up with him in the kitchen. He had a terrified man pinned against the wall by his throat.
'Where is he?'
The man hesitated so Shakir repeated his question and brought his sword up to touch the point of it against his face.
'Basement.'
He slammed him against the wall hard enough to crack the plaster before letting the unconscious body drop to the floor.
'Where's Nareema?'
'She's gone to the harbour. She thinks that Tong Li is after Molly.'
Shock and a dawning realisation passed across his face for a second.
'We have to get out of here and help.'
They moved to the door to the cellar and kicked it open. A set of stone steps led down to a heavy looking door at the bottom.
'Tobias? Are you here?' shouted Shakir as they descended.
There was no answer.
Marcus tried the door.
'Locked.'
Shakir sheathed his sword and put his shoulder against it.
'Help me.'
Marcus lent in and together they pushed. There was a grinding of metal before the frame gave way and the door crashed open and sending both men sprawling. As they stood, they took the room in at a glance.

There was a small bed, surrounded by empty wine bottles but no sign of the older man. The rest of the cellar was packed with barrels. A broken lantern was near the door frame, it's oil alight on the floor. Running from it were multiple detonators fizzing and sparking from the doorway to the barrels and in a second Marcus realised what was going on.

'It's a trap! Run!'

Shakir and Marcus turned and scrambled up the steps. Dashing out into the hallway, they made it as far as the front door before the house was rocked by a terrific explosion. The pair were thrown across the road and into the building on the other side as the barrels caught.

They hauled themselves up and Shakir threw Marcus into a doorway before jumping on top of him as a secondary explosion and fireball levelled the house and set the neighbouring buildings on fire. As the noise died away, Marcus pushed himself up. Shakir was sat up but had gone deathly pale. The Captain hurried across to the big man.

'Are you alright?'

He nodded but his breathing was shallow.

'Help me up.'

As he hauled him up he cried out in pain and then Marcus saw why. A foot-long sliver of wood was sticking out of his back, just below the left shoulder blade. Blood was flowing freely down his side. Marcus looked at it in horror.

'Sir...'

'Pull it out.'

'But...'

'Do it.'

Marcus grabbed the wood and heaved. Shakir grunted in pain as the wood slipped from his body.

'Are you alright?'

'I'll live. Get back to the ship. I will follow.'

'I can't leave you.'

'Do it. That's an order Captain.'

Marcus pushed away from him and snapped off a crisp salute.

'I will be back for you.'

Shakir nodded.

'Get out of here.'

'Sir?'

Marcus span to see Davis standing in the doorway. He was dirty and looked scared but otherwise unscathed.

'Davis. Here. Help him.'

The big man gritted his teeth through the pain as Davis helped him up and they headed out into the street as around them the town burned.

Nareema circled the harbour as behind her a terrific explosion erupted from somewhere in the town. Below her she could make out Molly and Brody. They were fighting a spinning, moving ball of fire that was Tong Li. Fighting and loosing. He was toying with them.

Each was bleeding from multiple cuts and Molly looked dead on her feet. As she watched, Tong Li raised his arm and conjured a lash of fire that caught Brody across the chest and then leapt at Molly. The ships' Captain fell back and beat at the flames on his clothes as Molly tried to counter with the Air Stone. Her gestures deflected the fire to her side but only just.

The buildings around the quay were burning fiercely and even some of the ships had caught light. Nareema dived towards the ground, the black mist spreading behind her once more as she changed. Tong Li glanced up just in time to see her come flashing out of the burning night and crash into him.

They both hit the ground hard but Nareema was up and drawing her sword before she had finished moving. She risked a glance at Molly and Brody. He had put out the fire and risen to his knees. Molly on the other hand had slumped down. Even in the reflected glow from the fires she looked weak and her skin looked pale. She called out as she turned back to face Tong Li.

'Captain Brody. Get her back to the ship.'

He glanced at her and then at the flaming madman before nodding. Gently he bent down, picked the girl up in his arms and began to take her back towards the Endurance. Tong Li moved to follow them but Nareema put herself between them. Slowly they began to circle.

'You're not going to take her.'

'I don't want her. I want the Stones. Although I will enjoy killing her.'

His voice was distant but held a power that was almost hypnotic.

'You'll have to get through me first.'

'Gladly.'

Tong Li feinted to the right and then brought a whip of fire slashing in from the left, Nareema ducked and rolled but felt the heat of the fire across her back. She rose quickly and attacked, her sword a blur as it swung towards him in a vicious upwards cut. He jumped back at the last second so her blade cut nothing but air.

'You'll have to do better than that.' he told her with a manic grin.

'I should have killed you when I had the chance.'

He cocked his head is puzzlement. The Princess took advantage of his momentary distraction and attacked, her blade becoming part of a spinning, whirring dance of death. Tong Li responded in kind. His own sword flashing to deflect every blow that the Princess threw at him.

He ducked a heavy swing and sprang forward, crashing his shoulder into her midriff and sending her flying. She cried out as the flames that shrouded him burnt her through the leather of her suit. Tong Li stood slowly and howled victoriously. Around him the harbour was a mass of flame.

The buildings were a roaring inferno and the larger ships were beginning to catch. The crews rushing to douse the flames before they could take hold. Nareema struggled to her knees, the wind knocked from her and she was unable to move fast enough to dodge the kick that he aimed at her. She crashed onto her back, blood flowing from her nose. Tong Li stood over her.

'Your father killed my family. Butchered my children and wife. They had no chance against armed soldiers.'

He kicked her in the side and she felt her ribs crack.

'And you wonder why I killed your sister?'

He raised his sword above his head and brought it down hard. The Princess managed to roll out of the way and the blade brought sparks from impact against the cobbles. As she rolled she drew her short sword from its scabbard on her thigh. Gritting her teeth through the pain she rose to one knee and drove the blade deep into Tong Li's side. He roared with agony and spun, catching her with the back of his fist and sending her crashing through some crates that lined the dockside.

Nareema struggled to stand but couldn't get up. She could hardly breath and she could taste blood. Once more Tong Li advanced, his sword a flaming beacon of death and there was nothing she could do to stop him.

'Goodbye Your Highness.'

He raised the weapon and she closed her eyes, waiting for the final blow. It never arrived. She looked up to see Shakir grappling with him. His hands and clothes were burning where they touched the flaming monster. Marcus dashed to help.

'No.' shouted Shakir. 'Help Nareema.'

He hesitated for a second before helping the Princess to her feet. As she stood, Tong Li managed to free his sword arm and plunged the burning blade into Shakirs chest. His grin as he did so dropped when the big man grabbed him again, forcing the blade deeper inside.

'Nareema.'

The Princess grabbed Marcus' sword and swung it hard at Tong Li. He pulled back and the blade sailed past his head but he couldn't shake Shakirs' grip on his sword arm. Nareema's strike continued down and severed his arm above the wrist. He fell back screaming, the fire around his body dissipating quickly. Seeing Marcus coming towards him he turned and ran.

'Marcus. Help me.'

He stooped his pursuit and went to the Princess. She was trying to hold Shakir up. Tong Li's sword was still deep inside him with his hand still wrapped around the hilt. His clothes and skin were badly burned.

'Help me get him to the ship.'

'We need to get that out first.'

Marcus pointed to the sword. Nareema closed her eyes and nodded.

'This is going to hurt.'

Shakir gritted his teeth as Marcus grabbed the blade and hauled it out. The big man cried out and dropped to one knee, blood gushing from the wound.

'We need to get him out of here.'

She slipped one of his arms over her shoulder and Marcus did the same. Together they headed back to the Endurance. Around them the quay was a raging inferno. The inn and warehouses were a mass of roaring flames and out in the harbour, the boats were burning.

They were all thrown flat as one of the warehouses exploded, sending burning wood and debris across the harbour. Some of the citizens of the town were trying to tame the fire and the rest were heading out of town.

Marcus hauled Shakir and the Princess back to their feet and stumbled along. They eventually made it to the ship and dragged Shakir up the gangplank before carefully laying him on the deck.

'Marcus, go to Brody, get us out of here.'

He nodded and ran off to find the Captain. Nareema knelt down next to Shakir. He grunted with pain and took her hand in his. His skin was blistered and raw from the flames.

'Nareema?'

'I'm here.'

He tried to reach inside his shirt but couldn't move his arm enough.

'Inside my...'

Carefully she reached in and took out a folded letter. the edges were scorched and it was marked with his blood.

'Take it. Read it when I'm gone.'

She took his hand once more and lent down close to him.

'You're not going to die.'

He chuckled a soft laugh.

'I am. Not even you can stop that.'

'No.'

He squeezed her hand.

'Yes.'

'You can't. I need you.'

'You haven't needed me for a long time. You've made me a proud father, so very proud...'

His voice tailed off and with a soft sigh, he was gone. She sat back on her heels, tears streaming down her face. One hand still clutched his tightly, the other held his letter.

Marcus ran up the deck. Brody was stood near the wheel, with Molly laid out beside him.

'Captain. Get us out of here!' he shouted as he ran.

Brody appeared at the railing.

'I can't. This isn't a bloody row boat. I can't fight the incoming tide and as soon as I get the sails down they'll catch fire.'

Molly pushed herself up and spoke softly, the weakness she felt in her body obvious in her voice.

'Captain. Put the sails down.'

He turned.

'What?'

She got to her feet, swaying slightly and head pounding.

'Put the sails down.'

'I can't...'

'Do it.'

There was a determination in her voice that made him hesitate.

'Trust me. Please.'

He looked at her for a moment before nodding and turning to the crew, bellowing his orders. Molly took in a shaky breath and stood in the centre of the deck, behind the wheel.

Taking out the sapphire, she looked at it for a moment. It sparkled in the light of the fires that burned behind her. It looked so beautiful. Slowly she closed her fist around it and concentrated.

Marcus was stood at the bottom of the steps to the upper deck when Captain Brody began to shout orders at the crew. They snapped into action and began to unfurl the sails. He began to climb the steps when he saw Molly. She was stood behind the wheel with a strange smile on her face. In her hands she held the sapphire.

As he watched she closed her eyes and folded her hand around the stone. In an instant he knew what she was going to do.

'Molly! No!'

He rushed up the rest of the steps but was too late. Molly threw her head back and cried out as the power flowed through her. It exploded out in a blast of wind that knocked him from his feet.

The torrent spread out all around with the force of a hurricane, smashing the burning buildings on the quay to pieces as it tore through them, spreading the fire to the rest of the town. The sudden force of the wind was so great that the deck beneath Molly's feet split and cracked and the back of the ship dipped in the water.

Marcus rolled onto his front and looked up. A bright blue corona enveloped her as the power flooded her body. The force of the storm around her caused her to float a few feet above the broken deck. Her eyes glowed with a brilliant light that was almost painful to look at. She looked down at him and smiled.

'I love you.'

Her voice was distant, as if she were in another room.

'Molly...'

She threw her arms forward and from behind her came funnel of wind that hit the sails hard. Brody was stood at the rail, holding on for dear life and bellowing at the crew. His voice barely audible above the roar of the wind.

'Get those sheets secure. Move damn you!'

As they dragged the sails tight, the wind caught them and slowly the ship began to move.

Nareema heard Marcus shout and glanced towards the wheel. She began to stand but was knocked back down by a ferocious blast of wind. Around her sailors picked themselves up and looked fearfully at the wheel as Captain Brody began to shout orders.

Nareema began shouting as well and they jumped to their appointed tasks, more scared of her than the bright blue glow from the bridge. The sails were barely down before more wind ripped in from behind the ship, bringing with it the smell of burning wood and death.

The ropes the sailors were hauling on snapped taught and the masts gave a warning creak. The Princess ran into the wind and grabbed a trailing rope.

'Help me.' she shouted at a group of men who were cowering out of the gale.

'Help me or we all die.'

They hesitated for a second before joining her and helping

to drag the sail tight. Slowly the ship began to move but lurched to a stop after a few feet. Nareema looked around to see it was still tied to the quay.

She ran to the nearest rope and hacked at it with her sword. The rope gave way with a snap and she turned to see the ropes at the back come away with a tearing of wood and metal as they wrenched the mooring posts from the deck. Nareema threw herself flat as one flashed over her head. It caught a sailor squarely in the chest and catapulted him into the water before it smashed through the railing of the ship and crashed onto the quay.

Before they'd even finished their flight, the ship began to move again, quickly picking up speed and crushing its way through the burning wrecks in the harbour. At the wheel, captain Brody struggled to stand up and guide the ship through the narrow opening between the harbour walls. There was a horrible grinding sound as it dragged alongside the port side wall before they were free and picking up speed towards deeper water.

Above her, one of the yard arms creaked and then began to split. Nareema shouted as loud as she could in the face of the wind but her voice didn't travel far.

'Molly. That's enough.'

Brody struggled with the wheel as the ship gathered speed. He heard a crack and glanced up to see one of the yard arms split, sending ropes and sail tumbling to the deck. Turning to Marcus he yelled at him.

'Get her to stop. We can't take much more. She'll tear us apart.'

Marcus bent into the wind and forced his way in front of her.

'Molly. Stop. We're safe now. Please...'

She looked at him for a long moment before nodding once. Slowly she closed her eyes and let out a long breath.

Suddenly the wind and light vanished and Molly fell limply to the broken deck like a discarded rag doll.

Marcus rushed to her side. Her skin was taught and pale, her shallow breath misting in front of her face and there was ice in her hair. He gently touched her cheek but snatched his hand back quickly. Her skin was so cold it almost burnt him. He glanced round as Nareema bounded up to the deck.

'She's so cold.'

Brody snapped into action, shouting for blankets. The Princess knelt down and Marcus looked at her.

'Shakir?'

She shook her head slowly.

'I'm sorry.'

'Don't. We need to look after Molly.'

Davis ran up on to the deck with an armful of blankets and passed them to Marcus.

'Thank you.'

He bent and wrapped them around Molly before he scooped her into his arms and carried her away.

## Chapter Thirteen

Aftermath

The crew of the Endurance were gathered on deck. Captain Brody stood in front of them, shadowed by Marcus to his left and the Princess to his right. Before him was a body wrapped in sailcloth. He turned to the Princess.

'Is there anything you want to say?'

She shook her head, her long black hair moving softly and a slow tear trickling down her face from her deep green eyes. There were words she should have said but couldn't. The body in front of them, Shakir, he had been her protector, friend and mentor since she was a little girl.

His last words had haunted her since their escape from Tong Li and the fires that destroyed the harbour a day ago. She hadn't opened the letter he had given her. She couldn't bring herself to read it. The Princess took a ragged breath and shook her head once more.

'No. I can't.'

Brody looked to Marcus. He looked tired. His eyes were dark under his mop of brown hair and he looked haggard and unshaven. He'd been up all night at Molly's bedside. She had saved the ship by unleashing an unbelievable power but it had cost her dearly. She was laid below in a cabin, unconscious and barely breathing. Her skin was pale and taught, as if she had had her very life essence sucked out of her.

'Captain Kane?' said Brody.

Marcus looked at him for a second before nodding and stepping forward. He snapped off a crisp salute to the man who had given his life to save not only Nareema but him as well. Marcus cleared his throat.

'General. I... May you be at peace.'

Marcus saluted again and Brody nodded to some of the

crew. They stepped forward and picked up the body before carefully commending it to the sea. Glancing back at the Princess he could see she was fighting hard to keep the tears from flowing. He turned to her.
'Your Highness...'
She shook her head.
'No. Please leave me alone.'
With that she left and hurried back to her cabin.

A little later Marcus was sat next to Molly. She hadn't moved since he had put her in bed and she was still cold to the touch, but it wasn't the icy, biting cold that it had been so that was an improvement. He gently touched her blonde hair, carefully brushing a lock of it away from her face.
'Come back to me. Please...' he whispered to her.
His thoughts were interrupted by a gentle knock at the door.
'Come in.'
Nareema opened the door and stepped in. Her eyes were rimmed with red from where she had been crying but he didn't say anything.
'How is she?'
Marcus shook his head.
'Still the same.'
Nareema looked at the girl for a moment.
'She is strong. She'll get better.'
'I hope so.'
They were silent for a moment, both lost in their own thoughts. Eventually Nareema spoke.
'Here.'
She handed Marcus a long cloth wrapped bundle she had been carrying.
'What is it?'
'Something I would like you to have.'
He began to unwrap it.
'I can't take this.' he said as he saw what it was.

'Please. It is too heavy for me and... Just take it.'

Marcus dropped the cloth on the bed and held up a big curved sword. The scabbard was polished metal, inlaid with gold while the blade was etched with swirling lines and whorls. It had belonged to Shakir. He swished it through the air.

'Thank you.'

'Use it wisely. To protect...'

They both glanced down at Molly.

'I will.'

'Good.'

Nareema turned to go but turned back.

'Marcus?'

'Yes Your Highness?'

'I said I would give you an answer to your question when we got back from looking for Tobias.'

'You did. But I don't think...'

She cut him off and spoke harshly.

'Do you want her hand in marriage? Do you want my blessing?'

He glanced at Molly and then stood straight.

'Yes. I do. On both counts.'

She smiled sadly.

'Meet me on deck in five minutes. Bring the sword.'

She didn't give him a chance to say anything else before she left.

Marcus stood on the deck with the sword slung at his side. It was heavier than the blade he was used to. It was not a weapon for fineness. It's lethally sharp edge was designed to do one thing and one thing only. To kill.

He waited for a while before Nareema strode up and stopped a few feet in front of him. There was a grim determination in her body language. He looked her over. She had pulled her hair back into a rough ponytail and was dressed in a tight fitting leather jumpsuit with a thin curved sword strapped to her back.

'You want my answer?'

He nodded, unsure as to where this was going.

'Yes. Please.'

She drew her weapon.

'Fight me. If you win the you have my permission. If not...'

'Your Highness... I can't fight you.'

The Princess began circling him, sword held ready.

'Why not? And don't you dare tell me you don't want to hurt me.'

'No. It's not that.'

She flashed in with a head height slash that he barely ducked in time.

'Draw your sword. Defend yourself.'

'No.'

She moved in again, swinging low towards his legs. He jumped back but she dropped almost immediately and swept his legs out from underneath him, sending him crashing to the floor.

'Why won't you fight?'

Marcus scrambled back to his feet as around them the crew begun to gather to watch.

'I don't want to fight you.'

'Not good enough.'

She lunged savagely and Marcus had to snatch the heavy blade from its scabbard to deflect to blow. The Princess smiled humourlessly and attacked again. Marcus countered, his military training kicking in, and he swung the blade at her chest. She danced out of the way.

'Better. Move faster.'

The air rang with the clash of blades until Brody stomped up on deck. Davis, the ships bosun, had obviously gone to get him when the fighting started.

'What the bloody hell is going on?' he roared.

Marcus looked across at him and in that split second of

distraction, Nareema took her chance. She jumped high, somersaulting over him and as she landed she spun and kicked him in the back, sending him sprawling. Marcus rolled and jumped up, spinning to face the Princess with his sword at the ready but he pulled up in shock as she was stood still, arms spread wide and sword hanging limply from her hand. She smiled at his confusion.

'I yield Captain. You win.'

Marcus was breathing hard. He lowered his sword warily.

'I don't understand.'

Nareema sheathed her weapon and stepped forward.

'Why wouldn't you fight me?'

He looked down and sighed.

'It would have been a fight I couldn't win.'

'Molly is special. I wanted to know how far you would go for her.'

'I would die for her.'

'I know that now.' said Nareema softly.

'Was that some sort of test?'

'Yes. And you passed.'

Nareema began to walk away from him.

'I love her you know.' he called after her.

She turned back and smiled.

'I know. And that's why you won.'

Marcus opened and closed his mouth a few times as she walked away.

Brody walked up to him.

'What was all that about?'

Marcus shook his head.

'I just don't understand her at all.'

They both looked in the direction the Princess had gone.

'I don't think you're supposed to lad. What was the fight about?'

'Molly.'

Brody looked at him strangely.

'I've just won permission to ask for her hand in marriage.'

'Congratulations. When she gets better you can get wed properly.'

'If she...'

'Don't start that. She'll be as right as rain in a few days.'

Marcus put his sword away and sighed sadly.

'I hope you're right.'

During their escape from the harbour, the power that Molly had been able to wield smashed one of the yard arms on the main mast, sending it crashing to the deck and it was five days later when they found a port they could put into for repairs. Molly was still unconscious and had hardly moved, but her colour was slowly returning. Marcus was at her side day and night with Brody and several crewmen frequently popping in to make sure she was alright.

Nareema had cut herself off from everything. She was on deck for most of the day, pushing herself through her training routines again and again before retiring to her cabin. She barely ate and when anyone dared to try and to talk to her she just told them to leave her alone.

She was in her cabin when there was a heavy knock at the door. She didn't answer and after a moment the door opened anyway and in came Captain Brody. He was carrying a tray with some food and a bottle of wine on it.

'I do not wish to be disturbed.'

'So you keep saying. But you need to eat.'

He put the tray down and sat on the bed.

'Punishing yourself won't bring him back you know. Or help Molly.'

She looked at him hard.

'I know but it will help me next time I meet Tong Li. He is going to die. He's going to pay.'

Brody sighed and shook his head.

'And you think you can beat him? While he has that power?'

'I have to.'

'I've fought him. He's something else.'
'So am I.'
'Have it your way.'
He stood.
'We're putting into port tomorrow. Why don't you get off the ship and get some clean clothes. Stretch your legs.'

She didn't reply so he left her alone, quietly closing the door behind him.

Nareema looked at the tray then at the door, before the tears began to roll silently down her cheeks. She had only felt such loss and such failure once before. It was while she was tied in the market square receiving her punishment.

Her father had come to her and had told her that it was her fault. Her own failure murdered her mother and sister. She might as well have wielded the sword herself. Now she had failed again. Failed to protect Molly. She had given her word that she would protect her, but now the girl was laid next door, unconscious and unmoving. And that was her fault.

She should have been there for her. And now Shakir was gone too. He had been her friend and protector since she had been a little girl. The Princess took a ragged breath. Her ribs still hurt from her fight on the quayside. She'd strapped them up and was pretty sure they weren't broken but they were still sore. She wiped her eyes. Maybe Brody was right. Maybe she did need to let it go.

But Tong Li would pay. Even if she had to die to achieve it.

Brody guided the ship into harbour and began organising the crew to fix the broken yard arm. Marcus headed into the town for clothes and other supplies. No one saw the Princess leave but her sword and other weapons were gone when Marcus checked on her that night.

'She can look after herself.' said Brody.

'It's not her I'm worried about.' replied Marcus.

They were sat at the Captain's table and the old sailor called Davis was watching over Molly. They seemed to have adopted her as an unofficial member of the crew and all were concerned for her. Marcus finished his drink and stared into the empty cup.

'Another?' asked Brody, offering him the bottle.

'No. Thank you.'

Marcus shook his head sadly.

'I think I'm going to call it a night. I need to see if...'

'She'll get better. I know it.'

Marcus didn't reply. He just smiled tightly and headed out of the cabin. Brody watched him shut the door and then sighed. He ran his hands across his face. God. He was tired. He wasn't as young as he use to be and that bastard Tong Li has nearly been the end of him. He owed his life, and his ship, to that girl and the Princess.

He stood and stretched, groaning as his tired muscles protested. Taking a swig from the wine bottle he pulled his shirt over his head and dropped it onto the chair. As he began to undo his breeches there was a soft knock at the door.

'Hold on.'

He put his shirt back on and opened the door, and was surprised when he saw Nareema standing there waiting.

'Princess.'

'Captain.'

He stepped aside to allow her to come in. She was wearing a long black dressing gown held closed with a wide satin belt. Her long black hair was loose around her shoulders and for the first time he noticed how small and fragile she looked. Inwardly he wondered why he hadn't seen it before.

'What can I do for you? We thought you'd left us.'

'I took your advice and stretched my legs. I did some thinking and just wanted to say thank you for the advice.'

Brody nodded.

'My pleasure. Drink?'

'No. Thank you.'

She hesitated then turned to go.

'What else?' said Brody, sensing she had more to say but seemed unwilling.

Nareema turned back.

'Look. If you want to talk then we can. I won't hold it against you.'

He gestured to the chairs at his table. Again Nareema hesitated.

'No. But thank you again.'

She stepped to the door and he followed, putting out a hand to stop her. She looked hard at the hand that rested on her shoulder for a second before closing her eyes and bursting into tears. Gently, Brody gathered her into his arms and held her close, half expecting her to explode with rage at the touch. She didn't. She just let herself be held.

'I miss him.' she said simply.

Brody didn't know what to say or do.

'He's always been there. From when I scraped my knee the first time, through everything with me. Like a father. Like my father. How can he be gone?'

'I don't know lass. It's just the way of things.'

The Princess took a deep breath and got herself under control before pushing away from him.

'I'm sorry Captain. I...'

'You don't need to explain.'

'He's always been there with me. To tell me everything is going to be alright. Now he's not and I don't know if it will be.'

'It will.'

'How do you know?'

'I don't. There's no point in thinking any other way.'

She moved closer to him again. He could feel her heart beating against his chest. Brody sighed softly and lent close.

'I'm going to kiss you. Promise you won't beat seven bells out of me if I do?'

She laughed quietly and pushed away from him. Slowly she turned her back to him and slipped the dressing gown from her shoulders, letting it fall to the floor. Underneath she was completely naked and Brody winced inwardly at the mess of scars that crossed her back. She looked over her shoulder at him and smiled coyly.

'What's the matter Captain, don't you trust me?'

He laughed before stepping behind her.

'Probably.'

She turned around as he touched her skin and kissed him deeply.

Marcus entered the cabin and Davis jumped up.

'Still th' same sir.'

'Thank you.'

'Will ye let us know when she wakes up sir?'

Marcus nodded.

'Of course.'

Davis left and closed the door behind him. Marcus looked at the Molly, still asleep and unmoving in the bed. She looked so fragile. He sighed and undressed before slipping into bed next to her. Gently he took her hand and kissed her on the forehead.

'Come back to me. Please...'

She didn't respond. He pulled the covers up and was soon asleep.

Marcus snapped awake as he felt a pressure on his fingers. He had fallen asleep holding Molly's hand and in the light from the dim lantern he could see her eyes were open. He shot up.

'Molly!'

She smiled tiredly.

'Marcus.' her voice was barely a whisper.

He kissed her, his joy of her being awake was beyond measure.

'Thirsty.'

'Right. Of course.'

He leapt out of bed and grabbed a glass, filling it with water from the jug nearby. She tried to sit up but was plainly very weak. Marcus helped her and held the cup to her lips so she could drink. She coughed and spilt some of it down her chin.

'Where are we?'

'Safe. We're aboard the Endurance.'

She nodded.

'I must tell Captain Brody and see if the Princess is back. Will you be alright for a moment?'

She smiled and nodded again.

'I'll be right back.'

He headed to the door but turned back, gave her another quick kiss and then left in a rush.

Nareema was lying face down in Brody's bed, resting her head on her hands. He was next to her, propped up on one elbow, gently running his calloused hands across the scars on her back.

'Is it worth asking how you got these?'

She shook her head.

'No.'

'Thought as much. What about the tattoo?'

She rolled over and pulled the covers up over her chest before opening her mouth to reply. Her words were cut short by a swift knock at the door before Marcus burst in.

'Captain...' he began but pulled up short as he saw them in bed together.

He floundered for a moment, unsure what to say. They both looked at him as he tried to comprehend the sight in front of him. Eventually he settled on two words.

'Molly's awake!'
Nareema and Brody looked at each other before diving out of bed.

Molly was still sat up and dozing as they all came in. The Princess sat next to her on the bed.
'Hey.' she whispered and touched the girls arm.
Molly looked up and smiled, tiredness written all over her face.
"You gave us quite a scare.'
'Sorry.'
'Don't be sorry lass.' said Brody 'You saved my crew and my ship.'
'Where's Shakir?'
Nareema looked down and took her hand.
'He... He isn't with us anymore.' answered the Princess softly.
They could all see the shock and pain that ran across Molly's face as she realised what that meant.
'How?'
'Get some sleep. We'll talk about it later. I promise.'
The Princess stood and walked out, followed closely by Brody.
Marcus sat on the bed.
'She's right. Get some sleep. You look very tired.'
Molly closed her eyes and nodded before snuggling down under the covers. Marcus lay next to her and took her hand.
'These last few days have been terrible. You saved us you know. That was the single bravest thing I've ever seen. Did you know what the Stone would do?'
'No.' whispered Molly. 'I just did what I thought was right.'
'It was right but please don't do it again. I nearly lost you and I don't think I could live with myself if I did that. I think you're so special and perfect and I haven't known what to do with you not here. I know we've only known

each other for a short time but I need to ask you. Will you marry me? Please.'

She looked at him and nodded.

'Yes.'

'You've just made me the happiest man alive.'

Her smiled said everything. Marcus gave her and soft a gentle kiss.

'Get some sleep.'

Her eyes closed and within moments she was asleep. He lay awake for a while, undeniably happy, before he eventually drifted off, still holding her hand tightly.

A few days later the repairs were complete and Molly was up and about. She had lost a lot of weight and was still a bit weak but there was no stopping her. They were due to head out of port on the morning tide and Brody had offered to marry them, "ships Captains duty and all that" and they had both agreed. Molly was resting in her cabin when there was a quiet knock on the door.

'Come in.'

It opened to reveal Davis and a couple of the other sailors. They looked uncomfortable. Molly smiled at them.

'Hello.'

Davis touched his forelock and glanced nervously at his companions. There was a brief muttering between them before Davis spoke.

'Begging your pardon miss but we heard that you was gettin' wed to Captain Kane. Proper like.'

'Yes. I am. We are. Captain Brody is going to do it when we're on our way.'

Davis wrung his hands and looked down.

'Me an some o' the lads... We...'

One of the other sailors gave him a shove.

'Well it's like this miss. We're all rightly grateful to ye for gettin' us out o' the harbour and stoppin' that fiery bastard...' he glanced at her before blushing '...beggin' your pardon miss.'

She looked at the men, puzzled.

'Well we thought that a lady needed a dress to get wed in so we all chipped in and got ye this. Cap'n Brody said it would be alright. He chipped in some too.'

He turned and took a carefully wrapped bundle from one of the other men which he handed to Molly. She took it and sat on the bed to open it. In the parcel was a simple white dress with a delicate lace around the hem and neckline. She stood and held it up against her.

'It's beautiful. Thank you.'

Davis and the other sailors smiled uncomfortably. Carefully Molly laid it on the bed and stepped close, giving each of them a little kiss.

'Thank you all.'

Embarrassment raged around them and they made some hurried excuses and turned to go.

'Mr Davis. If you're not too busy then I'll need someone to give me away.'

Davis turned back, flustered. He opened and closed his mouth a couple of times.

'I would be honoured miss.' he said eventually.

'Thank you again.'

He tugged his forelock once more and left, closing the door behind him. Molly grinned and picked up the dress from the bed. Holding it against her she did a little twirl. It was perfect.

'What did they want?' asked Marcus as he came in.

Molly jumped and quickly hid the dress behind her back.

'What have you got there?'

'Nothing.'

Marcus stepped closer and tried to see but she kept turning away from him.

'What is it?'

'Out.' she ordered with a smile.

He stopped and looked puzzled but Molly pointed at the door.

'Out. It's bad luck for the groom to see the brides dress before the wedding. So go on, out.'

He laughed and snapped off a crisp salute.

'As you wish my lady.'

He was almost out of the cabin before she spoke.

'I'm not a lady.'

He turned back, grinning.

'Yet.'

Molly had dressed and was getting ready when there was a knock at the door.

'Come.'

She looked up as Nareema came in. The Princess was wearing a long dress in a deep green fabric that matched her eyes. Her hair was tied in a braid and she looked every bit the Princess that she was.

'Ready?'

'I think so.'

The Princess walked over to her and took her hands.

'You look great.'

Molly smiled.

'The crew bought it for me.'

'I know. I helped them choose it. Here.'

She reached into a pocket and produced a small silver brooch. It was shaped like a bird in flight.

Molly pushed a lock of hair out of her eyes and took it.

'It's beautiful.'

Nareema smiled as she took it back and pinned it to Molly's dress.

'It's not much. I would have liked you get you something more and I will.'

Molly gave her a hug.

'You've given me enough. You've given me Marcus.'

'Still. I will give you a gift that benefits your status. I will except nothing less for my sister.'

Molly looked at her, puzzled.

'Don't look like that. You've saved my life more than once. Why wouldn't I consider you a sister. We both have little family of our own so I would be honoured if you will join mine.'

They hugged again.

'Thank you.' said Molly through teary eyes.

'You'll spoil your dress. And don't thank me yet. You've not met my father...'

The last words were with a forced smile. Molly knew that Nareema's father had had her flogged and they hadn't spoken since. The moment was interrupted by a knock at the door. It opened to reveal Davis. He'd brushed his hair and was wearing a new shirt. He grinned nervously.

'If'n you're ready miss...'

The crew were gathered on deck and Brody was stood near the forecastle with Marcus. It was a simple ceremony. They exchanged vows and simple gold bands before they kissed lightly to a cheer from the assembled men.

Brody had made sure there was food and wine and after they had eaten, one of the sailors produced a battered fiddle and played some jaunty tunes. Molly and Marcus had danced all evening and both were exhausted but very happy when they retired to their cabin as a real man and wife for the first time. Molly undressed and slipped under the covers and Marcus climbed in beside her. She snuggled close to him.

'So Mr Kane. I hope you will be able to keep me in the manner to which I have become accustomed.'

'Nearly getting killed and sleeping a lot? I hope to do better than that.'

'That's good.'

She smiled and he lent in and kissed her gently.

'I love you Mrs Kane...'
She giggled.
'I love you too.'

## Chapter Fourteen

Growing Power

They had been at sea for two days, heading for England, the late summer sun was high and the weather calm, when Nareema was in her cabin and heard raised voices from Marcus and Molly who were in the cabin next to hers. Puzzled she leant close to the wall to listen.
'You what?' said Molly loudly.
'I said, as your husband, I forbid you....'
'That's what I thought you said. Forbid? Who the hell do you think you are?'
'Your husband. That's who. Love, honour and obey? Remember?'
'Obey?' shouted Molly.
Nareema moved away from the wall as something made of china or glass smashed against it.
'Oh dear.'
She quickly went next door and met Molly coming the other way. She looked furious and was dressed in her leather jumpsuit with sword strapped to her back.
'Molly?'
'Don't. '
Marcus stepped into the door way.
'Your Highness. Will you see if you can talk some sense into her?'
Molly looked at him, opened her mouth to say something else but just sighed angrily and stomped away towards the deck. They let her go before the Princess turned and gently pushed him back inside the cabin, closing the door behind them.
'What's going on?'
Marcus paced up and down, gesticulating as he spoke.
'Her. Stubborn. Wilful....'

'Captain.' snapped Nareema.

He stopped and looked up at her.

'She wants the Stones back. And she said she wanted to start training with you again. She's still too weak and I don't know what the Stones will do to her. I said no. Forbade her in fact. On both counts.'

Nareema sighed.

'Marcus. If you wanted someone who would do as they were told you should have married Lady Samantha's daughter. Molly isn't that kind of person.'

He stepped forward angrily and prodded a finger at the Princess.

'This is all your fault. Filling her.... Aahhhhh.'

Nareema grabbed his outstretched finger and bent it back, twisting him as she moved, until his arm was up his back.

'Don't do that again or I will break every bone in your arm.' her voice was hard and full of steely determination.

She gave him a shove and he fell on the bed. He rolled over angrily and was about to say something else but saw the look in her eyes.

'Listen to me Marcus. Ordering her to do something isn't going to work. She's been fending for herself for a long time and knows what she's doing. And if you thought that would change when you were married then you're going to be sorely disappointed.'

Marcus sat up and looked at her dejectedly.

'What am I going to do?'

Nareema sat next to him.

'An apology would be a good start. She owes you one too but I'll talk to her about that. You can't treat her like a possession. She's worried enough about how she's going to fit into your life as it is. It's an alien world to her. She doesn't know what she's doing and ordering her about won't work. Like I said, she's fended for herself for a long time. Trust her. I do.'

'I didn't know.'

'No. She doesn't want to worry you. Where are the Stones?'

Marcus got up and went to a nearby trunk. He rooted around in it for a moment before producing a small velvet bag which he handed to the Princess.

'Here. Please make sure she's careful.'

Nareema nodded before heading out after Molly.

The Princess emerged on deck. She had changed into her own suit and had her sword ready. Ahead of her she could see Molly. She was going through the movements she had taught her, but not very well. It was clear she was angry and it was affecting her concentration.

'Molly. Stop.'

She turned at the shouted command, breathing hard.

'He's sent you to talk me into being a good obedient wife has he?'

Nareema walked up to her.

'No. Here.'

She handed the bag with the Stones in to Molly.

'He's worried about you.'

'He's got a bloody funny way of showing it. Did you know that he actually forbid me from coming up here like this? Who does he think he is? It's not like I've not done it before.'

'He doesn't mean it. I think he just doesn't want you to do too much too soon. I don't either.'

'So you're taking his side?'

'No. I'm not taking sides. You're both being as stubborn and stupid as one another.'

'Don't you start.'

'Apologise to him. You're at fault as much as he is. You don't know how worried we were after...' she changed tack slightly. 'You were so cold that he burnt himself on your skin but he still picked you up and carried you to the cabin. All I'm asking is that you take it easy. Please.'

Molly sighed.

'I'm not used to having someone look after me. I don't need protecting and I surely don't need to be told what to do.'

'I think he's revising his expectations of a wife as we speak. You must do the same. Allow him to be there for you.'

'I suppose. I don't know what he expects though. I don't know how to be a wife. I can't see myself hosting a party for lord and lady whatnot. I don't even know what his house looks like.'

'You'll work it out.'

Molly tipped the Stones into her hand. Immediately the sapphire glowed a brilliant blue. Nareema looked at her.

'Its' never done that before.'

'No.' replied Molly.

She closed her eyes and smiled.

'It knows me.'

'What do you mean?'

Molly looked at the Princess. Her eyes were a brilliant shining blue.

'It knows me. I can feel its power.'

'Be careful.'

'Trust me.'

The Princess stepped back as Molly raised her hand, and with gentle movement, caused a gust of wind to wash over her. Nareema looked at her, questioningly but Molly just smiled, eyes still shining brightly.

'How did you do that?'

'That's nothing.'

There was something in Molly's voice that caused her to pause.

'We will train for one hour. Then you will rest. This afternoon we will begin again with your academic studies.'

What're they?'

'Reading and writing.'

'Oh.' said Molly disappointedly.
'You need to be able to read and write.'
Nareema drew her sword.
'One hour.'
Molly nodded.

Three hours later they were still at it, both drenched in sweat and going hard. Marcus and Brody were watching along with some of the crew. Nareema flashed in with her blade, catching Molly off guard. She couldn't get her own sword up in time to block attack and the Princesses weapon was heading for her head.

Quickly, Molly gestured with her left hand and the oncoming attack was enveloped in a swirling maelstrom which stopped it in its tracks. Marcus could see Nareema pushing against the sudden change in the air, as if around her it had become thick and dense. Both of the women had a determined look in their eyes. He stepped forward.

'That's enough. Both of you. Please.'
Molly looked at him, her eyes shining unnaturally.
'Please.'
She nodded and let her concentration go as the Princess relaxed her weapon. They both put their swords down, breathing hard.
'How did you learn to do that?' said Nareema.
'I didn't. Saali knows what's she's doing. She guided me.'
'Who's Saali?'
Molly held up the sapphire.
'Since the harbour I've had a niggling voice in the back of my head. I never realised who it was until now.'
'What else does she say?'
Molly shrugged.
'Nothing much that I understand other than she knows that Daneep is close by.'
'Is that the Earth Stone?'
'I think so. I'll ask.'

'Wait. Rest first.'
Molly nodded.
'Alright.'
Putting the sapphire in the bag she headed off the deck towards their cabin. Marcus turned to Nareema, his concerned expression matching her own.

'I don't like this your Highness. What's happened to her? How can she do those things with the Stone? Is she still her?'

'I don't know. I think she opened herself to it completely when she got us out of the harbour. She and it are connected now more than ever.'

'Its' taken her over?'

'No? I don't think so. Its allowing itself to be used by her. Guiding her.'

'Why?'

'I don't know that either.'

Later that evening they were all gathered around Brody's table. Marcus sat next to Molly with Nareema and the ships Master to her left. Molly had been explaining how the sapphire talked to her.

'When I hold her I can hear her in my head. She knows things but I don't understand most of what she's saying.'

'Like what?' asked Marcus.

Molly shrugged.

'I don't know. What does philosophical mean?'

'How do you know it's a she?' asked Nareema.

'She sounds like one.'

'What does the emerald sound like?'

'I don't know. It's just muffled noise. But if I didn't know what I was listening for then I wouldn't know it was there.'

'Goodnight.'

Marcus closed the door to Brody's cabin behind him, leaving the ships' Captain and Princess alone. Quietly he went back to his cabin, opening the door to see that Molly was still asleep. She hadn't moved since she had retired after she had turned Brody's table into a bush. He had spent a good few hours with him and a couple of axes, trying to get it flat enough to use but as fast as the cut bits off, they just grew back again.

Brody had eventually cut it into small pieces and had it thrown overboard before it got too big to get out and up on deck.

With a sigh, he lay down next to his wife and took her hand. She stirred but didn't wake up. He brushed a lock of her blond hair away from her face and kissed her forehead softly.

'I love you.' he whispered.

Her lips parted slightly as she smiled in her sleep. He smiled back at her and let her go, rolling over to try and sleep himself. As soon as he released her hand, she grabbed his wrist tightly and her smile rolled away to reveal bared teeth.

'Molly?'

Her grip was solid and suddenly the temperature in the room fell. Ice formed on the furniture and his breath misted before his face. Molly went rigid. Her whole body locked stiff and straight.

'Mhh. Mhh. Molly...?' he stuttered as the temperature fell further.

He could feel the ice forming on his clothes and on the bed sheets. The glass of water on the table was solid. Inside his head a voice began to speak. It was soft and feminine but had an undercurrent of something dark and powerful.

'He's coming. Help her find us. We can stop him.'

Marcus was so cold he couldn't think straight.

'Wh.... what?'

'He. Is. Coming...'

The voice was loud and insistent, almost shouting. Molly released her grip and sat up suddenly awake. There was ice in her hair and next to her Marcus shivered, his skin blue with cold. She took one look at him.
'Nareema!'

The Princess had come running as soon as she'd heard Molly's panicked shout. That had been half an hour ago. Marcus was sat up, swathed in blankets to warm him up. Molly had sat away from him for a while looking sick before she headed up on deck. The sun was going down and in the distance she could see a coastline. She rested her arms on the railing and stared out to sea.
'Molly. What happened?'
She turned as Nareema came on deck.
'I don't know. I just remember a dream about somewhere dark and cold. There was something there. Something scary.'
'What?'
'I don't know. Then I woke up.'
She went silent for a moment and turned away.
'I nearly killed him.'
Nareema put a hand on her shoulder.
'No. You didn't.'
'I did.'
The Princess sighed.
'You can't control power from the gods. That is what the Stones are. They are more powerful than we imagined.'
'I didn't ask for this.'
'No. It is a burden. But not one you have to carry alone.'
Molly didn't reply.
'Come. Your husband needs you.'
'I'll be there in a minute.'
Nareema didn't push her. She left the girl standing and staring out across the water.

## Chapter Fifteen

Running Away

The next day Marcus found Nareema on deck. The Princess was practising. Running through her coordinated movements, the blade in her hand as much a part of her body as her arms and legs. He called to her.
'Your Highness.'
She stopped and looked at him hard.
'What?'
'Have you seen Molly? She wasn't in bed when I woke so I thought she might be here with you.'
Nareema's brow furrowed.
'No. I haven't seen her since last night. We made no plans to train this morning. Maybe she is with Captain Brody.'
Marcus shook his head.
'No. I saw him below. She's not there.'
The Princess sheathed her weapon, a sinking sensation in the pit of her stomach.

They'd searched the ship but couldn't find any trace of Molly. Her suit and weapons were gone. Marcus, Nareema and Brody were gathered in the Captain's cabin when there came a knock at the door. Brody flung it open to reveal the sailor that everyone called Skippy.
'What do you want?' Brody asked testily.
The man looked down.
'I know where Mrs Kane is.'
All three of them looked at him and he shuffled nervously.
'She's gone. I helped her get off. Said she had to get to the coast and wanted my help. She took the launch.'
'You did what?' exploded Nareema.
'Only what she asked.' said Skippy.

He was a big man in his mid-thirties with a bushy beard and weather beaten skin but was like a naughty schoolboy under the glare of the Princess.

'You put her off the ship?'

'No. I told you. She asked me to take her to the coast. I said no. She said she would steal the launch and do it herself. I told her not to be stupid so she went and tried anyway.'

'Why didn't you stop her?'

'She wouldn't listen. Threatened to jump overboard if I didn't help. What was I going to do?'

You could have got me.' said Marcus.

'Or me.' added Nareema.

'I didn't have time.'

'When?'

'They left just about midnight.'

'They?' demanded Nareema

'Mr Davis went with her. She doesn't know anything about boats and he said he couldn't let her go on her own. She asked me to give you this.'

He handed Marcus a letter. He frowned as he unfolded it and looked at it.

'I can't read it.'

Nareema snatched it off him.

'It's in French.'

'What?' said Marcus. 'She can barely write English. How can she know French?'

Nareema glared at him.

'Well she can't.' he said defensively.

The Princess held up the letter and read it aloud.

'Dear Marcus. Sorry. I have to do this. If I stay I will put you all in danger. I will find you again when this is all over. When I have the Stones I will find you. Love Molly.'

Marcus looked on.

'How can she write French?'

'The Stones I expect.'

Nareema shook her head.

'I'm going after her.'

'You can't. They've been gone a good few hours. You'll never catch them. Once we turn around we'll be running against the wind and tide.'

'I promised to protect her.' said Nareema angrily.

'And she's my wife.' said Marcus.

'You can't do anything about it now.'

'I have to try.'

Nareema looked at Marcus for a second. He nodded.

'Please find her.'

The Princess nodded back.

'I will.' she turned to Brody.

'Get your men below. I am going after her. If I see anybody on the deck I will kill them.'

She turned and stormed out as Brody went to protest.

'She will Captain. She's deadly serious about this. I know.' said Marcus as Nareema slammed the cabin door behind her.

What's she going to do?'

'You wouldn't believe me if I told you.'

Ten minutes later Nareema climbed up onto the deck by the wheel. She looked around and saw no one. All of the crew were below decks as she had requested. She had dressed in her leather suit and had a backpack along with her weapons. She closed her eyes for a moment and took a deep breath.

'Are you going to tell me what you're going to do?'

She spun, a knife in her hand in an instant.

Brody held up his hands. The Princess stared at him for a moment.

'Go below.'

'No. It's my ship. I go where I please.'

She gave him a hard look.

'How're you going to find her? She must have nearly a day's head start.'

'Go away.'

He lent back against the rail and folded his arms. Nareema walked over to him, brandishing the knife. He straightened as he saw the look in her eyes.

'Please. Go away.'

'No.' he said after a moment.

She raised the knife.

'I don't want to have to kill you.'

'Then don't.'

They both stood there in silence. The tension between them was palpable. Eventually the Princess swore and turned away.

'This will change things between us. Don't say I didn't warn you.'

Before he could reply, she began muttering under her breath. From nowhere, a thick dark mist descended and the temperature fell. Brody watched with a deep, growing, fear as the mist began to spin around the Princess until she was completely obscured by it. The wind fell and it even seemed as if the sea had stopped moving.

The ship's Captain swallowed dryly as an unsettling terror touched him. He wanted to run away but couldn't get his body to move. With a rush of air, the mist began to clear. Where the Princess had stood, there was now a huge black raven. It hopped around to face him, cawed loudly and then took to the sky, disappearing quickly into the night sky and as it left, the spell was broken. Brody had to grab onto the railing behind him to stop himself falling over.

'Bloody hell.' he muttered under his breath.

After a few minutes, he regained his composure and went below. He needed a drink.

Davis walked along behind Molly. He didn't understand her at all. First off, she'd tried to steal the launch, then threatened, then pleaded with him and Skippy to help her. He'd agreed eventually but knew that there was going to be hell to pay if he ever made it back on board the Endurance.

Once they'd got the boat in the water she was set to leave on her own but he could see she didn't know what she was doing. She'd have been drifting for weeks so, against his better judgement, he'd offered to help. He didn't know why but she looked so lost and sad.

They'd pushed off from the ship and it quickly left them behind. Once it was out of sight, she'd got him to rig a sail and then... He shook his head as he remembered... Then she took out a pretty gem and summoned the wind. It blew directly at the sail and carried them swiftly to shore, even though the wind was blowing off the land.

It weren't natural. Nor were the way her eyes glowed blue when she did it.

They'd pulled the launch up on a beach and had been walking for most of the day. Molly in the lead and Davis tagging along behind. She'd tried to get him to go several times but he wasn't having any of it. What's more, she was talking to herself. Having whole conversations. It weren't natural.

'Mr Davis, you can leave me now you know. I'll be fine from here.'

Her words snapped him out of his revere.

'Oh no miss. I'd never find the ship again now and I bet the Cap'n will have somethin' to say about me takin' the launch even if'n I could find it.'

'Tell him I made you.'

'He'd have more to say if'n I was to leave you all on your own in for'n parts too.'

She stopped suddenly and he almost walked into her.

'What?'

'I didn't say anything miss.'

She looked at him.

'No. Not you.' she cocked her head as if listening.

'Yes. I think we should.'

Davis looked at her as she turned off the road they were on and headed into the trees. He followed.

'Where're we going miss?'

'Off the road.'

She stopped suddenly again.

'Where are we Mr Davis?'

He shrugged.

'France I reckon. Somewhere north.'

She nodded.

'We could do with getting to England. But I need to do something first.'

'What's that?'

Molly looked at him.

'There's a cave ahead. We can stop there for the night.'

'How'd you know there's a cave.'

She shrugged.

'There just is.'

The cave turned out to be a hollow on the side of a small hill. Molly lit a fire in the mouth and then cooked a rabbit she had caught earlier.

'Tomorrow we need to find a couple of horses. We'll make better time that way.'

Davis looked uneasy.

'Can't ride a horse miss. Never needed one. Been at sea all my life. No room for horses on board ship.'

'It's easier than you think.'

They ate in silence for a while.

'If'n you don't mind me asking miss, what's going on? I mean, you can do things that I wouldn't believe if'n I hadn't seen them with me own two eyes and as for your servant! I ain't never seen anyone fight like that before. Not even the Cap'n' and I've been in a scrape or two with him in my time.'

'Nareema's not my servant. If anything, I work for her but

I don't think it's that simple anymore.'
 'Who is she then?'
 'She's a Princess.'
 'What about you?'
 'Me? I'm nobody. I just got caught up in something.'
 They went silent again listening to the crackle of the fire.
 'How old are you Mr Davis?'
 'Nearly fifty I think. Don't set much stock by birthdays.'
 'I'm only seventeen. Before I met Nareema I...'
 Molly stopped talking and seemed to listen intently.
 'What? Here? Now?'
 Davis looked on.
 'Alright.'
 Molly looked at the older man.
 'I need you to find the nearest village or town and get us some supplies. And a horse or two if you can manage it. Here's some money.'
 Molly handed him a bag containing a few gold coins and a small diamond.
 'What're you going to do?'
 'Nothing that needs to worry you. I'll be here when you get back. Just be careful.'
 He looked at her.
 'Go. Now please.'
 'I don't think I...'
 'Yes. You should. Go now and don't come back until tomorrow.'
 Davis stood but still eyed her suspiciously.
 'I promise I won't leave without you.'
 'I don't like it.'
 'I'll be fine. Trust me.'
 'If'n you're sure.'
 'I am. Now go.'
 Molly watched him turn and walk away, casting worried glances over his shoulder as he did. When he was out of sight she took out the sapphire and emerald from their bag.

Holding the sapphire tightly in her right hand she felt it grow warm against her skin.

'Now what?'

She doused the fire with a gesture that caused a brief but intense flurry of heavy rain.

'That's new.'

She listened.

'Well I just didn't think about doing that before. I know there's more to the air than just the wind but...'

She sighed.

'Fine. Let's do it.'

Moving to the back of the cave she sat down and picked up the Earth Stone. Holding it in her left hand she took a deep breath and closed her eyes.

Nareema stood on a rough pebbled beach. Just up the shore was the launch from the Endurance. She had spied the boat from the air. A simple mast and sail had been rigged and it had been pulled up the beach and abandoned. Crouching near the vessel she checked the ground around it and found some tracks heading off to the north. She took a deep breath and summoned the raven again.

Davis wandered into town. He was fed up. The nearest town was a good few miles from where they'd camped and not long after he'd left there had been a torrential downpour which had soaked him to the skin. What he needed was a drink. Setting his mind, he looked around until he found a likely looking building and headed over.

It was large and made of whitewashed stone with a stable adjoining it. He walked past the stables, his mind on a drink, but as he passed the last stall, a hand shot out and grabbed him. The grip was like iron and it hauled him back into the shadows. He felt a knife press to his throat and angry voice hiss in his ear.

'Where is she?'

He swallowed nervously, afraid that if he moved at all he would slit his own throat.

'Um...'

With an angry shove he was spun and pushed over into the hay. He rolled to see the Princess standing over him with a long knife in one hand and the other balled tightly into a fist. Gingerly he touched his neck and his fingers came away bloody from a small cut.

'Where is she? Where is Molly?'

She looked furious but there was something else. Something about the set of her body, like she was in pain. Davis gaped at her and she raised her fist as if to strike him. He cowered back and spoke quickly.

'Outside town. A few miles and there's a cave. She sent me here to get some supplies. Said there's sommat she had to do. Please don't kill me.'

Nareema took a step forward before swearing loudly and Davis couldn't help but notice a thin wisp of a dark mist escape from between her lips. She swore again before closing her eyes and taking a couple of slow deep breaths. Eventually she opened her eyes and lowered the knife.

'I won't kill you.'

Her anger seemed to have vanished or at least been brought under control. Nervously he stood.

'Take me to her please Mr Davis.'

He nodded and hurried out into the street.

Nareema had followed Davis out of the stable leading a couple of horses which they had ridden away before anyone noticed. She was tired. It had been a long time since she had called the raven like that and she was regretting it. In her head, she kept getting flashes of the darkness, the taunting voices and their cold grasping hands.

'Are you alright miss?'

She opened her eyes to see Davis next to her. He was

holding on to his horse for grim death but had managed to stop it next to hers.

'Yes. I'm fine.'

'If'n you're sure miss. You seemed to go blank and stop moving.'

'I'm fine. How far away are we?'

'Not far I don't think. I remember that broken tree there.'

The old sailor pointed to the remains of a tree trunk that looked like it had been struck by lightning.

'I came out the trees just past that.'

She nodded and dismounted, Davis gratefully following suit. Nareema walked into the wood.

'Where is it?'

Davis came up behind her.

'It was here.'

The cave wasn't there. The grass was long and tight tangle of trees and brush covered the small clearing. She crouched down and moved some of the long grass. Underneath was the choked remains of a fire. She frowned as she stood up.

'Molly?'

There was no answer.

'Where was the cave?'

Davis pointed to the far side of the clearing where the brush and trees were thickest. Nareema walked up to the bushes but couldn't see anything through the dense foliage.

'Molly?'

Still no answer.

'Maybe she left?'

The Princess shook her head.

'No. She's here. I know it.'

She drew her sword and began hacking at the brush. As fast as her blade cut the branches, they grew back. After five minutes, it was thicker than ever. She sighed and sheathed her sword.

'What now?' asked Davis.

She turned back to him.
'We wait.'

Nareema paced back and forth. It had been two days since she had found Davis and the clearing. They had moved their camp a small distance away as the ground around the cave was almost covered in thick briars and brambles now. She and Davis had taken turns watching the cave for any movement and it was his shout that brought her running.

The bushes were parting when she got there, splitting apart in the middle like a door. They both watched as into the dying evening stepped Molly. She looked pale and haggard with bits of twig and grass intertwined in her hair.

'Molly?'

The girl looked up at her name but said nothing. Nareema found see her eyes were dully glowing green orbs. There was a tense silence.

'What the hell were you thinking? You can't run away... ' said Nareema forcefully.

Molly's eyes flashed brilliantly, the green glow almost white. Suddenly branches flashed out from either side of the clearing, wrapping themselves around Nareema's wrists and pulling her arms apart. More branches swept in to wrap around her ankles. The Princess struggled but couldn't break free from their grip. Davis moved to help but was swept off his feet as creeping vines tangled around his ankles.

Molly stepped forward and the branches around the Princess tightened, lifting her clear of the floor. She cried out as her arms and legs were pulled tightly outwards. With a rush of wind and Molly floated up on a fusion of swirling air until she was eye to eye with her.

'Do not dare raise your voice to us, mortal....'

It wasn't Molly speaking. There were two distinct voices,

both slightly out of sync with each other. Both were distant, as if the speakers were in another room.

The branches tightened once more and Nareema cried out as her arms and legs were pulled in opposite directions. They were going to tear her apart. She gritted her teeth.

'Molly. It's me. Please don't do this. Please.'

She screamed as the pressure increased once more.

'Please. Don't....'

Suddenly Molly shook her head as if waking from a dream and her eyes returned to their normal bright blue. The wind that was holding her up vanished and she cried out as she fell the couple of feet to the ground. Around the clearing the trees seemed to relax and the pressure on Nareema's limbs vanished too. She fell to the ground next to Molly.

'Nareema?' whispered the girl.

The Princess crawled over and hugged her tightly.

'I'm here.'

Nareema stood shakily and helped Molly up. Davis had kicked off the vines that had ensnared him and helped too.

They guided Molly back to their camp and sat her by the fire. Her hands were curled into fists and she cried out in pain as she tried to open them. They'd been tightly gripping the Stones for days and the muscles had tightened.

'Here.'

Nareema gently took her hands and massaged a foul-smelling ointment into them and slowly they relaxed until the gems slipped from her grasp and onto the ground. Molly tried to pick them up again but could get her fingers to work properly. She struggled for a moment before bursting into tears. Nareema picked up the Stones and dropped them into the velvet bag before holding Molly tightly.

'It's alright.'

'I could have killed you. And I almost killed Marcus.'

sobbed the girl.

'It wasn't you. It was the Stones.'

'It was me. I used them.'

'But you stopped them. You're stronger than they are.'

'What if I can't stop them next time?'

'There doesn't have to be a next time.'

Molly pushed away and looked her in the eye, speaking softly.

'Yes there does.'

The Princess regarded her for a moment.

'Get some sleep. I'll find you something to eat.'

Molly nodded and lay down close to the fire, the bag with the gems in clutched between her still clawed hands. Nareema stood and walked to Davis who had stayed a little way away.

'Are you alright?'

'Aye. Is she alright?'

They both looked across at Molly who had quickly gone to sleep. Nareema sighed.

'Yes. I think so.'

Davis looked down.

'Me an' the crew... We sort of feel responsible for her, you know...'

The Princess nodded.

'I'd hate to see anything happen to her. She's...'

'Special.' finished Nareema.

'Aye. She's our good luck charm.'

Nareema laughed softly.

'Get some sleep your Highness. I'll keep a watch for a while.'

'My name is Nareema.'

Davis smiled.

'Nareema.'

She smiled back and went to settle down near the fire.

'Sister.'
Molly woke to a gentle shaking.
'What?'
'Molly.'
She sat up to see Nareema heading off into the trees. The Princess stopped and turned back, beckoning the girl to follow her.
'Come.'
Stiffly, she got up and followed.
'Where are we going?'
Nareema smiled and led her through the trees for a while until the emerged beside a secluded pool. A high waterfall fell from the far side and splashed noisily into it.
'Bathe. It is cold but it will help you muscles relax.'
Without another word, the Princess stripped out of her leather suit and dived into the water. Nervously Molly looked around.
'What if someone comes?'
'Then they will have a surprise. Come on.'
'I can't swim very well.'
'Then this is the perfect place to practice. Now are you coming in or will I have to throw you in?'
Molly looked around once more before stripping and jumping in. The water was cold but the Princess had been right. She could feel the tension in her body begin to melt away. She splashed her way over to Nareema who was near the waterfall.
'See. I told you. Turn around.'
Molly did as she was told and Nareema began to wash the dirt and twigs from her hair.
'If you're sure that you have no choice with the Stones then you need to learn to control them. Not the other way around.'
'I suppose.'
'There is no suppose. You need to do this. If not for you, then for me... And Marcus.'

Molly sighed.

'We're going to move today. To England. That's where Marcus is. From there we can see about the other Stones.'

'I think Saali and Daneep can help me find them.'

'How do you know?'

The girl shrugged.

'I just do.'

'Let's get head back to camp. You're going to show me what you can do with the Stones.'

'Is that a good idea?'

'Yes.'

## Chapter Sixteen

### Rami

The Endurance put into Plymouth a few days later and Marcus had been beside himself for the entire time. Sleeping little and pacing up and down.

'Don't fret lad.' Brody had told him. 'If anyone can find her then it'll be the Princess.'

Marcus shook his head.

'I don't doubt that but I should be doing something. I'm her husband. I feel so... So helpless.'

'There's nothing you can do.'

'I can get the first ship to France. I'll find them from there.'

Now it was Brody's turn to shake his head.

'She wanted you to go home. She said that she would come to you.'

'She can't take care of herself.'

'Do you really believe that?'

Marcus sighed and sat down heavily.

'No. She's more capable than I am.'

Brody handed him a drink.

'And she's with the Princess. I'd lay money on those two being waiting for you when you get back to Plymouth.'

'I suppose you're right.'

That had been two days ago but it hadn't stopped Marcus worrying. The ship drew into the harbour and as soon as the gangplank was down, a figure wearing a hooded black cloak was waiting at the foot of it. One of the sailors went to meet the stranger and after a few words were exchanged, the man went tearing back on board as if he'd seen a ghost. A few minutes later Brody and Marcus emerged. They walked to the top of the gangplank.

'I'm Owain Brody. What can I do for you?' he shouted.

The figure flicked back the hood to reveal a beautiful dark skinned Indian girl. Her jet black hair was tied in a neat ponytail which fell down her back and she was dressed in a loose fitting silk top and trousers held together with a wide black belt. There were three short knives in a bandolier on each hip.

'May I come on board? I have a message for you.'

Puzzled, Brody nodded.

'Aye. Come on up.'

'I also have something for you. It is on my coach. Would you have one of your men bring it please?'

Brody looked across the quay to a black coach and horses that was sat waiting. He glanced at Marcus, who shrugged but his hand had strayed to his sword.

'Aye.' said Brody before bellowing some orders.

The girl nodded in gratitude before ascending the plank and without another word, she followed the men below deck.

Five minutes later, both Marcus and Brody were sat in the Captain's cabin with an ornate wooden chest on the table between them. The girl had politely refused a chair and was stood between them. The chest was about two feet long by a foot wide and high. Intricate brass scrollwork covered the lid and sides and a solid looking lock sat at its centre.

Brody regarded the girl for a moment. There was something not right about this.

'So what can I do for you miss....'

'My name is Rami. I have a message for you and Captain Kane from my sister.'

'Both men looked at each other, each just as puzzled as the other.

'Go on then.' said Brody.

'Nareema wishes you well Captain Kane. She has found

your wife. She is safe and well.'

'How could you know that? Who are you?' stammered Marcus.

Rami ignored him.

'Captain Brody. This chest is for you.'

A slight smile graced her lips as she repeated the message

'For the inconvenience caused and that which is yet to come.'

She handed Brody a small key which he took and unlocked the chest. It contained gems and gold that were probably worth five times more than the ship.

'She hopes you will not forget the part your crew played in the matter. She would hate to find out that you kept it all for yourself and then have to kill you.'

Brody was speechless.

'How do you know these things?' asked Marcus again.

She turned to him.

'I belong to a very ancient sisterhood. We have our ways.'

'You're a Daughter of Kali?'

The girl nodded once.

Brody regarded her for a second.

'If you see the Princess tell her that the Endurance is ready for whatever inconvenience she has in mind.'

The girl nodded once more.

'Would you dine with us this evening?' asked Brody.

'No. Captain Kane and I are leaving now.'

'What?' stammered Marcus.

'Nareema has requested that I escort you to London. Please gather your belongings we will leave as soon as you are ready.'

She didn't give him time to answer before she turned and left. Both men watched her go.

'She can't order...' began Marcus.

Brody shook his head.

'If she's anything like the Princess then I wouldn't argue with her. It wouldn't be worth the bruises.'

'But she can't be more than twelve!'
'And she'd kill you as soon as look at you. If Nareema thinks it's important then it probably is.'
Marcus sighed in defeat and stood, offering his hand to Brody.
'Thank you Captain. It's been a pleasure.'
Brody stood and shook his hand with a smile.
'Take care. Look after your lass, if she gives you the chance.'
'I will.'
Marcus turned and left the Captain alone in his cabin.

Marcus had gathered all of his and Molly's belongings and Rami had picked up the few things that Nareema possessed and was waiting impatiently on the quay by the coach. Marcus walked to the gangplank but turned at a shout from Brody.
'Marcus!'
The ship's Captain came striding across the deck.
'Here.'
He handed him a small velvet bag.
'A wedding gift. Buy her something nice.'
Marcus smiled and shook his hand once more before snapping off a crisp salute.
'Thank you sir. With luck, we shall meet again.'
'Aye lad. That we will.'

Marcus left the ship and walked down to the coach. It was big and black with two large horses. The driver was also dressed in black and didn't look at him as he climbed in. As soon as he was in, Rami got in behind him and the coach moved off. She sat opposite him and they rode in a tense silence for a while before Marcus felt compelled to make conversation.
'So what brings you to England?'
'You do.'

'Oh.'
'Where are the Princess and my wife?'
'Safe.'
'Is she really your sister.'
'In Kali's eyes, yes.'
They lapsed into silence again.
'You're not much of a conversationalist are you.'
Rami looked at him hard.
'I do not feel the need to get to know you. I have been asked to escort you to London and see you get there safely by whatever means necessary. That in itself is an unusual request.'
'Why?'
'Traditionally our role is not one of protection.'
'I assure you, I don't need protection.'
'Tong Li is still alive. He will use you as bait to get the Stones. Then he will kill you. At least with me, you have a chance. The odds will not be good but they will be better than if you were on your own, now please be quiet.'

Her bluntness and matter of fact tone took Marcus by surprise. He frowned and then banged on the wall of the coach to signal the driver to stop. As it drew to a halt he got out. Rami followed.
'Where are you going?'
'I am going to find an inn. From there I will decide how I get to London and who with. Your company will not be required. Good day to you madam.'

He grabbed his bags and headed off into the town. Rami watched him go before sighing angrily. She turned to the coach driver.
'Wait here.'
'Yes miss.'
As he turned away she grabbed his arm.
'Do not cross me.'
There was something in her look and voice that made him hesitate. Eventually he nodded.

'Good.'
With that, she turned to follow Marcus.

He had only gone two streets before he saw her again. She was stood in the middle of the road, not blocking his path exactly but making sure he knew she wouldn't let him past. He turned down a side road and had gone no more than a hundred yards before she dropped in front of him from a nearby roof.
'Go away.'
'No.'
'If I wished the company of such a rude person as yourself I would have stayed with the army.'
'I am not rude. You mistake the truth for poor manners.'
'I don't believe I do.'
He turned his back on her and walked away. There were running feet behind him and she somersaulted high in the air to land in front of him.
'We will go to London. I don't wish to hurt you but I will if I must.'
'And that's going to get me there safely is it?'
'By any means necessary.'
She stood tall and drew a short tube from the small of her back. It was made of metal and about a foot long. With a flick of her wrist the tube extended from both ends and suddenly she was holding a metal staff about five feet long. The last foot of each end was a deadly looking blade. Marcus sighed.
'You're not going to let this go are you?'
She didn't reply.
'Ask me nicely.'
She stepped back in surprise.
'What?'
'Ask me nicely. Don't order or threaten me. Just ask me to go to London with you.'
The frustration was evident in her face.

'Come with me to London.'

He raised his eyebrows and could see her bite back a sharp retort.

'Please.' she said eventually.

Still he said nothing. Rami took a deep breath and spoke as if this was the hardest thing in the world.

'Please allow me to escort you to London.'

Marcus smiled.

'See, that wasn't so hard now was it?'

She fumed silently at him.

'Where is the coach?'

## Chapter Seventeen

## Visions

Molly, Nareema and Davis had moved north. The women were sharing a horse while Davis rode uncomfortably on the second.

'We are a couple of days from the coast. From there we should be able to get a boat to England.' said the Princess.

She turned in the saddle.

'Mr Davis. Will you ride ahead please. Secure us passage on a ship. Molly and I have things to do. We will follow you in a few days.'

He looked at her for a moment.

'Aye.'

'Thank you. Sell the horse if you like. We won't need it.'

She reached to her belt and pulled a small bag which she passed to him.

'This should cover passage and anything you need to get while you wait.'

He nodded and took the bag.

'Don't be long miss. Take care of yourselves.'

Nareema reigned the horse in and Davis continued down the path.

'Two days.' she called after him.

The Princess dismounted and Molly followed.

'Where are we going?'

'You're going to use the Stones. I want to know what they can do.'

Molly looked unsure.

'Don't look like that. You're stronger than they are.'

She still didn't look convinced.

'Trust me.'

They turned off the road and headed towards an old farm. It wasn't much more than a shell with the roof having been destroyed in what looked like a fire. They led the horse around the back before they went inside. The Princess moved to the far side of the room, picking her way through the rubble. Molly stayed by the doorway.

'What do you want me to do?'

'Open yourself to them.'

Hesitantly Molly took the emerald and sapphire out and held them, one in each hand.

'Concentrate.'

She nodded and closer her eyes. In her hands the Stones grew warm and she could feel their power begin to flood through her. It felt different this time. Instead of the uncontrolled rush of energy, it was a more gradual build-up. The power filled her from both the emerald and sapphire until she could feel it from her toes to the very tips of her hair.

Nareema watched Molly carefully as she channelled the Stones through her. She seemed to be more than herself. Even though her outward appearance hadn't changed, her very presence had. It was almost palpable. The air tingled with it.

'Molly. Can you hear me?'

Slowly she opened her eyes and nodded. Her pupils were a swirling, glowing mass of green and blue.

'Yes.'

Her voice was different. As if there were two people speaking but they were far away and slightly behind one another.

'Are you in control?'

Again the two voices spoke.

'Yes.'

Nareema slowly approached and drew her sword which she rested against Molly's neck.

'Let her talk or I will kill her. Then you will have no

power here.'

Molly hissed and closed her eyes again for a moment. When she opened them again her eyes were almost normal. They were her usual bright blue but there were brief flashes of the swirling morass.

'Are you in control?'

'Yes. I am.'

This time her voice was her own. Nareema removed the sword and put it away.

'They didn't like that.' said Molly.

'Neither did I but I had to know you were still in there.'

'I'm here.'

'Show me what you can do. Start with...'

The Princesses words were cut off as an invisible bubble surrounded her and lifted her from the floor, carrying her skyward. She pounded on the sides and even tried to slash it with a knife, but it was solid.

Molly followed her. A swirling vortex of air carried her up quickly until she was level with the stranded Princess, a good twenty feet from the ground. Nareema looked into Molly's eyes where the bright colours swam once more.

'Why do you continue to threaten us mortal? You cannot understand the power we have. We could destroy you with a thought.'

As the voices spoke, Nareema felt the air in her bubble prison begin to slowly ebb away. It was quickly becoming harder and harder to breath. She glanced up at Molly.

'Now. Show them that you are in control. Not the other way around.'

She slumped to her knees as she felt the air running out. Molly's face contorted into a grimace as she fought for control. After a second her eyes returned to normal and the bubble began to drift towards the ground but it was still five feet up when it vanished. Nareema fell heavily to the rubble strewn floor and gasped for breath. Above her Molly was descending slowly.

She reached the ground and put the Stones away before running over to the Princess.

'I'm sorry. Are you alright?'

Nareema rolled over, still catching her breath.

'Again.' she rasped.

'What?'

'Go over there and do it again. Control them.'

'But I could kill you.'

'You could but for the second time, you haven't. You've taken control. Do it again.'

Nareema stood and drew herself to her full height before speaking with a voice like steel.

'Again.'

'Again!'

Nareema stiffly stood, her face covered in tiny cuts from a shower of stones that Molly had thrown at her. Her left side and ribs were tight and sore after she had been slammed against the wall repeatedly. Across the room Molly was in tears.

'I can't.'

'Again!' Nareema shouted at her.

'No.'

The Princess moved quickly despite her injuries, closing the gap between them in a second. Molly barely had time to register the movement before Nareema struck her across the face with a strong backhand that sent the girl crashing to the ground. The Princess stood over her and shouted.

'Again. Summon them again. Do it. Control them.'

Molly pulled herself to her feet, tears streaming down her face and her eye already starting to bruise from the blow. Slowly she took a breath and closed her eyes.

'I can't.'

Nareema struck again but the blow didn't connect. Around her the air coalesced and became so thick her swung fist just slowed. Sweat broke out on her forehead as even though she was putting her full force behind the strike, it was like punching through molasses. Molly looked at her, perfectly calm and serene before speaking softly.

'Enough. Nareema please. Enough.'

She moved to the side before she reached out and gently touched the Princesses outstretched arm.

'We want to show you something.'

As Molly touched her, the air changed and thinned and suddenly she was free, the punch swinging into empty air. Nareema span to face the girl and she stepped back with her hands raised, almost expecting another attack. Fear was written all over her face, the calmness of a moment ago vanishing as quickly as it had come, to be replaced with tears.

Nareema saw the terrified look and a sudden realisation hit her. In front of her was not an enemy. Not a foe to be destroyed. She was just a frightened girl trying to cope with more than life should have bestowed on her. She was able to wield unimaginable power but hadn't asked for that responsibility.

Nareema's anger fell away in an instant. She had been forcing the girl to act and she was relying on the Stones for protection. Allowing them to come forward and control her as she knew she couldn't beat her any other way. There was no other way to prevent the threat. The Princess fell to her knees and bowed her head.

'I'm sorry.' she whispered softly.

Molly knelt down in front of her.

'I know what you were trying to do.'

'It was wrong.'

She looked up at Molly. Her right eye was swollen and red.

I can't dominate them like that.' said Molly. 'If I try it will take me somewhere I don't want to go. Make me into a person that I can't be.'

Molly sat back on her heels and closed her eyes. Nareema looked at her, shame burning bright within her as around her she felt the air change. It felt charged and full of unseen energy.

'Take my hands.'

Three voices spoke. One of them was Molly who had reached out to her. The sapphire lying in her right palm, glowing brightly with the emerald in her right.

'Take my hands.'

Tentatively Nareema reached up and placed her took Molly's hands. The Stones felt warm on her skin.

'Don't be alarmed. We want to show you something.'

Molly gripped the Princesses hands tightly and Nareema felt a shock run through her body.

Instantly she was transported to another place. She was stood on a rocky mountainside, a few scrubby trees and bushes dotted around the rough ground with a dusty path leading away higher up the mountain. Molly was stood next to her staring along the path.

'Molly. Where are we?'

'We are on the Gunjai mountain.'

Molly's mouth moved but the words weren't her own. Two figures coalesced from nothing either side of the girl. They were made from swirling mist, as insubstantial as the air but as real as the ground. Both were female and appeared to be dressed in simple robes. Nareema couldn't determine any specific features for them as the mist constantly moved and changed. The one to the left was a soft green while the right-hand figure was a pulsing blue. They looked at her.

'Come with us.'

Their mouths moved but the words came from Molly. Both voices floating out of her mouth on a breath of coloured mist.

'Not until I know she's alright.'

The girl turned to look at her and smiled sadly.

'I'm here. We need to see this. It is important. They are guiding me. Don't worry.'

It was with some relief that it was Molly's voice. Slowly she stepped forward and took the Princesses' hand.

'Come.'

Gently she led the Princess up the path, followed closely by the spectral figures.

The trail led them up the mountain for a way before it opened onto a narrow plateau. A hundred feet beneath them was a small village. Its consisted of a dozen or so ramshackle huts in between which sick looking cattle roamed.

'That is Gunjai.' said the voices. 'What it once was and what we were sent to help. Come.'

Molly turned and led the unresisting Princess along with her. She seemed to know exactly where she was going. The plateau narrowed again into a small path which ran to a dark cave. Nareema pulled up short and went to draw her sword. It wasn't there. The figures turned to her and spoke through Molly.

'You do not need a weapon. There is no danger here. You are merely an observer of things that have passed.'

Slightly reluctantly she let herself be led into the dark. The cave was not deep, running only about twenty feet back. At the far end a small pile of fruit and vegetables lay heaped together and from the smell, they had seen better days.

Prostrate in front of this was a man. He was painfully thin and dressed in a grubby loincloth with an equally dirty turban on his head. At first, Nareema thought he was dead and moved to check him but was stopped as Molly held her hand tightly.

'No.'

She looked at the girl in confusion.

'He is alive. Listen.'

Nareema strained her ears and could just make out a low and exhausted voice, chanting in prayer. The two swirling essences spoke, again Molly vocalising their words with snatches of coloured mist.

'This is Kenar. He has been praying for help for his village for three days. Before him is an offering. It was all of the food they had.'

Nareema looked once more at the pitiful heap of rotting food and felt sick. How could it have been like this?

'His life is almost at an end but still he prays. He is weak with hunger and riddled with sickness. But still he prays. He has hardly moved for three days but *still,* he prays. Not for himself. But for his village and its people. This is why we were sent to him. He was a good man. '

The Princess watched as a dim light formed at the far end of the cave. It slowly grew in intensity until the cave was as bright as day. Kenar struggled to lift his head to look but the effort was too great. He slumped onto his side, breathing fitfully. From the glowing light stepped four figures. Two male and two female, dressed in simple robes of green, blue, red and white. They knelt around the dying man and began a whispered chant.

It slowly rose in a gradual crescendo until there was a brilliant multi coloured flash and the figures in front of them disappeared. After a moment, the man sat up. He was still weak but there was a new vitality in his eyes.

'We gave him life. His mind was open and we entered. We left part of ourselves behind for him.'

The glowing figures pointed at the man who had turned to see four coloured gemstones floating in the air behind him. He reached out and touched them and suddenly the rotting pile of food became a banquet. Fruits, meat and vegetables spilled over where there had just been a sad heap. He grabbed a small apple and took a bite before beginning to gather the food together.

'We are the Stones. He was the person who opened

himself to us. We helped him. What happened next was not our intention. Come.'

Molly turned and led Nareema out but instead of leading out on to the plateau as they left the cave, she found herself in a large room. On a raised platform at the far end sat a young man with a crown perched on his head. It was gold and in it sat the four gemstones. In the centre was a small cube, about half an inch to a side and was a swirling mass of colours.

The man was laughing at a cowering couple who were grovelling before him while around the room a lot of heavily armed men stood and watched. The ghostly figures pointed at the man and once again, Molly mimicked their movements.

'This is Malor. Son of Kenar. His father built a city of splendour. None were hungry or in need. This man killed him for the power of the Stones and now things have changed. He did not want to open himself to us. He forced us to do his will. Bound us to the crown through dark magic. He is evil. Watch.'

Malor gestured to some of the men around the room and several stepped forward to haul the couple to their feet. It was a man and woman. Both dressed in rags and filthy. Malor stood.

'Why did you come here?'

'My lord we...' began the man.

A flash of lightning leapt from Malor's fingers and struck him. He screamed in agony as the power tore through his body.

'I did not give you permission to speak.'

Malor released the lightning and the man fell to the ground. His body was burnt and clothes smouldering but he was still alive. The woman cried out and bent down to him but she was hauled up again. Malor turned to her.

'How about you? Are you going to spread lies too?'

She shook her head. Tears were streaming down her

face. Malor cupped her chin in his hand before smiling cruelly.

'I will offer you a choice. My men require entertaining. Are you up to the task or shall I kill you now?'

Slowly he turned her head to look at the man on the floor. She tried to resist but he twisted her neck savagely so she had no choice.

'I'll make it easier for you.'

He lifted his free hand and sent a blast of searing fire into the prone man. He screamed and writhed as the fire consumed him. All the while, Malor forced the woman to watch. Once the man stopped moving, he turned her head back and kissed her roughly. She tried to push him away but strong hands held her from behind. He broke the kiss and ran a hand down her face and body, stopping to squeeze her breast cruelly.

'Take her to my chambers.'

The girl was dragged away, sobbing her heart out. He returned to his seat as a dark-haired beauty stepped from behind his throne to whisper in his ear. He smiled and waved her away as the vision faded. Now they were stood on a dusty road. Endless plains stretching away in all directions.

'When the Crown was created, a piece of us was ripped out and was bound to it. We cannot stop whoever possesses the Crown from using us in any way they see fit.'

'I don't understand.' said Nareema. 'Why show me these things?'

The spectres turned to Molly.

'This girl has opened herself to us completely. She must return us all to the Crown so we may be whole again. The man you call Tong Li. His will is strong and we cannot go against him. If he has the Crown then the world is finished. Not even Kali's chosen will be able to stop him. You, Daughter of Kali, must protect her.'

'You know of us?'

'We know who you are. We... Fear Kali. She is death. But only her daughters stood against the Crown last time, so we must put our trust in them.'

The figures stepped close to Nareema, their presence sending a chill down her entire being.

'Be warned. There is a shadow. One who's heart is dark and driven by anger. If Tong Li falls then another darkness may take his place. A darkness that would cast the gods down and destroy the world.'

Nareema swallowed nervously but nodded.

'Take care of her.'

The figures began to dissipate and Nareema sat up, a blanket falling from her shoulders. She was lying was outside the old farmhouse on the cool grass. Night had fallen and Molly was sat across from her, tending a small fire.

'Hey.' she said softly 'are you alright?'

Nareema nodded and looked around. The moon was high and a gentle breeze moved the nearby trees.

'How did I get here?'

'I moved you.'

The girl seemed distant and her tone was clipped. The Princess rubbed her eyes. She had never felt so refreshed after a sleep. She felt revitalised and suffused with energy.

'How long have I been asleep?'

Molly shrugged and turned a bird that was on a spit over the flames.

'A couple of hours I guess.'

Nareema sat up, pulled the blanket around her shoulders and stared into the fire.

'I'm sorry.'

'You were trying to do what you thought was right.'

'But it wasn't right. And you knew it. But I wouldn't listen.'

Molly shook her head.

'It doesn't matter.'

'It does. I'm sorry I hit you. How is your eye?'
'It's fine.'
'Let me have a look.'
'No. It's fine. The Stones fixed it. And they fixed you too.'

Nareema peered at the girl across the fire. The bruise on her face was gone and she looked fit and healthy. Quickly her hand went to her face to find the cuts and bruises were gone. The pain in her side from her bruised ribs was gone too.

'How...'

Molly shrugged.

'Don't know.'

'Molly... I have done wrong. I know that. My anger...'

She sighed before standing and drawing her sword. Molly jumped up and took a step back, looking on fearfully for a second before the Princess prostrated herself in front of her with her head bowed, her sword held out in front of her as an offering.

'Forgive me sister. My blade is yours to command. My life is yours to hold. The spirits told me I must protect you. I will do that with every breath in my body and every beat of my heart.'

Molly didn't know what to say.

'Please get up.' was the best she could manage.

The Princess straightened but remained on her knees. Molly knelt too.

'I don't want to command you. I don't know where we're going but I do know that we have to get the other Stones and then the Crown. Knowing you are there with me makes this easier.'

'Forgive me.' whispered the Princess, unable to look Molly in the eye.

Molly took the sword from her and placed it on the ground beside them before taking Nareema's hands.

'Why wouldn't I forgive you?'

'I hurt you.'

'Sisters do that, or so I've heard. I've never had one before.'

'You've got one now.'

The women hugged briefly. Tears falling from both. Molly pushed away.

'I need to get to England.'

'To Marcus?'

Molly looked sadly at the ground.

'I hope he's alright and won't be too mad about me leaving.'

'He'll be glad to see you. And if he isn't... Well he'll have me to deal with.'

'I need to find a man who can make things too. Make things from silver.'

She pushed a lock of hair from her eyes as Nareema looked at her quizzically.

'Why?'

The Stones said I should. I need him to make something for me.'

'What.'

Molly smiled and behind her eyes there was a brief swirl of blue and green. Gently she reached up and touched the side of Nareema's head.

'This.'

There was a small shock and then in her mind, Nareema could see it. It was a solid silver bracer that would fit over Molly's forearm. In it were four indentations, one for each of the Stones.

'If I can get this made, I can call the Stones without holding them. They told me they will allow it to be so.'

Nareema nodded.

'Then we will find a silversmith.'

Molly smiled again but it didn't reach her eyes.

'Please don't look so sad. We will find the Stones. And the Crown. Then you can come back to India with me and be a Princess.

'What's it like in India?'

Nareema moved to sit next to her and Molly lay down, resting her head on the Princesses lap.

'It is a beautiful place. Mountains higher than the sky. Forests greener than you can imagine. Magnificent temples and palaces rise on the banks of boundless rivers. It is my home. It can be your home too.'

Nareema looked down to see Molly had fallen asleep. Gently she moved the girls head and stood. Putting some more wood on the fire, she covered Molly with a blanket before picking up her sword and heading off into the night.

## Chapter Eighteen

### Trouble

'Why have we stopped?' asked Marcus.
Rami looked at him from the seat opposite and scowled. 'Wait here.'
She slipped the metal tube from her back and got out of the coach. Marcus shook his head. Ever since they had left Plymouth, she had hardly said a word. Frowning deeply whenever he asked her a civil question and blatantly refusing everything else.
She hadn't left his side either. Not even when he had gone to bed! She had just sat in a chair and watched. He hadn't seen her sleep and she had hardly eaten anything. That had been four days ago.
Now they were headed to London but for some reason the coach had stopped. He stuck his head out of the window to see what was going on. In front of them was a tree blocking the road and Rami was stood looking pensively around. There was no sign of the coach driver.
'What's going on? Where's the driver?'
'Shut up and get back inside.'
He frowned.
'Look. I say...'
He opened the door just as there was a crack from a pistol. The shot buried itself in the wood, not two inches from his hand. He dived back in and grabbed his sword. There was another crack from a gun as Marcus got back out but the shot disappeared into the trees. He took in the scene.
Three men were on the other side of the fallen tree, two hastily reloading weapons and Rami was running towards them. Behind the coach, another two scruffy looking men were coming in fast on horseback. Both had pistols drawn.

Marcus kept close to the coach as they fired. Their aim was off and the shots hit the woodwork. He stepped out as the first of the men reached him. Ducking under a hastily drawn and swung sword he brought his own weapon up. He didn't aim at the rider but the heavy blade sliced through the front leg of the horse. The animal screamed and came crashing down into the road, crushing the rider beneath it as it fell.

Marcus turned as the second rider thundered past heading towards the blockade across the road. Rami had reached the three men and in her hands the bladed pole span like nothing he had ever seen. She whirred it around her body and head, striking out to decapitate all three men before they knew what hit them. She slowed as the last of them fell but hadn't seen the horseman coming up fast behind her.

'Rami!'

She turned at his shout but could only dive to the side as the animal thundered past, its rider swinging a sword at her. The blade caught her shoulder and span her to the ground. The mounted man reigned the animal in and turned it around, raising his sword to finish the job as she pulled herself to her feet.

Marcus dived forward and fumbled a pistol from the belt of the man under the horse. He took a step and composed himself. Ahead of him the rider had spurred his horse on and was riding hard towards Rami. She stood dumbstruck in its path, her hand pressed against a bloody gash in her shoulder.

'Rami. Get down.'

She looked at him and then dropped to the floor as the horseman reached her and Marcus pulled the trigger. The gun went off with a bang and it bucked in his hand but the shot flew straight and true, catching the horseman in the neck and knocking him from his mount. He was dead before he hit the ground.

He hurried over to her. She was struggling to sit up and her shoulder was covered in blood from a deep gash the sword has opened. He bent down next to her.

'Are you alright? Here, let me look.'

She shoved him away with her good arm, smearing blood into his jacket.

'What do you think? Go away.'

Through sheer force of will she got to her feet and picked up her weapon.

'Let me help you.'

'No. I can manage.' her words were angry.

Using the staff like a walking stick she headed back to the coach. Marcus walked alongside her, ready to step in if she needed help. She made it to the coach and sat down by one of the wheels. Carefully she pulled back her top to reveal a deep cut. It was about six inches long and came from her back and across her shoulder to the top of her arm. She winced as fresh blood poured from the gash.

'Get my bag.'

Marcus did as he was told. Rami tried to open it but cried out as she moved.

'Let me help.'

She glared at him.

'In the bag. Find me a cloth or something.'

He opened it and grabbed the first thing he came across. It was a black silk scarf. She looked at him, an odd expression crossing her face.

'Not that.'

He grabbed one of his own bags and grabbed a shirt which he handed to her. She balled it up and pressed it hard against the wound.

'Can you sew?' she asked through gritted teeth.

Marcus looked at her.

'No.'

'Learn fast. In the bag there's a needle and thread. You're going to have to stitch the wound.'

Marcus delved in the bag and found what was required. He hurriedly threaded the needle as blood was soaking through the shirt she had pressed against her arm.

'Start sewing. Pull the sides together as much as possible.' Wincing, he got her to remove the shirt and began stitching the gash together. She cried out in pain as the needle bit her skin.

'Keep still. Please.'

'It hurts.'

She pushed him away.

'Hit me. Knock me out.'

'I can't...'

'Do it or I swear on Kali's name that I will make your life a living hell.'

Marcus saw the look of determination through the pain. He sighed.

'Sorry about this.'

'Don't....'

She stopped talking as he punched her as hard as he could. Her head snapped to the side and she slumped against the wheel. He quickly checked she was alive before continuing his work.

Rami woke suddenly and sat up, crying out as a pain lanced through her arm and shoulder. She closed her eyes for a moment while the pain subsided before looking around. She was lying on the floor of a small room with only one rotten looking wooden door to the left and a broken window in the opposite wall.

It smelled musty and damp, like no one had lived in it for a while. A small table and broken chair were the only furniture. To her right, a fire burned in the small stone fireplace and above her a drip of rain was coming in from a hole in the roof.

Her shoulder had been bandaged and her staff and a knife were on the table. She sat up, the thin blanket that was covering her falling away and she shakily stood and walked to the table. Leaning against it she slipped her top off and slowly undid the dressing across her shoulder. The wound was an angry red but wasn't bleeding. The stitches were quite even so the scar that it would leave would be neat.

With a satisfied nod, she began to reapply the bandage but noticed that it was some white material torn into long strips. One of the strips had a delicate lace edging and she wondered where Marcus had got such a thing from. She heard footsteps and grabbed a knife as the only door to the building opened. Marcus stepped in and immediately covered his eyes.

'Please put some clothes on.'

She relaxed slightly.

'Why? Have you never seen a naked woman before?'

'Yes, but...'

'Where are we?'

Still covering his eyes, Marcus stepped forward and grabbed the blanket from the floor.

'Here. Please.'

Rami sighed angrily before she put the knife down and snatched the cover from him.

'Better?' she asked sarcastically as she wrapped it around herself.

He peered through his fingers before dropping his hand.

'Thank you.'

'Where are we?' she demanded again.

'I don't know exactly. I left the coach and carried you away. I found this shack. It looked disused so I decided to stop here. I'm going to head back to the coach and pick up the rest of our things.'

Rami lent on the table for support.

'We need to leave.'

Marcus shook his head.

'No. You need to rest. It was a deep cut on your shoulder and you lost quite a lot of blood. Look, you can hardly stand now.'

Rami closed her eyes and willed herself to stop shaking. Despite her best efforts she could feel her strength leaving her quickly.

'For god's sake, sit down before you fall down.'

She gritted her teeth and stood as straight as she could. Marcus sighed.

'You're as bloody stubborn as the Princess. Fine. Have it your way. I'll go and check the coast is clear.'

He shook his head and left her. As the door closed she sagged dramatically and almost fell onto the floor. She hadn't felt like this before. This weakness was disturbing. As was the kindness that the Captain was showing her. These were not things she was used to. Slowly she sank down, back against one of the table legs. Wincing as she put any pressure on her arm.

A while later Marcus returned. He knocked loudly.
'Are you decent?'
Rami shook her head and bit back a sharp retort.
'Come in.'
The door opened and Marcus came in carrying a small loaf and some cheese.
'If you insist on leaving now then at least eat.'
He went to sit by the fire, adding some more wood from the broken chair. She looked at his back for a moment.
'Captain.' said Rami, surprised by her own voice.
'What?'
'Maybe you are right. Maybe I should rest for a while.'
He turned back but didn't say anything. Instead he nodded once before turning back to the fire.

Marcus woke suddenly. He had fallen asleep. Carefully he drew his sword and looked round. Outside it was dark and rain was pouring through the hole in the roof.
'Rami?'

The girl was nowhere to be seen. Her weapons were gone but her bag and blanket were still there. Suddenly there was a loud caw from outside followed by a heavy thump. Marcus put his sword away and pressed his ear against the door. There were shuffling noises from the other side. He took a breath and cautiously opened the door.

It was hammering with rain outside and in the dull moonlight he could just make out a body lying on the wet ground. He dashed outside to find Rami who was curled up into a ball and visibly shaking. The wound in her shoulder had reopened and her top was slick with blood and rain. He gently reached out to her and she screamed when he touched her.

'It's me. Marcus. Calm down. What has happened?'

She looked up, eyes staring wildly and not really seeing him.

'They came for me.'

'Who?'

She grabbed his arm and held it tightly.

'The souls. They came for me. They...'

She broke down into uncontrollable tears. Not knowing what else to do he picked her up and carried her inside. She screamed and kicked out at him as he did but she seemed calm down as he sat her on the floor near the fire.

Gingerly he sat down and put his arm around her. She flinched at the touch and he froze, fearing an angry outburst but she relaxed after a second and he held her.

'It's going to be alright. They can't get you now. You're safe.'

The fire had burnt itself out and daylight was flooding in through the hole in the roof when Marcus woke up. He still sat on the floor with his arm around the girl. After she had stopped crying she had quickly fallen asleep in his arms. He twisted stiffly. His shirt was sticky with dried blood from her shoulder but it looked like it had stopped bleeding on its own. Carefully he tried to move.

She stirred before snapping awake, a hand reaching for a blade before she knew what she was doing. She cried out at the movement as it sent a shard of pain through her injured shoulder.

'You're safe. Calm down.'

Still slightly wild eyed, she pushed away from him.

'What're you doing?' her tone was sharp and questioning.

Marcus shook his head.

'Do you remember anything about last night?'

The girl looked down, ashamed and unable to meet his gaze.

'Yes.'

'Well then...' began Marcus before she interrupted him.

'Why did you do that?'

'Do what?'

'Why did you hold me? Why are you being so nice to me?'

'You looked like you needed someone.'

They were silent for a moment.

'Why did you summon the bird? And don't you dare tell me that it was necessary.' said Marcus eventually.

She shot him a hard glance.

'How do you...'

'You are not the first Daughter of Kali that I have met.'

'Nareema.' said Rami, looking down sadly.

Marcus nodded.

'Yes. She threatened to kill me when I found out.'

'But she didn't. Why was that? It is death for anyone who isn't a Daughter to see such things.'

'Molly.' he said simply.

'The girl with the power over the Stones?'

'Yes. My wife.'

Rami didn't say anything for a moment.

'If she trusts you with that then maybe I should too. She

specifically asked for me for this. I didn't even know she knew I existed.'

Rami snuggled into Marcus's shoulder again and drew her knees in to her chest.

'This is my first assignment. I have never been this far away from home before. It's not going well so far.'

'You can never prepare for what will be thrown at you.'

'I summoned the raven last night to contact Nareema. We can use the darkness to communicate over great distances but it was different last night. Something felt wrong and I don't know if she got my message. Then the souls came.'

Rami shuddered and went quiet.

'Did you get a reply?'

'No.'

Marcus nodded.

'We need to move today. '

She looked up at him and all he saw was a frightened girl.

'How old are you?'

'I'm fifteen.'

'Come, let me redress your shoulder and then we will get our things together and take our leave.'

'Good idea.'

Marcus stood.

'Eat something and I will be back in a minute.'

He returned a few minutes later with a rough bowl with water in it. Rami had moved to sit on the table and had eaten the bread and cheese Marcus had brought her yesterday.

'Let me have a look at your shoulder.'

She shifted around before stiffly slipping her top off her shoulders. It was stuck and Marcus gently washed the dried blood away before it came off. Even though she didn't make any noise, he knew that it hurt her. Carefully he peeled the previous dressing off and checked the wound.

'You've pulled some of the stitches. It seems to have stopped bleeding by itself but you're going to have to be careful.'

She nodded through gritted teeth. Carefully he took a white cloth from his bag and tore some more of it into strips. Rami noticed some more lace around the edges.

'Where did you get the cloth?'

'It's my wife's wedding dress. It was the longest and cleanest thing I could find.'

'Oh. She's going to be angry about that. I know I would be.'

Marcus began to wrap the makeshift bandage around her.

'She's probably going to be furious but I'll cross that bridge when I get to it.'

He fished the dressing and tied it off.

'There. That should do it. We'll check it again later but please be careful.'

Rami nodded and looked down.

'Why are you being so nice to me?'

'Why wouldn't I be?'

She sighed and shrugged slightly which elicited a sharp intake of breath.

'I don't know. I haven't been that nice to you.'

'Well let's start afresh then shall we?'

The girl smiled sadly.

'I've been taught for such a long time not to rely on anyone. It's a lesson that the order is very, very serious about. Trust no one, show no weaknesses and do not rely on other people.'

'Sometimes you have to.' replied Marcus.

'Yes. I'm learning that now.'

'How long have you been with them?'

'I was taken to them when I was four. My parents couldn't support me and my brothers so I was gifted to Kali for food. I haven't seen them since and I don't even know if they're still alive.'

She turned and began to pull her top back up.

'We're not allowed to leave until our training is finished unless it is with a senior sister and no contact is allowed with family.'

'Nareema went to her family.'

'She is different.'

'Why?'

'She just is. She finished her training when she was ten and completed her trial that very day. I've only just finished mine and I'm five years older than she was.'

'Trial?'

'It doesn't matter.' said the girl dismissively. 'Nareema is destined for great things and the order knows it. They are more lenient with her than with anyone else. Some say she is descended from the very Daughter that killed prince Malor '

'Who's he?'

'Do you know of the Stones?'

'Yes.'

'The prince is the man who murdered his father and took the Stones for himself. She killed him.'

'Oh.'

They fell into an uncomfortable silence for a moment before Rami stood and picked up her weapons.

'We must leave.'

Nareema bent to wake Molly. The sun was rising but dark clouds on the horizon promised heavy rain.

'Molly. Wake up. We have to move.'

The girl looked up and her, sleep falling away from her quickly as she saw the look on her face.

'What's the matter?'

'Something's wrong. I received a message from Rami last night. She is injured.'

'Who's Rami?'

'She is a Daughter of Kali. She is with Marcus. I

requested her help to protect him.'

'Is Marcus alright? Is he here?' asked Molly, concern in her voice and face.

'No. They are in England. I do not know if he is alright.'

'How...'

'We can use the darkness to communicate over a great distance but last night something was wrong. The darkness felt different. The souls were angry. I don't know what is going on but we have to get to England quickly.'

Molly jumped up and began packing her things, a sick feeling in her stomach.

'Do you know where they are?'

'No. They have left the Endurance and are heading to London. Other than that, I don't know.'

'I hope he's...' began Molly before she stopped talking suddenly. She cocked her head to the side as if listening to someone.

'You can do that?' she said eventually.

'Do what?' Asked Nareema.

Molly wasn't listening to her.

'Are you sure?'

Nareema sat down as Molly took out the bag containing the Stones.

'Alright. If you think you can then we should.'

'What are you going to do?'

Molly looked at her as if it was the most obvious thing in the world.

'I'm going to find Marcus.'

'How?'

'I'm going to use the Stones. Saali has touched him and knows what he looks like. I think they leave a little bit of themselves behind in every mind they touch. The more they touch them, the more there is.'

'How does it know Marcus?'

Molly looked down.

'From the ship when I...'

Nareema nodded.

'I understand. Just be careful.'

Molly nodded and took out the sapphire. Holding it in her hand she sat down and closed her eyes. The Princess watched as the girl was surrounded by a glowing blue nimbus, the air taking on a charged and oily feel. There was a flash and Molly let out a slow breath before slowly slumping to the side and lying still.

Nareema jumped up to check she was still alive. Her breathing was regular but she was cold. The Princess gently covered her with a blanket and the sat down next to her to wait.

Molly felt herself rise from her body. She hovered for a second, floating above the field and saw Nareema rush over to her prone form and check it. A moment later a hazy figure coalesced in the air next to her. It didn't speak but raised a hand, palm outward, to Molly. She nodded and raised her own hand, placing her own palm against the figures.

There was a moment of cold so intense it hurt as the spectral mist flooded into her body before they suddenly began rushing across the early morning sky.

The speed was breath-taking as the land beneath them flashed past in a blur. In a second they had passed over towns and villages and then the sea.

'Where are we going?' asked Molly.

The reply formed itself in her head without seeming to pass through her ears.

'To find our brother.'

'What about Marcus?'

There was no answer as Molly barrelled across the waves. Ahead some huge white cliffs loomed and she thought she was going to crash into them. At the last instant, she swooped up and over them. She headed north for a while until Molly saw ten horses and all but two were ridden by more armed men.

Of these, one rode in the middle of the armed men and the other at the head of the column. Molly grew concerned as she slowed and swooped low. The voice in her head spoke.

'They cannot see us.'

Somehow that didn't make her feel any better. The man in the middle was Tobias. He looked tired and had his hands bound to the pommel of his saddle. At the head rode Tong Li. His right hand was missing, and had been replaced by a crude hooked blade.

As Molly flew close he suddenly stopped his horse and reached into his shirt. Pulling out the ruby he looked at it and then around quickly before ordering his men to dismount. They swiftly did as they were told and formed a cordon around him and Tobias.

'He knows we're here.' said Molly.

'No. Takahn does. We should leave.'

Without another word they soared high and then headed south.

'Take me to Marcus.'

'That is not wise.'

'And looking for Tong Li is? Take me to Marcus now.' replied Molly angrily.

As she spoke her flight became rough and she suddenly began to fall. She screamed as the ground began rushing towards her.

'Don't fight my control. Just let it be.'

Molly took in a panicked breath as the Stone regained control.

'Please take me to Marcus.'

There was no reply from the stone but her course altered until they were headed west. They flew fast for a few minutes until they found a small shack in field on the edge of a wood. Heading across the field were half a dozen

armed men. They looked rough and carried muskets.
'Where is he?'
'Think of him.'
She concentrated for a moment.
'He's inside.'

Her words turned into a scream as she suddenly swooped towards the roof of the house at breakneck speed. She flung her arms in front of her face as the roof rushed to meet her but in an instant she was through it as if it were not there.

'Warn me before you do something like that again please.' she said.

She found herself in a small room. Marcus was there with a young girl. Molly took in the scene and quickly spoke.

'There are six men. All with guns. Run. Head north. Tong Li is going that way so we must too. I will find you.'

She had barely finished speaking before she was unceremoniously dragged back through the roof and into the sky. The world span dizzyingly as she shot back the way she had come at terrifying speeds. Within a few seconds, she saw the field and the ruins farmhouse come into view and she plunged down to slam into her prone body.

Nareema was still sat near the fire when Molly suddenly jerked violently and took in a heaving, gasping breath. The girl scrambled to her hands and knees before being sick in a great wave. The Princess rushed to her side.

'Are you alright?'

Molly couldn't answer as she was sick again. Strangely, the vomit was tinged blue for a second but this disappeared in the blink of an eye and Nareema wondered if she'd seen it at all.

Molly retched once more before sitting back and wiping her mouth with the back of her hand. Nareema handed her a flask of water. The girl took a swig to swill her mouth out before spitting it out into the ground.

'Are you alright? What happened?'

Molly took another mouthful of water.

'I've felt better.'

The Princess waited until the girl was ready. Molly let out a long breath and then stood up.

'I found him. He's in trouble. There were men with guns. They were in a shack near a forest, I told him to go north but I don't know if he heard me.'

'What about Rami?'

'She was there but I don't know how badly she was hurt. She was standing if that's any help.'

'What about you? Are you alright.'

'I think so. It was all so fast. We saw Tong Li too. He was headed north. He had uncle Tobias with him.'

'Why did you go looking for him?' asked Nareema angrily.

'I didn't have a choice. Saali was in control. He had armed men with him.'

'Did he see you?'

'No. I don't think I was really there but he knew. I think the Fire Stone knew and he felt it. I think the Stones are getting stronger.'

'How so?'

'I don't know. Something is coming.'

'You said the same thing to Marcus. You told him that he was coming.'

Molly looked down.

'I'm scared. I don't know what to do. I'm afraid for Marcus. He's in trouble and I can't help him. Tong Li has Tobias and I don't know where they're going either.'

Nareema put her hands on Molly's shoulders.

'It will be alright. Rami is with Marcus. She knows her duty. We will find Tobias and the other Stones.'

Molly sighed.

'How can you be so sure?'

'I can't. A friend told me not long ago that there is no point thinking any other way. Let's go. We'll catch up to Mr Davis and then get to England.'

Molly nodded.

'It will be alright sister. Do not worry.'

'We have to move.' said Rami.

She turned to go but Marcus stood stock still, staring off into the distance. She put her hand on his arm.

'Come on.'

He snapped out of his daze.

'Did you hear that?'

'Hear what?'

He shook his head.

'There are six of them. We have to go north.'

'How...'

He grabbed her hand and headed towards the window.

'Just do as I ask. Please. Are you ready for this?'

She looked like she would protest but after a second she just nodded.

'Good.'

'Quickly. Head to the woods on the edge of the field. Don't look back. I'll be right behind you.'

Marcus threw their bags out of the small window and Rami climbed after them, swinging her legs over the sill and before dropping lightly to the ground. He heaved the table up onto its end before pushing against the door. There were shouts from outside as the men heard the noise but he didn't wait around to find out what they wanted.

Quickly he swung himself out of the window and scrambled to his feet as the door opened with a crash, but he was already sprinting across the field towards the woods. As he ran, there was a shout from the shack and the crack of a musket.

He feared no matter how hard he ran the bullet would chase him down and that would be it. He'd never get to see

Molly again. There was another shot which kicked up a puff of dirt to his left. Ahead of him, Rami had reached the trees. She turned and shouted at him.

'Move!'

He redoubled his efforts as volley of bangs sounded from behind him. He heard the first bullet whistle past his ear, its passing sounding loud against the morning air. The second caught him in the leg. Suddenly, and unable to stop himself, he staggered forward. His momentum carrying him for a few feet before he crashed down hard into the ground. He looked up to see Rami running back towards him.

'No. Run. Get out of here.'

She hesitated for a second before the ground around her erupted into a flurry of musket shot.

'Run!'

She turned and headed back into the trees. Marcus rolled onto his back as the first of his attackers reached him. They were scruffily dressed but had the look of fighting men. Marcus struggled to sit up but the man kicked him in the leg where the bullet had hit, sending a screaming wave of pain through him. He cried out as another man arrived. He pulled the first man back.

'Alive remember? We don't get paid if he's dead.'

'What about the girl?'

The second man smiled.

'Didn't say nuffin' about the girl. If you can find her she's yours.'

The man grinned evilly before heading off into the trees. Marcus tried to sit up once more, blood covering his leg.

'What do you want with me?' he asked through gritted teeth.

'Damned if I know.' was the reply as the man raised his musket and brought the stock crashing down against the side of Marcus's head.

## Chapter Nineteen

The kindness of strangers

Rami watched from the tree line as the man smashed his gun into Marcus and he flopped back to the ground. She couldn't do anything to help him as the other man was running towards the woods and behind him came the other four. She cursed silently and turned away into the trees.

A minute later she heard him, his tread heavy in the leaves and underbrush. He was unwashed, wearing a patched and grubby shirt and trousers. He had his musket held across his chest.

'Come out girl. I won't hurt you. We're just taking your friend for a little trip that's all. Come out and you can come too.'

He walked further into the woods.

'Come on you little bitch. Show yourself or when I find you I swear...'

Rami watched him carefully move beneath the tree she has climbed. He stopped directly below her as he found the discarded packs containing their belongings. He bent down, and with a cry she dropped onto his back from above with a knife in each hand. The first knife plunged deep into his shoulder and he shouted loudly, rearing up and trying to dislodge her. She hung on to the blade for grim death, the man floundering wildly.

He stepped back and slammed her hard into a tree and she almost fell, cursing loudly as she felt the wound in her shoulder open again and flood with the wetness of blood. He stumbled forward and span violently to his right, sending her flying. He dragged the knife from his shoulder and cast it into the woods.

'You bitch. You'll pay for that.'

He drew a heavy looking sword and advanced towards

her. She held the remaining knife in her hand and dropped into a crouch. He shouted and lunged with the blade but she was already moving towards him. His momentum carried him forward and at the last second, she dived to the right, slashing out with her knife. The blade entered on his left side and effortlessly cut through his stomach. She rose to a crouch and faced him once more. He staggered for a moment, turning to look at her, his sword falling from his grip.

His hands moved to his stomach as he desperately tried to hold his insides in. She shifted as he stepped towards her once more, a look of complete shock on his face before he toppled onto the leafy ground. Taking no chances, Rami leapt on his back and wrapped a hand in his greasy hair to drag his head back and slit his throat. She wiped the knife on his clothes before grabbing her things and heading quickly away.

She had gone no more than a mile before the woods opened up into an expanse of rolling fields and hills. She inwardly cursed as she touched her shoulder. It was bleeding freely. She had to do something about that. Looking around she could make out a small village in the distance, framed by a couple of small hills on one of which sat a large house. Gritting her teeth, she headed towards it.

Marcus woke suddenly. His head was pounding, while his leg was a ball of pain and he tried to sit up but his arms were securely bound behind him. In the end, he just settled to see where he was. It was dark and he was lying on the ground. Nearby was a campfire, around which sat five men. They all had their backs to him. He could hear them talking.

'Where are we takin' him?'
'Liverpool.'
'Liverpool? All the way there? That's practically another

country!'

'That's where we're meeting the for'n bloke. That's where we'll get paid.'

'I say we kill him and be done with it. That for'n one gives me the shivers. He's a shifty bastard that one.'

One of the men glanced round.

'Oh, he's awake.'

He stood and walked over to Marcus.

'Comfy?' he sneered.

This got a laugh from his companions. He drove his boot into Marcus stomach. He doubled up and gasped for breath as the man knelt next to him.

'Where's the little bitch what was with you? She killed one of our mates. She's gonna suffer for that.'

Marcus couldn't get enough breath to reply. The man lent in and grabbed Marcus by the hair, hauling his head up so he could look in the man's grubby face. His foul breath washed over him as he spoke.

'Good job for you that the for'n bugger wants you alive and he's payin' a lot of money for it.'

'We'll be there in a couple o' days. Be a good boy and do as you're told or I'll kill you.'

He raised his voice and shouted at the night.

'You hear that you little bitch. Try anything and he dies.'

He sneered once more before letting Marcus slump back down and heading back to the fire.

Rami stumbled against the wall of the blacksmith's. She could barely stand up as she carefully pushed the door open and fell inside. The forge was empty but warm, the coals having been banked for the night. She pulled herself up and found a length of iron about two feet long before thrusting it deep into the coals and hauling on the bellows to pour air into the fire. She could only manage a few pumps before she fell to the ground in exhaustion.

With the last of her strength she crawled to the furnace and pulled her top and the bandages from her shoulder. Gritting her teeth, she reached up and grabbed the iron rod. The end glowed a dull red and, taking a deep breath, Rami pushed the glowing metal against her skin. The pain was incredible as the hot iron cauterised the wound. She screamed in agony as the smell of burning flesh filled her nostrils. All her strength left her and the metal rod hit the cobbled floor with a clunk as she passed out.

Rami woke, reaching for a knife as her focus swam in to see three faces staring at her. She moved back, pressing herself against the wall of the forge in fright.
'Calm down lass.'
The man who had spoken was knelt in front of her and behind him were stood two concerned looking women, one older the other about the same age as her. The man was well built with thick brown hair and a kindly face that was partially hidden by a shaggy beard. He picked up the now cool iron bar with large hands and looked at it and then at her still bare shoulder. The wound was an angry red.
'I won't ask what you're doing in my forge. I can guess. You're screaming woke damn near half the village. What's a girl like you want to do something like that to herself?'
Rami didn't answer but reached up to touch the burn mark. Letting out a long and painful breath as her fingers probed the injury. She sat back and took in a few steadying breaths.
'It was necessary.'
He looked back at the women before speaking again.
'I don't know what sort of trouble you're in or where you're from but we don't need anything like that round here. Times is difficult as it is without...'
'William Stratton! She's hurt. Go and find something useful to do.' admonished the older of the two women.
'Martha...'

She pointed at the door with a determined look on her face. The man stood and took a last look at Rami before he shook his head and left, leaving the women alone. They eyed her with a mixture of curiosity and suspicion. Rami hauled herself unsteadily to her feet. Her legs were like lead and she felt light headed.

'I have to go.'

She took a step but stumbled and fell to her knees. The older woman was next to her in an instant. Long brown hair hung loose around her shoulders and soft hands with a caring look from her brown eyes. She pressed her palm against Rami's forehead.

'You've got a fever. You're not going to get anywhere like that.'

'I have to.'

Once more she dragged herself upright. The older woman moved with her and she got as far as the door before her strength left her once more.

'Grace, go and make up the spare room. Then get your father and get him to come back here.'

The younger woman nodded.

'Yes mum.'

She turned and quickly headed out of the forge as Rami slid down to a sitting position, leaning against a wooden workbench.

The darkness. It was all around her. It stretched off into unfathomable blackness in all directions. There was a noise from behind her and she span, but there was nothing there. The noise again sounded from behind her. It was a low moan and whispering. She turned again but there wasn't anything there.

'Who's there?' she shouted.

Her voice was muted with no echo in the vast space. More whispers joined the first, growing into a wall of sound that washed over her from all directions. She span again, her heart beating hard as a clammy hand touched her neck. Cold fingers brushed her skin from behind again.

She reached for a knife but found she had none. Breathing quickly with fear she turned once more to come face to face with an army of spectral figures. The glowed with an unnatural, sickly green light.

The closest of them was the man she had killed in the woods. His skin had begun to rot, revealing bone and muscle beneath his torn and tatty clothes. He smiled evilly and as she watched, his lips sloughed away, leaving a grin of bone. He began to laugh. It was a horrible sound. A coughing mixture of humourless noise.

Around him the army began to laugh as well, their noise growing into a deafening cacophony. She put her hands over her ears as it grew, screaming as it blasted her senses.

Suddenly it stopped and the ravaged figures lent in all around her. Their cold dead hands touching her all over. She span around, her heart pounding with fear in her chest and breath escaping in short misty puffs. As one, the spectral figures spoke. Their mouths moving in unison, but there was only the voice of the man from the woods, uttering quietly from hundreds of mouths.

'He's going to get you, bitch.'

Rami screamed as suddenly the army moved, pushing in on top of her from all sides, smothering her with their cold and foul bodies. She screamed again and again as they began to crush the life from her.

She sat up suddenly, a gentle hand on her arm steadying her.

'It was only a dream. You're safe.'

Rami looked up, still breathing hard and covered in sweat. She was in a bed with the young woman she had seen in the forge, Grace, was sat next to her. Grace had her mothers' brown eyes but her fathers' kindly face. She pushed a lock of her hair out of her eyes, tucking it behind her ear. Rami slumped back down and Grace put her hand on her forehead. It was cool against her skin and she shuddered involuntarily, the dream still fresh in her mind.

'Your fever has broken. Mum said I should get her when you woke up.'

She stood and left and Rami looked around. The room was plain with simple wooden furniture. She sat up again and threw the covers back to find out she was dressed in a plain nightgown. Swinging herself out of bed she took a deep breath. Her body felt heavy and weak. Gritting her teeth, she stood as the door opened once more. The older woman came in, followed by Grace.

'What're you doing up?' she asked.

'I have to go.'

'You're in no fit state to go anywhere. You've been asleep for four days.'

Rami looked at her in horror.

'Four days? Marcus...'

'He'll wait for you.'

'No. You don't understand. I have to go.'

She took a step but her legs didn't want to work properly and she sat down heavily on the bed. The older woman came over to her.

'You need to rest. Trust me. Grace will look after you. Now be a good girl and get back in bed.'

Much to her own surprise, she did as she was told. The woman pulled the covers back over her.

'Good. Now you need to eat something. When did you last have a proper meal?'

Rami shrugged, groaning as her shoulder flexed.

'I don't remember.'

The woman looked at her sternly and Rami looked down.

'Wait here.'

She turned and headed away, calling for Grace as she went. Grace smiled and followed her out of the room.

Rami sat back in bed. Four days! What had happened to Marcus? Was he still alive? She'd let him down. More importantly she had failed the Daughters. Failed her trial. As this thought began to sink in, the door opened and Grace came back in carrying a small tray.

'Mum said you should eat this.'

She handed the tray to Rami and sat on the bed. The tray held a small bowl of steaming porridge. Rami stirred it with the spoon but made no move to eat. She didn't feel like it.

'You've got to eat.'

'I don't want to.'

'Please. You need to get your strength back.'

Rami looked at her and nodded and began to eat the porridge. Grace watched her for a moment.

'What's your name?'

'Rami.'

'I'm Grace. Where are you from?'

'India.'

'You're a long way from home.'

'Yes.'

'I've never been further than the next village.'

Rami did answer her.

'Who's Marcus? You talked about him while you had the fever. Is he your...' she shrugged and looked down, tucking her hair behind her ear again.

'No. I was supposed to protect him. I failed.'

Rami looked up at her and put the spoon down.

'How were you supposed to protect him? What happened?'

'It doesn't matter. I failed. That is all there is to it.'

'Oh.'

'Will you find my clothes please. Where are my weapons?'

'Mum has your clothes. She's washed and mended them. Father has your other things. Why do you need so many?

I've never seen a girl with knives. None that I know anyway. I've never seen a girl with a tattoo either.'
'They are what I am.'
Grace looked at her puzzled.
'Why?'
Rami didn't have an answer for her. They lapsed into silence. Rami pushed the tray away.
'I have to go. I need to find Marcus.'
She tried to get up but her strength was not there. Weakness was not something she was used to and she shouted in frustration. Grace stood up.
'Please get some rest. I'll get your clothes but you'll have to ask father for your other things. They're in the forge.'

Rami woke the next day as the sun was beginning to break across the horizon. There was the soft patter of rain on the window and the air smelt fresh. She lay still for a moment before she closed her eyes and took a deep breath. Letting it out slowly she swung herself out of bed and stood. She still felt weak but her legs were able to support her without giving way like they had the day before.
Grace had brought her clothes and bag up the evening before and had sat with her for a while. Rami sat back down and stretched, wincing at the flare of pain in her shoulder. It hurt but it wasn't as bad as it had been. She reached into her bag and took out a pot of ointment. Carefully she applied some of the salve to the wound gritting her teeth as she did so.
The pain was only temporary, she told herself as she remembered the lessons that had been hammered into her. The stain of failure is forever.
She wiped her hands on her nightgown before letting out a long slow breath. Reaching into the bag again she took out the black scarf and ran it through her fingers. It was silk with a swirling pattern printed on it. Every Daughter was given one when they started their trial. It was their Ganta.

They carried it with them as a reminder of what they were trying to become.

When they returned to the monastery they were blindfolded using it and lead before the council where they would learn their fate. Success meant you were allowed to become a true Daughter of Kali. The Ganta was removed and your eyes allowed to see the light. To fail meant death and you would never see the light again. A tear ran down her face as she ran it through her fingers. She had failed. The light would never be hers.

Rami looked up suddenly as the door opened and Grace came in. Her smile fell as she saw the look on the Rami's' face.

'What is it?'

'It is nothing.' said Rami as she wiped her eyes and crammed the scarf in the bag.

Grace looked at her for a moment but didn't say anything else. Instead she sat on the bed next to her.

'It's the village fair in a few days. Would you like to come?'

Rami shook her head.

'I cannot. I have to go. I need to find Marcus.'

'Please. You're not well enough to go traipsing all across the country.'

'I have to.'

'One more day. Please?'

Grace put a hand on hers.

'There's not many girls my age around here. It's nice to have someone to talk to.'

Rami looked at her.

'I'm not much for conversation.'

'But you've travelled and seen things. You've come all the way from India. That's half way across the world! I couldn't do that. I'm probably never going to see more than the next village. I'll be married in a few years and that'll be that.'

'Is that a bad thing?'
Grace looked down and spoke quietly.
'I suppose not.'
Rami stood and stretched, wincing at her shoulder.
'Where're you going?'
'Right now? I'm going to get dressed and see your father. I need to be up and about. I have lost too much time already.'

Rami dressed and went downstairs with Grace by her side, feeling stronger with every step. They went into the kitchen to find her mother at the stove. She turned as the girls entered.
'You look better.'
Rami nodded.
'I'm feeling it. Thank you.'
The woman walked over and placed her hand on her forehead.
'You're still a bit warm.'
'I'm going to get some fresh air.'
'Don't get cold. Grace, go with her.'
'Yes mum.'
The girls headed outside, the rain had stopped and the yard was wet. Grace took Rami's arm and she tensed, pulling away. Grace looked at her.
'I'm sorry.' said Rami. 'Physical contact like this is not something I am used to.'
'Why not?'
'I have lead a solitary life so far. All of my kind do.'
'Your kind?'
Rami shook her head.
'It doesn't matter. Please take me to the forge.'
'This way.'
Grace led her across the yard to a stone building with large double doors. They were flung open and the sound of metal on metal rang out from within. Rami moved away

from Grace and went to the door. William was working hard, hammering a piece of metal that was glowing red hot.

He ignored her for a moment until the metal had cooled before he straightened and wiped his hands in his apron.

'You're up then.'

'Yes.' replied Rami from the doorway.

He looked at her critically for a moment.

'I suppose you want your things back?'

'Yes please.'

'They're over there.'

He pointed to a workbench on the far side of the forge and Rami headed over.

'I've cleaned and sharpened them for you.' he said as he came up behind her. 'Though why a girl like you needs so many weapons I don't know.'

He reached past her and picked up the metal tube.

'This is a piece of work. Must've been some skill that went into making this. Damn near had my eye out the first time I picked it up.'

Rami gently took it from him.

'It is old. I am the latest of a long line to have the privilege of using it. When I am gone it will be passed to someone new.'

She stepped back a few paces and with a flick of her wrist the pole extended, the foot long blades at each end glittered in the firelight. Slowly she began spinning it around her body, the speed increasing with each movement. It sang through the warm air of the forge and Rami began to add in kicks and spins of her own as the weapon danced around her body. She grunted with pain as she span it over her head before bringing the blade down to stop suddenly an inch from the cobbled floor.

In the doorway behind her Grace was stood open-mouthed and her father was regarding her with interest. Rami was breathing hard but flicked her wrist to bring the pole back in again before straightening.

'Impressive.' said William. 'Grace says you're from India.'

'Yes.'

'Is that where you learnt to do that?'

'Yes.'

William regarded her for a moment more

'Who's Marcus?'

'A man I was supposed to protect. He's probably dead now. Which is my fault.'

'But you don't know?'

'No. I will have to find out for sure.'

The blacksmith turned back to the forge for a second before looking straight at her.

'You're welcome to stay for as long as you need but I expect you to do as you're told and you pitch in with the chores. And I don't want those in the house.' he pointed to Rami's weapons. 'They can stay in the forge for now.'

Rami looked at him.

'Why are you helping me?'

He turned around and picked the piece of cooling metal up with a pair of heavy tongs, before thrusting it back in the hot coals.

'You need it.'

Rami watched him for a moment before she placed the knives back on the bench and went outside. Grace was beside her in an instant.

'How did you learn to do that? It was amazing.' she asked excitedly.

Rami smiled tightly.

'I've practice for a long time.'

'What else can you do? Will you teach me?'

'You don't want to learn to do what I do.'

Grace looked at her.

'Why not?'

Rami took a deep breath and then began to walk away. Grace hurried after her. They walked for a while in silence, absentmindedly following a winding path out of the village until they came across a small river. Rami sat down next to it and Grace sat next to her. The girls stared at the water for a while.

'I kill. It is what I have trained all if my life to do.' said Rami eventually.

'Why?'

Rami shrugged, wincing slightly at the movement.

'Things are different in India. My family was very poor. They couldn't support me and my brothers. I was taken and gifted to Kali in return for food. I was four. Since then I have been trained and educated in all sorts of things. But most of all I have been taught to kill. It is what I do. What I am.' she looked down.

'I'm a blacksmith's daughter. I spend my days helping mum around the house and running errands. It's not exciting.'

'Neither is what I do. This is my first time away from my home. It's scary.'

'But you've travelled. Seen places I'll only ever hear about.'

Rami shrugged and looked around.

'Why would you want to travel? You live in a beautiful country. The grass is green, the water is clear. It's perfect.'

'But boring.'

'Killing people is not fun. It is hard.'

'How many people have you killed?'

Rami thought.

'Six.'

'Oh. Why?'

'It came down to a case of me or them. I won.'

The girls were silent for a moment.

'You could be something else if you wanted.' said Grace.

'So could you.'

Rami sighed and stood up.

'Please don't tell your father.'

'He's not stupid.'
'Then why let me stay?'
'Don't know.'
'I'll be leaving in a day or two. I have to find Marcus. One way or another.'
'Why is he important?'
'He was my trial. I was supposed to protect him. He saved my life twice and I failed him.'
'Trail?'
'My initiation into the sisterhood. It doesn't matter.'
'Come on. Lets' get home.'
They stood and Grace took her arm as they began walking back to the village.
'You weren't in any fit state to do anything when we found you. How you managed to do that to your shoulder I don't know.'
'A man in a horse tried to kill me with a sword. Marcus called out at the last moment and I managed to get out of the way. Mostly.'
'Oh. I meant the hot iron. That must have hurt.'
'It did hurt. But it was the best I could do at the time.'
'It was brave.'
Rami shook her head.
'It was necessary.'
She went quiet.
'Maybe I can show you something after all.'
'Really?'
'Yes'

Molly heaved over the side of the boat. It was a good deal smaller than the Endurance and the crossing to England was proving to be rough. Waves and heavy driving rain tossed the small craft around. Nareema stood nearby, holding on to the single mast but seemingly oblivious to the lurching movement. Davis was below decks, sleeping, although how anyone could sleep in this weather Molly didn't know.

The boat crested a wave and dropped what seemed like a hundred feet causing Molly's stomach to flip up to her chest. There was a soft hand on her back and she glanced round.

'We'll be there soon.'

She retched again and wiped her mouth with the back of her hand.

'I hate ships. I don't like the ocean and I don't like...' she went quiet for a second, listening intently.

'Well yes, I could do something about it but I don't think that I should.'

Nareema watched her have a conversation with herself. It was strange and even though she'd seen it before, it still didn't sit well.

'I don't care what you think. I'll be fine once we get off the water.' continued Molly.

Across the deck, several sailors were giving her odd looks. Nareema glared at them until they went back to their duties.

'Alright, alright. Stop going on.'

She reached into her suit to take out the sapphire. The Princess laid a hand on her arm to stop her and shook her head. Molly glared at her, a bright blue flash of anger flared behind her eyes.

'No. You are in charge, remember.'

Molly took a deep breath and nodded before standing up.

'They're always there. In my head. Sometimes it's hard not to listen.'

'You're doing well. They have power but so do you.'

'If you say so.'

'I do.'

'How long until we get to England?'

'The Captain thinks it'll be another couple of hours yet. The weather isn't helping our progress.'

The boat lurched again and Molly dived for the railing once more.

They put into a port a few hours later and Molly had never felt so grateful to be on dry land. Quickly they found some run down lodgings near the harbour, owned by a foul smelling man with rotten teeth. He leered as he showed them the rooms but a look from the Princess sent him scurrying away. They took two rooms, the women sharing one and Davis having the other.
'These will do.'
'Couldn't we find somewhere nicer?'
'Probably but I want to stay out of the way. I've got a feeling Tong Li has eyes everywhere.'
Molly brushed some dust and dirt from a tatty wooden chair before sitting down.
'Alright. But can we at least go and find somewhere nice to have something to eat?'

Molly stood outside a reputable looking jewellers shop. Nareema was stood next to her.
'Are you sure this is the place?'
'I think so.' said Molly.
The Princess nodded.
'Be careful. I will see you later.'
They hugged and Nareema headed off into the bustle of the town. Molly cocked her head.
'Yes. I told you. I think this is where we need to be.'
With that, she entered the shop. The owner gave her a smile as she came in. The shop was tidy and well-kept with rings and necklaces decorating glass cabinets all around. The owner was a smartly dressed man in his early forties with slicked hair and well groomed moustache. A pair of thin wireframe glasses was perched on the end of his nose.

'How can I help you miss?'

She looked around at the expensive jewellery surround her.

'I need someone to make me something in silver.'

'What did you have in mind? A ring for a loved one? A locket perhaps?'

She stepped close to the counter.

'No, this...'

She reached up and gently touched the side of his face. He went rigid for a second as if he'd been shocked. Molly let him go.

'Can you do that?' she asked.

He nodded dumbly.

'Yes. How did you...'

'You don't need to know. How long will it take?'

'A week?'

Molly nodded.

'Please hurry.'

She turned to go and he came out from behind the counter, following her to the door.

'Who are you?'

Molly looked at him, her eyes flashing blue then green.

'No one important. I will see you in a week.'

When Molly got back, there was no sign of either of her companions. She sat on the rickety bed and took out the sapphire. Cradling it gently in her hand she closed her eyes.

'Show me Marcus.'

Again she felt herself rise above her body and then in a flash, she was gone but here was no flying this time. She just seemed to snap from one place to another but the disorientation still left her reeling. Her essence floated above a port. There were ships of all shapes and sizes and it was towards one of these that she drifted.

'Where are we?'

There was no reply for a moment before she snapped again to appear on the deck of the largest ship. Marcus was there, alongside Tobias with Tong Li and five men stood nearby. Both looked tired and beaten and were in chains. There was blood on Marcus leg and it was tied in a makeshift bandage.

'Marcus.... No!'

He looked up as if he had heard her but before she could say anything else she heard Tong Li. He was shouting at the men.

'I told you I wanted him unharmed.'

'He tried to run...' began on of them.

The leader of the group glared at him and he shut up.

'You wanted him, here he is. You didn't tell me that there was going to be a crazy girl with him too! She killed some of my men.'

'An oversight. Princess Vashti is more resourceful than I anticipated.'

The leader looked at his men.

'We want more money. You didn't say anything about her.'

Tong Li turned his back on them.

'More money? Didn't I pay you well enough?'

The man hesitated for a second before Tong Li moved. Like lightning, he span and slashed his crude hooked hand across the man's throat. The serrated blade ripping out his jugular without a pause. His hands went to his neck but he was already dead, blood gushing out of the deep wound as he fell to his knees. Tong Li looked at the other four.

'Anyone else wish to renegotiate?'

They stared at him in shock before they shook their heads.

'Good.'

He prodded the body with his toe.

'Get rid of that and then get out of my sight.'

He turned and then paused, looking straight at the space

where Molly floated. She was completely shocked by the casual violence.

Tong Li smiled.

'I know you're there Mrs Kane. I can feel you. The ruby can feel you. Enjoying the show? We are heading to get the Water Stone. If you want to see them alive you will follow me. Give me the Earth and Air and I will let them live.' he smiled cruelly and held up the blood covered hook. 'Probably.'

Before he could speak again, she snapped back and fell heavily into her own body which was lying in the floor of their room. She dashed to the window, throwing it open a second before she was sick. Marcus!

Nareema opened the door to their room and found Molly frantically packing.

'Where are you going?'

'Marcus. He's got Marcus. He's going to kill him. I need to follow them.'

The Princess looked at her.

'Slow down. What's going on.'

Molly looked at her, a panicked look on her face.

'He's got Marcus. He's going to kill him.'

'Molly.' snapped Nareema. 'Calm down and tell me what is going on.'

The girl burst into tears.

'Tong Li has got Marcus. I wanted to check that he was alright. I was worried.'

'You used the Stones?'

She nodded.

'It took me to a ship. Marcus was there with some men. Tong Li killed one of them. Oh, Nareema. He's hurt. Been shot I think.'

'What about Rami?'

'I didn't see her.'

'Then what happened?'

'Tong Li knew I was there. It must be something to do with the Stones. He said that if I didn't follow him to the Water Stone then he was going to kill them. Marcus and Tobias.'

'We'll find them.'

Molly disintegrated into a fit of sobbing and Nareema pulled her close and held her.

'It's going to be alright. Did you see the silversmith?'

The girl nodded.

'He said it would take a week.'

'We need to wait for that but I need to leave you and find Rami. I need you to promise me that you won't go after him on your own. Wait for the silversmith. Will you do that for me?'

'Yes.'

'Do you promise?'

'Yes. I promise.'

'Good. I will bring Rami back here and we will find out what happened.'

Molly wiped her face.

'How do you know she isn't dead?'

'She isn't. I would know. I fear that she has failed her trial and is hiding. I thought better of her than that.'

'Trial?'

Nareema sighed.

'Each Daughter of Kali is given a trial once they are deemed to have completed their training. It is their initiation into the sisterhood. If they succeed then they are welcomed. We call it the deliverance from the darkness.'

'If they fail?'

The Princess stayed silent.

'You kill them don't you? Is that what you are going to do to Rami?'

'If she has failed then it will be as our laws state.'

Molly pushed away from her.

'You can't. I don't believe that she failed on purpose. There's something wrong. You can't kill her for that.'

'It is not my choice. I will do what is necessary.'

'Please don't. You said that your blade was mine to command. I don't want to command you but please don't kill her. Even if she is hiding it is only because she's scared. I know what's that's like.'

Nareema looked at her and took a deep breath.

'If that is what you wish then it will be so.'

'Thank you.'

'I need to go. Please wait here. If you go anywhere make sure you take Davis with you.'

'I will.'

They hugged briefly before the Princess picked up her sword and headed out of the room, leaving Molly alone.

The next afternoon the girls returned to the sunny spot near the river. A few trees were dotted near the bank. Rami stopped and looked around.

'This will do.'

She reached into the small bag she was carrying and took out a wrapped bundle.

'What's that?' asked Grace.

Rami smiled at her and unrolled the black cloth to reveal half a dozen small knives. Grace looked on as Rami took three of them and weighed them in her hand for a second before throwing them in quick succession at a nearby tree. The blades thudded into the wood in a tight group. She smiled and removed another knife which she handed to Grace.

'Your turn.'

The girl looked at the blade in her hand. It was solid steel and about six inches long.

'I can't do that!'

'Yes you can. Give it a go.'

Grace bit her lip and held the knife in her hand.

'Hold it by the blade.'

Rami moved behind her and took her hand, showing her how to hold the blade and the action she used to throw it.

'Go on.'

Grace set herself and with an overhand throw, sent the knife whistling into the grass, missing the tree by a good three feet.

'Have another go.' said Rami handing her another knife.

They practised for a couple of hours until Grace could hit the tree nine times out of ten.

'Tomorrow I will show you how to defend yourself without a weapon.' said Rami as she carefully wrapped the knives up and put them away.

As the girls prepared to go there were loud voices from across the field. Grace looked up.

'It's Edward. Come on.'

'Who's Edward?'

'He's the son of Sir Henry at the big house. He's a bully. I don't like him. Please. Come on.'

Rami looked across the grass to see three young men coming their way. They were all well dressed and shouting and joking loudly. As they neared the girls they stopped and gawped for a moment before coming over.

'Please, let's go.' said Grace.

Rami made no move to leave as the men approached.

'Grace.' shouted the closest of them.

He quite tall with dark hair and an unshaven chin. He was wearing a white shirt, unbuttoned to his middle with cream trousers and black boots.

Grace turned to go, but he stepped forward and grabbed her arm roughly.

'Where are you going? Haven't you got a kiss for me?'

He span her around and tried to kiss her but she pushed him away to the amusement of his friends.

'You're drunk Edward.'

He glared at her and reeled her back in.

'Give me a kiss.'

'No.'

He wrapped his hand in her hair and mashed his lips against hers.

'She said no.'

Edward pushed Grace away and she fell on her bottom in the grass. He smiled cruelly at Rami.

'It speaks! So you're the monkey then. Can you do any other tricks.'

His friends laughed, one taking a swig from a bottle.

'None that you'd like.'

Edward moved forward and looked Rami over. There was a leer in his smile and mischief in his eyes.

'You're quite pretty for a monkey. What say you show me how respectful you are to your betters like Grace is. Isn't that right Grace?'

He turned to her and laughed, Grace couldn't meet his eyes. He reached out to touch Rami and with a move like a striking snake she snatched his hand and twisted his arm around. Keeping his arm straight she pushed down on his elbow with her free hand. He cried out.

'Owww. What're you doing? Let me go!'

Rami began running him towards the river. As soon as he saw where she was going he tried to stop but her grip meant he couldn't do anything about it with snapping his own arm.

'Let me go you crazy monkey!'

She sped up, but as she reached the bank, she stopped suddenly and let him go, his momentum carrying him forward headlong into the river. He floundered and splashed shouting for his friends to do something. Rami turned to them and gave them a little half smile. The men looked at each other before turning tail and running for it. Rami watched them go before walking over to Grace who was looking on at Edward as he struggled to haul himself up the muddy bank.

'I think that's enough for today.' said Rami with a smile.

Grace didn't know what to say, she just let herself be led away back towards the village.

Molly paced around her room. Nareema had been gone for four days and there hadn't been a word from her. All she could think about was Marcus. He was in trouble and all she was doing was sitting here waiting. She took the sapphire out if her pocket for the umpteenth time that day and stared at it. In her head, she could hear it.

'We could find him.' it said. 'We can get him back.'

She closed her eyes and put it down.

'No. I can't.'

'We can.'

The voice of the sapphire was joined by that of the emerald. Both were soft and full of promise.

'If we find your love we will find our brothers. We need them to be whole again.'

'Shut up!' shouted Molly. 'Shut up, shut up, shut up!'

She put her hands over her ears as if it would stop the voices in her head. Suddenly the door opened and Davis came in.

'Are you alright miss?' he asked, his voice full of concern.

Molly looked at him.

'I don't know.'

She stood up quickly.

'We need to leave.'

'I thought we were waiting for Nareema?'

'We were but I can't wait any longer. I need to find Marcus.'

He looked at her.

'Don't look at me like that.'

'Are you sure?'

'No. I'm not. Where will Captain Brody be?'

'Why?'

'Where will he be?' she shouted in frustration.

'When we're in England we usually put into Gosport. There's a woman who runs a bar room. She's pretty much the closest thing that he'll ever have to a wife.'

'Gosport? Where the hell is that?'

'Near Portsmouth.'

She closed her eyes and took a breath.

'Then that's where we're going.'

"If'n you're sure. What about Nareema?'

'She'll meet us there. I'll find a way to tell her. I've got to go and see a man before we go. Get ready we'll leave as soon as I get back.'

'Do you want me to come with you?'

'No. Just be ready to go.'

She didn't give him a chance to say anything else as she pushed past him and headed out.

## Chapter Twenty

All the fun of the fair

Molly practically ran to the silversmith. The door was locked and blinds drawn. She knocked but there was no answer. Cursing with frustration that drew disapproving looks from the people around her she headed round the back. There was a small door which was also locked. Molly began banging on it but again there was no answer.

She turned and sat down heavily, tears of anger, frustration and fear poured down her face as she leant back against the wood. Where was he? She wiped her face and sighed.

'Get a grip on yourself.' she muttered. 'You can't help him if you go to pieces.'

She sniffed and stood up. Turning back to the door she knocked again. After a few minutes it opened a crack and a pair of wild eyes looked out.

'What?'

'It's me. Have you finished it?'

There was a moment of recognition then the door opened fully. Molly looked at the silversmith. He looked dishevelled, as if he hadn't slept for days. His chin was covered in scruffy stubble and clothes were in disarray. He was far from the smartly dressed man she had seen earlier in the week.

'Come in, come in.'

He looked around nervously and ushered her inside, closing and locking the door behind her.

'Have you finished it?'

'Yes. Yes. It's done.'

He took her across to his workbench. It was covered in bits of paper and mess.

'Here.'

The silversmith picked up an object from the table. It was like the one Molly had seen in her head but with small differences. Instead of being solid, the silver had been worked into a twirling filigree with four indentations in two lines. Without testing them, she knew that the Stones would fit perfectly.

'It's beautiful.'

She gingerly took it from him and he grinned madly.

'Is that what you wanted? Please say yes.'

'It is more than I imagined.'

'Thank god.' he said with a pleased smile. 'I've never felt like this before. It's as if the design was in my head and I couldn't rest until it was out.'

Molly placed it over her forearm.

'It's perfect.'

He sagged and sat down heavily.

'How much do I owe you?'

'Nothing.'

'Why not? This much silver...'

'That is my masters piece. If I never make anything again it will be with the knowledge that I created that. That is payment enough.'

Molly didn't know what to say. Instead she just nodded.

'Thank you.'

He looked at her for a moment.

'Can I ask what it's for? I've had flashes of far off places and of fire and woodland and windswept water in my mind ever since you came in and I'm curious. What does it mean? What does it do? I know it's supposed to do something but I don't know what.'

Molly reached into her pocket and took out the bag with the Stones in. Carefully she took out the sapphire and with a gentle click and flash of blue light she slotted it into the bracer. As she had expected, the fit was perfect. The emerald followed, sitting snugly next to its sister Stone.

'What are they?' asked the silversmith, his voice hushed.

'They are the Stones of Gunjai. You are part of their story.'

Molly looked down and then back up at the man. With a gentle touch, she reached out and caressed his cheek. He closed his eyes as her fingers ran across his face. Molly opened her mouth but it was not her that spoke. Two soft voices floated out of her mouth, slightly out of sync with each other.

'Sleep now. You have done well.'

The man nodded.

'Our blessings are with you. When you wake, you will be refreshed and know that our light will be with you in your future endeavours.'

Molly let him go and stepped back. He was sat in the chair, snoring lightly with a perfectly serene look on his face. She knew deep down that he would be alright. Looking down at the bracer she felt the power of the Stones infuse her. In her head, they spoke.

'We are with you now more than ever. With our help, we can find your love and be reunited with our brothers. It must be so. We have been apart and incomplete for too long. You can make it right.'

Molly nodded.

'We will make it right.' she said in a whisper.

Leaving the sleeping silversmith, she headed out of the back door and into the town.

Grace and Rami wandered around the fair. It had been set up in a field near the village and had drawn crowds from all of the nearby settlements. Rami got many curious looks as she walked around, arm in arm with Grace.

'Why are they looking?' asked Grace, feeling embarrassed at the attention.

'I'm different.'

'But that's no reason to stare.'

'It is every reason.'

'I wish they wouldn't.'

'I'm use to it. I've travelled far and people are unused to others that are different.'

'Well I don't like it.' said Grace forcefully.

Rami smiled.

'Don't let it bother you.'

The girls walked around, Grace pointing out the people and relaying the gossip from the village. Rami stopped near a sideshow that boasted some short bows and targets.

'Hit the middle and win a prize.' called the man from behind the rope.

They watched several men have a go but none came close.

'How about you miss?' said the owner of the stall.

'I don't have any money.' replied Rami.

'I'll pay for her.'

They turned to see Edward and his friends swagger towards them. Grace stepped back behind Rami and looked down. He flicked a coin towards the man and grabbed a bow which he thrust towards Rami.

'Here. How about we make a little wager? What do you say to that monkey?'

Rami scowled at him.

'When I beat you I get that kiss from both of you then I'll throw *you* in the river.'

'What do I get if I beat you?'

Edward shrugged and smirked at his friends.

'What do you want?'

'Your respect.'

He laughed out loud.

'You can't be serious. Is that it?'

She said nothing. He looked at his friends again who egged him on.

'Go on Edward. She can't beat you.'

'Teach the monkey a lesson.'

'Tell you what. If you win then I'll give you my coin.'

He dropped a bag on the floor. It chinked.

Rami looked down and then back you at him.

'As you wish.'

She stepped back and Grace whispered in her ear.

'Don't do this.'

'Trust me.'

Around them a small crowd had gathered. The man whose stall it was picked up six arrows and handed them three each. Edward made a show of limbering up. Playing up to the crowd to cheers from his friends.

Rami looked at the bow, it was poorly made but it would suffice. The targets were only around fifteen feet away and were straw covered in cloth with rings painted on.

'Monkeys first.' said Edward with a bow.

'No.'

He looked at her, his smirk dropping away to be replaced by a frown.

'As you like it.'

'Come on Edward.'

He took a breath, notched one of the arrows and let it fly towards the target. It missed the centre ring by an inch but was firmly in the next circle out. He stepped back, smiling to himself, convinced he had already won. Rami was more measured. She raised the bow and notched the arrow, slowly drawing the string back as she sighted the target. She winced as her shoulder moved.

'Come on. I haven't got all day.' shouted Edward with a mocking laugh.

Rami loosed the arrow. It smacked into the dead centre of the target and Edwards face fell. Quickly he notched and fired the second arrow. It hit the centre of the target too this time but was still a good three inches from the middle.

Rami carefully notched her second and let it fly. It thudded home within half an inch from the first. Edward had lost his swagger now and the crowd around them had gone silent. He fired for the last time and the arrow hit the centre ring of the target.

He turned to Rami as she began to draw back the last of her missiles and as she turned her attention to the target, he reached forward with the end of his bow and poked her in the ribs. Her shot went wild and disappeared into the distance.

'I win.'

She shot him a venomous look.

'Where's my kiss?'

'Edward.' came a stern voice from behind.

Rami turned around to see William standing next to an aging man with thinning grey hair and a large moustache. He was well dressed with a silver topped cane held in his hand. He stepped forward and looked directly at Edward.

'Cheating is not the Cayhill way.'

The younger man held his gaze for a second before looking down and muttering to himself.

The older man turned to Rami.

'Have another go my dear. I won't let it be said that you were cheated out of your win.'

The stall holder handed her one more arrow and she notched it before turning to stare at Edward. He looked on aghast as, without taking her eyes off him, she drew the bow back and let the arrow loose. It thudded home tightly next to the other two.

'Oh I say. Well done.'

There was a polite round of applause. Rami handed the bow back to the stunned stall holder and picked up the coin pouch.

'So you're our little visitor then are you?' the older man asked as she stepped towards him.

Rami looked at him questioningly.

'Where are my manners? Henry Cayhill at your service.'

'Rami.'

He offered his hand and she shook it gently. Henry turned to Edward.

'Beaten by a girl eh Edward? Never mind.'

He clapped him on the shoulder.

'Don't think you've been introduced to my son eh? This is Edward.'

Rami smiled sweetly.

'We've met.'

'Really?' said Sir Henry. 'Edward, you never said.'

'He might not have. He was rude and I threw him in the river.'

Sir Henry looked between the pair. Rami was smiling like butter wouldn't melt and Edward silently fumed next to her. Suddenly he exploded with laughter.

'That explains his mood the other day. Well my dear I dare say he deserved it, what do you say?' he clapped Edward on the shoulder again.

The young man muttered under his breath and stalked off. They watched him go.

'Don't mind him. He's a sore loser. You'll have to come up to the house for dinner soon. I was in India back in ninety-six. Loved the place. You'll have tell me all about yourself.'

'Thank you but I really have to be going.'

'Nonsense! How about tomorrow eh? You can bring your friend too if you like.' he pointed at Grace with his cane and she flushed red.

'That'd be alright with you William eh?'

The blacksmith looked at Rami and his daughter.

'Of course Sir Henry.'

'Well that's settled then. Dinner at seven. I'll make sure Edward is on his best behaviour.'

With that he turned and wandered off to take in the rest of the fair. Grace turned to Rami, her excitement obvious.

'Dinner at the house!'

'I really need to be going tomorrow.'

The girl looked crestfallen.

'Please?'

Rami looked at her for a moment before nodding with a

sigh.

'One more day.'

Grace beamed and they turned to the stall holder who was still staring in disbelief.

'I believe I'm due a prize?' said Rami.

'Take anything you like.' he said distantly.

'Can I have that shawl?'

The man nodded and took a finely worked shawl from a low shelf containing the prizes. He handed it to her. Rami held it up then gave it to Grace.

'Here. For you.'

'Don't you want it?' she asked.

'No. Please. It's yours.' replied Rami.

'Thank you. I must tell mum.'

She dashed off leaving William standing in front of her and a small crowd of onlookers watching them. Rami handed him the coin pouch.

'Here.'

He looked at it and then at her before he handed it back.

'Be careful.' he said eventually before wandering off on his own.

Rami turned around to see a mother with a group of small children huddled around her skirts. They were looking at her with a mixture of awe and distrust. One of the older ones, he couldn't have been more than six, stepped forward.

'Is it true that you eat children?'

He was immediately chastised by his mother but Rami smiled and knelt down.

'Only the naughty ones.' she whispered.

She dug into the coin pouch and took out a shiny silver one. She handed it to him and he took it gingerly as if she were going to bite him. Rami smiled slightly and held his gaze for a second before she suddenly shouted.

'Boo!'

He ran away and hid behind his mother. Rami

straightened and with a cordial nod to the woman went on her way.

An hour later, William was uncomfortably sharing an ale with Sir Henry and a group of the local men at the inn. Having Rami stay with him seemed to have made him a bit of a local personality and he wasn't sure that he liked the attention.

'So what does she eat?' asked Bradbury, a farmer from across the valley.

'Same as you and me. Don't be stupid.'

'I was only askin'...'

Williams reply was cut short when Grace came running down the road towards him. He took one look at the panic on her face and he knew something was up.

'What's wrong?'

'It's Rami. He's grabbed her. Him and four of his friends. They've dragged her into the barn near home.'

'Who's grabbed her?'

'Edward. They're all drunk. They were shouting about teaching her a lesson.'

William dropped his mug and headed off at quickly with the men and Sir Henry in tow.

'If he's done anything to her...' puffed Sir Henry as he ran.

They skidded to a halt in front of the barn just as Rami came out, quietly closing the door behind her. She looked a little dishevelled but otherwise unharmed. Slowly she began to walk away, looking a little surprised at seeing the men and Grace standing there.

As she walked past them William put a hand on her arm to stop her. She looked at his hand for a moment and then up at him.

'What've you done?' he asked quietly.

'Nothing. We just had a conversation about respect.'

He held her for a second longer.

'Go home. Both of you. Now.'

Rami nodded, collected the distraught Grace, and went to the house. Sir Henry swallowed nervously.

'She seems alright....'

William didn't say anything. He just carefully walked to the barn and opened the door as if he were dreading what he was going to find. It was cold in the barn. There was a frost on the stalls and the animals were wild eyed and pacing. He opened the door wide and could see four of the young men were curled into little balls or sprawled on the floor, each deeply involved in their own private little worlds of pain.

Edward on the other hand was naked. He'd been strung up by his ankles and was dangling four feet from the ground. He was sobbing and from the mess and smell had soiled himself quite spectacularly.

'How'd she do that?' said Bradbury. 'It couldn't a bin more than two minutes since your Grace got us. There are five of em!'

'Shut up. Cut him down.'

He turned to sir Henry as the other men hurried over to Edward.

'I'm sorry sir, I....'

The older man looked furious but shook his head. William turned and headed home. He pushed the door open and went into the kitchen. Grace was sat at the table still looking a bit put out and her mother was stood next to her.

'Where is she?'

'Upstairs.' said Martha.

William looked at grace.

'You alright?'

'Yes. I think so.'

He nodded.

'What did she do? Did she...'

'No. He's...'
William sighed and shook his head.

Rami was sat on her bed when there was a knock at the door and without waiting for an answer William came in. He looked angry. Rami stood up.
'What did you do? I've not seen a man look that scared since...'
She looked at him defiantly.
'I defended myself.'
'There were five of them! We couldn't have been more than a few minutes. You can't do that to people.'
'What did you expect me to do? Stand there and let them beat me?' said Rami angrily.
'Don't you raise your voice to me my girl.' warned William.
'What if it had been Grace? I'm just the first girl that stood up to them and fought back. They've had a lesson that they won't forget in a hurry.'
William looked at her.
'You can't go 'round attacking people.'
'I didn't attack anyone. They're the ones that grabbed me. I...'
'He's Sir Henry's son!'
'He's a bully. I don't think I'm the first he's tried it with and I won't be the last. Did you know that Grace is scared of him? If you're not careful it'll be more than a kiss he steals from her.'
William looked concerned.
'When did he...'
'The other day before I threw him in the river. He went on about 'betters' and forced a kiss from her. She's not like me. She couldn't stop him. I took action and I will do it again.'
William clenched his fists, the news obviously upsetting him.

'He's not better than anyone.' said Rami.

'But he's still Sir Henry's son.'

'And is that why he's better? How is he better than you? You took me in when you had no need to. A stranger in your lives and country. You're a good man. A kind man. He is never going to be any of those things.'

William didn't say anything but was clearly uncomfortable.

'It's about money and status isn't it?' said Rami. 'He's the son of a lord and you're just a blacksmith.'

'That's got nothing to do with it.' replied William angrily.

'It has everything to do with it.'

Rami turned away from him and began stuffing her things into her bag.

'I've overstayed my welcome.'

William took the bag from her.

'Not yet you haven't. You're going to go up to the house and say you're sorry.'

She span round.

'Why should I? I have nothing to be sorry for!'

'My house. My rules. I told you that I expected you to do as you're told while under my roof and you're bloody well going to do it.'

'No.' shouted Rami.

William raised a hand.

'If you were my daughter I'd have my belt to your backside before you knew it.'

Rami stared at him for a moment before she sighed softly, her anger gone in an instant.

'No you wouldn't. I doubt you've ever lifted a hand to Grace and I don't think you will. I can see it in your eyes. '

William lowered his hand.

'That's as maybe but you're still going to march up there right now and tell them that you're sorry for what you did.'

She held his gaze for a second longer before lowering her head and nodding.

'I will do as you ask.'

He dropped the bag back on the bed.

'Better get that unpacked.'

He turned to go but looked around as she put a hand on his arm. She smiled softly and gave him a gentle kiss on the cheek.

'Grace is lucky to have a father like you. I wish I had been so blessed.'

He opened his mouth to say something else but shut it again just as quickly before heading out and quietly closing the door behind him.

William went down to the kitchen. His wife was sat at the table waiting for him.

'Where's Grace?'

'I sent her to get some milk from Mr Ford.'

She looked at him as he sat down across from her.

'Are you alright?'

He took a deep breath and shook his head.

'It's that girl...'

Martha put a hand on his arm.

'You're doing the right thing.'

'Am I?'

'We are.'

He sighed.

'I'm going to the forge. I need to think.'

Martha nodded and smiled.

'You are a good man William Stratton.'

'That's what she said.'

'Don't be too long. I'll sort out something for tea.'

William stood and gave his wife a kiss on the head before heading out of the kitchen. He entered the yard to see the forge doors swinging open. He frowned. He was sure he had shut them. Cautiously he walked over and peered in. There was no one around but his eyes were drawn to his anvil. On it lay a small black velvet bag and a note. He picked it up and read it.

"Now you can be the better man."

William quickly glanced round to see the table where Rami's weapons had been was empty. Holding the bag tightly he rushed inside. Martha saw the look on his face.
'Will?'
He didn't say anything but headed upstairs.
'Rami.' he called as he opened the door to her room.
It was empty. There was no sign of the girl but the window was wide open. Her bag was gone too. He took one more look around before he closed the door and went back downstairs. His wife was stood near the fire.
'What's wrong?'
'She's gone. She left this.'
'Gone? Gone where? What is it?'
William shrugged and pulled open the bag. Puzzlement furrowed his brow as he peered in.
'What is it Will?'
Martha took the bag from his unresisting hand and emptied it onto the table. She gasped in shock as a dozen diamonds, rubies and emeralds clattered out. They were as big as her thumb.
'My goodness.'
'Better man.' whispered William to himself with a half-smile.

The raven flew through the gathering night. Rain began to lash down as it singled in on the point it had seen earlier. The flash of light in the darkness. Inside its head, Nareema knew she was close.

## Chapter Twenty-One

## Judgement

After collecting her weapons from the forge, Rami took a circuitous route out of the village, avoiding all of the people she saw so it was late in the evening by the time she reached the big house. A strong breeze had picked up and dark clouds were beginning to drop heavy spots of rain onto the ground

She walked up to the large oak double doors and knocked loudly. After a moment, it swung open to reveal an imperious looking butler.
'Yes?'
'I need to see Sir Henry.'
'He is indisposed at the moment and not receiving visitors.'

Without giving her a chance to say anything else he shut the door in her face. Staring at the door for a moment, she quietly made her way around the house. There was a light on around the back and she carefully peeked in through the window.

Sir Henry was stood near a large fireplace while nervous looking Edward was stood in the middle of the room. His head was down and she listened as Henry gave his son a verbal lashing.
'What the hell do you think you were doing eh? Dragging the poor girl off like that.'
Edward muttered something that Rami didn't hear but she did hear Henry explode.
'I don't care what she did. Man up for god's sake. You're supposed to be a Cayhill! She's a little girl. There's no shame in being beaten by her at a fair. It's nothing like being found naked and tied upside down after you and four, four no less, of your so called friends dragged her into the barn. Seen by at least half of the village I might add. What

were you going to do with her eh?'
Quietly she opened the window and dropped into the room.
'Teach me a lesson was what he said.'
Both men span round to look at her. Sir Henry gawped and Edward whimpered before a tell-tale patch appeared on his trousers as he wet himself. She looked at him pointedly and he quickly left the room. Sir Henry watched him go in disbelief. He turned back to Rami.
'What the hell do you think you're doing? You can't just break into my house!'
'I needed to see you.'
He opened his mouth to say something else but Rami beat him to it.
'I'm leaving but I came to apologise. Not to Edward. He's a bully and a drunk and I would do what I did again without hesitation. I came to say sorry to you. I'm sorry if I caused any embarrassment or distress to you earlier.'
Rami stepped further into the room.
'Please don't blame William or his family. They are not at fault. I take full responsibility for my actions. Your anger is for me and me alone.'
 Sir Henry seemed to sag as if all if his bluster had been taken from him at once. He turned away and looked at a painting of a woman that was hung above the fireplace. She was pretty with long brown hair and brown eyes that looked like she didn't have care in the world.
'I'm not angry with you.' he said quietly. 'In all honesty it's me that should be apologising to you for my sons behaviour.'
He turned back to face her.
'Since his mother died he's gone a bit wild. I don't know what to do with him.'
Sir Henry sighed.
'Maybe I'll buy him a commission in the army. Maybe a stint abroad will make a man of him.'
'You should do what you think best.' said Rami.

He nodded.
'I will give it some thought.'
'I have to go but I am sorry sir for any harm to you.'
'Nonsense girl.' said sir Henry with a sad smile. 'I'm sorry for the behaviour of my son and I won't hold it against anyone but him.'
'Thank you.'
Rami turned and walked back to the window.
'There's a front door you know.'
She smiled as she pulled herself up onto the sill.
'I know.'
'Wait!' he called as she began to climb out. She leant back in.
'What did you do to him?'
Rami thought for a moment.
'There is a darkness in all men's hearts. I just showed him his.'
With that she dropped out of the window and was gone.
Sir Henry hurried over to window but there was no sign of her in the steadily falling rain.

  Rami began to walk away from the village. She was headed in roughly the direction she had staggered from a few weeks ago. She had to find out if Marcus was still alive. The trail would be cold but she had to try. She had waited too long. She set her backpack and began walking into the driving rain.
'Rami!'
She turned to see Grace come running up behind her.
'Father said you'd left.'
'I have to.'
'Without saying goodbye?'
'I...'
Grace stepped close and gave her a hug.
'I'll miss you. It's been good to have someone to talk to.'
'It's been nice having a family.'

'Then stay.  Father won't mind.'

Rami wavered.  She hadn't felt wanted for such a long time that it was almost overwhelming.

Grace pushed her away gently and looked over her shoulder.

'Who's that?'

Rami turned and her heart sank.  Stood in the rain in the middle of the road was a woman dressed in black leather.  She had her arms folded and looked severe.

'I can't stay.  I have no choice now.  Thank you for everything.'

They hugged again.

'Be careful.'

'You too.'

She wiped her face.  The tears mixing with the rain.  She un-slung her backpack and took out the cloth pouch containing her throwing knives.  She handed it to Grace.

'Here.  Practice.'

Grace looked at the pouch in her hand and when she looked back up Rami was walking away towards the woman in black.

'Sister.' she said as she reached her.

'Sister.'

Nareema's tone and face were like stone as she stood, seemingly oblivious to the torrential rain.  Without another word, she turned and walked away, expecting that Rami would follow without question.  The girl let out a long breath before following even though she knew where this was going to lead.

They followed the muddy road out of the village in silence for a while before Rami eventually broke it.

'How did you find me?'

'There was a light in the darkness.  It was the briefest of flashes but I knew it had to be you.'

'I see.  I showed a man the darkness within.'

Nareema glanced at her but didn't say anything. They carried on in silence for a while longer. Around them the rain continued to fall.

'I failed.'

'I know.' was the Princesses hard reply.

Suddenly Nareema turned and headed off the road and headed towards a small clump of scrubby trees. Once undercover of the branches, she stopped and turned.

'Give me your weapons.'

She held out her hand and reluctantly Rami did as she was told, handing her the bag. The Princess took out the metal pole and allowed the rest to clatter to the wet ground. She flicked her wrist and the pole extended. With practiced ease, she span it around her body, the blades slicing through the rain with a hum as they cut the air. She stopped and looked at it.

'This was Aleena's'.'

'Yes.'

'She must have thought highly of you.'

Rami looked down.

'Tell me what happened.'

The girl sighed, the beginnings of a tear forming in her eyes.

'I failed. That is all.'

Nareema nodded.

'You understand that there is no middle ground on your trial. You either succeed and are brought into the light or fail and end in darkness. There can be no excuses.'

Rami felt sick. She knew what was coming. She dropped to her knees in front of the Princess and bowed her head.

'I understand.'

'You have the choice of waiting until we return to our home so you may go before the council or you can accept my judgement. Here and now.'

'Your judgment.' she whispered.

'Speak up.' snapped the Princess

'I accept your judgement. I cannot bring my shame before the council.'

'Where is your Ganta?'

'In... In the bag.'

Nareema bent and took out the black silk scarf. Slowly she walked around behind Rami and placed the cloth across her eyes.

'Please.' whispered Rami.

'We are Daughters of Kali. We do not beg for our lives. We give them willingly.'

She heard Nareema walk around in front of her.

'You have entered the dark.'

Rami nodded. Behind the blindfold, she could feel the tears stinging her eyes before running down her face to mingle with the pouring rain. Nareema spoke once more, her voice icy.

'By your own admission you have failed your trial. Our laws state there is only one outcome for this.'

She was silent for what seemed an age. Rami could feel her heart pounding.

'I have made my judgment.'

Rami nodded, bowed her head and waited for her death. Above the sound of the rain she could hear Nareema spin the metal staff around and Rami tensed. With a whistle, the blade came past her head and thudded into the ground. There were footsteps and the blindfold was removed.

Rami blinked through the tears to see Nareema crouched in front of her, the scarf in one hand. To her left was the metal pole, one of the blades buried deep in the ground. She spoke softly.

'You have been delivered into the light. Your failure will be with you for a long time and you will know it. I expect you to learn from it. Grow from it. Do you understand?'

The girl nodded.

'Tong Li has moved north and is headed to the Water Stone as we speak. We cannot let him get it.'

'What about Marcus?'

'He is alive. Molly has seen him in a vision. He is being held prisoner.'

'Thank you sister. I owe you my...'

She bowed her head again in respect but the Princess interrupted her.

'Do not thank me.' she paused for a moment. 'You owe your life to Molly. She asked me not to leave you in the darkness. She...' Nareema shook her head and handed the scarf back to Rami.

'Failure is not an option again and you will do a penance for your mistakes. What form that penance takes is for Molly to decide.'

Rami nodded.

'Come. We have work to do.'

## Chapter Twenty-Two

### Into the Dark

Molly headed back to their lodgings. Davis was waiting for her. He had his bag packed and was ready. He followed Molly to her room as she finished packing her bag and gathering the few things the Princess had.
'I still think we should wait for Nareema.'
Molly looked at him.
'I can't wait.'
'How's she going to know where we've gone?'
'I'll let her know.'
'How?'
'I...'
She closed her eyes for a moment. When she opened them they were a swirling mass of blue and green.
'Wait outside.'
Davis looked at her, suddenly feeling uneasy as around him the temperature in the room began to drop.
'Got out. Now!'
He almost fell in his haste to get out, such was the growing sense of fear and darkness that pervaded the air.
Around Molly a heavy black mist began to swirl and envelop her. She cried out as an intense cold flooded her body as the mist was drawn into her. The pain was incredible. It filled every nerve in her body with icy fire and just as she thought she couldn't take any more it vanished.
She looked around, instead of being in the run-down bedroom she was surrounded by darkness. Unfathomable blackness stretched out in all directions. It was cold and she shuddered.
'Where is this?' she asked.
'This is the darkness beyond. We dare not linger here.

We fear it. It is death. Hurry. Find your sister.'

Molly turned as a deathly low moan floated in from behind her. The was nothing there. Just the endless expanse of black.

'Hurry.'

Fighting a rising panic, Molly called out.

'Nareema. It's me. Molly. I can't wait any longer. I'm heading to Gosport. There's a bar there where Captain Brody will be. It's called the Old Ship Aground. Mr Davis says it's run by a woman called Nancy Johnson. Meet me there. Please hurry.'

She span round as cold fingers brushed the skin of her neck. Again, there was no one there.

'Get me out of here. Please.'

She was scared. A deep primordial fear was pulsing through her body. Behind her she felt an icy breath but she was too scared to turn around. A rough hand grabbed her arm and she could feel its chill seep into her body as around her a white mist began to form. It span and whirled and then there was the intense pain again. She screamed as it tore through her, ripping her very being asunder as she felt herself falling forward.

With a crash, she hit the wooden floor of the bedroom. She looked around, the fear and pain still coursing through her but after a few moments she realised where she was and the sensations began to fade. Gingerly she pushed herself to her hands and knees, then sat up.

'What happened? Did it work?'

There was no answer from the Stones. She closed her eyes and let out a long steadying breath, a thin stream of black mist escaping from her lips. Dimly she became aware of a throbbing in her arm.

She rolled her sleeve up and was shocked to find a huge bruise on it. It was shaped like a hand. She shuddered again as she remembered the coldness that had touched her just before she left. After a few minutes she stood, collected her bag and went to find Davis.

Rami and Nareema had moved further into the trees and made camp for the night. The thicker branches of the canopy kept most of the persistent heavy rain off them but it still crackled and fizzed when it touched the small fire they had made.
Nareema was sat on one side with Rami on the other. The younger woman couldn't meet her eyes. She was looking down and kept running the silk scarf through her fingers.
'Tell me what happened after he was shot.'
Rami was silent for a moment.
'He told me to run. I didn't want to but he gave me no choice. The men were on him in a second and they took him. One of them followed me. I killed him but reopened the wound in my shoulder. After that, it's a bit of a blur. I don't know how I made it to the blacksmiths or what happened after that really.'
Nareema looked at her. She was young and inexperienced and deep down she felt a pang of guilt. It had been her request that had brought her here and she should have been with her. Once again, she had underestimated Tong Li and once again it had cost her.
'Show me your shoulder.'
The Princess moved around to sit next to the girl as she pulled her clothing down to reveal the deep angry red gash. It had puckered at the edges where the hot metal had done its work and it still looked very sore.
'Does it hurt?' she asked as she gently touched the area.
Rami flinched as she ran her fingers across it and nodded.
'Yes. But it's better than it was.'
Nareema sat back on her heels.
'Keep it clean. Do you have ointment?'
'Yes. I have some. It's in my bag.'
'Good.'

The girl pulled her top back up and looked at the silk in her hands.

'I'm sorry I failed you.' she said after a while.

Nareema didn't answer.

'The family at the village. The blacksmith and his wife and daughter. They were kind to me. They didn't have to be.'

'No. They didn't.'

'Then why did they do it?'

'Some people are kind. Some are not. You must learn to see the difference and accept that and see people for whom they truly are.'

They lapsed into silence again. Eventually Rami spoke.

'Grace asked me to stay. Be part of their family. If you hadn't have been there I might have done.'

'Why?'

'I... I felt wanted.'

'Wanted?'

Rami sighed.

'The Daughters are like my family. But it's not like having a family of your own. I've not known that before. It's different for you. You have a family that you see often. I don't. I never have. They were kind and I felt like I belonged. I don't know.'

She glanced up at the Princess who was staring at her intently.

'I know it is hard to be a Daughter of Kali. There are many sacrifices that must be made but you *are* wanted. Why haven't you spoken of this before?'

'I never realised that I needed it until I found it.'

'I understand. Discuss this with the Seer when we return.'

Nareema stood up.

'Get some sleep. We have an early start tomorrow and a great distance to cover.'

Rami nodded and lay down, pulling a thin blanket over

her. The Princess watched her for a moment before she picked up her sword and headed into the rain.

She followed the path and eventually reached the village. There were few lights in the windows and no one about but when she reached the blacksmiths, the forge doors were wide open and he was stood at the anvil working hard. She walked up and stood in the doorway.
'You're working late.'
He glanced up, gave her a calculating look and then returned to his work.
'It helps me think.'
He turned and thrust the cooling metal back into the coals.
'Grace said that Rami had gone with a woman in black. You I suppose.'
'Yes. She is my sister. I came to find her.'
'So you've found her. What do you want from me?'
'To say thank you.'
'She's already done that.'
He motioned with his hammer at a small velvet bag that sat on his workbench.
'I don't know where she got that but...'
'It is a gift. Please accept it. We always pay our debts.'
He pulled the metal out of the fire and began beating it again in silence. Nareema watched him intently sensing he had more to say.
'She's a good girl you know.' he said eventually. 'We would have looked after her without that.' again he pointed at the bag on the bench.
The Princess stepped into the forge proper.
'And that is why she gave it to you. She is a long way from home for the first time and it has been good for her to see that not everyone is unkind.'
He turned to her and wiped his hands.
'Who is she? Who are you for that matter?'
'We are sisters. That is all you need to know.'

He seemed unsatisfied with the answer.
'She and my Grace got on well.'
'So I hear.'
'She was proper upset when she didn't say goodbye.'
Nareema didn't say anything. William sighed.
'If she wants to stay she can. I have no problem with that. As long as she doesn't attack anyone else and does as she's told. She's already the talk of the village.'
'That is very kind of you.'
'But...?'
'We have work to do.'
'Is it to do with this Marcus character she's been on about?'
Nareema nodded.
'He has been taken and we need to get him back. His wife is very worried.'
The blacksmith shook his head.
'Sounds like dangerous work and if I hadn't seen her beat five men this afternoon I would be more worried.'
'It will be difficult.'
Nareema stepped forward and handed him a piece of paper and an envelope.
'If you wish a new future for your daughter then send her here. It is my house in London. I will guarantee that she will be well looked after. I will also provide for her financially and give her an education. It is my gift to you for what you did for Rami.'
'She's better than a maid.' he pointed to the bag. 'And with that we can look after her ourselves.'
'I do not need a maid. I am offering her a chance to grow. I do not doubt for a second that you can look after and provide for her but think about it. Discuss it with your wife and daughter. If you decide to let her go, make sure she hands the envelope to Mrs Kettering or Simcox.'
With that she turned to leave.
'Wait.'

She turned back. William picked up a pair of tongs and lifted the metal from the anvil to dip it into a barrel of water. It hissed as it cooled. Drying it off he handed it to the Princess. It was about six inches long and was four thin strands of iron worked together to form an intertwining spiral which ballooned in the middle and tapered down to a point at each end.

'Give her that. It's not much but it's something to remember us by.'

Nareema took it.

'I will.'

She turned again and walked out into the night.

The rain had stopped as she headed back to camp and the moon bright in the sky. As she walked she felt a deep chill begin to settle over her and she stopped and looked around. The night had gone silent. Heavy dark clouds massed and obscured the moon, plunging the road into a thick twilight.

Carefully she drew her sword, alert for a danger that she could sense but not see. Slowly she turned around in the silent night before the darkness smashed into her. She fell to her hands and knees in the muddy road as the icy pain flooded through her and she cried out as it wracked her body. She could feel every inked feather of the raven tattoo on her back as if it were on fire.

Sprawling forward, a voice hammered into her head. It was Molly but it was like she was standing right next to her shouting at the top of her voice.

'Nareema. It's me. Molly. I can't wait any longer. I'm heading to Gosport. There's a bar there where Captain Brody will be. It's called the Old Ship Aground. Mr Davis says it's run by a woman called Nancy Johnson. Meet me there. Please hurry.'

Just as suddenly as it had come, the darkness left her. Tearing itself out of her and leaving her breathless in the mud. She forced herself to her knees as from the trees towards their camp she could hear screaming. Struggling to her feet the Princess headed back as fast as her lead like legs would let her.

She barrelled into the camp to find Rami screaming at the top of her voice. She was curled into a ball with her eyes screwed shut and hands over her ears. Nareema laid a hand on the girl and she went rigid, her eyes flashing open and she grabbed Nareema's arm so tightly it hurt.
'He's coming. He's going to get me. He's coming.'
The Princess looked at the girl and in her eyes there was nothing but abject terror. She gently reached out and laid her free hand on her head.
'Calm down. It's going to be alright.' she said softly.
The girl looked at her for what seemed like an eternity.
'He's going to get me.' she whispered.
'No one is going to get you. I'm here. Nothing can harm you. Here.'
Nareema handed the girl the metal sculpture that William had given her. Rami looked at it for a moment then clasped it tight to her chest before she relaxed her grip and drifted off into a fitful sleep.
Nareema sat with her, gently stroking her hair and feeling absolutely exhausted. Her head pounded and body ached. How had Molly entered the darkness? It must have been the Stones. How did they know about it? Through Molly, she suspected. She sighed wearily.
The Stones were more powerful than anyone had thought and they seemed to be getting stronger. Their link with Molly was being forged tighter and harder and she was beginning to worry that they would destroy her. What would it be like when she had all four of them? Would she be able to control them? It was with this thought running round her mind that she drifted off to a disturbed sleep herself.

## Chapter Twenty-Three

Gosport

Marcus shifted uncomfortably. His leg was stiff and ached. He tried to move as best as he could without waking Tobias. The older man was exhausted and sleeping fitfully.

As far as he could gather, Tong Li had taken him from his house and used him to find the location of the Earth Stone. Then had used him as bait at the port before shipping him off. Tobias had unwillingly discovered the location of the Water Stone and that's where they were headed. It was north of England in a frozen area called Iceland.

He shifted again and the chains around his wrists clinked against the stout iron ring set hard in the bulkhead. Tobias was similarly shackled and together they shared a small brig in the hold of a ship that Tong Li commanded.

The little he had seen of it was depressing. There were at least five cannon on each side and the men were hardened sailors, ruled over by a despotic Captain who they feared. And rightly so. On the one occasion Marcus had been on deck since they set sail he had seen him take a man's fingers for a suspected theft. There was no argument about it, he just grabbed him and cut his fingers off one by one. He even seemed to enjoy the pain he was inflicting. But even he, as evil as he was, looked scared of Tong Li.

Since he'd seen him last at the harbour he had fitted himself with a cruel hooked blade in place of his right hand. It was a brass tube, about ten inches long that fitted over the stump of his arm, topped with a bladed serrated steel hook. It replaced the hand that the Princess took from him as they fought in Portugal. Marcus laid his head back against the damp wood and closed his eyes. He hoped Molly was alright.

Molly walked silently along next to Davis. They had left their lodgings early that morning and were headed to Gosport looking for Captain Brody. Davis kept giving her sideways glances as they plodded along the road.

There was something different about her. He'd seen something like it when she'd used that gem of hers to push the small launch along but this seemed like something else. She seemed as if there were more to her. Not physically but... She was just more... He shook his head.

'How far away are we?' she asked

He shrugged.

'Don't rightly know miss. A week me' be. Might be a bit longer.'

'That's too long.'

They walked in silence for a while longer until they saw in the distance a small group of men on horseback coming towards them. Molly stopped in the middle of the road and they slowed as they approached, with Davis moving away to the side. The lead rider, a well-dressed man in his early forties called out to her.

'Stand aside girl.'

Molly made no move to get out of the way. She just stared straight at him. He looked at his companions before riding closer.

'Get out of the way.'

Still she regarded him silently.

'Stupid girl.'

He went to ride around her but she moved too, staying in front of his horse. The animal sensed something was wrong and brayed nervously.

'We need your horses.'

He looked at her in disbelief.

'What? Nonsense. Get out of the way or I'll run you down.'

Still she didn't move and he slashed at her with his riding crop, catching her across the cheek and drawing blood. She didn't seem to notice.

'Miss...' hissed Davis from the side of the road but she ignored him.

'Give me your horses.'

There was something in her voice that made him hesitate before he raised the crop to strike her again. With an open palm, she thrust her hand towards him and a strong blast of air slammed into his chest, knocking him backwards off his mount. He crashed into the ground hard and Molly turned to his friends.

They looked at her nervously but before they could say anything she casually flicked her hand towards them and sent them flying from their horses.

'Get the horses Mr Davis.' she said distantly.

The man who had struck her had scrambled to his feet.

'What the hell do you think you're doing?'

He moved towards her angrily and she raised both hands. Out of nowhere sprang a swirling vortex which snatched him from the road and carried him upwards. When he was six feet from the ground, Molly began to turn her hands in a slow circle. As her hands moved, so did he until he was suspended upside down.

The man's friends took one look at what was going on and began to run back the way they'd come. Davis gathered the horses and watched as Molly regarded him with interest.

Slowly she bent down and picked up his riding crop where it had fallen in the dirt and examined it curiously.

'What.... What're you going to do?' he asked, a tremor in his voice and all trace of his earlier bluster gone.

Molly flexed the crop between her hands and the struck him across the face with it, cutting his cheek as he had done to her. He cried out.

'Miss.' said Davis. He put a hand on her shoulder and she turned to him. Her eyes were wrong. They were a swirling blue and green. He stepped back as she looked right through him.

'Miss. Are you alright?'

She blinked and for the first time seemed to realise who he was.

'Horses.' she said simply.

'Yes miss. Horses.' he replied softly, as if talking to a child.

She turned back and seemed genuinely surprised to see the man floating upside down.

'Let me go. Take the horses but please don't hurt me.' he shouted.

Molly frowned and with a gesture sent him flying into a nearby field.

'Well done Mr Davis. Horses are just what we needed. Let's go.'

She mounted up and began to ride away. Davis clambered up onto one of the others and followed, leaving the other unattended by the roadside.

Nareema woke suddenly. The sun was high and she closed her eyes again for a moment while she got her bearings. She had fallen asleep with her back against a tree and Rami lay with her head in her lap. She rolled her shoulders stiffly and gently stroked the girls head.

'Rami. Wake up. It's time we were leaving.' she said quietly.

The girl stirred and looked up at the Princess through the fog of sleep.

'Please don't let him get me.'

Nareema smiled sadly at her.

'No one is going to get you. I'm here. But you need to wake up. We have to move.'

Rami laid her head back down for a second before she sat up. Nareema noticed she seemed to be very anxious, looking around as if she expected an attack at any moment. She laid a hand on her shoulder.

'Sister. Trust me. We are safe.'

The girl nodded and looked down.

'I'm sorry. I shouldn't show my weaknesses. Again, I have failed in my teachings.'

'It is from weakness that we become strong, and besides, Seers are allowed a little leeway in all things.'

Rami looked at her, confused.

'Seer? I'm not a Seer. Jamail is the Seer and she was the first for two hundred years. I'm not like her.'

'And yet, she grows old. It's about time another were found to take her place. Something is changing in the world and I think you are changing with it. Make yourself ready. We need to be away.'

Rami stood and stretched.

'Are we going to Gosport?'

Nareema looked at her.

'You heard that too?'

'I couldn't help it. I was dragged into the darkness and it was like a hammer to my head. How did she do that? She's not a Daughter. I thought only we knew the way.'

Nareema stood.

'Molly is special. She has the power of the Stones with her. I do not know what she is capable of. I suspect that neither does she.'

'How far away is Gosport?'

'Three or four days.'

Rami looked down.

'We would get there faster if we summoned the ravens.'

'Yes we would.' answered Nareema.

'I don't think I can call it. I can't... I'm scared of the darkness. I feel like if I go there again...'

'He's going to get you?'

'Yes. And I won't come back.'

'Who is he?'

'I don't know. Something evil. Something blacker than the darkness. He can control the souls. Please don't make me call the raven.'

Nareema looked at her. There was a definite tremor to her voice. She was truly scared.

'We will walk.'

'You can go on ahead. Leave me behind. I'll only slow you down. I'm a liability. Who heard of a Daughter that was scared of the darkness?'

'Jamail is scared of the darkness.'

'She isn't. She is strong and...'

Nareema cut her off.

'You do not know what goes on behind closed doors, although she will not thank you if you were to mention it to anyone else.'

'How do you know then?'

The Princess smiled.

'The council knows more than you realise.'

'You're on the council?'

Nareema didn't answer her.

'We have to go. Gather your things.'

Nareema and Rami had waited until dark before entering the town. They kept to the shadows before heading up onto the tops of the buildings where they could move unseen. Quickly they made their way across town before dropping back down at the waterfront. After a look round, they found a disused shed set back from the water. It was dirty and stank of fish.

'This will do. We will rest here for tonight.'

Rami nodded.

'I will watch.'

The Princess looked at her for a moment.

'Wake me if anything happens.'

'Yes sister.'

She took out her thin blanket and made herself as

comfortable as possible on the hard floor. Rami slipped outside before scrambling up onto the low roof. Drawing her metal pole, she sat and began to keep a lookout.

Molly and Davis stopped on a hill a few miles from the outskirts of Gosport. In the distance was the sea and a veritable forest of masts from the multitude of ships that filled the harbour. The setting sun behind them was making the shadows long.
'Where now?' she asked.
'It's a few streets away from the waterfront.'
'Right.'
She dismounted and took her bag from the horse before she shooed it away.
'We'll walk from here.'
Davis dismounted too and stretched stiffly.
'Don't think I'll ever like horses. I'll take the sea any day.'
Molly smiled.
'I think I'll disagree with you on that one.'
Davis shrugged.
'It's what you're use to I suppose.'
'Guess it is. Let's...'
She stopped talking and listened intently.
'Really? Where?'
The old sailor watched her for a moment. It still didn't sit right with him.
'Are you sure?' asked Molly.
'Well yes if she's here then we need to find her.'
The girl turned to Davis.
'Nareema is here already. We're going to find her first.'
'How? There's lots of people in Gosport. How're we going to find her in all that?'
'I told her the name if the inn but she's not there yet. I can find her. Follow me.'
She set off at a brisk pace and Davis followed but he

couldn't help but notice the flash of swirling blue and green behind her eyes.

Rami had been watching for a few hours before out of the darkness came a woman, closely followed by an aging man. Rami watched them walk along the street, the woman heading directly towards the building.
'Are you sure this is right?' he asked.
'Yes. Come on.'
Rami slipped off the roof and back into the building. Quickly she went to the sleeping Princess.
'Sister. Someone is coming.'
Nareema was awake in an instant, reaching for her sword.
'Who?'
'I don't know. A man and a woman. They're coming here.'
They moved over to flank the door, Rami on one side and Nareema on the other. The door opened and in stepped the pair.
'Nareema...' began the woman but like lightning, Rami grabbed her from behind.
'Rami, no!' shouted the Princess as she realised who the people were but it was too late.
Molly twisted in the girls grip and lashed out, sending a blast of air smashing into her chest and sending her flying. Rami hit the wall hard and dropped to the floor.
Molly span, her eyes blazing with power. Nareema stepped forward.
'Molly. Stop!'
She blinked a few times and her eyes returned to normal.
'Nareema?'
She smiled tightly before a groan from across the room caused Molly to turn. Both women hurried over to Rami and helped her sit up.
'What happened?' she asked groggily.
'Sorry. You surprised me.' said Molly.

Rami looked at her.
'Rami. This is Molly Kane. Marcus's wife.'
'The Keeper of the Stones?'
'Yes.'
Rami's' face fell and she dropped to her knees, bowing down before Molly.
'Please forgive me. I have failed you. I failed to protect your husband...'
'Stop it. Please.' said Molly uncomfortably.
Rami straightened and looked up at her before nodding once. The Princess turned to her.
'Get some sleep. It's late.'
The girl stood, still slightly shaken.
'Yes sister.'
Nareema and Molly watched her walk away across the room.
'I didn't mean to hurt her.'
'She is having a difficult time at the moment. She reacted as her training taught her.'
'She just surprised me. I wasn't expecting to be grabbed.'
'She'll be alright. I will speak with her in the morning.'
'Why did she do the whole bowing thing?'
'She is grateful you delivered her into the light and sorry she failed to protect Marcus.'
'But...'
The Princess ignored her and continued speaking.
'How did you find us?'
Molly held up her arm so Nareema could see the silver bracer and Stones. They were glowing faintly.
'With these. They've touched you remember?'
The Princess nodded.
'Then why use the darkness? Why send me a message through it instead of using the Stones? Surely they could do that?'
Molly looked at her.
'I don't know. I didn't think of that. I remembered you

said you could talk across long distances in the darkness so that's what I tried.'

'Did you go there?'

'Yes. It was scary. There was something in there. Something...' she tailed off and Nareema put her hands on her shoulders.

'Don't do it again. The darkness is not a place you need to go. Do you understand?'

Molly looked down as even though the Princesses words had been soft there was still a feeling of being chastised.

'Yes. I understand.'

'Good. Now we need to get some sleep. We'll go and find Captain Brody in the morning.'

Molly nodded and turned to go but Nareema put a hand on her shoulder before hugging her tightly.

'It's good to see you safe, sister.'

Molly returned the hug.

'And you. I'm sorry. I couldn't wait. I'll say sorry to Rami tomorrow.'

'She thinks she owes you more than an apology.'

'She doesn't.'

'Get some sleep.'

The Princess let Molly go and watched as she settled herself on the floor near the wall.

Rami woke as she rolled over. Her shoulder ached from where she'd hit the wall. It hadn't reopened the wound but it had bashed it a lot. Quietly she sat up and looked around. The old sailor was asleep and nearby lay Molly. Her blonde hair falling over her face in a cascade.

As Rami watched, there was a faint glow pulsing in time with Mollys breathing. It seemed to be coming from under the thin blanket that covered her. Gingerly she rose and as carefully as she could, she pulled back the cover. On her wrist was a silver bracer, in which sat two gemstones. It was from this that the glow was emanating. A gentle pulsing brightness, a blue and a green that moved in time with her breathing.

'It's been doing that for the last hour.'

Rami turned quickly as the Princess spoke softly from the shadows behind her.

'What is it?'

'The Stones of Gunjai. Earth and Air. She and they are linked.'

'What're they doing?'

'I don't know.'

They went quiet for a moment, each lost in the gently pulsing light.

'She has power.' said Rami.

'Yes. More than she knows. We must protect her.'

'I will.'

The Princess moved and placed a hand on Rami's shoulder.

'*We* will.'

'Dawn is coming.'

'Yes. It is. I'm going out to find us some food. Look after her while I'm gone.'

Rami nodded.

'Yes sister.'

Molly was still asleep when Nareema returned a few hours later. She had food and water. Davis was awake and sat slightly away from Rami. Both were watching the sleeping woman. The glow from the bracelet was barely visible now.

'She's hardly moved.' said Rami.

'Then let's leave her. She will wake when she's ready.'

The trio had eaten and were resting when suddenly Molly cried out in her sleep.

'Marcus!'

They turned to see a brilliant flash from the stones and Molly go stiff for a second before slumping down.

Nareema went to her side. Her breathing was shallow and she was cold.

'What's the matter?' asked Davis.

'I don't know.'

Molly found herself on a ship. Tong Li was stood near a table at which sat a cruel looking man with a ragged beard. Tong Li smiled to himself and turned around. She could feel him staring right at her. Slowly he moved towards her.

'I know you're there. I can feel you.'

He waved his hand where she was standing and it passed right through her, she shivered.

'I suppose you are looking for your husband? Very well.'

He snapped his fingers and the seated man jumped up and began bellowing orders.

'He'll be here shortly.'

He smiled but there was no humour in it.

'I want the Stones Mrs Kane. You're going to give them to me.'

'Get up. Captain wants a word.'

Marcus looked at the sailors through the bars of his prison. There were three of them. Two were armed while one carried the keys to his shackles.

'What for?'

'Don't know. Didn't ask.'

He opened the door and unlocked the restraints from his wrists and those of Tobias too. The older man rubbed his wrists. He looked tired and exhausted. Marcus stood stiffly and helped Tobias up.

'Thank you, dear boy.'

The sailor who had unlocked them stepped back and drew his sword and motioned with it.

'Out. Make a move I don't like and we'll kill you.'

Marcus nodded and despite the stiffness and pain in his leg he drew himself up straight. They were roughly pushed up onto deck and then into the Captain's cabin. He was stood to the side grinning nervously and casting odd glances across the room while Tong Li was sat at his table. The Chinese man smiled and stood up as they were escorted in.

'Captain Kane. Mr Callahan, I hope you're being treated well and enjoying your accommodation.'

Marcus stood straight.

'What do you want?'

'Straight to the point. Although I would expect nothing else from His Majesties Army.'

Marcus didn't reply. Tong Li smiled again and turned to look towards an empty corner of the room.

'Here he is Mrs Kane. I told you that I would prove he was alive. I also want you to know I am not to be trifled with.'

Tong Li walked round the table and took a sword from one of the guards. He hesitated and held on to it for a second before Tong Li wrenched it from his grip with a scowl. He went to test the blade with his thumb and realised he didn't have one on his right arm as it ended in a bladed hook.

He stared at it for a moment before driving the blade into the man he'd taken it from. The sailor looked down in shock as Tong Li twisted it and pulled it out. As the man fell to his knees, Tong Li held the sword up in front of him.

'Not perfect, but it will do.'

His eyes flashed with fire and before him the blade began to heat up, quickly turning from orange to a glowing white hot. Tong Li turned to the men near Marcus and gestured to the table.

'Hold him there.'

They manhandled a struggling Marcus to the table.

'Right hand.'

The Captain stepped forward and grabbed Marcus right

arm, pinning it against the wood. Marcus tried to push them away but one of the sailors hit him across the back of the head with the pommel of his sword and he slumped forward in a daze. The three men pushed him down and held him still.

Tong Li smiled darkly before he raised the blade and slashed down. The glowing metal crashed through Marcus arm to bury itself in the table which began to smoulder from the heat. Marcus fell backwards, screaming in agony as the hot blade cauterised the wound instantly. He hit the ground hard and stared in shock at the stump where his right hand used to be.

Tong Li turned away from the table and addressed the corner once more.

'You have two weeks. We will be anchored off Iceland. I know you will be able to find us. If I do not see you on a ship by that time I will take his other hand. Then his legs. This will be your doing Mrs Kane. How much of your husband is left depends on you. Two weeks.'

He turned away from the corner.

'Get him out of here.'

The stunned sailors hauled a shocked Marcus to his feet and dragged him away with Tobias following on behind.

Molly snapped awake and immediately burst into tears. In an instant Nareema was by her side.

'What is it?'

'I saw Marcus. I was dreaming about him. Then Tong Li was there. He's cut off his hand! He said I have two weeks to get to Iceland or he'll cut his other hand off and then his legs. I don't even know where Iceland is.'

She dissolved into a fit of inconsolable sobbing.

'We will find Brody today. We will get there.'

She stood and went outside to get Rami and Davis. A few minutes later she returned. Molly had stopped crying but the pain was written all across her face.

'It's my fault. I should have been faster.'
'Nonsense. Gather your things.'
Molly nodded and grabbed her bag.

Davis lead them to the waterfront. It was a mass of ships and men and they threaded their way through the bustle to a side road.
'Where will he be?'
'There.'
The old sailor pointed towards a large two storey house with a sign swinging outside.
'That's the Old Ship Aground. Nancy Johnsons place. That's where he'll be.'
'Right. Thank you, Mr Davis.'
Nareema strode purposefully towards the inn with Rami barely a step behind. At the door stood a large man with a many times broken noise jutting from a bushy beard. He saw two armed women coming towards him and straightened, squaring his shoulders. As Nareema reached him he put himself between them in the door.
'There's nothing in here that's for you. I'd find somewhere else to be if....'
Nareema didn't give him chance to finish before she kicked him in the head, following up with a series of furious punches which sent him crashing backwards through the door.

Everyone in the bar looked up as the door smashed open and the doorman came flying through to land heavily amongst a group of sailors. Nareema and Rami stepped in with Molly and Davis close behind.
Two more heavy looking men dashed towards the intruders and Rami glanced at Nareema who nodded slightly before they both exploded into a series of spinning kicks that dropped the men to the floor.

Molly looked around the stunned bar. It reminded her of the inn on the quay in Portugal. There were groups of drinking sailors and dotted between them were women in various states of undress. Unlike the Portuguese inn though this was clean, light and airy. A large staircase led up to the second-floor landing and several women were perched on the balustrade, watching the men below and flaunting everything they had. Across to the right was a small stage and several barely dressed women were looking fearfully at the newcomers.

Several sailors stood and looked ready for a fight but Nareema drew her sword and next to her, Rami flicked her metal staff which snapped into place with a metallic snick which was loud over the sudden silence of the bar. The sailors looked at each other and then at the women before sitting back down again.

'I'm looking for Captain Owain Brody. I know he's here and if someone doesn't go and find him now I'm going to tear this place apart.' said Nareema with a voice like steel.

'And what do you want with him?' said a female voice with a heavy Irish drawl.

Everyone looked up to see a woman coming down the stairs. She was doing up a red dress with black lace edging that barely concealed her bust. She had a pale face with deep blue eyes but the most stunning thing about her was her long red hair which was swept over her right shoulder. She reached the bottom of the steps and walked straight over to Nareema, standing close.

'What d'ya want with him? He's not been here for months now.'

'He is here and I need to see him. Now.'

The two women stared at each other, eyes locked, neither backing down.

'Bloody hell. Nareema, what're you doing here?'

They both turned to see Brody coming down the stairs. His shirt was unbuttoned to the waist and he was still doing his trousers up. He quickly crossed to the two women.

'What the hell is going on?'

'Friend of yours is she Owain?' said the red headed woman.

'Not now Nancy.' he replied.

'Not now? She's come in here and started smashing the place up. Who's going to pay for it?'

Nareema gave her a withering state.

'Go away before I make you.'

Nancy bristled.

'Make me? Come on then missy, I'll show you who...'

Molly stepped forward.

'Stop it! Both of you.' she turned to Brody.

'Captain, I need your help. Please.'

Brody looked at her. He could see the hurt and anguish in her eyes. He nodded.

'Aye lass. Come on.'

Ten minutes later they were all sat in a small room off the main bar. Molly had told Brody what had happened, only just managing to keep herself together as she recounted what she had seen on the ship. Nancy was there too. She took a swig from a cup of wine and banged the empty cup back on the table.

'What a load of rubbish.' she exclaimed. 'You can't believe this stuff can you Owain? Visions? Magic stones! I've never heard the like.'

'Will you just go away and leave the grownups to talk about important things please?' snapped Nareema venomously.

'Grownups? Why you...'

Molly jumped to her feet and shouted at them.

'Shut up! I'm wasting time. Marcus is going to die and it'll be my fault.'

Everyone looked down at the table apart from Nareema and Nancy who were glowering at each other. Molly looked at Nancy, seeing the disbelief in her eyes.

'Right. You don't believe me. Fine. Want a demonstration?'

Molly grabbed the empty wine cup and threw it at the wall.

'Steady on lass...' began Brody, as he went to duck out of the way, remembering her last demonstration which had cost him the back windows of his cabin and half a dozen silver cups.

Molly eyes flashed blue and a thin stream of wind caught the cup before it hit the wall. She pulled it back in towards her but stopped when it reached Nancy. Slowly a swirling vortex began to spin the cup around until it was whizzing so fast around Nancy's head that it was a blur. With a flick of her hand, Molly sent the cup hammering into the wall where it smashed into a hundred pieces. Nancy looked on open mouthed.

'Do you want me to show you again? Something bigger this time? Which part of the building don't you want? I haven't got time for this. I need to get to Marcus.'

Molly sat down heavily and dissolved into a fit of tears with her head laid on the table. Nareema put a gentle hand on her shoulder and looked at Brody.

'Will you help us?'

He nodded.

'Of course.'

Nancy looked at him, quickly recovering from the shock of the spinning cup.

'Now hold on a minute Owain Brody. Don't be thinking you're leaving me like that again.'

'Nan...'

'Don't you "Nan" me...'

'Nancy. Shut up.' said Brody forcefully. 'This girl saved my life, my crew and my ship. If she needs help then she's going to get it.'

He turned to Davis who was sat across the table from him.

'Good to have you back Mr Davis.'

'Good to be back cap'n.'

'Skippy and a few of the others are out front. Go get 'em and then round up the others. You know where they'll be. Any you can't find don't worry, just make sure we've got enough to go on the tide. Hire more if you have to.'

Davis stood.

'Aye cap'n.'

Davis left them and Brody spoke to Molly.

'Come on lass. Let's go and find your husband.'

## Chapter Twenty-Four

### Calling the Raven

'Come on, shift yourselves. Get that gangplank up and loose those lines so we can be away.'
Just as the gangplank was being raised there was a shout from the quay.
'Wait!'
Brody turned to see Nancy run up and on board ship with a bag in each hand.
'Nan. What the hell d'ya think you're doing?'
'If I can't beat you then I'll join you. You keep promising to take me to see for'n places so I'm coming with you.'
She dropped her bags and hitched her skirts up to climb to the wheel as Brody shouted down to the crew.
'Hold those lines.' he turned to Nancy. 'You can't come.'
'Why not?' she demanded. 'Is it because of her?'
Nancy's tone made it quite clear what she thought about Nareema.
'What? No. Don't be so soft.' said Brody quickly.
'Then why not?'
'It's going to be dangerous. I mean properly dangerous.'
'Then it's a good job I've got you to look after me then.'
She smiled sweetly and draped herself around him before whispering in his ear.
'I'm staying put so you'd better get use to it. I don't like that for'n woman and I don't trust her as far as I can spit.'
He pushed her away.
'Well I do trust her. You ain't staying and that's it.'
He grabbed her arm and began to march her towards the stairs but as he neared the rail he saw the harbour floating out of reach.
'I told you to hold those bloody lines.' he roared.
The sailors on deck looked sheepish but continued to stow

the ropes that had tied the ship to the quay. Nancy grinned.
'Well it looks like you're stuck with me. Where's our bed?'

That evening they were stood on deck. Davis and the others had rounded up most of the crew and had mustered along with a few new hands who were looking on confused at the four women, three of whom were armed and dressed in black and stood behind the Captain. Brody stepped to the rail and addressed the assembled men.

'Most of you know what happened in Portugal. We owe our lives to Molly and now she needs our help. The bastard that nearly burnt us all to death is still alive and has got Captain Kane.' he glanced at Molly before continuing. 'And by all accounts he's not in a good way. I've a feeling that this trip is going to be hard and we'll be putting into port up country to resupply.'

There was some murmuring amongst the crew, especially the new hands. Nareema stepped forward.

'It will be hard. We are going north as fast as we can.'

One of the sailors held up his hand.

'Where are we going?'

'Iceland.' said Brody.

'We're going to find Tong Li.'

There were some more mutterings. Nareema vaulted over the railing, drawing a knife as she did so. As soon as she hit the deck, she span and threw the blade hard. It thudded solidly into the mast.

'We will be putting into port in a few days to resupply. Anyone of you who isn't up for this can leave then. Unless you want to discuss this further now. Draw the knife and you and I will talk about honour and debt.'

Even the new hands caught the ice in her words and no one moved. She cast her stony gaze around the men before stalking below. They all looked up nervously at Brody.

'Well? What are you lot waiting for? Get to it!'

Nareema was sat alone in her cabin when there was a knock at the door.

'Come.'

It opened to reveal Davis. He looked down and nervously wrung his hands but didn't come in. The Princess looked up at him.

'Come in. What can I do for you?'

He stepped in and closed the door behind him.

'Beggin your pardon miss but...'

'You know that my name isn't "miss". Just being back on board the ship doesn't change what we've seen and been through together. My name is Nareema.'

He glanced down.

'Come on Mr Davis. Out with it.'

The older man took a breath.

'It's about Molly. I'm worried and I thought you ought to know.'

She looked at him for a moment before speaking softly.

'Sit down.'

He did as instructed, sitting in the narrow bed next to her. He waited for a moment, composing himself before speaking.

'She's not right.' he said eventually.

'What do you mean?'

'While you was away and we was heading for Gosport she seemed different. Like she wasn't there all the time. Not there in her head.'

He shrugged.

'I thought it was prob'ly me bein' daft but we took some horses off some gentl'men and it was like she'd never seen a man before. Even when one of them hit her with his crop she didn't move or make a sound. She just knocked him off his horse and then spun him upside down. Then she hit him back an...'

'And what?'

Davis looked at her.

'I think that if I hadn't stopped her, spoke to her, she'd have taken him apart just to see what made him work. She had that sort of look in her face.'

Nareema looked at him for a long moment before nodding.

'Thank you for telling me.'

'I don't want to get her in any trouble but she's like a lucky charm to lots of lads on board and me especially. Bit like a daughter I never had. But I don't want her to do nothin' to hurt herself or anyone.'

'I'll keep an eye on her. Thank you.'

Davis stood up.

'Just thought you ought to know. That's all.'

Nareema nodded as Davis tugged his forelock and left. The Princess sighed and sat back. How much had the Stones got into her head? She would have to keep a close eye on her.

'Nareema?'

The princess sat up at a knock on her cabin door.

'Nareema?'

She blinked, rubbing the sleep from her eyes and spoke.
'Come.'

The door swung open slowly.

'Molly. It's early. What can I do for you?'

The girl was dressed in her black jumpsuit with sword at her back. She looked tired. Her blue eyes were rimmed red from where she had been crying and her blond hair was tangled.

'I can't sleep. I can't get Marcus out of my head. What Tong Li has done to him... Will you train with me?'

The Princess looked at her.

'Don't think that I'm going to let you go after Tong Li alone. He is more dangerous than you know.'

'I'm not going to go alone. I'll have your blade next to me. You said that it was mine to command. Well here is the only order I have. I want you to kill him. I want him dead. I don't want him to hurt my family anymore. Shakir told me that his head was yours and yours alone. When you've taken it I want to see it. So I know he's gone.'

There was something in Molly's voice that Nareema didn't like.

'Don't let revenge and anger get the better of you. He will use it against you and you will fail. Do you understand?'

'No.'

There was a tense silence.

'Wake Rami. We will train together.'

Molly smiled sadly, the tension of the last couple of seconds vanished.

'Thank you.'

'Go.'

She closed the door and Nareema swung herself out of bed. She hadn't thought about Shakir for a while. She grabbed her bag and rooted around inside for a moment before pulling out the letter Shakir had given her. It still bore the marks of the fire and his blood. Slowly and with a heavy heart, she opened it and began to read.

Three days later they had put into port to resupply. As well as food, they had bought cold weather gear and, much to Molly's unease, guns.

'Just in case.' Brody had told her.

Of the crew, all but one of the new hands had jumped ship leaving only a young and inexperienced sailor called Tom Keenan behind. Nancy too had refused to go despite Brody's best efforts to get her to leave. In the end, he'd just given up trying.

Now they were headed north and the further they got the rougher and colder the weather got. For the last few days Molly, Rami and Nareema had been training hard. Brody and Nancy had watched them.

'She's got quicker.' said Brody

Molly moved to the left, deflecting a blow from Rami's staff with her sword while shoving Nareema back with a blast of wind. Rami spun the staff and flicked Molly's sword out of her grip, sending it skidding across the deck. With the staff a spinning blur, Rami pressed her advantage, bringing it thundering down towards Molly's head.

She gestured with her right hand and the staff stopped suddenly, as if it had hit a solid wall. Molly followed up with a blast from her left hand which hit the younger girl in the stomach and sent her flying.

Nareema lowered her sword.

'Enough.'

Molly was breathing hard as she stepped over to help Rami up.

'How did you do that?' asked Rami. 'It was like hitting a stone wall.'

'I don't know. It just seemed to be the best thing to do.'

Now the weather had closed in and Molly lay on her bed feeling terrible. The ship was rolling through the waves as they lurched towards Marcus. Despite Brody's assurances that they were making good speed it didn't seem quick enough. She rolled over. Why was sailing so awful? Although, she admitted to herself, it was getting better.

She thought back to her first trip on the Endurance which seemed like a lifetime ago now. That had been calm but she still hadn't been able to leave the cabin for four days. The ship dropped suddenly and her stomach flipped. She groaned weakly.

'I hate ships.'

Her self-piteous wallowing was interrupted by a knock at the cabin door. It opened and Rami came in carrying a small bowl. Molly sat up and the girl sat next to her.

'Nareema said that you don't travel well.'

'I don't like being on the water. The way it moves...'

She swallowed dryly.

'Here.' said Rami, handing her the bowl.

'What is it?' asked Molly

Inside was a steaming brown syrupy liquid which smelled terrible.

'It should help to settle your stomach.'

Molly looked at it and her insides rolled.

'I don't think I can face anything.'

'It will help. Trust me.'

Taking a deep breath and fighting the rising sickness inside she swallowed the thick contents of the bowl. It tasted worse than it smelled.

'That's horrible.' said Molly, pulling a face.

'Yes. But it works.'

Rami took the bowl and placed it on the floor.

'I have something else for you.'

She reached inside her robes and took out a black silk scarf that was printed with swirling whorls and lines.

'I want you to have this.'

'What is it?' asked Molly.

'It is my Ganta. It is to say thank you for delivering me from the darkness.'

Molly looked at her, confusion on her face.

'I don't understand.'

Rami looked down.

'Nareema acted on your words. She delivered me from the darkness and into the light. I can't explain this. It is a thing only another Daughter of Kali would understand.'

'Is this something to do with your trial?'

Rami nodded.

'Oh.'

The girl got up and knelt in front of Molly with her head bowed.

'I owe you my life. My blade is yours to command.'

'I don't need your blade or to command you.'

'I understand. But still, you have it.'

Rami stood and with a reverential bow, she picked up the empty bowl and left.

Molly looked down at the scarf in her hands. She didn't understand. The boat lurched again and she let out a long breath. Maybe that nasty tasting stuff did work. She didn't feel quite as sick as she had done. Once more she lay back on the bed and thought of Marcus.

'They are close.'

Molly jumped up in surprise at the sudden voices.

'Don't do that. At least warn me before you're going to drop words into my head.'

'Our brothers are close.'

'How do you know?'

'We can feel them.'

'So Tong Li has the Water Stone then?'

'No. Norek and Takahn are not together. But they are close.'

'Why aren't they together? Surely Tong Li has had enough time to go and get the last Stone by now.'

The voices were silent for a moment.

'We do not know. They are not together.'

Molly stood up as a realisation hit her.

'He can't find it. That's why he needs me. I have the sapphire and he needs it to find the Water Stone.'

She held the bracer up in front of her, the gemstones glowing with power.

'With this Stone I can find the others...' she said to herself, an idea forming in her mind.

Nareema, Rami, Nancy and Brody were gathered in the Captain's cabin. Molly had brought them all together.

'I know why Tong Li needs me here.'

'To get the other Stones from you.' said Nareema.

'Yes. He needs the Air Stone to find the Water. Tobias has only been able to get him so close. He can't find it without this.'

'So?' said Nancy.

'So what if I were to get to it first?'

'We're still a good two days out I reckon.' said Brody.

'That's not a problem. If you were to carry on to meet him, Nareema and I can go looking for the Water Stone. Once we've got it we can use it to rescue Marcus and Tobias.'

'You can't just give him the Stones.'

'I'm not going to. He has the Fire Stone. He's also a much better fighter than me. How well do you think he'll fare against all three Stones and a Daughter of Kali.'

'Two Daughters.' added Rami.

'No.' said Molly. 'I want you to find Marcus and Tobias and get them safe. I'm going to use the Stones to draw Tong Li away from them. Then...'

'Then this ends.' said Nareema.

'How're you going to get to the land? I said we're still a good couple of days out yet and you can't put the launch out like you did last time you jumped ship. In this weather, you'll be smashed to pieces in five minutes.'

'There is a way. I know about the darkness...'

Molly looked at Nareema who held her gaze for a moment before she shook her head.

'No. It cannot be done.'

'It can. I know it.'

'Know what? Will someone tell me what the hell is going on?' said Nancy angrily.

Nareema glared at her before turning back to Molly.

'The darkness is not a place for you. You are not marked. The raven will not come.'

'What raven?'

'The bird?' said Brody with a shudder.

He looked at Molly.

'No lass. That's not a good idea. Fair gave me the willies that did.'

'I can do it.'

'No.' Nareema was adamant.

Molly sat back closed her eyes. They opened a second later swirling with blue and green. Two voices spoke but neither was Molly's.

'We will protect her.'

'No. Last time she entered the darkness it was like taking a hammer to crack an egg. She smashed her way in there, dragging us along with her whether we wanted to go or not. The darkness is not the place for her. It is a path she will not travel.'

'And yet, chosen of Kali, you know she must.'

Nareema stared at Molly. There was a tension in the room that everyone could feel. The assembled people held their breath. Eventually the Princess looked down.

'If it must be done then so be it. But I do not have to like it. Give Molly back to us.'

Molly closed her eyes and when she opened them they were her usual blue. Nareema stood.

'Molly, get yourself ready. This is not going to be pleasant.'

She stood and left them as Nareema turned to Rami.

'Go as far down and away as you can. I don't want you near the darkness when I call it.'

The girl looked nervously at her.

'As you wish.'

'Rami. It will be alright. Trust me.'

She nodded and left, following Molly.

'What the hell is going on?' demanded Nancy.

'Something dangerous.'

Finally she turned to Brody.

'Captain Brody. Get everyone below deck. That includes you this time. I don't know what's going to happen when we do this but I want everyone as far away as possible.'

Brody nodded.

'Aye.'

The ship rolled in the cold wind and rain as Molly clambered up on deck. Her breath misted before her face and she shivered as she pulled up the fur lined coat that Captain Brody had given her. The Princess was already waiting near the wheel. She was similarly dressed and had her sword in her hand.

'Are you sure about this?' she asked Molly for the hundredth time.

'No.'

Nareema stepped forward.

'We can find another way.'

'No. There isn't another way.'

The Princess sighed and then nodded.

'Take my hands.'

She held out her hands and Molly took them.

'Whatever you do. Don't let go. I don't know what is going to happen.'

Molly nodded and closed her eyes. Nareema could feel the power of the Stones begin to flood into her through Molly.

'Now.' said two disjointed voices.

Nareema began to speak the words to summon the darkness. Around them both the black mist began to swirl and the already cold air dropped further. Molly felt the darkness begin to enter her and cried out at the intense cold as it burnt through her. She could feel Nareema gripping her hands tightly. The pain grew in intensity until Molly felt it was going to tear her apart then it suddenly vanished and she was surrounded by the darkness. She looked around but the Princess was nowhere to be seen.

'Nareema?'

'She has called the dark raven. Her mind is elsewhere. We need to do the same.'

Part of her mind lurched and she felt herself splitting between her body and something else. Her vision swam for a second and the she was back in the deck of the Endurance with a huge black bird in front of her. It cocked its head to the side and the cawed loudly. She jumped back in fright. Nareema's voice floated into her head. She sounded amused.

'Well it's not a raven but it will do.'
'What?'
Molly spoke but instead if her voice there was a shrill cry.
'Come my little magpie. We need to go.'
'Magpie?' thought Molly.

The huge raven turned and took to the wing. Molly watched it go and even as she wondered what to do next, a deep instinct took control and within a second she took to the sky herself. She turned her head and could see her wings spread wide, feathers fluttering in the wind. This was fun!

'Follow me.'

Looking up she could just make out the form of the raven above her. It turned north west and sped off with Molly following close behind.

Below deck, Rami had gone as far down and forward as she possibly could but she still felt the darkness calling her as it was summoned above. She felt the beginning of the icy burning that heralded the call. She cried out and screwed her eyes shut, fighting the pull.

'Are you alright?'

She looked up as the young sailor called Tom came to her. He was carrying a lantern and in the pale yellow light it cast he looked as scared as she felt.

'Are you alright?' he asked again. 'Captain Brody sent me to check on you but you've hidden yourself away pretty good.' he swallowed nervously.

She shook her head.

'You're shivering. Here.'

He turned and picked up a thick bundle of woven cloth from a pile to his left, which he handed to her. Rami gingerly reached out and snatched it from him as if he were trying to coax her into a trap.

'I'll go and get the Captain.'

He turned to go but as he moved, the darkness stabbed through her and she cried out. It's coldness seeping deep into her body as above the raven was summoned. She could hear it caw in her head as around her the temperature dropped suddenly.

'Don't leave me.' she begged him, fighting with everything she had not to be dragged into the dark.

The sailor hesitated and turned back, a deep fear setting over him. It felt as if his life could be extinguished at a thought. Fighting his own rising panic he knelt down in front of the terrified looking girl. She had her eyes closed tightly and had pulled her knees up in front of her chest.

Gently he reached out and touched her trembling body and she jumped and screamed at the touch. He jumped too, falling back on his bottom. The girl opened her eyes, deep blue eyes that at that second held nothing but fear.

'Hold me.' she whispered.

She held her arms out to him and he almost fell towards her, needing to feel the realness of another person against the pressing chill and dread that surrounded him. She held him tightly, burying her head in his shoulder and he could feel her heart hammering in her chest, almost in time with his.

He didn't know how long they stayed like that but eventually he felt her relax slightly and around them the temperature began to rise. Slowly she pushed him away as her composure returned.

'They've gone. '
'Who has?' he asked.
'Thank you.' she whispered.
He swallowed nervously.
'What... What was that?'
'The darkness.'

He looked at her with a puzzled expression and she smiled, her whole face lighting up and he could feel himself beginning to blush.
'What's your name?'
'Um... Tom miss. Tom Keenan.'
'Rami.'
He moved to go but she put her hand in his arm.
'Please stay with me.'
'I'd better tell Captain Brody that I found you...'
'Please. I don't want to be alone.'
He looked at her for a second before nodding.
'Alright.'
He sat back down and she snuggled in tight next to him, pulling the makeshift blanket he had given her around them both. Gingerly he put his arm around her shoulders and there they sat, in silence until they both drifted off to sleep.

Dawn was beginning to break and the rain had stopped. The two birds were flying fast and had covered miles since they had left the Endurance the evening before.
'There. Land.'
Nareema's voice entered Molly's head and as she looked the coastline began to swim into view.
'Is that where we're going?'
'Yes. A few more minutes and we'll be there.'
Nareema turned her head to watch the small bird flying next to her. She would regret calling the raven later. There was a deep feeling of dread at the back of her mind. The souls had gathered and she could feel them around her body as it wallowed in the darkness. The transition back would not be good. She shook the thought from her mind. That would come later and there wasn't anything she could do about it, and she didn't even want to comprehend what it would be like for Molly.
'Nareema!'
She snapped out of her revere to see the magpie dip

suddenly and sharply towards the sea. It recovered and began to climb again.

'What? What's the matter?'

'Can't you feel it?'

'Feel what?'

'The cold.'

Before Nareema could ask her what she meant there were two voices in her head. The Stones spoke like a hammer on an anvil.

'He has found us. We have to flee.'

The bird dipped again and it was obvious it was struggling to regain height. Something was happening to Molly's body in the darkness. The coast was still half a mile away.

'Hold on.'

Diving swiftly she snatched up to the smaller bird in her talons and began racing towards the land as fast as she could.

Molly felt herself began to fall as the coldness began seeping into her mind. She could feel herself slipping away from the bird and into the dark.

'Hold on. Concentrate. If you enter the darkness now then we will both die.'

Nareema's voice was distant.

Using every ounce of willpower she had she thought about the bird she had summoned. The Stones spoke to her and Molly could sense a tremor in their voices, as if they were afraid.

'He is coming. We cannot hide from him any longer. He has found us.'

Molly felt rather than saw the land appear beneath them. It flashed past a few feet below.

'Nareema!'

Molly called out as she was dragged back into the darkness, her essence and mind slamming back into her body. She span as a heavy hand fell on her shoulder,

accompanied by a deep mocking laugh. There was no one there. A deep fear flooded through her and she screamed as something brushed her neck.
'Nareema. Help!'

The raven has just made it across the land when the mist began to form around the magpie, stretching out behind them as they sped forward. Nareema could feel the weight beneath her begin to change as Molly came out of the darkness. She dropped as low as she could and slowed before letting go.

The mist covered the form below as it bounced along the rocky ground before dissipating to reveal Molly. She rolled for a few more feet before sprawling face down.

Nareema circled once more before she began to speak the words that would bring her from the darkness. As she spoke, her mind was transferred back to her body and she was taken aback at the number of souls around her. They stretched off into the distance in every direction. The closest grasped and pawed at her, their cold dead hands sending deep chills through her body. Her head snapped up as from far away the souls began to part like water in front of a boat. Something was moving towards her quickly, pushing the bodies out of the way, riding a wave of fear that spread out before it.

The Princess could feel it and the panic began to rise inside her. It was only feet away, radiating its evil presence in every direction. A hand made of nothing but blackness reached out towards her and she screamed before the transfer was completed and she was ripped out of the darkness.

She fell to her knees on the rocky ground, the black mist escaping from her lips in a smoky rush. With a deep rooted and unsettling fear still inside her she looked around for Molly who lay on her side a few feet away. Nareema scrambled over to her.

'Are you alright?'
Molly rolled over and clutched her side, moaning loudly.
'Let me look.'
Nareema helped her sit up and to struggle out of her coat and get her left arm out of her suit. Molly's left side was a mass of purpling bruises. Gently the Princess checked her over.
'I didn't think you hit the ground that hard, what happened?'
'I don't know.' she said, wincing as she shrugged her suit back on. 'Something in the darkness. I didn't see what it was but I felt it. It threw me around like a rag doll.'
'I've never heard of this happening before. The damage done by the darkness has never been physical. It might have felt like it but there were never any signs once outside.'
'Well this feels pretty real to me.'
She rose to her knees.
'I've never felt so scared of anything in my entire life. It was...' Molly shook her head. 'I'm never going back there again. Ever.'
'I felt it too. There is something evil in the darkness. Rami senses it. She is scared that it's going to get her. Although she refers to it as a "He". Who "He" is, I do not know.'
'The Stones said something similar. "He has found us..."'
'And back on the Endurance. They said that "He was coming". What do you think it means?' said Nareema.
They looked at each other before Molly spoke eventually.
'I don't know.'
'We need to be away. Can you walk?'
'Yes.' said Molly as she pulled herself up with a grunt of pain.
Nareema stood and readied herself.
'Which way and how far?'
Molly closed her eyes and pointed west.

'That way. We're close. Maybe five miles. It's near the water.'

'Then let's go. We need to find it before Tong Li realises what we're doing.'

'He has found us...'

Rami snapped awake as the words entered her head and she glanced around in a panic until she realised where she was. Beneath her she could feel the ship move and she closed her eyes again, leaning back against the wall while she composed herself. Next to her sat the young sailor, Tom. He was asleep and she had been nestled up next to him. She moved slightly and he stirred.

'Time to get up I think.' she whispered.

'What?'

He looked around frantically.

'I was supposed to take third watch. It'll be my guts for this.'

'Calm down.' she said. 'It will be fine.'

She stood as stretched before they both headed up to the deck. They passed some of the older members of the crew to jeers and suggestive remarks.

'Had fun Tommy boy? Mr Davis wants you. I'd find him before he finds you. Proper angry he is.'

Rami glared at them and they quickly went silent, much to the deepening embarrassment of Tom.

'They think we, you know...'

Tom went red as Rami winked at him then took his hand and led him away.

'Where're we going?'

'To see Captain Brody.'

'Oh I don't think that's a good idea...' stuttered Tom.

Still, he let her lead him right up to the Captain's cabin where she banged loudly on the door. After a moment the door opened to reveal a half dressed Brody.

'What?' he asked grumpily, running a hand through his

sleep tousled hair.

Rami pushed past him and into the cabin proper, dragging an unresisting Tom behind her.

'Hey, you can't...' began the Captain.

'I can and have.'

He sighed resignedly.

'What can I do for you?'

'Mr Keenan has been the perfect gentleman and it is not his fault he was derelict in his duties. It was mine. I asked him to stay with me and he did as I asked.'

Brody shrugged.

'Fair enough. But I pay him to work, not to...'

Rami interrupted him.

'Please can you make it clear to the crew that whatever he and I did or did not do is our business and I will have words with anyone who may suggest otherwise.'

Behind Brody, Nancy rolled over in bed and cast an amused glance towards them. The Captain looked at her and then back at the pair before he shrugged again.

'Look. I don't care. It's not worth the hassle.'

'Thank you Captain.' said Rami before walking out of the cabin, leaving a bewildered Tom behind.

'Sorry Captain... I, um...'

'Get out of here.'

'Yes sir.'

He headed quickly to door but Brody called him back.

'Do you have any idea who she is or what you're getting in to?'

Tom shook his head.

'No sir.'

Brody sighed.

'You're excused all duties for now. Stay with her, don't let her leave your sight and keep her out of trouble.'

Brody couldn't tell if the boy was excited or terrified. His Adams apple bobbed up and down a few times before he spoke.

'Yes sir.'

He turned to go but Brody called him back once more.

'Watch yourself lad.'

Tom nodded and left the cabin. Brody watched him go.

'She's going to eat him alive.' said Nancy with an amused grin.

## Chapter Twenty-Five

### Water

'We're nearly there.'

Nareema looked around. The land was snow covered, featureless and flat. To their left stood a cliff that dropped to the sea a hundred feet below. A wide river flowed in front of them, cascading off the edge in a thunderous waterfall.

She squinted out to sea, just able to make out a large ship at anchor a few miles down the coast. Tong Li was aboard that she guessed. So close and yet so far from his prize. Glancing further out to sea she could see another ship, the Endurance, heading inland and barley half a mile from the one at anchor.

There was a bang from the anchored ship and she saw the muzzle of a cannon flare. She watched the shot plough through the front of the Endurance, smashing through the forecastle. She prayed no one was hurt and that they could keep up the deception long enough.

'Are they shooting at Captain Brody?' asked Molly in disbelief.

'Yes. Although they seem to have stopped now. We need to hurry. Where is the Stone?'

Molly shrugged.

'I don't know. Somewhere close. Do you think I should ask the Saali and Daneep?'

The Princess considered this. The Stones reacted together and consulting them would surely alert Tong Li through the ruby he possessed. But without their help they would wander fruitlessly for too long, allowing Tong Li to find out that they weren't on board the Endurance.

'I don't think we have any choice.'

Molly nodded, grunting with pain as she moved. The last few miles had hurt her but she hadn't said anything. The darkness had not been kind. It was something that she had to discuss with Jamail when and if she ever got home.

Ahead of her Molly stopped still and closed her eyes and Nareema could sense the power of the Stones as she let them run through her. It was different to the time they found the emerald in Portugal. Molly had attuned herself to them since then, they knew her inside and out and their power was greater. This wasn't just her trying to find them using her limited knowledge. This was unexplained forces searching for their like.

The air tingled with the energy and she couldn't help but think that Tong Li would feel this too. Molly opened her eyes.

'We need to go down. Down the waterfall. There is a cave behind it, near the base.'

The Princess looked at her and then walked to the cliffs edge. It was a sheer drop to the raging sea below.

'Are you sure.'

'Yes... I think so.'

Nareema regarded the rocky face of the cliff.

'I can climb that, but I don't think you can. Is there no other way?'

Molly closed her eyes again and when she opened them they were a blinding green.

'We can climb.'

'You might be able to. Molly can't. I listened to you before, about entering the darkness. That didn't end well did it?'

Molly's eyes flashed green with anger.

'Do not question us mortal...'

'No. You listen. You asked me to protect her. That is what I'm doing. There must be another way.'

'There is... But it is not subtle.'

Nareema glanced across at the ships again. They were side by side now. It wouldn't be long before Tong Li found out they weren't there anyway. Subtle and quiet was one thing but they didn't have time for that.

'Whatever it is, do it.'

Molly nodded and walked to the edge of the cliff. She knelt down and placed her palms flat against the rocky ground. Around her the air tingled with power.

'What...' began Nareema.

'Silence.' said Molly sternly.

She closed her eyes and deep beneath Nareema's feet, the ground began to shake.

'I said a warning shot. I don't want them sunk!' shouted Tong Li.

He grabbed the closest sailor and threw him to the deck as his eyes flared with power. The man screamed as he burst into flame. Tong Li watched on as his friends rushed to put the fire out.

'Leave him.'

The sailors pulled up short and looked at him.

'The next man who doesn't do as I say will suffer a worse fate. Do you understand?'

Without another word, Tong Li drew a sword and drove it deep into the man's chest, leaving it sticking out of his body and pinning him to the scorched deck beneath.

'You.' he pointed at one of the men with his bladed hook. 'Fetch Captain Kane and Mr Callahan. I want them up here now.'

Brody looked through his telescope as Marcus and Tobias were dragged up on deck where they were roughly thrown down. He snapped the spyglass shut and then looked at the damage to his own ship. Part of the forecastle was smashed and the rigging was in pieces. He turned to look at the other people on the deck with him. Rami was stood near the boy, Tom Keenan, with a steely look on her face. Nancy was next to the rail at the back, a look of disbelief on hers. He called Davis forward.

'They've got Marcus on deck and he doesn't look like he's in a good way. We can't go toe to toe with them. I count five cannon on this side. We're going to sail up close. Prepare the men for boarding.'

Davis nodded.

'Aye Cap'n.'

The Endurance had approached the other ship, its hands armed and ready but they were still unprepared for the ferocious attack that the Captain had launched against them. They were boarded and after an intense fight which lasted for mere minutes, Brody ordered them to stand down. He couldn't let his men be butchered.

Reluctantly, they threw down their arms and were rounded up and herded onto the deck. The girl, Rami had taken down quite a few but the last he saw of her was as she was forced over the side of the ship by four men and into the freezing water below. The boy Tom had tried to help her but had been slapped down hard before they threw him overboard too, laughing as he splashed into the freezing water.

A few minutes later, Tong Li came aboard and quickly despatched sailors who tore through his ship searching for Molly. When their search turned up nothing, Brody was hauled in front of him.

'Where is she?' the Chinese man demanded.

'She died.'

Tong Li drove his fist hard into Brody's stomach and he doubled up, gasping for breath.

'I have felt her using the Stones. She is somewhere here and you will tell me.'

'Drop dead.' gasped Brody.

Two sailors came forward at a gesture from the thin

oriental man and began laying into the Captain. Finally, he was dragged up and Tong Li rested his bladed hook against his throat.

'Tell me!'

Brody smiled through bloodied teeth and spat in his face. Tong Li roared with anger and raised his hook, bringing it screaming down towards the Captains neck.

'Wait! Don't!'

Tong Li stopped his hand barely an inch from Brody's throat. He turned to look at Nancy who was stood nearby, tearful and terrified.

'You have something to add?'

'She's not here. Her and the other one, Nareema, they went ashore to find some sort of magic stone.'

'Nan...' said Brody.

Even as Nancy spoke all eyes turned towards a deep rumbling from down the coast. As they watched the cliff seemed to move, pushing boulders and large rocks from its face to fall into the sea below. Tong Li smiled and turned back to Brody.

'I will enjoy killing you later. And your woman as well, although maybe I'll just give her to the crew first and then I'll kill whatever they leave.'

Brody shouted in anger and surged forward but was dragged back by the men either side of him. Tong Li walked across to the other ships Captain.

'Bring Captain Kane. We'll go and get my Stones back and then we can finish here.'

'What about them?'

'Lock them all in the hold. If they do anything at all, sink them.'

The man nodded with an evil grin and began giving orders to his crew.

As the ground stopped shaking, Nareema crawled to the edge of the cliff. Where there had been an almost vertical drop, there was now a winding and narrow path where the rocks and stone had been forced out. She stood up and walked over to Molly who was still knelt on the ground and put a hand on her shoulder.

'Molly, are you alright?'

The girl looked up. Her eyes were swirling masses of blue and green.

'She is fine. We must hurry, our brother is coming.'

Nareema glanced up at the ships.

'Give her back to me.'

Molly blinked and her eyes returned to normal, just with an occasional flash of blue or green behind them betraying the lurking power.

'Are you alright?' the Princess asked again as Molly stood up.

She nodded but winced as she straightened.

'Yes. I'm fine. We have to go. Tong Li couldn't have missed that.'

'Come on.'

With Nareema leading the way, they made their way down the newly created path. It was about two feet wide but covered in loose rock and stone from the cliff.

'Not subtle.' said Molly with a smile.

'No. Not really.'

They reached the bottom after around ten minutes careful walking. Ahead of them the waterfall roared into the sea which was only ten or fifteen feet below. It crashed against the rocks, sending spumes of water up the cliff and making the path wet.

'Look.' said Molly, pointing ahead. 'There's the entrance.'

Just behind the waterfall, there was a black cave into which the path ran.

'We're going to have to be quick and careful.' said Nareema. 'If one of those waves catches us, then we've had it. Ready?'

The Princess watched the waves and after a particularly large one had smashed against the cliff, she dashed forward and into the cave. Molly watched her go.

'Now you.' shouted Nareema, but Molly could barely hear her over the roaring of the sea and waterfall.

Taking a deep breath, Molly watched the water as it threw itself against the stone wall of the land and as soon as it began to retreat she ran for it. She saw Nareema ahead of her and jumped the last few feet into her waiting arms. They both crashed backwards onto a damp and rocky floor.

'Made it.'

'Yes. You did. I'm going to have to teach you about balance I think.' said Nareema as they untangled themselves and stood up.

They looked around. The cave ran back about twenty feet to disappear into the dark.

'We'll need some sort of light.'

'Here.'

Nareema took off her coat and tore the sleeves off before wrapping one of them around her sword to make a makeshift torch. Molly did the same.

'Ready?' Nareema asked in the flickering light.

'Yes.'

They walked back towards the rear of the cave. It ran for about another thirty feet before it narrowed into a dead end. Molly looked around.

'This is it. I'm sure of it.'

'There must be a door or something.'

Molly closed her eyes and the Stones flared into brightness.

'Here.'

She stepped forward and held her torch near the wall at the back. Just visible was an old carving. It was four teardrop shapes, points touching, set in a circle. Molly brushed some of the dirt off it and with a heavy shove, pushed it backwards. There was a solid thud and to their left a section of wall began to sink into the ground. It dropped about two feet and then stopped with a loud grinding noise.

'I think it's stuck.'

Nareema put her torch through the gap.

'There's another tunnel. Come on.'

She handed the sword to Molly and clambered over the stone, dropping down and turning to take the torches. Molly followed, shrugging out of her coat first and wriggling through the gap. Dropping onto the floor on the other side, the women began to make their way down the tunnel. It wound along for a few hundred feet before beginning to slope sharply downwards. As they walked they both became aware of a roaring noise from in front of them.

The tunnel continued, with the noise getting louder until they emerged in a cavern. It was roughly circular and about fifty feet across. A very narrow ledge ran from their left to about halfway, where a rickety wooden rope bridge it crossed to a stone spire with a flat top in the middle. A matching bridge crossed to the other side where another narrow ledge continued around the edge. Molly looked down. Below them was water. It rose and fell with a violent swell, sending sprays flying high before dropping ten or twenty feet.

'It must connect to the sea outside.' shouted Nareema over the crash of the water.

'How do we get across?'

'The ledge.'

'I hoped you wouldn't say that.'

'I don't think we've got any choice in the matter.'

Gingerly they began edging along the ledge, hugging the wall tightly. The stone underfoot was damp and covered in loose rock. Nareema made it to the wooden bridge first and tested one of the wooden planks with her foot. It creaked alarmingly.

'We're going to have to be quick. I don't think the wood is going to hold up for long.'

Next to her Molly nodded.

'I'm right behind you.'

'Quick and light. Don't look down and don't stop. We're going over this bridge and the next one in one go.'

The Princess pushed away from the wall and bounded across the bridge. She made it almost to the middle before one of the planks gave way, pitching her forwards. She hit the bridge hard and the last couple of wooden planks gave way too and suddenly she was falling.

'Nareema!'

Frantically she threw her arms out and just managed catch the edge of the stone spire with her fingertips. Below her the water crashed, sending a freezing spray of water up.

'I'm coming.' shouted Molly.

'No. Wait. I'm alright.'

She looked down and managed to find a foothold in the uneven rock before hauling herself up. She lay on her back on the cold stone for a moment to catch her breath.

'Are you alright?'

The Princess sat up.

'Yes. I'm ok.'

They both looked at the bridge. The last four or five planks were missing.

'What now? I don't know if...' began Molly before she stopped and closed her eyes.

'Why didn't you say something before?' she said to herself.

'What is it?' called Nareema

'I'm going to try something. Remember what I did to Captain Brody's table? I'm going to see if the planks can remember when they were a tree.'

'Is that a good idea?'

Molly grinned at her, the flickering light from her torch turning it into something disturbing.

'Probably not, but when has that stopped me?'
'Just be careful.'

Molly pressed herself back against the wall and closed her eyes. Across the cavern Nareema could feel the air change as the girl channelled the power through her.

In front of her, the old wooden planks began to creak until the closest to the wall burst with new shoots and green leaves. Suddenly, the new growth shot forward, intertwining with itself to make a new bridge. Nareema jumped out of the way as it went past her at speed to crash into the far wall, taking the other half of the bridge with it. She turned back as Molly came striding over the new bridge, her eyes glowing a bright green.

'Come. Our brother awaits.'

'I'm sorry Owain. I thought he was going to kill you.'

Brody was sat next to Nancy in the forward hold of his ship. They'd been locked in with the crew, some of who were sporting cuts and bruises from the fight. Brody turned to the woman, wincing as he did so. His left eye was swollen and he was pretty sure he'd got a couple of broken ribs.

'It's not your fault. He would have killed me. He's a vicious bugger.'

'What're they going to do?'

'Well if the Princess and Molly get to the Stone first then there's a good chance they'll sink us. If they don't then they'll kill us then sink us.'

'Oh.'

Outside the hold he could hear the three men who were guarding the hatch as they paced around.

'Well cap'n. It's been an honour to sail with ye.' said Davis who was sat nearby.

'Shut up Davis. We're not done yet.'

He pulled himself up as from above him came the sounds of a scuffle followed by three heavy thumps. A moment later the hatch opened and Rami dropped in, closely followed by the boy Tom. They were both soaking wet and she was covered in blood. Nancy looked at her.

'Is that blood?'

'It's not mine.' she said dismissively. 'Captain. There are four more men on the Endurance, the rest have gone back aboard their own ship. I suggest we take the men here and then sink their ship. They got enough gun powder aboard to start a small war so I think it might be wise to do something with that.'

'How'd you survive? I saw you both go over the edge.'

'I can swim quite well.

'Me too.' added Tom.

Rami smiled.

'We must hurry. Those three I've just killed will be missed soon. The rest are in your cabin.'

'What about weapons?'

'There are three swords and muskets on deck, and the others are similarly armed. The rest have been taken I'm afraid. We need to move quickly and quietly. They have all five of the cannon on this side of their ship aimed and loaded. If they find out you've escaped then they'll blow the ship apart.'

The Captain sat back down.

'Right. Here's what we're going to do...'

Molly and Nareema had worked their way around the second ledge and into the tunnel beyond. It led downwards for another hundred feet before emerging in a huge cavern. Light filtered in from cracks and holes high in the left-hand wall. They stopped at the edge of a narrow rocky beach that ran down to a vast area of water and looked across the cavern at a large ship that was moored at a tired looking wooden jetty.

'How the hell did that get in here?'

Nareema shook her head.

'I don't know.'

The left hand wall was solid rock apart from the cracks and holes near the top but there was nowhere a ship could have got in.

'Where now?'

'There.' said Molly, pointing at the ship.

They both began walking towards the galleon and as the neared they saw it was listing to the starboard.

'How old do you think it is?'

'I don't know. A hundred years at least. We're going to have to be careful.'

As they neared the jetty they could take in the ship. The sails were rotten and holed and the fading paint may once have been yellow but was now peeling badly. Nareema hauled herself up onto the sloping deck and turned to help Molly. The girl winced as she scrambled up next to her, clutching her side as she moved.

'Are you alright?'

'Yes. Just a bit sore.'

They walked towards where the Captain's cabin would be.

'Where are the crew?'

Nareema shrugged.

'I don't know. There's no sign of anyone.'

Carefully the pushed the cabin door open. It was empty. Rotting furniture and bedding were the only indication that there had ever been anyone on board. The women gave the place a quick search but turned up nothing.

'Where now?' asked Nareema.

Molly closed her eyes and felt the power of the Stones flow through her. She could hear them calling out to Norek, the Water Stone, and feel its response. More disturbingly, she could feel a reply from the Fire Stone as well.

'Water. It's in the water. We need to go down. But we have to hurry, Tong Li is on his way.'

Quickly they headed out of the cabin and then below. It

was as a mess. Several rusty cannons had slipped across the deck and lay in a tangled heap to one side. They cautiously picked their way past and the down again.

The second set of steps dropped them into waist deep water. Molly took a step and the tripped on an unseen obstacle, sending her headlong into the cold dark water. She emerged a second later splashing wildly and spluttering for air. Nareema helped her up.

'Be careful. We don't know what's under the surface.'

Molly wiped the water from her face.

'Now you tell me.'

The Princess grinned at her.

Working their way forward they came across a pile of barrels and crates that had been stacked to make a wall across the entire hold. Over time some of them had shifted and tumbled out of place, and Nareema peered through the gap they had left.

'Molly. Here.'

The girl hurriedly splashed her way over. As she moved, her foot bumped against something solid and she screamed as three grinning skulls floated up out of the murky water. The Princess was with her in a second.

'It's alright. They're dead. I guess that explains what happened to the crew.'

She picked one of the skulls up and examined it. There were no obvious wounds or damage and she dropped it back into the water. She took Molly's hand and carefully led her to the gap in the crates.

'Look.'

She pointed through to the desiccated corpse that was slumped on a barrel just out if the water. The clothes it worn were tattered and rotten, the skin it had left was dry and stretched Molly couldn't help but retch at the sight. On its left hand was a ring. It was large and had a teardrop shaped diamond the size of a man's thumb set into it.

'Norek.' said Nareema quietly.

Molly put her hand to her mouth and swallowed dryly.
'Can you go and get it? I don't think...'
Nareema smiled and nodded before she clambered over the barricade. Cautiously she made her way to the body. The clothes it wore might once have been finely made but now they were little more than tattered rags. On its head perched an equally battered brown tricorn hat with feathers stuck in it. She reached up and slipped the ring from its finger. The movement suddenly caused the corpse to shift and it splashed noisily into the water. She turned and headed back to Molly.
'I've got it.'
She handed the ring to the girl and hauled herself over the crates. Molly took it and stood looking transfixed at the gem.
'Molly!'
'What?'
She looked up and her eyes were swirling blue and green.
'Come on. We have to go.'
She nodded as she popped the gem out of the ring and with a click, she fitted it into the bracer on her wrist. All three gems flashed brightly as it slotted home and Molly smiled.
'Come on.'
Nareema grabbed her arm and began to haul her along.
'I can feel it. All through the water.'
'Move.'
Molly allowed herself to be dragged as far as the steps before Nareema turned and grabbed her shoulders.
'Molly! Focus! We need to get out of here and go and get Marcus.'
The girl looked at her, eyes returning to normal but still with flashes of green white and blue behind them.
'Marcus?'
'Yes. Marcus. We're going to get out of here and rescue him. Remember?'

She took a breath and seemed to pull herself together, snapping out of her daze.

'Marcus. Yes. Marcus. Come on, we're wasting time

Leaving the Princess standing in the water she pulled herself up the steps. Nareema followed, seeing Molly hurry ahead, past the rusting cannons and then up on to deck.

'Molly, wait.'

She quickly followed but was only halfway to the stairs before Molly disappeared up them and onto the upper deck and had only got as far as the bottom of the steps before the unmistakable sound of gunfire erupted from outside. She scrambled up, keeping her head down.

Molly was crouched behind one of the gunwales and across the beach she could see Tong Li. He was accompanied by three armed men, one of which was dragging Marcus along with him. She was pretty sure that they hadn't seen her. Molly stuck her head up and took in the scene. She dropped down again as another shot cracked towards the ship.

'Go and get Marcus.' she whispered to the Princess. 'I'll keep him busy.'

'You can't fight him.'

'Watch me.'

Without another word, Molly stood with her hands up.

'Don't shoot.' she shouted. 'I'm here. I have the Stones.'

Nareema cursed silently before slipping back down below and looking for another way off the ship.

Marcus stumbled along. His leg was stiff and he cradled his right arm against his chest. He heard that shots and then saw Molly stand, his heart filling with joy and immense sadness at the sight of her. She jumped over the side and into the wooden jetty at the end of the beach. Ahead of him, Tong Li and his guard stopped.

The men reloaded their muskets and aimed them at her. Next to him, the last guard pushed him roughly to his knees and pressed a sword to his back.

'Where is the Princess?' shouted Tong Li as Molly walked towards them.

'Dead.'

'Forgive me if I don't believe you. Where is she?'

'Dead. She fell into the water in the room with the ledges. There was a bridge. It gave way beneath her.'

Tong Li turned to the man with Marcus who nodded and the struck him across the back of the head with the pommel of his sword. Marcus fell sideways onto the pebbles.

'I will ask you one more time. And then I'll kill him.'

Molly looked at Marcus as he tried to sit up. He looked terrible. He was gaunt and tired with a scruffy looking beard. Inside she wanted to cry.

'If you kill him then you will never get the Stones.'

'And why is that?'

'I will destroy them.'

Tong Li smiled.

'I don't think so. I've read enough to know they cannot be destroyed without the Crown.'

Molly groaned inwardly.

'I can do it. If I give them my life then they'll break free of the crown. Then they'll disappear.'

'Good try Mrs Kane. But sadly, that isn't the case. Kill her.'

The men next to him snapped into action and suddenly things seemed to go into slow motion. Off to her right and behind Marcus, she saw Nareema rising out of the sea and start running up the beach. The men next to Tong Li tensed and pulled the triggers of their guns. The muzzle flashes became drawn out as the lead shot span across the cavern towards her.

She flung out her left hand and an invisible wall of air formed between her and the bullets, slowing them down to a walking pace. With her other hand she conjured a hail of stones from the beach which hammered into the men knocking them senseless. It all happened in a second and before she knew what she was doing she found herself running at Tong Li, drawing her sword as she went.

## Chapter Twenty-Six

### Vengeance

Rami and Tom quietly slipped out of the hold, followed by three sailors. The men picked up the weapons from the dead guards and shoved the bodies back down in the hold. Night had begun to fall and they began to pace backwards and forwards, as if they were on guard. Rami moved into the shadows and gave a whistle. Four more men followed, crouching down next to her.

'We move quietly. We need to take all four of them as fast as possible.'

The men nodded, their faces grim.

'Come on.'

They followed Rami across the deck, keeping low and to the far side, away from the other ship. The girl drew two short knives as they came up to the door of Brody's cabin. She knocked loudly. There was a silent pause before footsteps were heard from the other side. The door was flung open to reveal a drunken sailor.

'What...'

He didn't get chance to finish his sentence before Rami drove one of her blades into his throat. She pushed past him and let the other knife fly, catching one of the other men in the neck who fell backwards off his chair. The remaining two sailors stood and fumbled for weapons but the Endurance crewmen were on them before they realised what was going on.

Rami recovered her knives and was cleaning them on the clothes of one of the dead men when Brody arrived with Nancy and Tom in tow. He looked around his cabin at the blood but more noticeably at the empty wine bottles that littered the table. He picked one up sighed.

'That was my best stuff.'

'I'll buy you a bottle if we get out of this Captain.' said Rami. 'First of all, we need to get out of here. I'm going aboard their ship. It's going to go out with a bang so I need you to be ready and get out of here as fast as possible.'

I'm coming with you.' said Tom quickly.

Rami turned to him with a hard face to say something but after a second she just smiled and nodded.

'Thank you.'

'Slow down lass. The two of you aren't going to be able to take on a whole ship.'

'We need to be quiet...'

'No lass. The time for quiet has passed. We're going to go over there and give them a bloody good hiding they won't forget.'

'What about the cannons?' piped up Tom. 'As soon as they get wind that something is up they'll blow us out of the water.'

Brody looked like he was going to say something else but Rami interrupted him.

'Look for our signal. As soon as you see it, cut the lines and make for open water as fast as you can. They'll be too busy to fire. Trust me.'

The Captain sighed.

'Bloody stubborn. Just like the other one. It's going to get you killed one of these days.'

Rami smiled.

'Hopefully not today.'

She turned to Tom.

'Are you sure you want to come?'

He nodded.

'Cap'n said I was to look out for you.'

Rami glanced at Brody who shrugged.

'Here.'

She handed him two short knives and he took them before looking up at Brody.

'Nice to serve with you sir.'

'Shut up lad. If your both not sat round my table tomorrow then there's going to be hell to pay.'
'Aye sir.'
Rami just nodded and without another word left the room with Tom following closely behind.
'I hope she don't get him killed.' said Nancy.
'She's sweet on him. She'll be careful.'
'Well if she isn't she'll have to answer to me.'
Brody turned to her with a grin.
'Getting all motherly are ye Nan?'
She glared back at him.
'Don't you dare start Owain Brody. I ain't going to forget that it was you that dragged me on this trip in the first place.'
Brody opened his mouth to say something but thought better of it. In the end he just shook his head with a sly smile.
'And if we do make it back then I'm going to fix that boy up with as many girls as he wants.'
'I wouldn't do that if I were you. I reckon Rami would have something to say about that.'
'She's not his mother.'
'No. But neither are you.'
Nancy pulled a face and crossed her arms.
'She's not the sort of girl I'd want my son to know.'
Brody just smiled and shook his head once more.

Rami and Tom headed up onto the deck and across to the side facing away from the other ship.
'Ready?' she asked him.
He hesitated.
'What?'
He looked down for a second before lunging in and giving her a kiss. She stepped back in shock, hand going to her cheek.
'Just in case we don't make it.' he muttered,

embarrassedly.

Without giving her a chance to say anything else he swung himself over the edge and began climbing down the side. Rami stood still for a moment before her shock was replaced by a mixture of embarrassment and joy. She smiled to herself before following him.

They quickly scaled the side of the ship and into the freezing water. Carefully they swam around until they were near the anchor chain of the other vessel. Rami pulled herself out of the water and began to climb, followed by Tom. She clambered up to the gunwales and peered over the edge.

There were six sailors on deck and towards the rear of the ship she could see the Captain talking to another couple of men. As she watched, he turned and went below with the men close behind. She ducked back down and whispered to a shivering Tom.

'There are six of them. That's too many, we're going to have to find another way in.'

He nodded and then pointed along the length of the ship.

'There. The cannon ports are open. We should be able to get in those.'

She followed his arm and nodded before climbing along the side of the ship. They reached the first open port and Rami glanced in to find the cannon was pulled back from the opening. Across the deck a dozen men were lounging around the guns that were facing the Endurance but none were paying any attention. They were too engrossed in the dice game they were playing.

Rami looked back at Tom and pressed a finger to her lips to silence him before she slipped aboard. Tom followed and they crouched in the shadow of the cannon.

'Where will they store the gunpowder?' she whispered.

'It'll be in the lower hold. Probably under lock and key.'

Rami looked across the deck. The sailors were in between

them and the steps down below.

'We need a distraction...'

Even as she spoke there was a thunderous explosion from somewhere outside and the sailors looked at one another before racing away to see what was happening.

'Move! Now!' said Rami as they quickly scurried across the deck and down the steps.

They reached the bottom as two armed men came hurrying in the opposite direction, obviously going to see what the noise was. The sailors pulled up in surprise when they saw the young pair.

'What d'ya think....'

Rami darted forwards and drove one of her short blades into his neck. He fell back and was dead before he hit the deck. The other looked on in shock as she span towards him, a second knife slashing at his chest and opening him up from sternum to stomach. He cried out and lunged towards her, more out of desperation than anything else but she sidestepped and grabbed him as he went past.

She wrapped an arm around his neck and with a twist, pulled him backwards off his feet. As he went down, Tom couldn't help but wince at the snap his spine made as she broke his neck.

'How did you do that?' he asked as she picked up and quickly cleaned her weapons.

She just smiled at him.

'Practice.'

Rami stepped forward and pecked a little kiss on his cheek.

'Just in case.'

Tom couldn't help but blush furiously. Trying to hide it, he bent down and pulled a ring of keys from the body of one of the men.

'These should get us where we need to go.'

They moved towards the end of the hold.

'Remind me never to get you angry at me.' he whispered.

'This isn't me angry.' she said sweetly. 'I'm a whole lot nastier when I'm angry.'

'Right.'

At the far end of the hold there were two locked doors. One had a grill set in it. Tom peered through.

'There's a man in here.' he whispered.

Rami joined him at the window and he became uncomfortably aware of her as she pressed close to him. He blushed despite himself.

'That must be Tobias.' said Rami.

'Who's he?'

'Nareema's uncle. We have to get him out.'

She pulled the bunch of keys they had taken and tried one in the lock. It fitted perfectly and with a rusty clunk, the lock opened. Tom swung the door open and Rami darted inside to the man who was chained to the bulkhead. He was old and looked tired. His clothes were a mess and he sported multiple bruises and cuts across his face.

'Are you Tobias?' ask Rami as she knelt next to him and began to undo the shackles. He looked up at her.

'Nareema?'

'No. I'm Rami. Nareema has sent us to rescue you.'

'Oh. Where's Marcus?'

'He's with Nareema.' said Rami, inwardly wondering where they were.

'That's good.' he replied tiredly.

Tom helped him up and out into the hold and Rami followed.

'We have to get out of here.'

'What about the gun powder?'

'There isn't time to look for it. But...'

She began poking through the contents of the hold, quickly turning up a few bottles. Smashing the top off one of them she took a sniff, recoiling at the smell.

'Rum.'

Tom looked on as she smashed all but one of the bottles,

splashing the contents around the rest of the hold. Tom looked at her quizzically as she tore a strip of cloth from a bundle on the floor and stuffed it into the top of the last bottle. She opened one if the hooded lanterns that hung from the wall and lit the trailing cloth.

'Get ready to run.'

She smiled at him before throwing the bottle as hard as she could against the bulkhead. It smashed and caught light sending burning streams of liquor in all directions. The flames took hold quickly as the other pools of alcohol caught.

Rami turned.

'Let's get out of here.'

They began to move towards the stairs, both supporting Tobias as from somewhere outside, another huge explosion sounded.

Brody slipped back into the hold and addressed his crew. He had left Nancy in his cabin with instructions not to leave. Even though she knew the danger they were facing she had still protested but he'd convinced her in the end. She'd stay put and out of harm's way.

Now he turned to his men. Good lads all and all knew what they were facing. They'd seen the power Tong Li held and they'd agreed to help Molly but first they had to help themselves.

'Alright lads. I ain't going to lie to you. We're in the shit but we've got a way out. The other ship thinks we're beat. So they're taking no notice of us. We're going to go out there and give them the hiding they've got coming.'

'What about the cannons?' asked one of the men.

'The girl Rami is sorting them out and giving the other crew something to worry about other than us.'

'Can we trust her? Sorry cap'n but...'

Brody looked at the man. He could understand their concern. She was just a young girl. Yes she could fight but was that going to be enough? Could she do as she had promised. He pushed the thought from his mind.

'Molly trusts her so that's good enough for me.'

There were some nodding heads and a ripple of assent passed amongst them. Molly was their mascot. They were protective of her in a way that made him smile. Women on board ship were never a good omen and so far that theory hadn't been proved wrong what with Portugal and now this but they still looked out for her. If she said it was going to work then it would. Hell, they'd probably march behind her in an army if she asked.

He looked around the crew once more. He'd sailed with each and every one of them for years.

'We're going to go up there and get our ship back. I want all of you to arm yourselves with whatever you can find. We're going to go over there and kick their arses. Are you with me?'

It was Davis who spoke first.

'Aye cap'n. I'm with you and Molly.'

The rest of the crew sounded their agreement.

'Then let's bloody well get to it.'

Brody turned and had climbed almost out of the hold when from up the coast a huge explosion sounded, throwing a ball of fire high into the air. He ducked back down as sailors on the other ship flooded into the deck to see what was going on.

With their attention away he began to pull his men out of the hold and up on deck. It took them a few minutes but as the last of them crouched behind the gunwales, the Captain of the other ship stomped onto deck and began bellowing orders and abuse at his crew. With his back to the Endurance, Brody gave the signal and his men stood, ready to go.

As he opened his mouth to give the order to attack, another explosion ripped into the night, lighting the sky like daylight and overhead heavy thick clouds began to mass.

At that second the other Captain turned. They both stared into one another's eyes, faces lit by the billowing fire from the land. The other Captain smiled and drew a heavy looking sword. Brody cursed before turning to his men.

'Get them!'

He scrambled across the planks that connected the two ships while around him his men swung across from the rigging. He hit the deck and came up swinging, catching the first man he came across with a huge punch that laid him out completely. He grabbed the sword from the unconscious man and looked round for his opposite number. He was stood a little way off, easily parrying an attack and despatching his opponent with a vicious backhand. He stepped over the body and began to walk towards Brody, an evil grin on his face.

One of his own men ran in front of him and began to head towards Brody but the Captain hauled him out of the way, driving his sword into his back and throwing him aside.

'He's mine.' he shouted.

'Right,' muttered Brody. 'If that's what you want then that's what you're bloody going to get.'

With a yell he launched himself at the man, their swords meeting with a clash.

Molly ran across the beach and with a gesture, sent the two men in front of her flying to the sides, leaving the way clear to Tong Li. He stood his ground and grinned as she swung her sword at him.

He deftly deflected the blow with his metal hooked hand punched her square in the face. She fell back, blood spurting from her broken nose, but she barely flinched before she leapt back towards him. This time he entangled her blade with his hook and wrenched it from her grasp, sending it skidding across the beach.

He moved like lightning and wrapped his right arm around her neck, the hooked blade an inch from her neck, before driving a series of hammer punches into her kidneys. She cried out and he span her away into the surf.

Molly fell to the ground clutching her left side unable to avoid the kick he drove into her that knocked her sideways into the water. He stepped forward into the water himself and hauled her up by her hair before smashing her in the side of the head with the brass casing of his false hand. She dropped down into the water and he dragged her up again raising his hooked blade to finish her.

'Tong Li!'

He turned to see Nareema standing on the beach, over the dead bodies of his men. He smiled evilly.

'Princess. You know I almost believed you were dead.'

'This ends now.' her voice was steely and ice cold.

He laughed before smashing Molly into the water again and then dragging the dazed girl up the beach by her hair where he dumped her on the stones.

'Don't die on me. I've not finished with you yet. I want you to watch as I kill her and then your husband.'

He drew his own sword and the pair began circling.

'I've been looking forward to this.' he said with a humourless smile as his body burst into flame and he roared his defiance.

Suddenly he launched himself towards her but Nareema jumped back into the shallows near Molly.

'You can't protect her. She is going to die. The question is, how quickly?'

Tong Li threw his arms forward, sending a ball of fire searing towards the Princess. Even as she dived to the right, Molly struggled to her knees and deflected the ball with a powerful gust of wind which sent it flying skyward to smash into the sea wall of the cavern. It exploded with an ear-splitting boom, sending fire and burning rock in all directions. As the dust cleared, Nareema was at Molly's side, helping the girl stand.

'Impressive.'

His voice dropped and around him the fire burnt brighter.

'Give me the Stones and I'll let you live.'

'Not a chance.' spat Molly, clutching her injured left side.

'Well don't say I didn't offer.'

He swung his sword down vertically, sending a stream of fire slashing towards the pair. Nareema jumped left but Molly didn't get out of the way in time and it struck her in the side.

She screamed as the flames burnt her, and fell backwards into the water, he hair singed and smoking. Nareema spluttered to the surface and moved up the beach, only just getting out of the way of Tong Li's blade as he brought it crashing down towards her. In the water, Molly had risen to her knees and was obviously in pain.

'Molly!' shouted Nareema. 'Use the Stones.'

Tong Li caught her in the knee with a kick and dropped her to the ground before kicking her in the face, sending her sprawling. He span round to face Molly and launched another ball of fire towards her, easily twice as big as the first.

Around him the air crackled with the heat. Molly drew herself up and closed her eyes as it sped towards her. A second later she opened them, they were a swirling mass of colour. With a gesture, the wind and ground rose to meet the fireball, sending it hurtling across the cavern where it destroyed a huge section of the sea wall in a blossom of fire and rock. Three voices spoke, only one of which was Molly's.

'This ends now.'


Rami and Tom help Tobias up the steep steps to the deck with the cannons on.

'There's no way he's going to get out the way we came in.' said Tom.

Rami looked round.

'Then we'll go the long way round. But first, give me a hand.'

They carefully sat Tobias down and hurried to the nearest cannon. With a swipe of her blades Rami cut the heavy ropes that anchored the gun to the deck. Above them there was shouting and the sound of fighting.

'Must be cap'n Brody.' said Tom.

'Help me.'

Together they manhandled the gun into the middle of the deck, facing along its length and towards the steps up. Tom checked the weapon.

'It's loaded.'

'Good. Get Tobias and get up the steps...'

As she spoke, four sailors came down, grinding to a halt as they saw the cannon. Rami didn't hesitate, she grabbed a smouldering taper and thrust against the gun. It fizzed for a second before it went off with a deafening boom.

The recoil sending the gun crashing down into the lower deck. The heavy ball ejected from the barrel and smashed its way through two of the men, the steps and destroyed part of the back of the ship. The other sailors picked themselves up and took one look at her before scrambling up what was left of the steps and away. Tom picked himself up, ears still ringing. Behind them, a thick smoke was beginning to pour upwards.

'Subtle.'

'Necessary. Come on. We have to get out of here.'

Between them they hoisted the dazed Tobias up and headed away from the fire.

Brody locked blades with the Captain as from below them came the unmistakable retort of a cannon. Both men glanced at the Endurance but she looked fine.

A puzzled expression passed across the other man's face and Brody took advantage of his distraction and headbutted him, driving his forehead hard into the other man's face. He fell backwards, clutching his broken nose.

Brody didn't give him a chance to recover, he followed in quickly, stamping as hard as he could on his knee, feeling it break beneath his foot. The Captain fell down, unable to stand and Brody drove his sword into his chest, pushing him back until the blade erupted from his back. He glanced up as two panicked sailors emerged from below deck.

'Fire. We're on fire.'

He grabbed the Captains sword and for the first time, saw what it was. The blade was heavy and covered in swirling whorls. This was Marcus's sword. He grabbed the matching scabbard as from below came an explosion and the ship lurched to the starboard.

'Cap'n! Look out!'

Brody span at the shout to see a man baring down on him with a sword raised high. With a cry the man brought his blade down, Brody slipping to the deck as he tried to get out of the way. The sword missed him by an inch but he wasn't going to get out of the way a second time.

He raised the weapon again but suddenly went rigid as a blade pushed its way through the front of his shirt and he toppled sideways to reveal Nancy. She was stood with a heavy club in her left hand, the right had been holding the sword. She smiled at him.

'Well don't just sit there you lump, get...'

She fell to her knees as an explosion spewed from the prow, sending burning timbers across the water. The ship lurched again and Brody scrambled to his feet, dragging Nancy up with him.

'Back aboard the Endurance, cut us loose or when she goes, she'll take us with us.'

The sailors around him bolted back towards their ship. He turned in time to see Tom and Rami struggling across the deck, almost dragging Tobias with them. He rushed over to help.

'She's going down. We've got to get off.'

Rami nodded and between them all they manhandled the older man across onto the Endurance where they laid him on the deck. As soon as they were all on board, the lines and planks and ropes tethering the two ships together were cut and the Endurance began to drift away.

The other vessel was fully alight now and listing heavily to the starboard. Brody glanced round. Most of his men had made it back, along with some of the other crew. They had surrendered and were corralled in the centre of the deck. Davis came running up, bleeding from a cut on his forehead and arm.

'What shall we do with them?'

He pointed to the men with his sword. Brody looked at Nancy before answering.

'Give em some food and water. Then find something to clean any wounds they got.'

'But cap'n, they tried to kill us!'

'I know Mr Davis. But they didn't succeed did they. It'll take more and that lot to finish us off. What they done was under orders from a couple of bastards. I won't hold them accountable at the moment. The Princess can decide what to do with them. Make sure our lads get some rum. Not too much mind. I don't want any trouble.'

Davis nodded.

'Aye cap'n.'

Brody looked up as a heavy splash of rain hit his face. Above him the clouds were boiling with a storm. Lighting was flashing in the heavy swirling mass.

'Davis, stow the rum for now. We need all hands to the mast. I think things are going to get rough really quickly.'

The old sailor looked up.

'Aye.'

Tong Li stood his ground as in front of him Molly rose out of the water, supported by a column of spinning air and water. Her eyes were glowing orbs and the power that was flooding into her made the air crackle.

'Give us our brother.'

The man on the beach roared his defiance and sent a ball of fire tearing across towards Molly. She casually flicked her hand and the flames were deflected with a blast of wind.

Tong Li laughed.

'Always with the wind.'

Molly smiled.

'There is more to the air than just the wind.'

Behind her, the night sky erupted into light. Through the huge holes blasted in the rock came lighting. It flashed in and struck Tong Li. Arcing across the water to hit his raised hooked hand.

Nareema crawled up the beach to where Marcus was still slumped as another jagged line streaked in. It was followed by another and another until she could see the flashes of blinding light from behind her closed eyes.

With a final titanic blast the lightning stopped and she pulled herself wearily to her feet, blinking at the after images of the light. Molly was still floating above the water, arms outstretched and eyes burning with power. Tong Li had slumped to his knees on the beach, body smoking and spasming as the electricity still powered through him. The Princess picked up her sword and walked over to the man. He turned to look at her, his face burnt by the fury of the sky. She raised her sword.

'You killed my mother, my sister and...' she hesitated as if the thought was difficult, '...and my father. This is for my family. The one you have destroyed and the one I have left.'

The blade spoke once and the man knelt still for a second before his head tumbled to the rocky floor and his body dropped sideways. Nareema looked at it for a second before she sagged and sat down heavily. It was done.

Suddenly she felt tired. The adrenaline and her own thirst for vengeance left her. Across the water, Molly floated down to stand near the body. She reached down and plucked the ruby from the decimated corpse. Without a word, she fitted it into the bracer on her forearm.

As soon as it clicked into place, all four gems glowed brilliantly, their light illuminating the entire cavern. Nareema had to shield her eyes from the brilliance. It dimmed after a second and Molly turned, heading out over the water again.

'Molly. What are you doing?'

Three voices spoke.

'We are becoming one with our brothers.'

Slowly the girl sank beneath the surface and after a second the water began to boil sending steam high into the air.

'What is she doing?'

Nareema looked up at Marcus. He was filthy and blood had run down the side of his face from where he'd been struck. His right arm was cradled across his body, wrapped in a dirty cloth.

'I don't know.'

He moved across to Tong Li's body and gave it a brutal kick before reaching down and taking the bladed hook that had covered his severed arm. He looked at it for a second before coming and sitting next to the Princess.

'What do we do now?'

'Wait.'

Dawn was beginning to break when the launch from the Endurance rowed to the cliffs. The night had been rough, wind and heavy driving rain had lashed the ship but at least it had pushed them away from the wreck of the other vessel. Now as the sun came up the sea was calm and peaceful.

As soon as it was possible, Brody sent the launch across to the cliffs. There was a huge hole near the base of one of them, with another near the top. The sailors, led by Davis, rowed through the breach and into the cavern. It was steamy and hot, the water beneath their boat boiling and rolling. They put ashore, where Nareema and Marcus were sat.

'Mr Davis.'

The old sailor smiled.

'We didn't know if you was dead or not.'

'We're fine.'

He handed her a water bottle and some bread. She took a long drink and passed it to Marcus.

'Where's Molly.'

Nareema pointed out across the water.

'In there.'

As they watched, the water parted and Molly rose out of the rolling steam. Her arms were spread and her entire body seemed to glow. She floated across to the beach where she gently set down.

'We are one.'

There were four distinct voices, all slightly out of sync with each other. Nareema turned to face the girl.

'Give Molly back to us.'

'For the first time in a thousand years, we are one...'

'Now.'

Molly looked at the Princess, eyes swirling with red, blue, green and white. She stared for a second before nodding once. The girl tilted her head back and with a slow sigh allowed the power to flood out of her. She looked back at Nareema, eyes now their normal bright blue but the Princess couldn't help but notice the occasional flashes of colour behind them.

'Nareema?'

She smiled.

'Yes?'

'Did we win? Where is Tong Li? Marcus?'

'I'm here.'

He stepped forward and she burst into tears, throwing herself at him and hugging him tightly.

'I thought I'd lost you. I'm sorry. I'm...'

He hugged her awkwardly back.

'Stop. Don't. It's not your fault.'

Marcus kissed her gently and pushed her away slightly. For the first time, she seemed to notice his injured arm.

'Oh my god. I'm sorry. I...'

'No. Don't.'

He smiled tightly.

'Don't leave me like that again. Please.'

She burst into tears again. He gathered her close.

'I love you.' he whispered.

'I love you too.'

They stood in each other's arms for a moment before they separated. Molly turned to the Princess.

'What now?' asked Nareema.

'We find the crown.'

'How?' asked Marcus.

'I can show you.' said Molly with a smile.

She stepped back and held up her arm. All four gems flashed brilliantly and around them the cavern changed.

They were suddenly standing on a plain. In front of them was a city and to their right was a high mountain range. The world span towards the mountains and flashed forwards through a thick jungle towards a huge cave mouth, hidden deep beneath the canopy of trees. The vision stopped outside. To the left and right were stone monoliths, carved with deep bass reliefs of grinning skulls.

'It is here.'

Nareema smiled.

'I know where this is.'

Molly looked at her.

'How?'

'I have seen that city before. Many times. I grew up there.'

She turned to look at Molly and Marcus.
'I'm going home.'

Printed in Great Britain
by Amazon